HIDDEN SANCTUARY

HIDDEN SERIES OF ELARIA: BOOK 2

BY TIFFANY SHEARN

Hidden Sanctuary by Tiffany Shearn

Published by Tiffany Shearn

Auburn, Washington, U.S.A.

www.tiffanyshearn.com

Copyright © 2022 Tiffany Shearn

This is a work of fiction. All names, characters, and events are the product of the author's imagination. Places are either the work of the author's imagination or are used fictitiously. Any resemblance to actual people, living or dead, or historic events is coincidental.

Cover design by Jonathan Lebel.

Edited by Maxine Meyer

ISBN: 978-1-7377111-3-1 (Paperback)

For my husband, who is the calm center of my storm. Thank you for the love, help, and support in making this series a reality.

PROLOGUE

Deathwind filtered through the murmurs and noises of the prey-prisoners below and lamented his own captivity. His kind knew to beware the transitive power of blood. Such was the domain of vampires, but there was no escaping *this* master. It was better to reap the benefits of falling in line than pay the price of opposition. So, the pact was made and their colony bound. He pulled his supple lips back to reveal double fangs on each side of his wide mouth in a silent snarl. It was little comfort the dogs and lizards had it no better. They were given different boons, but all equally ensnared.

The gilar were alpha in the trinity. There were times a colony or pack could subjugate gilar for a time after a long war with the vulpes, but such stupidity always ended with decimation. The survivors died slowly beneath their rule. Smarter by far to kill the lone gilar, bury the bodies, and stay away from the revenge slaughter.

Deathwind scratched his long claws against the stone wall in frustration. There was no way to avoid them here. He reported to gilar and the pet mage in charge of the camp; ordered around like a servant and given scraps unless there was a Punishment. Then the blood flowed, and he drank deep.

What he wanted to do was kill something, but there were 'rules' they were forced to follow. The only rules should be those the colony queen decides when she made up her mind each night. There should be no schedules, no 'do this and not that' all the time. You did what you wanted and took what you wanted, or you died making the wrong decision. While the smart survived, the stupid fell into the dust of the ground dwellers.

Here though, he had to watch this section of the camp perimeter every night. Every. Night. He listened for attacks from beyond or escape from within. His red-gray vision scanned for motion in the darkness, a task for which vampires were best equipped. One sweep of the area at the beginning of his shift, and one at the end when the next perimeter scout had *just* finished a sweep.

Worst of all the rules was 'no killing the prisoners.' Not for anything, or you died in the next offering in their place. Not if they tried to run. Not if they attacked him. Not even if they managed to kill another guard. Only the pet mage and lizards could decide to kill, and then they took all the food the death brought, wasting the blood most of the time. Letting it fall to the ground. Slowly torturing the prisoner to death as his fellows watched.

He knew how to frighten prey-prisoners too. Rip out a throat, drain the sweetest death blood, and leave the body to rot in the pen. Simple, and so much more satisfying than wasting the blood until the prey lost consciousness.

But Deathwind would not be a sacrifice. He would follow the rules until he needed to no longer. Then he would take one of the vulpes and fly away to feast on elf blood before flying back to the main colony. Tonight would not be that night. There was too much order and too much recent success for those in control. So, he would scan the area yet again.

Hearing something to the north, Deathwind snarled a toothy smile and took wing into the darkness. Out over the dead fields, poisoned by the forges and denuded to feed them. The dead ground was why the vulpes—the 'elves' as they called themselves—were brought to his camp above all others. They were no good for the herds because they did not reproduce. You either ate them immediately or sent them here.

Stronger humans, sometimes dwarves, were kept for the work the vulpes could not do, but the male vulpes did most of the work. Killing and cutting their precious plants to feed the fires, manning the forges, making weapons for the people killing their kin more every day. Deathwind laughed silently at the beautiful cruelty as he clawed through the air.

From miles away he heard a shout and a whip crack, and he knew more gilar were coming with new prisoners. The pet mage sent for more workers after the last Punishment. He made a satisfied sound deep in his throat at the thought of all the fresh blood from the Punishment even as he effortlessly made a complicated maneuver in the air to change direction back toward the wall.

A fly might claim superior maneuverability, but *he* brought your end from above. Deathwind was one of the best. That was why he was there, and how he caught one of the vulpes trying to escape in the uprising. Stupid prey-prisoners thought every attempt was an uprising. Calling it something they thought gave it more power in their minds.

Stupid prey-prisoners thought we could not hear them plotting and planning. Do they think the vampires are stupid beasts? We destroyed the birds until their species was no more. If anything, we are the superior race of Elaria, he thought to himself and sneered.

And yet, they talked and planned and failed to notice the silent fly clinging to the wall. The guards knew about the uprising, and they knew about the plans and the hidden scraps of weapons and armor secreted away when the vulpes thought no one noticed. Vampires reported to the gilar, and the gilar told the mage, and they waited.

Deathwind laughed again about the gilar and vampires placed on watch for the planned time. The ones who thought they escaped punishment for not following the rules were put on watch at the time so the vulpes had *someone* to kill. So they would think their plan worked.

Idiots should have known there was no escaping

discipline, but they forgot, and so they died. Vulpes and humans killed the watch, only to find guard forces massed against them. Some knew what was coming and fought to the death to avoid it. Most could not find death and instead found themselves killing the weak among them the next day.

That was the brilliance of the Punishment. Those plotting and planning were not killed or tortured, at least not for an uprising. No, the weak were tortured, and the strong were given the means to end the torture. They could watch those they protected fade beneath the constant pain, or they could take those lives with their own hands.

A vampire would love either option, selecting whichever was most desirable on any given day. The 'good' races, though, were destroyed by it, haunted by the choice no matter what it might be. Their love for each other weakened them and ate away at everything that might make them strong; turned their love into weakness. On a day of Punishment, everyone ate well, except the prisoners, and they ate well for all the days it took the prisoners to learn the lesson being taught.

Forty-eight of their captives fed the guards at the last Punishment, and more were coming to take their place. Deathwind relayed the information to a gilar upon his return and settled onto the wall to wait. Hours passed, and he waited and waited still. Finally, near the time for the end of his shift, the gilar were seen herding their chattel before them.

More vulpes from the north with their skin the color of the dirt on which they made their homes. Many were brought from that place, where the gilar penned them in and harvested a full crop every year.

They trudged along, weary from running in chains, but mostly uninjured. The injured were killed and eaten along the way. There was no use wasting good food, and it meant they could push for a faster pace to move the prey-prisoners to their new positions.

He smiled to himself again. Captivity and the rules pressed upon him were bad. It was not worth the regular provision of his preferred diet, but he would enjoy the bounty. New prey-prisoners meant prey-prisoners not beaten down by the last Punishment. It meant another uprising would come. Another feast in the making.

CHAPTER ONE

Even after watching Annalla stretch her wings and practice flying, rebuilding their strength, the sight of them still took Larron's breath away. A few months were enough time to come to terms with the fact she was a fairy, but those wings were too fantastic to yet be commonplace. It was easy to forget as she usually kept them wrapped around her like a little dress.

They were wrapped then so they could follow Rolandor down the hallway without her taking up the entire width. He smiled as Thanon fell in beside her, with Geelomin and Bealaras right behind. His unit had been strangers when their mission began. He selected from among the volunteers with consideration of the limited likelihood any of them would return home. They could vanish into the unknown as all the messenger pairs had before them.

The Derou, and elves in general, were not known for approving suicide missions, but his Woodland was dying, and without aid, they would no longer exist within a year. The gilar siege was overrunning them already. In the spring, King Zeris had been ambushed and captured during a surprise raid. Search attempts were made for months. They continued until they yielded hundreds of acres of Woodland in a summer surge by the enemy. It was either retreat, or lose the defenders holding the lines. They were being squeezed until they burst and fell. So Larron's nephew,

Prince Erro, decided they could wait no longer.

Larron was ordered to select a larger messenger unit and make a run for the Palonian to request help. They sent aid to others earlier in the war. They held out as long as they could alone. Then it became time to call in those favors. He was authorized to do whatever it took to make that happen. Erro conveyed royal authority to negotiate. It was the only reason for his involvement, as otherwise, Geelomin would have led the unit.

No previous messengers returned. They were counted among the dead. His unit comprised those with fewer close ties back home. Fewer to worry over them and wonder if they lived. One of their numbers had not survived.

Palanthuiel was lost in the Claws to a gilar ambush. As their scout, he ranged ahead, ensuring the way was passable. One rainy evening, he failed to return. Larron did not think they would have survived then without the warning his absence conveyed. He died protecting them, and they mourned him still.

All five might have died had they not saved a wayward woman early into their journey. Larron smiled at the memory. She was one of the few who might match him in skill for combat, had hearing beyond the other races, and, of all possible wonders, she could *fly*.

"That was one monumental secret you kept," Prince Tyrus said, walking at his side.

The human prince traveled to the Palonian on orders for Ceru, seeking the northern war council, to discover the reason for missing shipments from their northern supply lines. Larron's scouts found them contemplating how to pass through the minor siege of humans surrounding the Palonian, so their two groups entered together.

"Don't get me wrong," he continued, "I'm not complaining. Just... Wow, you are really calm about this."

His perspective widened Larron's smile. "We have had time to accustom ourselves. Annalla joined our party nearly three months ago."

"It must be quite a story," Tyrus prodded, but Larron was

not going to share it just yet.

"We should maintain the secrecy, if you have no objection, until our grievances are addressed by the council. I would prefer neither of our needs become overshadowed by a discussion on a lost race."

Tyrus looked at him in confusion. "You do not think the fairy could help?"

He sighed and lowered his voice further. "It is not for me to explain further, but Annalla knows nothing of the fairy. Not whether they still live nor where to find them if they do. If we need the council's help, it is best to keep the fairy out of the discussion for now."

"I will order my men to remain silent on the matter. It will need to be discussed, but we have more pressing matters if she cannot offer immediate aid." His head bowed in concession, if not in satisfaction.

"Would you prefer to first be settled in your quarters, or shown to the bathing houses?" Rolandor asked as they approached the main doors.

Tyrus and his men requested quarters and were led away, but only Annalla had showered recently, so his party preferred a bath first, and he spoke for them at the wistful glances sent his way.

"I'd rather wait with you all once you are decent enough, if that is alright," Annalla said when both Rolandor and Larron looked at her.

"Please, follow me."

As they trailed him outside and through the forest toward one of the common bathing houses, he watched Annalla's head turn back and forth to take everything in. Larron had been raised in a Woodland. He could not guess what those who'd never entered one would think and feel. It must be even more...complicated for an elf in such a position.

She felt the border crossing at the Heartwood, and she seemed to be quietly focusing on the forest as they passed through it. Having traveled to all three Woodlands, he knew the connection was strongest with the Woodland one called home. Larron could not help but wonder which would call loudest to her. He wanted to be there as she traveled the world and found out.

Two elven women met them before the bathing house. If anyone were to assess the faults of elves, Larron could admit vanity would be at the top of the list. It was something that struck him every time he returned from his travels and was no different that time. Elves were beautiful. They knew it, and they enjoyed the fact it was acknowledged by others. Everyone not actively involved in the defensive efforts at that moment was dressed in resplendent attire, and the moment those scouting and defending rotated back to the Heartwood, they changed to match.

The two women before them were no exception. Both wore light, flowing gowns draped around them in layers. Perfectly coordinated with their individual elven features, the two glowed. One wore her light brown hair in only a couple of loose braids pulled back to hold her hair together gently. Her brown eyes held a tint of reddish umber, which her softly pink skirts and sleeves highlighted. The second also wore colors to accentuate her eyes. The bright jewel green flashed in the sun, complementing the soft sunrise color of her hair.

It was exactly the type of clothing Annalla would hate to wear. Elven clothing was always soft, strong and comfortable, but the clothing made for wearing in the Heartwood took the visual aspect to another level. Everything coordinated and worked well with the forest, which did not always mean blending. King Oromaer's clothing had been rather subdued for the Heartwood. Larron thought he made concessions in case of a sudden defensive need. Others they passed wore the more traditional exotic styles.

"Rolandor. Prince Larron." The brunette spoke first. She seemed to be in charge and nodded to them. "We have come to take the lady's measurements in order to bring suitable clothing."

He nearly laughed at the play of emotion crossing Annalla's face. First was excitement for the possibility of clothing that might fit properly, followed immediately by utter dread as she scanned the two women. Her eyes widened, nostrils flared, and lips pursed as she took in their loud, draping clothing. He wondered if she might faint and eagerly anticipated her response.

"Uh…" The sound extended, as though she did not want anyone else to feel compelled to fill the stretching silence while she thought fiercely for the right words. "I appreciate the…offer of clothing, and…would like to request that it includes nothing that…flows or swirls."

For all her skills, they would not be counting 'polite' or 'political' conversation among them. The second woman shook her head at the request, and both their faces clearly indicated they did not approve of her preferences in the Heartwood.

Larron thought it likely they were told to treat her as a visiting elven lady. The term did not have the same political or status meaning as for the humans, but it would indicate a preference of position or occupation. To be fair, even an elf soldier would probably prefer leisure attire within a Heartwood. Annalla acted more like a visiting human soldier.

"Very well, nothing that flows or swirls," the first sighed out in agreement, capitulating more easily than Larron expected. Her following whispered words explained it though, "I would also like to see these magnificent wings of yours. We will see what we can do to accommodate them."

An eager fascination entered her voice, and the whispering meant they knew to keep it confidential. She turned back to face Larron again as the two women squeezed in on both sides of Annalla, hooking their arms through hers.

"Your horses have been seen to and your belongings taken to your quarters," she called over her shoulder as they pulled along their skittish charge. "Clean attire will be brought for you all shortly, and your own will be taken and laundered. Prince Larron."

They gave a quick head bow to him and ushered Annalla through the opposite door from the one Rolandor held open. He had to bite his cheek to keep from smiling at the look of mild desperation on Annalla's face before the door closed behind her.

"As Jaria mentioned, clean clothing is being brought for you. I will return shortly with the healer." Then he too bowed and showed himself out.

It would feel good to be clean again. Elves had the fortune to rarely take on an unpleasant odor, but with the blood and dirt clinging to their clothing and bodies from the journey, they were far from appealing.

He disrobed and took a turn in the rainfall. It was a spot in the bathing house where cool water fell from the ceiling for someone to scrub off excess dirt before entering the warmer baths. The baths themselves operated with a constantly replenishing supply of water, which reduced the maintenance required. The use of the rainfall prior to entry also helped keep the pools clean and free-flowing.

It was a cold shower reminiscent of the rain they endured frequently of late, but there was soap here. They could finally remove every clinging layer of grime.

As Larron finally lowered himself into the steaming water, he felt some of his worry lift for the first time since their departure from the Derou. He forced his mind away from any speculation on the war, but it landed on a far more confusing and possibly dangerous subject: Annalla.

When he first made the decision to help her, he decided to bring her to the Palonian. She could be both watched and protected there. Her story and claim of having no memory convinced him she would need to be watched and guarded more than given their protection. Nearly three months had passed since those judgments and conclusions. They survived much together. In that time, he had come to respect her, care for her, and trust her.

But how far does that trust go?

Trusting her completely before meant risking his companions and his mission, but then it could mean risking the safety of the Palonian. He could not make the choice for them. It was a decision for their king, but he would be asked his opinion. It was not something to which he looked forward. His loyalties were torn, and he would need to find a way to confess the truth of his situation to Oromaer tonight when they spoke.

"—forget sometimes how different she is. We came to

expect and rely upon her unique appearance and abilities as time went on. Their reaction simply served as a reminder." Larron drifted back to the discussion around him to discover he was not the only one thinking about her.

"Her existence is a difficult truth to accept. Many long-held beliefs are put into question."

The opening of the door to the bathing house interrupted their conversation. A blond elf, to whom they had not been introduced, entered and laid out clothing on a bench. He left as quickly as he entered, giving them little time to offer thanks.

He was immediately followed by Rolandor's return with an incredibly old man leaning on him for support. The contrast between the two highlighted the immortality of elves.

Rolandor was an ideal figure of a man in his prime. He had the slim, toned frame common to elves, with shoulder-length dark brown hair tied back in elegant loops at the base of his neck. His every movement was full of grace, purpose, and strength.

Contrasting this picture of eternal youth, the man beside him exemplified one in the waning years of his life. His thinning hair and coarse beard were cut short, both completely white without even a hint of gray remaining. Though his muscles were loose, based on remaining mobility, he must have maintained fitness well into his later years. There were age spots and wrinkles clearly visible on the skin not covered by his robe—all of which translated to a feeling of frailty.

The old man relied on Rolandor's arm to help him move into the room and take a seat on the bench, but he carried himself in a way showing he did not give into age easily. His joints may have been protesting the movement, but his stubborn strength supported him as much as the elf at his side. There was also no lack of life in his blue eyes. They almost had an elven quality; the look of knowledge and experience deepening as years passed.

Those eyes moved slowly around the room, taking in each of the four elves soaking in their baths. As his gaze met Larron's it felt as though all his fears, hopes and desires—his very soul—were as exposed as his naked body immersed in the warm water. The sensation should have been unsettling, but the man put people at ease with the small smile playing on his lips.

"May I introduce you all to Healer-Mage Gregry?" Rolandor spoke once the mage sat on the closest bench. "Mage Gregry, this is Commander Larron, Prince of the Derou elves, Lieutenant Geelomin, Thanon, and Bealaras. I would have introduced you under more appropriate circumstances, but the mage heard of your fairy and wished to perform his healing in a location he thought he would be likely to encounter her. Of course, I told him the *male* bathing house was not such a location. Alas, he would not be deterred."

"I also heard she entered the Woodland clothed and armed as a full member of your party. It did not occur to me that something so small as gender distinctions would hinder her." His voice came out as strong as his gaze and filled with what Larron thought to be both humor and admiration. Mage Gregry waved a hand. "Please, do not let me rush your baths. I know how relaxing a good soak can be for weary bones after a long journey. We will deal with the healings whenever you are ready. These may be the fading years of my life, but I will not pass today."

Geelomin dipped his head to the mage. "Healer-Mage, it is good you come seeking our friend, as she too suffered wounds that would benefit from your skills, should you be willing to offer them."

"That I had not heard," he responded gravely. "I suspect everyone was so enchanted by the wings it did not occur to them to ask."

"Mage Gregry, please forgive me for my curiosity," Larron spoke up, "but I suspect you are older than the average magai lives to be."

His smile widened. "Not at all, young elf. I am over fifteen hundred years old now. I must admit I stopped counting at some point, so it is only an estimate. You are correct in believing I have seen more years than most magai ever will. I have been gifted with strong magic, and with it comes a longer life than most of my people. At least, so long as I do not meet with any unfortunate circumstances along the way." He winked one of his bright eyes.

Over fifteen hundred years meant he was older than all in Larron's party, other than Geelomin. Magai, those descended from the people originally from the realm of Scorcellen, naturally had longer lives than humans, living to around six hundred. To survive more than double those years was extraordinary.

All magai possessed some level of magical ability, ranging from simply feeling the magic in the world to possessing vast strength in one of their five power concentrations: combat, healing, architect, chemical, and artist. This strength often determined how effective they were at using the magic in the world in their selected area. Those with greater magical strength could perform greater feats or smaller tasks with greater speed and ease.

As for aging, a few magai in each generation whose power rose far above could live much longer. Judging by his age, Mage Gregry was a Power in the world. It was unfortunate for the allied people his aging body forced him to remain away from the front lines.

"I find it surprising I have not even heard of you in my travels," Larron said as he rose from the water to dry and dress. He had learned much of the magai visiting their strongholds across Elaria and thought he knew all the strongest alive in recent generations.

"Not so surprising. I too traveled a great deal, rarely staying in one place long or dealing with any injuries serious enough to turn my abilities into local legend. There has not been a war such as this before in my lifetime."

"There has never been war such as this in the history of the realm," Geelomin commented.

"Just so. Neither side had a habit of combining forces historically. And, as elves tend to remain healthy and uninjured, I never visited a Woodland until recent events necessitated my arrival here. It was decided I would bring some students escaping the academy massacre here. It is a large world, and even in all of my years, I have not met everyone worth knowing."

"We are fortunate to have someone of your abilities to

assist us and to teach the next generation of magai. I—" Larron stopped at a quick knock on the door.

"Is everyone clothed in there? Or are you all still lounging about in the water?" came Annalla's muffled voice.

He looked around to see the other three fighting smiles and shaking their heads. Those who had not gotten out before him had followed his lead, emerging from their baths and putting on the clothing. "We are dressed, Annalla."

Taking it for an invitation to enter, Annalla opened the door and was followed through by an exasperated woman, looking at Annalla as one might a naughty child, and apologizing for the intrusion. Annalla ignored the elf. The hint of a smile on both faces told him they were both more entertained than irritated by the interplay.

"It is nothing to be concerned about, lady. Our healer expected her." With an uncertain glance between him and Annalla, she sighed and shook her head before bowing herself out.

Rolandor adjusted quickly enough to introduce them. "Annalla, this is Healer-Mage Gregry. Mage, this is the elven-fairy Annalla."

"Nice to meet you. I'm sorry if I interrupted your bathing time. I can wait outside if you need me to."

"No need!" he exclaimed. "I am here as a healer."

She looked confused. "Okay, but Larron already patched us up pretty well."

"Annalla," Larron kept forgetting about her memory issues, "he is a Healer-Mage. That means he can heal with magic rather than relying on medicine and bandages."

"Oh." He could see her pondering. "How does it work exactly?"

Gregry smiled. "It is quite straightforward. I take magic from the world around us, shape it to my will, and send the power into you so I can see your injuries and repair them near instantly rather than requiring a natural healing process and duration."

Larron could see her flinch at the 'into' part of his explanation. It made him wonder if a mage was responsible for her transformation with some combination of healing and architect skills.

"Perhaps a demonstration would help," Larron offered. "You could watch him work on Thanon's arm injury and decide if you are comfortable with him healing you after."

He peered between Gregry and Thanon as he said the last to gain concurrence; one smiling serenely and the other nodding with a knowing grin. With their approval, he looked back at her with a question on his face.

She took a bolstering breath. "I suppose that's an acceptable compromise."

The old mage laughed out loud. Looking around, he said, "Well then, to business, I suppose. Which one of you is Thanon, and where is this arm I am to look at?" Thanon stepped forward, smiling. "Come, come sit over here and let me see."

The mage's fingers moved lightly over the fresh scar tissue. His face smoothed as his concentration shifted to a place no one else could see. Gregory's eyelids fluttered before his eyes regained their former alertness. The entire act took no longer than the span of a couple of breaths. During that time, Thanon's eyes closed as though in slumber, waking the moment it was done.

"You were right to ask for a healer. It would have retained limitations otherwise, as you strained the original injury more recently. Muscle is always a little trickier once healed magically. You need to treat it carefully. Gradually increase the intensity of any exercise so you do not pull what has newly grown together. I recommend nothing strenuous for at least two days." He turned toward the rest of the room. "Now, what are the other injuries I can be of assistance with?"

They turned to look at Annalla expectantly. She stubbornly bit her lip. Larron was not going to give up easily, so he raised his eyebrows and did not look away. He could feel the gazes of their friends lingering as well. With a sigh, she took Thanon's place on the bench, looking uneasy but resigned.

"My first fairy healing, how exciting. So, what have you injured recently?" Gregry asked when she sat down, but did not touch her or move closer.

Larron grunted but said nothing.

With an ironic, slightly bitter laugh, she replied, "What have I not? That would be an easier question to answer."

"Why don't we start at the top. Head and neck injuries?"

"This slice under my eye missed anything vital. My ears were injured months ago, but I think they are fine now, same with the earlier bruises."

"Shoulders, arms, torso?"

It hurt to hear the recounting of her injuries, but he did not interrupt. "Trakin bite to one shoulder and the other dislocated months ago, broken forearm from an arrow injury, a sword cut on my other arm... I think that is all of those."

"Wings," Thanon chimed in helpfully.

She made a face. "How could I have forgotten that?"

Her friend grinned. "Blocked the memory," Thanon suggested.

She grinned back. "Yes, my wing joints were injured badly and re-injured while still healing. I also think I may have cracked some ribs a few months ago, but I don't know for sure."

Gregry nodded, still not reacting. "Hips and below?"

"Cut on one leg from a sword, an arrow to the other leg did some damage when I rode a horse with it still in there..." She thought further. "Uh...trakin stab to the calf, a likely sprained ankle, and my feet were damaged from walking barefoot for a while, but the last few were a while ago too."

He stared at her for a moment as she listed off her recent injuries before shifting closer and gesturing toward her. "May I look and try to heal you? You need only pull away to stop me."

Her nod was slow, but it came, and Gregry held his hands toward her as if feeling along a wall. His face transformed to the same relaxed, distant look as his fingers moved. While his eyelids fluttered again, his gaze did not return immediately that time. Instead, he held them both still before his hands moved to settle against her skin.

One rested beneath her hair at the base of her neck, while

the other moved beneath the shirt she wore to rest against the skin of her abdomen. Frozen in time, the two seemed to barely breathe, completely oblivious to the rest of the world. Before anyone could begin to worry something was wrong, they came back to themselves.

"What in the world has happened to you, child?" The light exasperation in his voice held an edge of pity. "You have more recently healed wounds than the last twenty I healed from the field combined. You said all of these were within the last three months?"

She shrugged. "Yes, that's close enough of an estimate. As to your first question: a tree attacked me and then the ground joined the fight. Rats, cats, and giant bugs, then rocks and lizard people. Removing the arrows wasn't exactly pain free," she sent a wink in his direction, "so we can add elves to the list. Last, but certainly not least, the humans surrounding this place had a go at killing me."

"You forgot the nettles," Bealaras added.

Gregry appeared amused by their antics. "Well, some of the injuries are more than three months healed, so cheers to your medic and the healing of the fairy."

He eased back and sighed. "I put the finishing touches on your older injuries, so they will be as good as before. The last broken bone is ready for full use. Bones do not need to be worked back to their former strength when healed by a properly trained magai. I will give you the same caution on the flesh wounds as your friend. Nothing strenuous for at least two days, but you can both begin light exercise immediately."

"I thought bones took longer to heal."

"That will depend on the injury, but when it comes to magical healing, bones are easier. We put them back to the way they should be. With muscle, it is more difficult because the way they should be structured is not necessarily the same as how strong they need to be for what their owner intends."

"So, it's basically that strength has to be developed. You can't make someone strong."

"Basically. Though there is always some level of base strength, it depends on the person. So, did anyone else receive an injury on this perilous journey?"

Larron was glad she agreed to the healing and felt relaxed around the mage. He worried about the extent of her recovery and whether the injuries might permanently limit her. With a mage as powerful as Gregry declaring her healed, there was little risk of that.

Unless she puts herself in another situation where she can become injured, he thought to himself with a resigned sigh and laughed at the inevitability.

CHAPTER TWO

By the time the mage had finished healing the cut on Bealaras' head, it was well into the evening. Larron left for his invitation to dine with Oromaer.

Mage Gregry was fascinating to Annalla, and she liked him immediately. She would have remained there, speaking with him the rest of the evening if her stomach had not betrayed her at the mention of a meal being sent to their rooms. Their conversation had barely begun, but he shooed her off with her friends on the promise they would meet to talk again.

"Doesn't he need help back to his own room?" she asked as they stepped onto the path leading deeper into the Heartwood. "He isn't exactly a spry sapling of a man."

"His students are coming to aid him. They were told of his location and when to attend him," Rolandor assured her.

"If they are learning to be healers, why did they not come with him to observe?" she asked.

"They have other lessons in the afternoons. It has also been decided to keep knowledge of your heritage restricted until the matters Prince Larron and Prince Tyrus wish to bring before the council are addressed. If you are agreeable to this plan."

Was this the rejection she'd feared? Could she take the words at face value? "About how long will that be? I don't want to get too far behind on my training."

"The council meets every third day. The last was yesterday, and neither prince specified a need for an emergency session."

"Two days is acceptable. Thank you for asking." She tried to sound more like an elf. He did not appear to notice, but Thanon gave her an odd look.

They followed their guide back toward what she thought of as the palace, though it bore no resemblance to what she would expect visually from the term. Buildings in the Heartwood were built around, between, and even *in* the trees growing everywhere. Beautiful carvings covered every inch of exposed wood that was not a still-living tree and every large chunk of stone. Based on the guard post, she expected the Heartwood to blend everything together and look exactly like an empty forest, but she had been very wrong.

While the trees were an integral part of the buildings and structure of this sprawling city, the blending and camouflage were structural, not cosmetic. Like the beautiful dresses of the two elves who had taken her measurements, the buildings and streets were lined with color. Stained woods, carpets, canopies, curtains, and more were all strung about and decorating the Heartwood in a beautiful array. It was a fantastical mixture of happiness, serenity, and exuberance.

The people were as beautiful and colorful as their city. They draped themselves in flowing swaths of color from head to toe. Elegant dresses, tunics, and robes were paired with hair in delicate loops and braids. Only a few of the elves were brown and tan, like her friends. Thanon told her the Derou were the elves with dominant skin tones in the range of browns and reds. The Auradian dominant tones were gray, blue, and green. Most they passed there in the Palonian were fairer, with pink or yellow undertones, and with hair ranging from golden yellow to bright red, and even to pale white.

The elves themselves were diverse, but she was caught off guard when they passed an individual not even five feet tall with golden fur, large eyes and ears, and a muzzled face where the upper lip was more connected to the nose than in elves or humans. Something about the person prodded at the edge of remembrance, but she could not bring to mind whatever knowledge of those people lay dormant in her memories.

There were fewer people out and about at that point. Annalla suspected they were indoors for dinner or settling in for the night. The building she called the palace was a cluster of interconnected rooms spanning between a few sections of trees. The building extended up into the branches, in some places up to one hundred feet into the air.

Rolandor led them along one wing of the palace and up about three stories off the ground to an area within one of the larger and taller structures built wide around a central tree. The hallway circled the trunk, with rooms spreading off along the perimeter. He indicated two pairs of doors at the far side of the loop, letting them know whose belongings had been taken to each room. The door closed behind her and Annalla leaned against it, sighing deeply and shaking her head as if shaking off nerves. Only then did she look around the room given to her.

It was a simple but elegant little bit of space. There was a bedroom, with a small privy room off to the side, and a sitting room. All the exterior walls curved. The bedroom was similar to the one given to her at the guard outpost, but half again as large. The quality of the fabric was better and there were touches of decorations like wall hangings, a potted plant, and curtains. All colorful but muted, as though they did not want to overwhelm visitors with a conflict between the personality of the person and the space.

Along with the soft bed, there was a small table with a washbowl and pitcher in the bedroom with a large, empty trunk standing open at the foot of the bed. She wondered absently how much clothing it would take to fill it. A little trepidation crept in at the thought that the two seamstresses would try. She had nothing against the clothing worn in the Heartwood other than that it would be impractical to travel with and in.

There were four chairs around an oval table in the sitting

room where she'd first entered. All five pieces boasted beautiful carvings resembling the trees from which the wood for them must have come. That room contained a fireplace, tucked into the wall adjacent to the bedroom and lined in thick stone. The promised food waited on the table.

A knock sounded at her door as she started toward the table, so she changed direction to answer it.

"Thanon," she said unnecessarily when the door opened.

He smiled and held up his tray. "I thought I might join you, if you do not mind."

"Come on in," Annalla laughed at his meek expression and stood aside.

"Oh! Wait for us!" She poked her head out to see Bealaras, with Geelomin trailing behind him, headed her way, both with trays in hand.

While Bealaras went in to join Thanon at her small table, Geelomin stopped before her and spoke quietly, "If you prefer solitude this evening, I can make that happen."

Her eyes softened at his consideration. "I wouldn't know what to do with myself alone another night. You are all more than welcome."

She closed the door after him, and they rounded out the group sitting down to eat. It was a simple meal of soup, bread, and fruit, with some cold tea to drink. She wondered if there was a way to get hot tea.

"How do I get food in the morning?"

Geelomin paused. "I expect it is done as in the Derou. You place your dinner tray out in the morning when you wake, and it will be exchanged for a breakfast tray. Plan for a quarter to half an hour before food will arrive. Tomorrow evening there will be a feast in honor of the visiting leaders. Instead of bringing a tray, a guide will lead us to the correct location."

While she nodded her understanding, Thanon spoke up, "Do you think your father was Palonian? Larron was correct that your coloring is most common here. Based on when you entered the Heartwood, does this one feel right to you?"

Annalla thought back to the moment they entered and the feeling of deep connection. She wiggled her head in indecision. "I will not deny I felt something, but so did all of you. Larron described it as 'staggering' when he spoke of the difference. I would not describe what I felt that way."

He wrinkled his nose. "I was in and out of the Heartwood enough to know it is stronger at home, so I do not think this is your home Woodland either, based on your response. You still have two more to try, though."

She smiled but was quiet while the three of them talked about the differences they noticed between there and home. They compared the colors and the people and the food, discussing differences and preferences between the little they'd seen so far, speaking as though the survival of their home did not hang by a thread.

Annalla sat there and wondered more and more what was for show and what was real. If they could pretend then, the friendship they showed her might also have been pretense. In what way were they looking out for her?

"Annalla?" Thanon called her name, bringing her out of her thoughts.

"What was that?"

"You have not been listening at all, have you?" He started to laugh, but something he saw made him change his response. "Is something wrong?"

She looked between them and saw concern. Annalla *wanted* to believe they were her friends. "You didn't trust me," she said. "You all lied to me. I understand why, I really do. I just thought it wasn't like that after a while. I thought it had changed."

All three looked confused for a moment. Thanon's eyes cleared first. "You are referring to Commander Larron being Prince Larron."

Annalla was most angry with Thanon. He encouraged her pointless infatuation in the guise of friendship, so she let a little of her hurt and anger onto her face as she acknowledged his guess.

It was Geelomin, however, who responded, "I do not

believe you understand fully in this case, Annalla. You know of our dire situation, and you know the message and request we carry. If that was the whole of it, then you are correct, not telling you as we came to know you would have been a choice we made."

"So, what is different?" she asked, trying for patience. "If this is some honor about protecting your leaders, then it is still about you not trusting me not to betray you."

"Our orders to bring a message of our plight to the council are effectively our secondary mission. Larron has dispensation from Prince Erro to negotiate on behalf of the Derou elves. He alone has the authority to authorize a debt on behalf of all Derou. The primary orders were to see Larron to the Palonian at any cost and to reveal to no one his position until we were safe with our allies. If we had met any elf along the road, or any known ally, who possessed no prior knowledge of Larron, then we would have proceeded the same with them."

"We more than trust you, Annalla. We are family now." Bealaras looked around the table. "All of us are family."

She gave him a weak smile as the others nodded in agreement. "Thanks. I guess I just feel embarrassed about everything. I probably should have acted differently all this time."

"Does this mean you are going to stop arguing with him?" Geelomin asked with a grin. "I am not certain you are capable of such restraint."

At the same time, Thanon grabbed her arm with an intensity unlike him. "This changes nothing."

"It changes everything," she said with the same intensity, before looking at Geelomin and grinning back at him. "And it changes nothing. I also don't think I could maintain the necessary level of restraint for long, so the *healthy disagreements* will probably continue."

Thanon was not happy with her reply, but he let himself be led back into the conversation, which turned to talk of the feast the next day, and what different dishes they hoped would be available. Annalla shook off his worry.

She was glad she had asked them about her concern. It

would have continued to fester and taint their relationship with her hurt and confusion. They were her friends, her family, and she needed the trust and stability she felt with them on their journey to remain strong.

CHAPTER THREE

Larron shook his head at the sight of two guards in the hallway as he headed for Annalla's door. *Any chance she did not notice?* he thought wryly to himself.

It turned out Tyrus had been there before, so not even the visiting humans had a guard at their hall. That meant the only chance she failed to notice Oromaer's caution was if she inexplicably went blind from the healing the day before. It was the last time he had seen her because of an early invitation that morning to hear a report on the siege surrounding the Palonian.

The main force did not settle into their current positions until most of the shipments from the harvest season departed. As they were relatively ineffective there, the decision was made to leave them alone to prevent the men from supporting the enemy elsewhere.

Oromaer expected to leave them there through the winter, or at least until late in the season. Deprivation would make their enemies slower and weaker when they did attack. It would need to be far enough before spring planting for injuries to heal and able bodies to serve. At that moment, there was nothing to do except wait and watch.

"Lady Annalla is not in her room," the guard spoke before Larron reached her door to knock, and he shifted to face him. "The lady Jaria came to collect her for a fitting a short time ago. I believe she will be heading straight to the feast from there."

"Thank you. Do you know if clothing arrived for me?"

"It has and was put away in your rooms."

He would have happily remained in what he wore were they not guests of honor at the feast. As it stood, something specifically tailored was more appropriate.

"Commander." Geelomin leaned out of his door and gave one pointed look from Larron to the guard before continuing, "We are changing. Lady Jaria wanted to make some final alterations to Annalla's clothing and pulled her away. She told us not to wait as they left."

"Thank you. I have come to change myself and should only be a moment."

He put action to word and soon stood in the hall with the rest of his unit. They looked clean and respectable for the first time since leaving home. Larron felt relieved they were getting time to rest and recover. No matter the physical healing Mage Gregry provided, hearts and minds needed *time* to heal.

"King Oromaer placed guards in our hall," Geelomin stated. His voice remained neutral, but he knew him well enough to hear the disapproval.

Yes, he did, even knowing she is my life mate and has saved our lives multiple times. He thought it but would not say the words out loud there and then. He settled for an agreement. "I have told him such is unnecessary. This is his Woodland to protect. He has his own people, as well as the refugees, to consider."

"This goes beyond distrust of the unknown. He is stating we may have been compromised by her and *we* are not to be trusted either. Even I do not appreciate the implication, and you know as well as I that Annalla is unlikely to hold her tongue."

They approached the queue to enter the large dining hall. Larron stopped and looked at his lieutenant, a slow smile spreading. "Then tonight's feast should prove entertaining."

Still laughing, they followed directions from one of those serving that shift. His three companions were seated together, while Larron proceeded further up the tables. As the highest-ranking elven guest, he took his place at Oromaer's left hand.

Shortly after they arrived, servers emerged with food heaped upon platters, setting them along the center of the tables. It was not a large feast by usual elven standards, but in a time of war, they rarely spent that much effort on one meal. Expertly prepared game, vegetables, and fruits were spread before him. A few bottles of higher-quality wine were passed around. He could not help but remember the plight of his own Woodland as he looked at the array before them.

Many years had passed since the Derou had enough people to spare in such preparations, and it would be many years, many generations of men before they recovered enough. If they recovered at all.

There was no malice in his mind toward the Palonian, no desire to see them suffer as his own people. It eased some of his sorrow to see there remained intact Woodlands. At the same time, it made it impossible to forget, for even a moment, that he would never again return to the same place he recalled from childhood.

"I should have thought this would be painful for you. You do not need to stay."

"I am sorry?" Larron startled and turned his head toward Oromaer.

"Your face, my friend. We must seem heartless throwing our better fortune at you, and I would not have you suffer."

Larron shook his head. "It is good to see a Woodland with so much life. I would not have it subdued on my account. Do not worry about me." He paused. "I hope my melancholy is not the reason you are delaying."

"There are still seats to be filled before we begin, and not everything has been brought out yet." He smiled. "Shortly now."

Annalla was one of the last to enter, though Larron needed to look again before he recognized her. He had never seen her properly healthy, clean, and attired before. It was startling the change the combination brought to her appearance. Her figure was athletic and strong, but the clothing she had worn to that point did nothing to flatter her. Skilled elven tailors had altered simple scout clothing to fit. Her wings wrapped smoothly around her, working with the fabric rather than causing it to bunch up or tangle, appearing like a fine lace wrap. The colors of her wings blended perfectly with the uniform. Forest greens and browns shifted and merged with every movement.

Her hair was pulled back into one tight braid, both practical and elegant. He recognized the style as a combination of one used by elven fighters with decorative loops along the main line. It brought attention to her bright blue eyes and exposed her ears, reminding everyone of her elven heritage. Annalla's fair, smooth skin was free of blood and bruises, and she walked without a limp.

She had the purposeful and graceful tread of an expert fighter, with no wasted motion. Annalla screamed of hidden strength and danger. He could not take his eyes off her, and barely registered the fact she was led to his own table and the king indicated she should sit next to his wife.

"Are you certain this is where you wish me to sit, Majesty?" she asked sardonically when she reached his side. "I was sure I would be relegated to eating in my rooms tonight…for my own safety, of course."

The guards had not gone unnoticed. Larron pursed his lips against a smirk. *If Oromaer is concerned about her, though, it is odd to place her at Arbellie's side.*

Oromaer did not take insult from her tone, neither did he change his mind or offer apologies.

"Lady Annalla, my son has command of the watch tonight, so there is a place open at my table. I would speak with you, if you are not opposed." He smiled at the last and was given a small smile in return.

"Honored, Majesty. But, please, call me Annalla. I believe I have proven myself far too stubborn, blunt, and uncultured to ever qualify as a lady. At least in comparison to the esteemed Lady Jaria."

"Please, Annalla, have a seat. We will do what we can to change this underfed look about you." Lady Arbellie had always been the more parental of the pair. During his fostering there, she took on that role for him. It was a fitting personality trait for an elven consort.

Annalla took the seat while Oromaer looked around the room. He seemed to be counting guests. Finally, he stood to offer a brief, traditional toast to friends and allies, indicating an official start to the meal. Arbellie turned to engage Annalla once more.

The seating arrangement suddenly made perfect sense to Larron, and he bit back amused irritation. She was there at Arbellie's invitation, providing her access to interrogate his life mate.

"Our visiting fairy," she said conspiratorially and patted her hand. "Are you comfortable? Finding everything you need here?"

Annalla was clearly caught off guard by the caring gestures, likely wondering if they were feigned. "Um, sure, I guess."

Arbellie pressed on, undeterred by the stunted response, "A stellar review. Is there nothing we can do to improve your situation?"

"Doubt it." She shook her head as if to clear it and adopted an expression Larron was certain she thought to be placid. "Sorry. No, I am fine, really. This is better than I have known. I appreciate your hospitality."

"So, there is nothing we can do for you?" she pressed.

"What I would ask is not feasible at this time."

"If it was? What would you ask?"

Annalla blinked at her, then shook her head, fighting back a laugh at the persistence. Arbellie simply waited with a gentle smile until Annalla sobered and sighed. "Weapons, as those entrusted to me seem to have gone missing. Permission to fly without the risk of being shot down. Information. I find neither dependence nor ignorance to my liking."

"Perhaps you could think of it as a reward, rather than dependence?" Larron asked, even though he agreed with her.

A non-committal grunt was her first response. The placid

expression was gone, replaced by a sneer. "Nothing says 'thank you' like a guard at the door and crossbows aimed at your back."

Larron noticed the guards around the room. It had only been a faint hope Annalla would not observe them as well. Arbellie raised an eyebrow at her life mate—one of her more open public expressions of surprise.

"My guard thought it prudent. You disagree?"

She sent him an incredulous look. "An *elf* could climb down from my window. I have wings. If you are going to guard me, it would be *prudent* to place guards there as well. And if I wanted you dead, Majesty, you would already be dead."

He doubted anyone else saw the flick of her wrist. The guards certainly did not react. Larron watched closely because he knew she was willing and able to try something insane.

Few would have noticed the momentary look of shock crossing Oromaer's face. Larron was impressed with the level of control it took to not jump out of his seat. While others did not see a reaction from the king, all sitting nearby noted the small dinner knife quivering in the arm of the king's chair between two of his fingers.

Annalla's expression echoed the frozen shock seen on the faces around her. She had shielded the movement perfectly from the guards watching and waiting with loaded bows.

"As I recall, you are plenty dangerous without carrying around weapons of your own." Larron was the first to speak.

"I manage," she said with the hint of a sad smile. Looking at Oromaer again, she took a deep breath. "I will hold to your decision. If you want me to leave, I'm gone. If you want to lock me up, point out the prison. If you want me to help, then point me to the fighting. It is one of the few things I know I am good at."

Oromaer set the knife gently back on the table, meeting her stare. "Why should I trust you, Annalla? Why should I believe anything you have told Larron?"

"You shouldn't. A chance meeting with an amnesic half-elf—thought to be an impossibility—and half-fairy—thought to be extinct. On top of that, I have shown the capability to kill you easily and without warning should I ever betray whatever trust you place in me. I can identify and evade your scouts, which would make it possible for me to lead your enemies in an attack against the Woodland. Four elves have already been taken in by my act and led me straight into your Heartwood.

"Everything about me is preposterous. The awful theories about me seem more plausible than any explanations I have been able to think of over the last three months. I have shown I can be an asset, but is it worth the risk I could betray you?"

The king's face looked sad to Larron's familiar eye as he said, "Probably not. That much information is too great a risk in the hands of someone capable of acting on it, to the detriment of my people. I would be acting foolishly."

"Better you than me having to make such a decision. I'm not a nice person when threatened."

The exchange was light, but Larron sensed the underlying tension. Burdens and responsibilities of leadership weighed on Oromaer. He had witnessed similar stress add years to a human's face and body. Oromaer's hair would not turn gray, his face would not wrinkle, and his back would now bow beneath the pressures, but the signs were there if one knew how to look.

He had aged. Not in body, but his soul was older since Larron had seen him last, and more so than for which the years could account.

Annalla was...different. It might have simply been his perception, but she was constantly handing him contradictions. She was young, he thought, no more than three decades into her life, which would still make her a juvenile if fully elf. Yet even with no memory, he believed she had seen more than most would in a lifetime.

What happened to age her so, even when she could not remember it? Whatever it might be also gave her confidence and a natural sense of authority. There was no fear in her. What he sensed from her, beneath the banter, was irritation.

Lady Arbellie placed a hand over Oromaer's where it rested next to the knife. "And yet..."

The depth to their gaze spoke volumes, but it was a language only the two of them understood. The bond between them was centuries old and drew them closer with every year. She could be saying any number of things with those two words. Larron suspected most of them were about him and the bond to which he admitted the night before.

Oromaer sighed and smiled with a love in his eyes so deep Larron could only fathom. "And yet..."

"The guard will remain until after the council meeting," he said finally. "I wish to stop further rumors until after such time as the leaders can be informed simultaneously. They have no orders beyond keeping the curious out at this time. I will not be guarding your window."

"Annalla." Arbellie considered the conversation concluded. "I heard you and young Thanon were lamenting the lack of pie during your travels, so we opened some of our jarred fruits for the occasion. Many people like the apple pie, but I am partial to berry pies myself."

Larron knew it would not be the end of the conversation. One way or another, there would be a situation to call both their actions and responses into question again. He could only hope it continued to leave both alive and well...and not holding him accountable.

"It is good to see reunions. They are so infrequent of late." The voice came from further down their table.

"Mage Gregry!" Annalla called out. "I did not even see you there when I came in. I'm usually more observant."

"I arrived late. With the wine—as is my preference—so I was not here for you to notice. You look lovely and dangerous."

"Thank you. I suppose I should say something like, you are looking rather chipper this evening?"

"I like that. So, my dear, how are you enjoying the Heartwood thus far?"

"I can't say I have seen much of it. I'm afraid I overslept this morning, and most of my day was spent in repeated fittings and clothing alterations. Thanon dragged me on a small tour, though. I love the color and artistry of the buildings here."

"As do I. The visual pleasure is one of the reasons I regret not visiting the elves sooner. I'm afraid I always expected everything to blend more and just look like a forest." He laughed at himself.

Annalla grinned. "I thought the same thing. Like you would need to squint and unfocus your eyes to see any of the buildings."

"No matter how many times I describe a Heartwood to humans and magai, that misconception persists," Larron grumbled with a shake of his head.

"That's because all of your travelers wear green and brown," Gregry explained. "No variety at all."

Annalla looked thoughtful as they bantered. "I have to say, I thought the races were still separated for the most part, but there are so many others I saw as we walked around."

"And they still are, for the most part," Gregry replied. "The Palonian is different because it was the most secure Woodland and still serves as a sanctuary or waystation for many refugees."

Larron took the explanation further, "The beginning was bad. The initial surprise made it difficult to offer aid in those early years. War dragged on, and our forces were squeezed more each year. Areas we have control over tightened steadily over time. We were bound to cross over more as our lands shrank. You see more of the interspersion than previously in most places, but the Palonian is further along that path."

"As to the current residents of the Palonian Woodland," Gregry continued, "I only know specifically how the majority of the magai arrived." He paused dramatically. "They came in with me. I was teaching at the smaller academy attacked by Kahnlair's vampires a few years into the war. It is a tragic tale—I will not burden you, nor shadow this feast, with the details—but my orders were to take care of the students, sent with me and a handful of other teachers, leaving before his full force arrived.

"Only the fully trained combat magai and a few others for

support stayed behind to defend the stronghold. No one suspected the strength Kahnlair had in the way of magic until that attack. The academy was lost, and with it, so many, so much power. We escaped with the students.

"To avoid having all of us caught at once if there was a pursuit, the remaining teachers decided it would be best to split up. We could never defend the students and face attackers with most of the combat magai gone. Some headed for the human capital, some to the Auradia Woodland, others to our capital city and the primary academy.

"The group I was with came here. King Oromaer is kind enough to allow us to remain, and we continued teaching and practicing our magic within the Woodland to aid the elves and other refugees."

"I am pleased you made it here safely. If you don't mind my asking, what does he use it for now, the academy he took over?"

"As far as I know, he was only there one time, just after it was taken. It was given over completely to the attacking colony of vampires shortly following. They hold it still. Why do you ask?"

"No reason. I just wondered if you had some magic weapon hiding there. It seems strange he would make such a grand showing and not take it as his own base, right?"

"I never gave it much thought, actually."

"Kahnlair has not changed his base at all. He remains within the desert, but it does not hinder him. Some aspect of his magic allows him to work through others," Oromaer added. "We suspect he does not trust most of his commanders, which is wise when considering gilar, vampires, and windani. He can remain where he is well protected and work against us from a distance."

Annalla shook her head with pursed lips. "There is nothing I can say other than, 'I'm sorry for your loss.'"

There was silence for a moment, but Gregry broke into it with a kindly, sympathetic smile and changed the subject, "We do what we are able. Now you can tell me what you think of these wines. I dare say we need Oromaer's kin to visit more often. He is usually rather stingy with the best vintages."

Arbellie joined in his jesting, and they deftly turned the conversation back to the topic of food and drink, with Oromaer taking most of their good-natured fun at his expense. The feast continued. Idle conversation with the inevitable war-time dips into sorrow and fear. They did the right thing at those times: they acknowledged the moment and moved on. Larron relaxed as the evening wore on, more so than he had in years. He wondered if he would ever feel that at home ever again.

CHAPTER FOUR

Geelomin's sword flashed toward her side and was met by her own blade well in advance of finding a mark. She was content to retreat for a pass or two, testing her body's responses to the different positions and postures now that she was healthy. Their little group—without Larron—had taken her on a tour of the Woodland farms that morning and decided to linger in one for a training session. She suspected Geelomin tested her skill as well.

The fields were all harvested and stored or shipped as needed. The elves called them fields, but they were more like meadows to her mind. Each one was planted more like a kitchen garden, with rows of varied crops rather than one crop per field. Instead of fences, they used hedges to keep larger animals out. Smaller creatures coming in to sneak away with the crops were trapped to use in stews and such.

About a quarter of each meadow-field grew outside the hedges. Most of those crops were probably lost to the forest animals. Elves working the fields considered those areas their contributions to helping maintain the Woodland herds.

Along with varied crops—which included fruit and nut trees clustered here and there—were scattered forest trees and brush. It looked like they had simply not taken the time to clear them out to plant, but Thanon said it was intentional to keep the forest connected and present in cultivated land.

"Isn't all the green and growing stuff connected to the elves?" she asked him.

"You felt the difference when you entered the Heartwood." He gave her a look that said, 'use your head' and continued, "It is a matter of degree, and a Woodland is degrees more *connected* than other plants. We are somewhat symbiotic with all flora, but the relationship with wild Woodland is deeper."

"I do not know if the elves as a race would continue to exist should all the Heartwood die," Bealaras added.

So, they let the forest grow into their fields and the forest creatures take some of their crops. The field they were in had lain fallow that season, so wild grasses along with some random vegetables from those not harvested last year grew around them as Geelomin and Annalla put on a fighting demonstration for the other two.

Back and forth their sparring went. They still pulled their hits in case of a trip on questionable footing, but gently tested her strength, agility, and stamina in a steady routine. It was somewhat more difficult to push just to the edge of danger with her strikes. Annalla needed to hold back rather than press full out, and the control was a test in itself.

"Enough!" Geelomin called a halt, and they stepped apart before accepting the towels held out by their entertained assistants. "You are as talented as I have long suspected. I still profess you should ask Larron to perform the complete weapons dance with you. You obviously know it, based on the routines we completed together. It has not been performed in its entirety in some years now, to my knowledge."

"I believe that is because nearly a quarter of the performances end in a serious injury for one or both of the participants," Bealaras said incredulously. "Are you not usually the voice of reason and restraint, Geelomin?"

His comment had Geelomin lifting an eyebrow while Annalla and Thanon laughed.

"I may not be a dancer myself, but I am extremely skilled at identifying weapon proficiency in my students. I also witnessed a completed dance many centuries ago. It inspired me to become a trainer," was his response.

"Do not worry, Bealaras, we can make sure Mage Gregry is there to watch, just in case Geelomin is wrong."

Annalla grinned at Thanon. "Very true. I know I can perform it, but we wouldn't want to risk Larron becoming permanently injured."

That set the two of them off again, slumped together cackling, while Bealaras rolled his eyes and Geelomin threw up his hands as though done with them. She saw him look to the sky before he spoke again.

"We should start back. I want time to bathe before the mid-day meal."

"Oh! Me too!" She jumped up. "Did one of you mention my desire for hot tea to someone, or does its sudden inclusion in my morning meal mean the guards are spying on me?"

"Annalla, you complained about the lack of hot tea *all day* yesterday," Thanon bumped her with his elbow. "Of course, we requested it for you."

"You did ask numerous times as we toured the Heartwood," Bealaras agreed.

"Are you trying to tell me you do not relish all the hot food and hot water available now that we are no longer traveling?" Her tone conveyed distinct disbelief.

"Ha! No. I am more subtle in my appreciation of such things, however."

"Thanon, I do believe a comparison to Annalla is the only time I could agree with subtle as a suitable description for you." Geelomin's statement, made in a flat tone, had them both stopping.

"Hey!" they both complained at the same time, which resulted in Bealaras and Geelomin chuckling as they continued walking.

The council meeting was about to begin, so they wanted to get back for it. She suspected at least Geelomin would attend with Larron, and she wondered if she would be invited. Annalla hoped she would. She was invested in these people and this war. With her skills—as recognized by Geelomin—she could be an asset. However, she knew assets were not always consulted in how they were to be used.

The meal she found after her shower was made of easy to prepare and store foods. Annalla expected they would be called on soon, so she ate quickly and listened intently. The presence of the elves was requested soon after she had finished eating. She was not asked to join them. Their invitation was given quietly, and it was only by virtue of her fairy hearing she knew what took place. To their credit, her friends did not attempt to sneak past her door.

Bristling again, Annalla quashed the feeling of becoming a caged bird. It frustrated her because she wanted a say in her future and to go into it well informed. She could just leave. On the wing, she could escape most things, and she was obviously skilled enough to take care of herself.

Still, she owed the elves, especially the Derou. Looking at the empty road below her window, Annalla remembered another avenue available to her.

If he did not want me to attend, he would have added a guard, she reasoned mentally. *I did tell him to do so, after all.* With a quick leap out and a snap of her wings, a weightless feeling swept over her body as she caught the air and drifted down.

She had to rein in the feeling of freedom and the urge to soar. There was still a high probability the elven guards would take aim at any form flying above. Rather than taking to the skies, Annalla dropped swiftly and silently to the ground and wrapped her wings about her again.

The sounds of her friends being led away receded to the north, so she turned to follow. Even overcast, the early afternoon offered no deep shadows in which she might hide. She would stand out more if she tried to sneak. Instead, she tried to look as though she belonged in that section as much as anyone else. Her walk was purposeful, her eyes friendly but addressing no one. People crossing her path waved as they had the last couple of days while she was out with Jaria or her friends.

It was a few minutes before she caught up enough to

distinguish the king's voice making introductions. Enough time for her to consider how much of a bad idea that was. She showed disrespect for their wishes and generosity by spying on them. An overwhelming frustration pushed her forward despite those reservations.

Oromaer's voice came from around a corner. Annalla stopped and peered around. Before her stood an open courtyard. With foliage acting as exterior walls, it looked like more of a forest clearing turned into a courtyard. At the center was a modest stone structure the size of one large room. The room was eight-sided, with an archway on every other wall. The roof was constructed of elegantly carved stone and a translucent material she could not identify. Thick wooden beams supported the thin, flexible dome, tapering as they came together, and meeting at the center.

Through the nearest opening, Annalla distinguished the edge of a table amidst the people crowded around it. She cautiously moved forward into the open area, staying opposite where the attention of those inside focused. As she neared the gathering, she identified figurines and colors on the table. Annalla guessed the figures were arrayed on a map, though she could not make out details.

She came up behind some elves, both seated and standing. If she interpreted the organization correctly, the leaders or highest rank were at the table. Those standing behind them or at the walls were subordinates or guards. Just to her right were three short, sturdy, and hairy people.

Dwarves. They were nearly as wide as they were tall, and most of the girth would be attributed to muscle rather than fat. Beside each was at least one axe, and all were in full armor. Like humans, dwarves were from Aryanna, but the humans procreated much faster and were wiping out the people they feared for their differences. Larron mentioned once, during their journey, that he suspected they would be extinct if the connection to Elaria had not opened up, allowing them to escape and make a home there.

Beside the dwarves were four of the small feline people— *What are they called?* she wondered to herself once more—

including the only woman in the room she could see. Not simply large cats—though they did have fur, slit pupils, and other feline facial features—their form was distinctly humanoid. The way they sat gave the impression they were as graceful as the elves, with the same agility or better.

Across from the dwarves were Tyrus and Harndorn. It looked like they had displaced the usual humans based on the unknown men standing against the wall, deferring the seated positions. Closer to the king at the head of the table was another small group of humans dressed like Gregry in tunics of varying colors. They were likely magai, based on her experience with the healer-mage. Rolandor and Larron, with his group behind, sat next to the king.

Annalla could have listened in from the far edge of the clearing, tucked away in some corner. It would have been safer than standing within sight of an opening.

A niggling twist in her gut, a nagging voice in her head, told her neither choice was right. Eavesdropping, spying on people she would call friends and their allies was a far cry from a demonstration of trust. Damn it if the exclusion wasn't frustrating and insulting, though. Especially after their discussion at the feast.

Okay, I can't claim some grand leadership position anywhere, but neither can Thanon, and I took an arrow for one of their princelings.

Her stubborn streak would not let her walk away, and her conscience would not allow her to remain where she lingered. The king's notice took the decision out of her hands. He stopped mid-sentence. In moments, the rest of the room turned to look at her. Elven guards drew and aimed in her direction.

"Annalla, I wondered when you might join us today," Oromaer said calmly. "Please, if you do not mind waiting there for Prince Larron and Prince Tyrus to share their information, we will then proceed to your announcement."

His acceptance caught her off guard. She nodded and fell in beside the dwarf at the wall. Oromaer's face gave nothing away. Annalla could not tell if he was angry, surprised, amused, or furious, which made her more worried than any of the expected emotions. The only explanation she could think of was that it had been a test of some sort. Annalla was not sure what sort of test exactly. She had not been explicitly told to remain in her room. But it was done, and all she could do was wait for her time to come.

"Prince Tyrus," Oromaer continued, "I believe you wished to address the council."

Tyrus was a broad man with olive skin a little lighter than Larron's. His tilted gray eyes gave a brief, confused look between her and the king, but he rose to speak.

"Thank you, King Oromaer. I was dispatched by His Majesty of Ceru, King Garrett, to investigate the northern supply lines and report to this council on our situation. We received only half of the northern harvest last fall and have seen nothing this year as of the time I left." He paused and looked down with a grim expression. "The lands around our farms have been hunted to near extinction and the farms are either overworked to produce little, or too dangerous to man.

"When the supplies slowed as we moved later into the harvest season, my father ordered additional supply runs into our lands. We know severe weather has caused shortages before, and he acted on such an assumption even as we sent messengers due to the corresponding reduction in communication. We emptied the stores to keep everyone fed this year. Were it not for the fact so many are dead, we would have lost more to starvation.

"Auradia is doing what they can to supplement our stores, but most of their able-bodied are on the lines with our people. We made a push this spring to take pressure off some of the farmlands for what might grow by summer. I was sent out after the planting was completed and hoped to find deliveries traveling opposite along the way.

"We had a party of fifteen upon setting out. Only eight of us made it to the Palonian. Instead of supply shipments, there are roving groups of enemy humans along the river. I suspect they have been sent over specifically to disrupt our supply lines. They cannot establish their own lines in the east while we hold the main swaths of the river north and south.

"King Garrett bid me discover the reason for the supply disruption and ask for your aid in putting a stop to it. His words are that with the combined efforts of Ceru and Auradia, we can survive another winter, buying that time with the lives spent in the spring.

"We cannot afford more. There will not be another push. We will not survive another winter after this one to come. If we cannot reinstate the northern supply lines in time for the next harvest, within two years, the southern lines will be broken. Ceru will become a gilar stronghold."

"Paraeceus, do you have last year's reports?" Oromaer asked.

"No, sir, not with me today."

All eyes turned with Oromaer's to focus on an elf to his right. Everything about him was fair; his coloration lighter than any elf she had seen. The hair plaited in intricate, interwoven braids looking like fragile icicles was silvery white. The frost-blue of his irises was nearly indistinguishable from the whites. Combined with his slender build and pale skin, he possessed an extraordinarily wraithlike appearance. One might expect his voice to come out in a faint whisper, but it was confident, with command and volume enough to carry across the room as he addressed the king and assembly.

"I have this year's report. I know we were low on what we sent due to the minor drought resulting in harvests smaller than usual. However, I do not recall last year being exceptional in either direction. We sent as many shipments south on the river as we have in the past."

"We sent our own people with the shipments this year. Along with volunteers from the refugees," Rolandor noted. "The people have changed so often, we thought this year there was no one to spare for a trip north and back south, so we sent our own when none returned. It was not done blindly. Additional guards were provided, but it would seem they were not enough."

Annalla saw Oromaer's lips purse, but he remained composed. "We can hope some will escape to return to us, but we must presume them dead at this time. This is troubling news, and we will discuss it further, but Prince Larron has also come to us with word from the Derou I would like us to hear and consider before we delve too deep into one situation alone. Larron?"

Larron's presence stood out as *more* to Annalla's senses. He kept his raven dark hair pulled back in tight, precise braids. The lean muscle of an agile fighter stood out beneath his tan complexion, and the contrast of his green eyes was piercing whenever he turned them in her direction.

"Thank you, Majesty." He rose as Tyrus took his seat. "We come from the Derou Woodland on a mission to seek aid. After years of unrelieved siege, we can no longer hold out against the gilar on our own. Even as we departed, a retreat from our long-standing border was underway. We have sacrificed a significant part of the Woodland perimeter to gain what time we can."

Cries of disbelief and despair from other elves met his announcement. It was difficult and painful for any to conceive of sacrificing a part of their Woodland. The other races recognized the relinquishing of territory, but the elves knew a true connection to the land Annalla had only begun to explore. Based on Thanon's earlier words, it was akin to cutting off one's own arm more than simply moving from a long-time home.

"We have fought alone against the gilar siege for nearly sixteen years, but there are no longer enough of us to maintain the Woodland border. The new perimeter lies nearer the Heartwood.

"With the elves withdrawn, and so many gilar surrounding and invading, the rest of the Woodland will not maintain its defenses long. Our influence will quickly wane with the enemy presence. It had been so long since we heard a word from outside, we could not be sure our messengers made it through. The decision was made to send a final party asking for help by using the withdrawal as cover for our departure…"

From the beginning, their tale was clearly—at least to her—difficult for Larron to tell. Derou was his home Woodland,

and the pain the others could scarcely imagine was a reality for him and his companions. If they did not bring help, all his people would be lost.

He told of the Derou's situation in greater detail with an impassive expression, but she could see the faces and voices of those lost floating in his eyes. Palanthuiel's face was one she could not help but remember as he told of their journey. Her father's was another. Both were killed by gilar. He described the transformation of the eastern forest into one of suffocating desolation. Trakins roaming and attacking freely within, having invaded the area.

Coming to the point of her rescue, he only hid one key detail. Larron went over details she had not been conscious to hear, including the condition in which they found her. Geelomin's reluctance to sacrifice supplies was not left out, nor was her hostility upon waking on the horse the following day.

When telling her story, of how she ended up in such a situation to begin with, he had to admit the same disbelief she saw on the faces around him. Annalla knew they would never trust her if they thought him careless with his own trust. She said nothing to defend herself or otherwise interrupt him.

Along with the aggressive and incredulous moments, he told of the helpful and positive impacts of her presence. She trusted him enough to return his weapon, found additional supplies whenever possible, and aided how and when she could. He outlined the trakin attack in which she risked her life to protect Bealaras. Then he came to the gilar attack upon the Claws.

"She saved our lives that day," he said, "and she saved my life specifically by taking an arrow meant for me."

The remainder of their journey was easier for him to tell. There was no personal loss attached to the land through which they traveled at the end. He went into detail about the layout of the encampments they found, likely to aid in future planning for actions the Palonian might make against them.

Larron asked his people and Tyrus to add anything they felt was missing from his report. Annalla waited, offering nothing and still expecting Oromaer to kick her out. His guards continued to wait with arrows nocked but not drawn. They likely thought her unaware of them. She knew they only worried over their king.

"Paraeceus, would you please provide a quick summary of our status for our guests?"

"Of course, King Oromaer." The fair elf rose again. "Other forces supporting Kahnlair have been at work in the north. To the northeast, the Trazine Range Caverns—as Controller Karntag and Sub-Controller Nurtik previously reported—is under increasingly frequent attacks by vampires from deeper within the range and windani gathered in the foothills.

"Those two groups might be the lesser organized of the enemy races, but they are no less brutal. Their swarming attacks can be overwhelming. The Trazine Clan continues to keep them occupied with raids to prevent their attention from shifting to the closer farmlands.

"There are also gilar and human contingents spreading from Kahnlair's eastern base to the southeast. I suspect this is the source from which the bandits along the river have come. They have not yet been reported this far north, but there is a strong indication they are ranging in this direction.

"The Palonian and the magai capital remain in the best situation to send aid. Our forces here, after sending all we could to help, are now such that we have only enough defenders to maintain our own Woodland borders. The encampments Prince Larron described beyond are but a few of those surrounding us. They are small enough in number to easily defend against them, but attacking would mean leaving a large area of the border vulnerable for long periods. At this time, we expect to leave them as they are through winter.

"As for the magai capital in the east, they sent the majority of their fully trained magai, who could be spared from teaching and defending their city. We are all reaching into the last of our resources to hold the enemy at bay and still have hope of defending our own lands. It pains me to say it, Majesty, Highness, but I believe the Derou are beyond our aid," Paraeceus concluded. "The distance and need are too great."

Gazes around the room flicked over Larron and his party, doing their best to avoid catching their eyes. Annalla did the opposite. She met Larron's eyes and held them until he gave a hint of a wry smile. He looked at the king. "Not until the tide turns, at least. You have the stores to send south if there is a way to keep them secure along the river."

Oromaer tipped his head toward Larron with respect and understanding. "It would seem our best course of action is to aid the alliance lies along the river. We may need to accelerate our plans for dealing with those outside our border."

There were nods around the table, but Oromaer forestalled the conversation, speaking again, "We will proceed with the planning after supper. There is one further revelation I wish to make before we break." His eyes turned to her, staring. Confused gazes followed and darted between them. "You have heard Larron's tale about the events leading to lady Annalla's joining his group. He called her elf, but you may notice she appears…different from most of us. If you are willing, Annalla?"

He gestured for her to proceed but was allowing her the final decision to reveal herself or leave them all pondering. There was not really a choice, so she swallowed and unfurled her wings.

"I'm only half-elf," she said into the silence, looking around the table.

"The fairy went extinct. The vampires killed them off, we all know that," one of the cats—*irimote!* she suddenly recalled the name—stated, starting everyone talking at once.

"It's clearly a trick," a human not from Tyrus' group muttered to a smattering of agreement.

Oddly, the youngest person at the table, one of the magai, stood and pointed at her and looked at his companions triumphantly. "I knew it was real. We should be seeking out an alliance!"

Oromaer stood and raised his hands to call for silence and order. It gradually quieted, but the dwarf at her side leaned back and sneered.

He spoke over the dying clamor, disgust lacing his grunted

words, "If they exist, the fairy are cowards! Hiding away and letting the rest of us take the beating. I would not suffer an alliance with them." He turned and spat in her direction. "Your vampire of a father probably forced himself upon an elf maid and ran off before they could hunt him down, leaving her with a filthy half-breed."

Annalla froze as he spoke. Her entire body still faced the king, but her gaze narrowed and shifted to take in the speaker. They might say what they would about her and the fairy, but her father gave his life for her and this realm.

Her lip lifted in a snarl, and her vision went into a battle focus. From stillness she became motion, and a fraction behind her sudden movement, two elven guards fired. Larron stood and shouted, but he was slower than the flying shafts.

She'd expected the attack. In a movement born of combined instinct and training, she spun low to the ground, dropping below the arrows and kicked out a foot. The dwarf's axe leaning against the wall fell forward at her touch. She caught it just below the blade, spun it for a better grip as she rose, and came up swinging toward its owner's neck.

"I should use your own axe to make you shorter by a head, dwarf. Perhaps speaking from your gaping neck would improve your words."

Annalla held the axe still, the blade halted a fraction into his bristly beard. It was sharp enough to trim the hairs it pressed against. All who had started moving froze with the halted momentum followed by her calm words. His eyes, wide with more surprise than fear, stared down upon the blade at his throat before following it up to take in the one who held it. With another swift motion, she pulled the axe away and placed it against the wall as though it had never moved.

"And my father…was the elf."

Still staring at her in disbelief, and a surprising amount of respect, he said, "You speak Dwarren?"

"No, I—" She sighed, realizing she was yet again speaking another language without noticing. "Apparently."

She could feel all eyes in the room upon her and knew she would not survive the next round of arrows and flash of swords so close to her. Even in the north, those were people hardened by war and ready to act. Retreat would be her only option, so she shifted her feet appropriately as she turned slowly to face King Oromaer. He opened his mouth to speak, but the dwarf beat him to it again.

"Huh. I like 'er," he huffed out.

The older dwarf at the table sighed and shook his head. "'pologies, Y'er Majesty. Insult was given, an' 'er actions warranted. Nurtik 'll face any punishment you 'r the lady decide."

He looked at her, and Annalla shrugged with an apologetic smile. Oromaer had a moment of looking at a loss. She swore Thanon laughed, covering it with a cough into his hand.

"I do not believe punishment will be necessary, Karntag. However, I do believe we should break for our meal and to regain our composure after such an interesting demonstration. We will reconvene in two hours, and I will hold a special council daily until our plan revisions are complete." He received indications of agreement before continuing, "Very well, we are dismissed."

"I should apologize, lady." The dwarf, Nurtik, turned to her. "It is no excuse, but I did not think you would understand me. Anyone who speaks Dwarren, has that much skill and control with an axe, and has the guts to do it in a room full of armed soldiers, has my respect."

Annalla felt herself smile. She liked him, too. His was a response she could understand. "It is appreciated, and apology accepted."

Well, that could not have gone worse, she thought to herself about the council session as people filed out toward another room where food waited, and she followed.

***

"Nurtik, what did you say to her?" Larron asked after she was well ahead.

The young dwarf looked decently guilty. "It wasn't nothin'

nice, an' nothin' I should be repeatin'." His primary language must have been the dwarven tongue. He spoke through a thick accent in Market, the common language used for interactions between the races of Elaria. "Karntag be right ta say it warranted."

"She has trainin' wit' a dwarven axe, though. Tha' handwork was beau'iful." Karntag's accent was less pronounced.

"It would not surprise me," he said and followed them through the hall of trees to the dining room. "Are you still in contact with your clan, then, based on what Paraeceus reported?"

"Ay, coded message pigeon relay. We have more'n a year lef' on'r station 'fore replacements wi' new coded book arrive." Larron followed as they filled plates and found seats. He saw Thanon and Geelomin bracketing Annalla to one side, but Larron remained with the dwarves. "Is bad all aroun'. We sen' half our forces ta tha Karasis Valley, an' they been under siege as yer people fer years now too. Jus' less directly."

"We need a new strategy. I fear we will need to sacrifice my Woodland and other strongholds as well." Though he did not see how consolidating would win them anything other than time and a slower death.

"Wha' we need's help." He tipped his head toward Annalla after eating for a while. "Ya trust 'er an' er' story?"

"I do. She will help us, but she cannot offer us the fairy as well, at least not yet."

Karntag shrugged. "We'll survive. Jus' make sure she does."

Larron laughed. "That, my friend, is a more difficult task than you might believe, with her propensity to throw herself at danger."

Nurtik grinned on his other side. "I 'spect she c'n protect 'erself well 'nough."

Karntag and Nurtik traded barbs back and forth. He could tell from the gestures involved it included a replay of Annalla trimming his beard. They seemed to find the entire event hilarious and respectable rather than insulting or intimidating. It pleased Larron that she could win over one group so quickly. He hoped the rest of them did not expect more of her than she could offer.

"Were you smoothing things over for me with the dwarves?" Annalla asked him as she fell in beside him, heading back to the council room after the meal had concluded.

He looked from her to Nurtik and back. "I do not believe that is necessary. You honored them with your knowledge of their language and weaponry. I am not certain Oromaer is as impressed with your attack on an attendee of the council, however."

"Mmm, yeah...about that," she started. "Geelomin helped me make a peace offering."

The eager and amused way she said it worried him, and he glanced over in confusion. "Why does this sound like something *I* am going to regret?"

"Well, it will require your assistance. Geelomin has assured me you are perfectly capable of executing your part in the agreement. As long as I can get you to agree."

"What *exactly* is it to which I am supposed to agree?" Larron asked with growing concern.

His stoic lieutenant had not been a troublemaker before their journey. So much time around Thanon and Palanthuiel seemed to change most of them. He also had a growing suspicion his Derou contingent was aware of the life bond and taking pleasure in making his life more complicated by having fun at his expense.

Annalla wrung her hands and fidgeted. That was bad. "There were some comments made—maybe some boasting to impress people—and I said that, in a gesture of apology, we could maybe provide some entertainment...tomorrow morning."

He stopped, closed his eyes, and took a deep breath. "Annalla, nothing about that sentence was exact. Exactly what entertainment are we expected to provide tomorrow morning?"

When his eyes opened again, she was standing before him, looking nervously into his eyes. "Dance with me?"

"Dance?" He blinked. Most women asking that of him would be referring to dancing to music. His mind did not even stop to consider the option, knowing Annalla as he did.

"Spear, long knives, and sword. I've been told you're capable of performing it completely and at speed," she clarified unnecessarily, but looked at him with confidence. "I know I can too, Larron. I want to show what I can do."

Elation and terror crashed through him. To flow through the moves against a skilled partner was freeing. To do so at speed with this partner would create a connection beyond imagining. The danger of the dance was part of the exhilaration. At speed and with this partner, the danger might be too much for him, but looking at her excitement, he knew he would do it.

Larron sighed. "Granted."

She beamed at him, and he hoped his inability to crush her enthusiasm would not lead him to kill her. "This is going to be amazing!"

"This is a very bad idea," he grumbled in reply. "You have practiced with the sword and long knives, but I have not seen a spear in your hands. Are you certain you are ready to perform a complete dance tomorrow?"

"Yes, I am. Though if it is any comfort to you, if there is no spear that suits me, I will postpone until one can be altered."

"I could easily kill you if there is even the smallest error by either one of us. There are reasons few perform this as a dance countering rather than in unison. If you are not perfect and completely committed to the strikes, it will mean death."

She stopped and met his eyes again, serious. "I will not falter, and you will not kill me. Though, as you well know, there is also a great deal of trust required in successfully dancing counter. I trust I will not err. I trust you are capable of completing it to perfection. I have seen you in combat. Larron, if you have any doubts about your own ability or mine, tell me now. I have no desire to kill you either."

His green eyes bore into hers, searching, reading, assessing. "It will be a worthy performance."

"Thank you."

"With one decision behind us and a brilliant display to look forward to, we should continue with our council." Oromaer had stopped behind him along with Larron's people.

"Whose brilliant idea was this?" His dry question had his group moving quickly ahead, back to the council chamber, as though they had not heard him, while Oromaer laughed and walked with him.

"Do not expect me to reveal the instigator," he said when Larron sent him a questioning look. "She dodged elven arrows and took a dwarf's axe. I plan on enjoying the demonstration of skill tomorrow."

"I will call it off if conditions are not right," Larron warned.

Oromaer nodded. "I would expect nothing less, but the crowd will be disappointed if such becomes necessary."

"Crowd?"

He laughed at him again. "My friend, it was very loud boasting. I am surprised you did not hear it where you sat. Everyone else certainly did."

Larron shook his head in disbelief at how the situation had spun out of his control before he even knew about it.

"Come now. We should return to the council so we can begin planning how to free our supply lines once more. I welcome your thoughts on the matter, as we will be facing greater numbers."

"I am interested to hear your scouting reports on the enemy encampments. We found their patrols to be poorly disciplined, though Annalla did report facing some with more fighting skill than expected."

They would need to free the Palonian before they could send scouts along the river to identify the parties responsible for the missing shipments. Maybe if they went too late into the evening, he could postpone the dance to another day and she would forget about it.

And maybe she will ask me to dance amores with her instead, he joked to himself, thinking about the romantic elven dances. Impossible things had happened to him before, what was one more?

CHAPTER FIVE

Morning dawned crisp and clear and saw the two of them out at the training field early. It was made of soft earth to absorb falls from practice and raked daily. They needed to know its flaws to avoid small stumbles that could get them killed.

The presence of the quickly forming audience surprised Annalla. Word of their plans seemed to have spread to the entire Heartwood overnight. Those who might normally have been training themselves moved to the fences to observe Larron and Annalla's examination. It was unlikely any could duplicate what they were about to witness.

They walked, ran, shuffled, crawled, and even moved across the ground with their eyes closed to feel their way. There was some laughter from non-elven fighters as they continued their detailed examination. The elves present, showing both apprehension and excitement, gave disapproving glares to such jokers but refused to say anything about what was to come. A large crowd gathered and swelled with those emerging from their morning meal by the time they were both satisfied and moved to the weapons.

Annalla had been practicing with Palanthuiel's sword since receiving it after his death. She was comfortable with it, so it would serve as one of her blades in the dance. Bealaras allowed her to train with his long knives when there was time, so she asked to borrow them that morning. It was the spear that would be the most difficult to find.

She knew she could fight with any weapon brought out for her inspection, but the dance required more familiarity. Having to compensate for one not *right* in her hands would make what they were about to do more dangerous. Annalla gave her word she would call it off if she did not find one. She started down the line of spears but stopped when Larron did not follow.

"You only brought a sword with you from the Derou. Don't you need to select your other blades?"

"I was fostered here in my youth," he said and shook his head. "There remains a complete set here for my use."

"I did not think elven children left their Woodland."

"Some do, others do not. Only those of the royal family are required to foster in another Woodland. As we do so, we are no longer royalty even in title, just another elf."

"I thought royalty was not treated differently."

Larron raised one shoulder in a 'sort of' gesture. "The royal line is the conduit for the connection between elf and Woodland. I will always be royal on some level to Derou elves."

"Interesting."

Annalla turned back and continued along the line of spears presented to her. Some she dismissed with a glance, others she touched, held, handled. It was when she took hold of the fifth in line that she thought she may have found one.

"This one," she said after using it for only a short time. It was not the smallest brought before her, but it was cut slightly shorter and suited her lesser height. The lighter metal of the rings and the narrow blade in the staff also suited her weight. When she was sure it felt right in her hands and claimed it for the dance, she turned to Larron.

"You were hoping I would not find one." It was a statement, not a question, and he did not respond. "I told you last night if you did not trust—"

"This has nothing to do with trust," he cut across her. "Trust cannot eliminate caution and concern. If you eliminate the possibility someone could be hurt from your mind, it is almost certain someone will."

"I know the risks, but you will not harm me in this."

"You are certain you know the dance?"

She rested her hand on his arm. "I'm certain, and Geelomin confirmed it. Once more over the terrain and warm up before we begin?"

Larron looked at her hand on his arm, and she saw a change come over him. The reluctance and fear melted away, and a fierce, eager light took their place. "Agreed."

When they finally completed their preparations, they were both ready and properly armed. Long knives at their backs, swords at their hips, and spears in their hands. They settled into the starting positions and it seemed everyone in the Woodland not on guard turned out to watch.

The atmosphere was filled with hushed anticipation as they faced each other in the ready stance. There would be no one announcing their movements or the start of the dance, no one cheering for one side or the other. It was not a fight, not a contest between competitors, but a deadly dance in which two would move as of one mind. The only sounds they inspired would be awe or horror.

Taking the part of point in the dance, Larron would make a quick, simple count before beginning to allow her to time her first move on counterpoint. In some respects, this was the most dangerous part. Even performing every step to perfection could not save you from poor timing at the start. They were staring at each other, bodies stretched and loose for sudden movement, breathing deeply in the calm morning air. She nodded.

"One, two, three!" Larron thrust the blade of his spear at her chest. Their timing was on as she smoothly stepped aside and spun along the shaft. Her own blow with the staff end of her spear was already descending toward his head, but he, too, was in motion. A spear might seem a bulky weapon compared to many other blades, but it made up for that with dual functionality.

They moved in a synchronized blur where the spear

became part of their body. Attack, defend. Strike, block. *Clack. Clack. Clack. Ching.* Larron drove her back across the training ground as the spear staves met time and again, giving and halting blows aimed at the other's body.

A hard slash up with the blade aimed to gut her as she backed against the fence, but she ducked low beneath it and spun the spear around her back to strike with her own blade from the other side. *Thun-klick* as it stopped on a metal ring in the shaft of Larron's blocking spear.

Then, she was the one pushing him along the fence line. A feigned thrust to the head, and she spun the shaft around to take out his legs. He jumped over and thrust out and down on his descent; the blade entering the ground where she had crouched less than a second before. They both had cuts in their clothing where skin could be seen, it served as a reminder to the crowd of the danger they courted. A fraction slower or off-step and there would be blood.

They were at it for nearly a quarter-hour and approached the point of a weapons change. After another exchange of blows, they spun away from each other, only to quickly twirl the spears around and head back for another clash. In a flash, as spear blades came down to strike, swords rose to meet them in defense and thrust the blows aside. Spear shafts were released to hold the sword with both hands for the next series of strikes.

The *clack* of spears was replaced by the *ching* and *shing* of exquisitely crafted metal meeting and sliding. With this change, the pace of their dance increased as they held weapons half the weight of those discarded.

Again, Larron made the first attacking run, forcing her to the center of the field with hard stabs and slashes at her torso and head. Her blade met every one, and at the center, she spun away from a strike, deflecting it slightly before slashing up at his weak side.

His sword maneuvered back, barely in time to deflect the blow enough to spin out of the way. His clothing took another cut, and the fight continued. Twirling, thrusting, slashing, the two fighters moved across the field in all directions, their blades coming within a hair's width of skin time and again.

Audible gasps of fear and exclamations, growing in volume as they continued, rose more frequently from the crowd. Over it all, Annalla heard a brief and slight *crack* of wood nearby. The sound was dismissed as quickly as the noise from the audience as she concentrated fully on her part of the dance.

Their breathing grew heavier as they traded blows for the final weapon exchange. Training and endurance were enormous factors. The last stage would quicken, even as the dancers became more fatigued.

They spun apart, pushing off with their blades, and immediately came back in an attack. In that brief time to disengage and attack, they sheathed their swords and drew the long knives. With a blade in each hand, the timing of the blows doubled.

Shing-shing. Shing-shing. Each blade became an extension of an arm, and they attacked from multiple directions, only to then bring them together on the same course in a combined strike. Coordination was paramount, with each limb moving in its own direction to dodge, strike, or block.

There were flashes of steel, grunts of exertion. Both sweated and breathed hard as they spun and struck, but neither slowed nor eased off on their strikes. Force and purpose remained behind every thrust, slash, and deflection.

Annalla became the defender again, backing away from Larron's attacking run. They both knew the line would take them under the young maple tree, with branches reaching out over the training field from behind the fence.

Crack. There it was again, but this time a muffled scream accompanied the sound. Annalla's eyes flew wide as Larron's blades circled his head to swing at her in unison. She would need to duck beneath them, rolling and rising for an attacking thrust from below.

Her ears told her something was wrong. Someone was in danger. In that instant, she jumped, and both long knives connected solidly with her chest.

CHAPTER SIX

Time stopped for Larron. He could not breathe, his heart stopped. There was nothing for him the moment his blades met flesh instead of air.

She was supposed to duck and roll. That is the step. Why jump? Why would she jump?

It had been a perfect, flawless dance, minutes from completion—one last attacking run on her part and they were done—when she made a fatal error. Tears welled unbidden in his eyes, and he struggled to swallow as he stared at her pained face. Anger, grief, sorrow. All those thoughts and emotions went through his mind as his long knives pinned her against the fence beneath the tree.

In the next moment—*had it only been a second?* —he had his answer as an irimote child screamed in pain behind her legs. The facts arranged themselves in his mind. The boy must have been perched on a branch in the oak tree to watch their dance. It broke just as they were passing beneath it. Had she not jumped in the way and taken the blow herself, the boy would have been cut in two.

Clarity brought undeserved guilt with it. Her crumpled form fell over the boy's body on the ground. He should have heard, known, adjusted, and stopped his attack. Mere seconds were all that had passed, only the time it took to finish the strike and pull back.

It felt like a lifetime. Larron fell to his knees at her side, and he took her hand. His mind remained fixed, caught in a moment of loss and despair, unable to respond.

"It's just a bruise... Are you hurt?" The voice was pained, but strong.

Larron's mouth dropped open in incomprehension. She not only spoke to him, but rolled around to look over the boy. He shook his head to clear it, blinking stupidly at the crowd now tightly surrounding them. Geelomin cut through them, carrying Mage Gregry in his arms.

"Let him through!" Larron shouted as he pointed at the elf and healer, and a path was made.

"What is the worst of it?" If the mage expected Annalla to be lying in two pieces surrounded by a pool of blood rather than examining a crying youth, he hid his surprise well.

"Broken leg. Pretty bad, the bone is sticking out. Other than that, he is scraped and bruised from his fall."

"Larron, you have some medical training. I need your strength to push the bone back into position. Do not worry about dirt; I will take care of any foreign material."

I am trained better than this, Larron scolded himself. He should have already been examining them both, but there he was processing through too many shocks. He could at least follow orders.

"Sherdan!"

The female irimote struggling through the crowd must be the boy's relative, with such panic in her eyes. Annalla scooted back, and the wince as she did so did not escape his notice. The woman took Annalla's place at the boy's side, and Gregry told her he was going to sedate him.

Bringing about unconsciousness without the aid of a chemical mage's blending was something few healers could accomplish, but it was done shortly after Gregry placed a hand on the child's forehead. Opening his eyes, he nodded to Larron, who gently took up the broken leg and began the grisly task of manipulating the bone back beneath the furry skin and in alignment with the other half. When it fell into place, it almost seemed to give an audible click. He knew it was only his imagination, but every bone he ever set felt like the same.

"Wonderfully done! Hold it there a moment... You may remove your hand now, Larron. Thank you."

He did so and watched the concentration on the mage's face as he performed his healing. When he was done, Gregry looked to the child's guardian.

"Healing on the young takes time to settle into their system. He will need to stay off it for at least a week and then gradually exercise it back to its former strength. There will be an aching pain as his body adopts the healing as its own." He glanced at a female mage in the crowd, who nodded and turned to move away. "Mage Sharie will bring a chemical blending to you for his pain and will give you instructions on its use."

She beamed at Gregry as she hugged the boy to her, tears streaming from her eyes. As she gathered his sleeping form in her arms, she thanked Gregry, then Larron, and finally Annalla as she carried him past her through the crowd. Larron stared at Annalla when she turned back toward him, and it was Gregry who gave voice to everyone's confusion and curiosity.

"Well, young one, how in Elaria is it *you* are not dead on the ground?"

She laughed, then grimaced. "My dear mage, what is the one thing you do not aim for when attempting to shoot down a vampire with the wings of a fly?"

"Their wings," Larron answered on a whispered exhale, still clinging to her hand. When had he grabbed it? It must have been after he finished working the bone. "They are as tough as armor, but even they could not have turned that blow."

"All four wing types have different advantages. Bat wings are truly silent, bird wings are better for altitude flying and speed, and insect wings are impervious and more agile. Fairy insect wings having more of the former and vampire, the latter benefit."

"I thought I killed you," he said in another whisper, so

softly only Gregry next to him and Annalla could have heard over the murmuring crowd. A little louder he said, "You mentioned bruises, and I saw you wince, there could be fractures. Allow Mage Gregry to see to you as well." He turned to the mage. "So long as you are not tired from your healing of the boy."

"Not at all. Come here, young one." She rolled her eyes and shook her head but, he was happy to see, did not protest. No one told him to let go, so he kept her hand in his.

"Only a small crack," Gregry said when he was done. "You would not have noticed it for some time under all the bruising, but I have taken care of it and eased those as well. There will be tenderness for a few days. I left it to remind you to take it easy as the healing completes and give Larron an excuse to refuse a rematch."

Her smile turned back toward him. "So close, Larron. We will have to try again sometime, but perhaps not right away."

"It would be a pleasure." He was surprised to hear the truth in the statement. "Right now, though, I would rather clean up and head for a late breakfast. And I think I need a drink— something strong, despite the hour."

They helped Gregry up, and Geelomin gave the mage his arm to lean on as Larron and Annalla led the way through the crowd. They received praise and words of admiration from many they passed. The performance was impressive, no matter the manner of its conclusion, or perhaps even because of it.

Oromaer stepped before them, and they held up for a moment. "Well done, to you both. Some of my people requested the honor of cleaning your weapons and returning them to you, if you are agreeable." They both nodded in agreement. "I will see to it, and I will see you both at the council."

They parted at the bathhouse. He would have lingered within, but his stomach protested a longer soak and pressed him toward the dining hall. Nerves kept him from eating in the morning. With the dance concluded and everyone safe, he could appreciate it more.

He enjoyed the challenge, the movement. Only two other

elves had ever been able to counter him at full speed. He had seen neither of them in many decades. It was something he would have liked to think back on, but every time he did, the image of his knives cutting into her tore through.

She was alive and whole, but for that moment, he thought her dead at his hands. The image continued replaying as he absentmindedly joined his friends at a table. It took him a moment to notice with whom they were seated.

"Prince Tyrus, it is good to see you again."

The charismatic human smiled at him. "Just Tyrus, please. That was an impressive display of skill this morning."

He shook his head. "One nearly ending in disaster, but no one was seriously injured."

"You at least took some precaution and gave your girl some armor," a man further down the table commented.

He was a blind idiot to miss the level of capability displayed countless times in front of those men. Larron looked at him, thinking his name was Brandon.

"She is no one's 'girl,' and neither of us was wearing armor. Without her wings, she would have died to save that boy."

"Let us hope the enemy never take fairy wings as armor, then," Tyrus gave his man a look of clear disapproval and warning.

"Haven't you ever killed a vampire before?" Annalla slid gracefully into the seat across from him. "Same principle; wings are like brittle paper when they die."

"Lady Annalla." Larron saw the wince as Tyrus addressed her and remembered Thanon saying something about her thinking the honorific something of an undeserved title. "I should ask who your trainers were."

"My father mostly," she replied, "but he couldn't do that either. There are few who can."

"It was luck, nothing more. A woman should not be allowed to fight."

"Brandon, enough," Tyrus scolded his man. "Human culture is not the only way things may be done."

He became extremely focused on his meal, but Larron

could hear continued mumbling. He knew most human cultures in Elaria still placed their women in more of a protected and secondary role. Even among the elves, there were fewer women electing to enter a martial profession. Gender roles among humans, however, were more often prescribed. Many of the men with Tyrus looked uncomfortable.

Tyrus turned his smile back to Annalla. "I'll not claim your level of skill, but perhaps we could spar sometime? I'm sure I would find it educational."

Larron held back a snarl as she leaned forward and smiled back. "We can carve out some time. I could probably teach you a thing or two."

"Ha! As long as you have your personal healer around," he teased her. "You do seem to be injured often."

She rolled her eyes and jabbed back, "An unfortunate byproduct of defending the innocent and seeing them to safety. We need not take Larron away from his meetings with the king for something as trivial as training."

She thinks of me as her personal healer? he wondered even as Tyrus smirked at him before responding. "I meant the mage, but it is good to know you have two healers to aid you."

Annalla's face scrunched up and she blushed a little. "That was good." She held up a finger. "I don't have a response now, but I'm sure something witty will come to me in the middle of the council meeting."

"Be sure to speak up when it does." He laughed. "Everyone enjoys your council interruptions. They are so entertaining."

Her face reddened further, but she still smiled. "I'm wondering why I was starting to like you, Tyrus, but I bow to my better in verbal sparring."

"You still like me." He winked at her before turning back to Larron. "I wanted to ask your thoughts on the plan to free the river."

The polite smile remained frozen on his face, and he hoped the desire to teach Tyrus a thing or two himself was not in evidence as he took up the new line of conversation.

"It will depend greatly upon the enemy numbers holding the river, but the plan is sound. I believe significant supplies will be delivered to Ceru before next fall."

"Part of me worries about waiting to start the attacks," he admitted.

Harndorn nodded. "The stores will be empty by the time replacements arrive. I feel uncomfortable waiting as well."

Larron knew their worry and the reason for their impatience. "It is understandable to feel so, but clearing the river will be the work of seasons. It will cost many lives. If we control the time and place of the confrontations, it will go better for us and mean a greater chance of successfully maintaining the lines."

"You believe they will be worn down by the weather?"

They had discussed the matter in council the night before, but he sensed the young man needed confirmation from someone else dependent on the Palonian in some way.

"This is their first winter in the area. They will be unprepared, no matter how well they planned, and it will provide an advantage. Holding new territory is always more complicated than one imagines. Nothing is guaranteed, but the plan is solid and adaptable. Your father has dealt with the situation well, and the Palonian will see to it that your people do not starve."

He heard a deep, bolstering breath behind him as Tyrus nodded in agreement.

A new voice broke into their discussion, "Lady Annalla?"

"Mage…?" she said, asking for a name.

"Uh, Mage Marto." It was the young combat mage from the council. He had a child's face. Larron suspected he would still look young well into middle age. At that point, it remained accurate. Marto was a student when the academy fell and was not a year into his full mage status. Despite that, he was the eldest combat mage in The Woodland since his teacher had passed from old age two months before.

"I was hoping for some of your time before the council. I could walk with you if you are not opposed."

"Of course." Annalla brushed off her hands, took up her plate, and nodded around the table. "I guess I will see you all there."

Tyrus looked at him as she walked off with the mage in tow, still in their conversation. "My people are suffering now. It's difficult to wait."

"It is." He felt the same, and there was nothing they could do to help the Derou.

CHAPTER SEVEN

Annalla wondered if something had gone wrong with her healing that morning. The room spun briefly as she rose from the bath after their dance, and an achy pressure built in the back of her head. As she ate with the elves and joked with Tyrus, she could barely stomach the food and mostly just drank water.

The dizziness dissipated by the time Marto approached her, but the headache had lodged firmly and gave every indication it intended to grow. She would ask Gregry to check her again after the council meeting.

"Thank you for agreeing to speak with me," Marto said as they left the dining hall, pausing to collect his thoughts. "I have a proposal for you, one backed by the mage council here in the Palonian."

Her lips firmed against a smile. *Someone has practiced this delivery in front of a mirror a time or two.*

Marto was young, and his round face made him appear even younger. His light brown hair was cut closer than most men wore their hair there and had just enough of a curl to it to look unruly despite obvious efforts to tame it. He was shorter than most of the elves and humans on the council, which made him look stocky, but she suspected the impression was inaccurate. The robes he wore likely enhanced the illusion, but his arms and neck were toned. He was probably in better shape than most people would first assume.

"Go on," she prompted.

"After the mage academy was taken, the Magai Council in our capital saw the full power and threat Kahnlair represented. His ground forces were always greater than our own. With his attack, he showed that the magai loyal to him gained a strength we could not hope to possess while he is supplementing them. When his aerial fleet is considered, it adds a dynamic we cannot directly combat and makes gaining an advantage on the ground or with our magic impossible.

"The Council began to look into the history of this realm for any advantage such information might illuminate against the gilar, windani, or vampires. Nothing critical was discovered about those races or about magical energy in Elaria. There was one historical aspect, however, with a chance to balance the scales in the fighting to some extent.

"The idea was dismissed as hopeful wishing on which the council would not risk lives. No one was even sure they still existed, so any efforts to find them were abandoned before they began. Your people, the fairy, were that idea."

"An air force of our own is a wonderful idea, and I might prove the existence of the fairy, but I have no idea where to find them." Annalla sighed and looked away. "I wish I did."

"I might."

The realization of what he said struck her hard through the headache. She stopped him with a hand on his arm. "How would a mage know how to find my people?"

He looked nervous then, squeezing one hand with the other. "Walk and talk, remember?"

"Where are my people?" Her mind didn't remember grabbing the front of his shirt, but his eyes were large as he looked down at her hands and into her face.

She smoothed the wrinkles her hands caused. "Sorry. Sorry, please continue."

He began walking again. "I don't *know* exactly, but I have an idea where to find the fairy. First, how much do you know about artist magai?"

Annalla shook her head. "I probably remember less than I know. Assume the answer is: absolutely nothing."

"A fully trained artist can recreate your image and voice exactly in a construct both visual and auditory. Someone who knows you would not be able to tell the difference unless the creation did something out of character for you or they tried to touch the image. To be considered a full artist, you need to be flawless.

"There was a story my mother told me almost every night; one passed down through generations before me. It was about one of my ancestors traveling with a fairy back to her lands."

"Marto, I'm sorry, but how is a story you were told when you were…two going to help us?"

"I was near six," he responded defensively. "And it helps because every generation the images passed through, including my mother, were artist magai."

She knew she was still missing something. "I see what you are hinting at, but stories will still change over generations, especially the longer magai generations."

"Not in this case, Annalla." Marto shook his head with conviction. "One of the tests to be accorded Artist Mastery is to memorize another mage's story and present it without alteration. Their training allows them to memorize images with unfailing accuracy. The reproduction takes effort, but they would have made it for such a story."

"The Derou explained a little about the magai, so I know your people originated elsewhere, in another realm, and came to Elaria at some point. Were the fairy still around when the magai came to Elaria? How could this ancestor have met a fairy if there were none to meet?"

"How could you exist, if there were no fairy to meet?" Marto countered. "There are a number of circumstances to explain how you exist that would align with my mother's story. All of them mean the fairy are only hiding and potentially isolationist, not extinct.

"My ancestor never went into the fairy lands in our family story. Mother always changed the ending as inspiration took her. The fairy's image also varied. I suspect the first to replicate the images did not pass that piece on to maintain her anonymity.

"The route taken in the tale, though, *that* never changed." There was a sad smile on his face.

Annalla could almost feel the pain he felt at losing his mother, but she pushed emotion to the side and considered what he was saying. He believed the bedtime story told in his family through generations was based on true events. Not only true, but he thought it held a path to find fairy lands hidden away from the world since time long passed.

"Can you map out the route?" she asked after a moment.

"No. The journey shown was not a trip of roads, towns, and signs. We jumped from landmark to landmark in each scene shared, avoiding the tedium of travel in between. And no, the landmarks were not major ones that would be on any maps. If we do this, I have to go."

"None of the artists can recreate the images for us?"

He shook his head. "We kept it in our family. I'm one of about four people alive to have seen the story images. None of the others are here, and I'm the only person to have witnessed it numerous times. This was my mother's. I'm seeing this through."

What he offered her was invaluable, and she wanted to shake him and demand he put the images in her head or share it with her himself. From his story, though, he was no artist mage, and she would likely end up lost without him.

"You said you have the approval of the other magai. What, exactly, are you proposing? And what do you need from me?" she finally asked.

"I have requested to speak at the council today. I am going to propose an expedition to follow the landmarks and find the fairy in my family's story. We all need help, and we have more to offer in exchange as a group, but I intend to go regardless of the council's decision. I want to tell them you have agreed to come with me."

She nearly laughed at him then, her pain momentarily forgotten. "Marto, you could not keep me away from this."

As they grinned at each other, his eyes finally looked his age. They decided to change the subject before approaching the council chamber where Oromaer told her a seat next to Larron's had been added for her. Marto and she took their seats, and others soon filed in after them.

Oromaer stood at the front, and the quiet chatter silenced. "We have a request to address the council this afternoon, so I will cede the floor to Mage Marto."

"Thank you, King Oromaer." Marto's voice betrayed nerves, despite his obvious efforts to control it, and color rose in his round cheeks. Oromaer ignored the nerves, nodding and sitting to give him the room. "As a representative of the magai, and with the authorization of the Magai Council, I will be leading an expedition to find the lands of the fairy and solicit their aid in the war against Kahnlair.

"Lady Annalla has agreed to join me in the attempt and offer what help she can in gaining entrance to their lands should we find them. The magai masters here in the Palonian have recommended we wait three weeks to draw up plans and prepare for the trip. If any others wish to send representatives with us in our plea for aid, we ask them to put forth a name before our departure."

Silence and a few gaping mouths followed his short speech, and she felt Larron stiffen in his seat beside her as Marto spoke. He was likely unhappy with her for agreeing to go without consulting him.

Tyrus looked at Annalla when he spoke. She could tell he tried to be diplomatic with his words. "You know where the fairy are and have not spoken of this before now, Fairy Representative?"

"I have no idea where they are. It's the mage who will be leading the way." With that, she put the attention right back where it belonged, which was away from her.

Marto swallowed under the scrutiny before explaining about the artist mage story passed down through his family.

"You would place your trust in an ancient story?" Tyrus asked her, incredulous enough to again speak out of turn.

"I would be gone with the mage now if mine were the only considerations in play," Annalla shrugged. "The magai are right, though. The voices of all the races combined might hold more weight for your cause than the magai alone."

The council peppered Marto with questions, covering the same ground, in greater depth, that they had on their walk there. Many focused on the fact the magai had not shared this idea with their allies sooner, but Marto proved himself well by deflecting the accusations lightly and skillfully.

Of course, the same people on the council would have thought it a laughable idea only a week before, which is exactly why the magai did not share it.

Annalla let them talk through the matter. Larron served as a mediator, and Marto was clear, patient, and gained confidence with each successful answer. Annalla, meanwhile, drew further back in her chair to try to get away from the sunlight shining through the thin roofing. The headache spread from the back of her head to plant itself firmly behind her eyes, making her feel like the light stabbed right into her brain. Her sight remained fixed on the shaded floor beneath the table to ease the burn.

"Annalla?"

"Yes? What? I'm sorry, I missed the question." She had to put effort into focusing on Paraeceus's face.

How long have they been talking? she wondered.

"I was just asking if memories have returned to you that might provide insight into what sort of reception we might receive."

"I don't know." Annalla slowly shook her head. "I'm sorry to say, I don't even know what their reaction to me will be. The best I can offer are speculations based on the same information available to you. They are likely an isolationist culture, but that does not immediately translate to hostility toward outsiders, especially if it simply means outsiders cannot reach them. Impenetrable defenses would be protection enough without having to raise a hand against someone from another race."

"Granted. We best proceed with caution in any case, and anything you recall about fairy etiquette will need to be shared with whoever is sent. Such an alliance is too important to risk with a breach of protocol or unintentional insult."

Someone else asked a question, but she could not convince her head to turn in their direction. Conversation faded from her awareness once more.

The headache worsened. The light and voices in the room became explosions of color and sound behind her eyes. Annalla clenched her hands into tight fists and folded her arms to keep them from shaking. A bead of sweat trickled down her spine and her breathing quickened as though from some great effort.

Something was happening to her, and it was dangerous.

"Annalla?" Larron's gentle voice penetrated through the haze of pain as he set a hand on her back. "What is wrong?"

At some point, her eyes had squeezed shut. Her head tilted toward him, but she could not gather the will to make them open. A force shuddered up through her body to reach her hands. They shook so violently that the rest of her body moved with them and panic enveloped her. Her eyes flew open to focus on Larron's.

"Run," she whispered through clenched teeth.

"Rolandor, find Mage Gregry and request he join us," Oromaer called out in concern.

They are not listening!

Annalla held Larron's eyes, grabbed his hand with her shaking fist, and put all her desperation and alarm into the look. "Run!" Her voice remained a whisper, but it had the force of a pleading shout. Her gratitude was surmounted only by the pain her head swam in and the feeling of something crawling beneath the skin of her hands and arms as Larron reacted immediately and without question.

CHAPTER EIGHT

"Everyone out of here! Now!" Larron shouted and peered around, his gaze coming to rest on King Oromaer.

"Do as he says," Oromaer echoed in a calm, but firm tone. "Everyone out."

"And away from this room!" he shouted to be heard by those already leaving. The panic Larron allowed to edge into his voice beside the command had the desired effect. No one knew what was going on, but the combination had them hurrying to comply.

Larron was the last out and paused at the entryway to look back at Annalla. She no longer stared at him with desperation to be heard. Instead, she slid from her chair and curled up in agony on the stone floor. He wanted to run toward her, not away. Part of him understood she would never forgive him if he did, so he turned and hurried to follow the mass exodus.

"What is this about, Larron? What is happening?" Oromaer asked when he joined the Derou at the edge of the courtyard where they gathered.

He started to say he had no idea, but the words were cut short by a trembling of the ground. A heartrending scream of agony from inside the evacuated room preceded something crashing through the roof.

"What in…" Larron trailed off as he stared. He covered his

slack jaw loosely with a hand, taking in the scene with wide eyes. An evergreen tree, with centuries of growth, shot from the ground in moments, breaking through the thin, delicate roof.

It was only the first to appear. More quickly followed, both within the building and in the clearing surrounding the room. Soldiers with years of battle experience scrambled away from a scene they could not comprehend.

Trees of all kinds erupted from the earth. Vines snaked their way up walls and new tree trunks. Bushes, flowers, and ground cover sprouted randomly among the newly-erupted boles. The room crumbled as walls cracked and broke, and Larron cried out with the others when those walls tumbled inward, collapsing completely.

The destruction ended as quickly as it began. Everything became still, silent after the roar and rumble, but nothing in the courtyard or the surrounding area was the same.

Foliage covered the ground like that of a densely packed forest. Thick bushes and vines crowded around the trees, making an impenetrable barrier. Larron heard Marto order someone to get the architects, but he was too busy cutting a path through the underbrush to turn and see who hurried off to obey. Distantly, to his mind, others began their own attack on the tiny forest.

It could not have been more than twenty large paces from where the plants began thickening to the edge of the collapsed room. He walked the distance often enough to know without looking, but time dragged on in his fight against the vegetation.

When his blade finally met stone, the only thing he found was rubble. There was so much overgrowth that the structure appeared more like an ancient, buried ruin than the well-kept chamber from less than an hour before. There was nothing resembling the arched entryways, only dark holes leading down and in.

Larron was about to start climbing and sifting through the stone in a desperate attempt to reach her when a sharp voice stopped him from behind.

"Do not touch anything."

A disheveled female mage pushed through his thin path. Her auburn hair fell around her face, pulled loose from the knot at her nape by the snagging branches. There were cuts on her skin and clothing from those he had not taken time to cut back far enough.

She must have rushed there, as she was slightly out of breath. Despite that, her words were firm and confident. "I am Mage Nessa, an architect. If you start moving things, it will only disrupt what little stability exists in this chaos. Let us do what we can."

Not trusting himself to speak, Larron nodded once as she crowded in next to him and placed her hands on the stone. The same expression of concentration Gregry had when healing consumed her face, but she maintained it for longer. He waited as she worked, and waited again as the other Derou widened the path. Not until three other magai reached them did she come back to herself.

"Where was the woman last seen?" Nessa asked him.

"Across the way, to the right there." He pictured the room with Annalla huddled beside the table and pointed toward their spot.

"Good." She turned back to the other magai. "One of the larger pockets is over there, so she may still be alive. That is the location we will work toward first. Fortunately, this is one of the better places from which to begin, as it is less likely to collapse as we progress."

Nessa assessed the gathered magai. "I reinforced the entire structure. Andre, you will need to maintain the stability as the rest of us change it."

Larron stepped back, and Andre took his place by the fallen stones and reached out to touch them. Nessa and the other two adopted a slightly different stance. Their heads bowed, and they stood with one hand clenched at their sides and the other loosely extended toward the ruined room. The magai countenance of concentration settled on all their faces, but it looked to Larron as though nothing happened. Geelomin, Bealaras, and Thanon stood beside him and silently watched the architects work.

After an eternity, the stone began to shift and take on a fluid appearance. Ever so slowly, it reformed; merging, pushing out, and becoming two low walls curving upwards. He had seen architects work before, but there had always been a larger group working on a less drastic change in structure. These four would not be walking away from this fresh and unruffled.

Step by agonizing step, they crept forward as the hallway grew before them. Reforming stone should be slow work, and the rush strained the magai beyond what they could maintain. One by one, they crumpled where they stood until only Nessa remained conscious.

"The pocket is not far." She sat on the ground with her head in her hands. "But I cannot continue without another to support the walls I expose and stress in the working. We must wait for one of the others to rest and regain strength enough to assist me."

"They are supported." The voice came through faint but clear enough to have all their heads snapping up to look at the wall.

"Annalla?!" Larron jumped past Nessa, crouching at a crack in the stones.

"Yes, and the walls are supported."

She sounded exhausted, but evidently alive and conscious. Larron felt a weight heavier than the stones around them lift from him.

"Not much," Nessa called through the stone, answering the question he forgot in his relief.

"Enough," was the reply, so calm and certain Larron could not help but smile.

Nessa appeared less assured and entertained by Annalla's relaxed tone. She looked around before shrugging. With a sigh, the mage returned to her stance and concentration for one last push.

A hole materialized in the wall at a painstakingly slow pace. Larron would knock Nessa out of the way if he tried to maneuver around her to peer in, so he forced himself to stand still as the hole expanded. The groaning and grinding of stone scraping along stone heralded an imminent cave-in.

He stood poised to move in to pull her out when Annalla came rolling through just ahead of the crush. She lay on her back, panting as though she had performed two weapons dances in a row.

"Are you injured? What happened? What took you so long?"

"You have...the worst habit...of asking...numerous questions...at the...most inopportune times," she managed between breaths, then lay her head back and closed her eyes. He collected her in his arms to carry her out before she opened them again. "Put me down. I can walk. I'm not hurt, just tired."

Her breathing still sounded labored, but less than initially. That did not mean he believed she had the strength to walk out of there.

Larron knew it would be less effort to prove her wrong than to argue the point. Her shaky legs gave out beneath her on the second step, and he caught her on the way down. There were no more protests as he gathered her up again and carried her out. She fell asleep with her head pillowed on his shoulder before they reached the edge of her little forest. Not even the cheers of the crowd woke her.

"Geelomin, bring Mage Gregry to her rooms," he ordered as he walked past everyone, not caring enough to answer questions or curiosity when he remained worried himself. They could wait until he satisfied himself with the healer's answers.

Twice in one day was too much for his sanity. He was going to have a conversation with her about taking care of herself and caring about her own health.

Larron's grip tightened and his steps quickened as the fear hit again. He had to consciously slow himself and make his arms relax around her. He only realized he was crying when a glance down at her face showed a drop on her cheek. It was too much for one day, too much for one person.

She looks drained, he thought, seeing her skin pale against the sheets he laid her upon once they reached her room. Her chest rose with steady breaths, and he knew her heart beat, but nothing detracted from the wan complexion and dark circles, like bruises, beneath her eyes. He intended to remain at her bedside.

"Larron, sir," a messenger called from the doorway. "Your presence is requested."

Geelomin arrived, once more carrying the healer-mage in his arms.

"Go. Out. All of you." Gregry shooed them away with flicks of his hands the moment he stood upon his feet.

Larron looked from the messenger to the mage and back, sighing.

Thanon placed a hand on his arm. "We will stay nearby."

Despite his intentions, events and people quickly conspired to pull him away. Soon enough, he stood outside Oromaer's public rooms.

"Larron, what in all hells is going on here?" Oromaer asked the moment he entered.

He had been summoned—as he refused the initial request, sending the messenger away and waiting with the Derou—to join the king and council members in the king's meeting house. Intended for private audiences with visiting ambassadors, there was not enough room for all of them in there, and he felt suffocated.

The king stood accompanied by Paraeceus, Rolandor, and Oromaer's son, Orion. Larron entered alone, having left Geelomin with the rest of the Derou to make sure no one would be harmed if Annalla had another attack and to make sure of her safety. He trusted them with her.

Controller Karntag was present, as was Prince Tyrus, with Harndorn, Matriarch Patrice, and Mage Marto.

"You know as much as I do at this point, Your Majesty," Larron responded to the question. "Mage Gregry sent us from the room shortly after arriving, and he had not emerged when I was summoned." His back remained firm as he stood at attention before the king.

Irritation suffused the king's response as he waved a hand. "Oh, sit down, Larron. You might not *know*, but I certainly believe you speculated on the matter while you sat outside her door." He sighed, and his eyes softened. "Please, old friend."

Larron's shoulders relaxed, and he eased himself into the only open chair. "She is a manifest essence. I can think of no other explanation for what happened."

"If she was a manifest, her power would have presented itself in adolescence." Patrice spoke without accusation. "Those abilities emerge slowly so the child gains control over time. Could this have been intentional?"

"I do not know the answer, but I do know what happened the first time she remembered an event from her past. She shouted and screamed into the night, flailing so violently it took three of us to hold her down. If something, or someone, could forcibly repress her memory, perhaps it had a similar effect on her power. Obviously, the effect was not permanent, but the possibility remains."

Harndorn snorted. "You expect that to…what? Comfort us? Ease our minds about her? She is dangerous."

"Everyone in this room is dangerous."

"Different, and you know it," he countered Larron's sarcasm.

Patrice shrugged. "It appears she regained control. She stopped the growth."

"Did she?" Rolandor asked. "Was it control that stopped it, or did events stop when she passed out? Will the destruction start again?"

"She regained consciousness briefly when we pulled her out. It should not start up again when she wakes based on that example," he offered.

Tyrus shook his head. "Not necessarily. If she was…out of power, like the magai, she might not have been able to do anything at that time."

"We are housed in a remote wing, so if your concerns prove true, the repercussions would be limited."

"Larron, perhaps you and the other Derou should relocate," Oromaer said gently.

He looked at his friend and just stared, raising his eyebrows. The look asked if he would be content to leave should he find himself in the same situation. No, they were not in love, but some basis existed for the life bond to build upon. He and all the Derou with him cared about her. She was one of them.

"No," Oromaer said, "that is probably not for the best."

Orion appeared confused at the exchange. "An entire structure collapsed when this power presented itself. If this does happen again, and if it is uncontrollable, we need a plan. She may need to be moved to a more remote location."

A knock at the door stalled further argument, and Rolandor moved to open it.

Thanon entered. "Mage Gregry wishes me to pass along a message. She is awake and asking questions. I am sure you have questions as well, so please join us as soon as possible. I should add that Annalla is not being the most cooperative of patients. Gregry says she should not leave her bed, but he knows she has every intention of doing so if he leaves. Chairs are being brought into the room for everyone."

"Thank you, Thanon," Oromaer said with a bow of his head. "It sounds as though you may all join us if you wish. Larron?"

Nodding his thanks at the gesture for him to precede them, he walked out of the room with Thanon ahead of the king.

CHAPTER NINE

"When you're in a forest like this, insects can be a great source of protein if you have nothing else. Fallen logs like this one are a great place to look," droned the host on the television.

Mrs. Cransky liked her survival shows. After dinner, Mr. Cransky went to play some games, their son Turner went out for practice, and she turned on her shows. They were okay. They mostly ignored Alexis. They even turned a big pantry into a spare room for her, so she had her own space there.

Her room was small though, and she found the shows entertaining and educational. Alexis brought her books out to the living room floor to finish her homework and listen to the survival shows with Mrs. Cransky.

That place was much better than her last home. She ended up breaking the nose of her previous foster father and getting him arrested. Too late to help his victims, but she ensured he would not be doing bad things to anyone again. Alexis thought the note of violence on her record would mean worse homes and worse places from then on, but she had ended up there a few months before.

She was fifteen and making her way through high school, doing her best to remain unnoticed and get out. Math sucked, and history was boring. Alexis still had trouble reading because she started so far behind. When they first found her, she couldn't understand anyone at all. She caught onto the language quickly enough, but reading remained a challenge.

Sports were her favorite, but there was no chance of anyone paying for any fees or uniforms, so class time was the only chance she had to play. Her clothes were donations, but they did not stand out too badly. Overall, things were pretty good.

"Ugh, gross... That is so awful," the man said on the show as he ate a giant larva. She wondered absently why he bothered chewing the thing instead of just swallowing it.

Alexis chuckled to herself as she watched him take another bite to finish the grub off before heading out again for the next essential wilderness survival thing. Food, water, and shelter.

He was always licking rocks and drinking dirt along with the copious amounts of bug-eating. She was pretty sure she could survive anywhere just from watching that stuff. It did not matter in her mind that the playground down the street was the closest she had ever come to wilderness. His advice was gold, otherwise, he wouldn't be paid to do the show.

Her chuckle must have been louder than she thought. Mrs. Cransky looked over, glanced pointedly down at her books, and back up. The message was clear: one more sound that she was not working and she would be doing homework in her room instead. So, she got busy on the next problem and only glanced up occasionally.

A few more years, that's all she had to make it through. A few more years and she could watch whatever she wanted whenever she wanted. She could go out into the wild and test her skills. She could survive all on her own.

"A few more years," she said, putting a hand to her aching head, which had faded to a dull throbbing at that point.

"What was that, young one?" asked a kind voice.

Annalla wiped her hand across her eyes and blinked over at Mage Gregry, feeling both disoriented and more than a little appalled. "I based all my survival skills on a show made for entertainment. It's a wonder I didn't poison myself or lose a limb."

He smiled at her as he sat on the edge of the bed. He placed a hand to her forehead before nodding to himself and meeting her eyes. "Sometimes, I advise you don't think too hard on your fortune and simply be grateful. Hmm?"

She gave a laugh, but it took about all her energy. Her body felt like one giant bruise, or as though she had pushed through a very thorough exercise routine the day before.

Maybe the dance is part of this, she thought to herself. *That was yesterday morning, after all, and maybe Gregry did not heal the exercise aches like he left some of the pain in my ribs.*

"What happened?" Annalla asked him aloud. "I feel like I fell off a running horse. Did something go wrong with the healing this morning?"

"There was nothing wrong with my healing," he scolded gently. "You destroyed the council hall and nearly took yourself out with it."

"What?!" she started to push up out of bed. "Is anyone hurt? What happened?"

"Stop! Stop!" he pushed against her shoulders. She fell back, more to avoid hurting him than because of the meager force he brought to bear.

"The trees," she breathed out in vague recollection.

An image and feeling came to her of enormous growth pressing up from the ground and through her. Annalla thought that had been part of another dream. A forest sprang up around her, imprisoning her in stone and wood.

"It was real. Wasn't it?"

"It was," Gregry responded.

"And I did that. I made the trees grow so fast." She looked at him. "But how? I'm not a mage. Am I?"

"You did make the trees grow, but I sense no magic in you." He patted her hand as he continued, "In Elaria, we call it a manifest essence. There are some among the races—those originating in this realm—who have abilities beyond the norm. It is said the essence of the person is too powerful for their physical form to contain."

"Wait," she stopped him. "I thought essence had to do with the creation of the races in Elaria. How does this relate to me?"

"Ah, yes, the beginning then." He smiled, a mischievous quirk on his lips. "It might be best to provide all with an overview of essence, if you think you can wait for the council to arrive?"

"Arrive?" There was no chance she wanted them to see her as an invalid or even so incapable as to need to stay in bed. "I can wait until we go to them."

Mage Gregry's smile turned pleasantly patronizing. "No. I'm afraid I want you to remain resting in bed until tomorrow. They can see you here, or you can all wait."

Annalla narrowed her eyes at him. She knew she could escape him, but he was such a nice old man—and she so often needed healing—that she hesitated to push.

"Why don't you go get them, then?" Annalla asked, with the brilliant idea of rising and arranging herself more to her liking before he returned.

She did not like the grin he turned on her before calling out toward the door. Thanon entered. The furthest Gregry went was over to her friend close enough to tell him quietly to go call the council and mention how bad of a patient she was being.

That is rather unfair. I have not actually voiced any protests or acted against his advice. Thinking about doing so should not count toward him being able to tattle on me.

Annalla gave the mage her unamused look when he returned to her side.

"I am only allowing this meeting at all because I know everyone wants answers and will be even more difficult should I not allow the conversation to happen." He sobered. "Annalla, you could have died from this. Do not take your need for rest lightly."

Annalla thought back to the power rushing through her, crushing in its grip on her body and mind. "I know, and I'm not. Will you at least allow me to sit up against the headboard?"

"Of course." His smile became amused. "Allow me to help you."

He was not much help, but she managed to push herself up to a sitting position, breathing hard by the end of it.

"Gregry." She studied him when they settled and her friends started bringing in additional chairs, likely from their rooms. "Why are you here and not closer to the front lines? You have to be a Power in the realm."

He shrugged. "The front lines are fluid and rough. I putter around here well enough, but I am old. It would likely be too much for me."

"What about one of the larger cities down there?"

"We thought about it," he said. "Ceru remains a human place filled with political machinations. The royal family and their ambassadors do well enough, as they must interact with the elves frequently. Unfortunately, much of the city is run by the aristocracy.

"I would have found myself healing the rich and doing nothing for the soldiers or poor. As I understand it, one of Tyrus' brothers are set in Ceru specifically to keep the lords in line with the war efforts.

"Auradia was another option, but with much of their forces and support out of the Woodland, they are not allowing outsiders into the Heartwood. It would have restricted my efforts as much as Ceru. Many with serious wounds come here with the supply fleet returning north. I am able to heal them even much later, after the initial healing, so they can return south whole again.

"It is a compromise, but I hope I am doing enough good despite the limitations."

Annalla was glad he wanted to do more than be a pampered healer pet for the Ceru elite. "I'm sure you are helping more than you think. I hope I am not taking you away from others in more need than I."

Gregry shook his head. "I believe you heard in the council that the transports did not return from the south this year. As a result, my skills have been less in demand of late. I may head south for a time to assist once the river is cleared."

"I'm sure they will appreciate any time you can spend with them," she said before yawning.

"Tired? I will try to keep this meeting short."

While she felt exhausted, it was more of a drained sensation and was better than she'd felt since before the headache had begun. The pain faded more with each moment, and she could regain her energy with a little rest, as Gregry suggested.

A voice called from the doorway, "May we enter, Lady Annalla?"

She failed to stifle an exasperated sigh at the honorific. "By all means, Majesty."

The door opened and a good portion of the council filed in, taking seats on the chairs they managed to cram into her little room. She found their obvious discomfort at being in her sleeping quarters entertaining and struggled not to laugh.

They were unlikely to notice her weakened state much when they were avoiding looking directly at her, even though she was fully clothed in the bed.

When they settled, King Oromaer cleared his throat. "You look well."

"It was nothing a few hours' sleep couldn't cure. I'm only still here because my captor over there will not let me leave yet." She added a conspiratorial tone to her voice and leaned forward. "If you ask me, I think the old mage is going a bit daft."

"Ha! Youth are always far too careless with their health. And from the injuries you have tallied recently, young one, you are among the worst offenders," Gregry shot back at her with a grin, playing along.

Their banter eased some of the tension in the room, enough for King Oromaer to call them to order. "Mage Gregry, I think we would all appreciate an explanation."

"I am sure some of you have already reached the correct conclusion. It is simply that our young friend here is a manifest essence. Not everyone is as familiar with the concept though, so let me think for a moment on how to best summarize it for everyone…" When he continued, his voice changed. Annalla could imagine it as the voice with which he lectured his students.

"The basics are needed, I believe, so we are all working from the same foundational understanding. Essence, not only in

Elaria but in all realms, is one of the three aspects necessary for life. Your body, or physical form, ties you to the physical world. Your soul is your will or personality to dictate and control your decisions, actions, and behaviors.

"Your essence is your potential, power, or capability. Potential for *what* exactly depends on the individual. Few people truly reach the limits of their potential, as it takes a great deal of drive and effort to go beyond what comes naturally to the extent of one's ability.

"Essence within each individual person, creature, or thing is finite. That individual essence is concentrated within one or more of the seven essential elements. Earth, water, fire, air, communication, thought, and pure essence.

"The first four are often referred to as the base, or physical, elements. Someone with an essence concentrated in one of these often possesses the greater potential for physical endeavors of some kind. The next two are referred to as the higher, or mental, elements. An essence concentrated in one of these would have a higher potential for the mind. No person is completely bereft of either physical or mental ability. The concentration of essence simply determines where the greatest potential lies for each individual."

Annalla held up a hand to stop him. "What do you mean by the term *elements* here? The world isn't just made up of those seven things. Fire is not an object, but rather heat or energy. Thought is certainly not part of the physical world around us as a building block."

"We have given the elements terms with which we are more familiar, but they are not an exact application. It is not rock, water, flame, wind, and such to which I refer. The elemental names are representations of aspects or characteristics these essential elements embody in the world."

Gregry paused and looked away in thought before snapping his fingers. "Let us take the dance you and Larron performed. I am told it is extremely challenging, requiring significant physical and mental prowess to accomplish. The two of you likely have at least one strong concentration in both a base and higher element. Knowing which is nearly impossible unless you can *see* essence because the aspects and characteristics of the elements often overlap.

"Strength might be the solidity of earth or the fierceness of fire. Agility could come from the fluidity of water, air, or fire. The mental aspect might be communication through reading body language or thought through memorization. There are a multitude of combinations, and people with the same aptitude could easily come by their natural abilities from different elemental concentrations."

She nodded. "Okay, but not everyone with an aptitude makes trees grow crazy."

He smiled consolingly. "If essence is powerful enough in someone, that person can manifest their essence in the physical world beyond a body's natural capability. This manifestation takes the form of the element in which their essence is concentrated.

"An example of such a manifestation, and the elemental connection, is an irimoten healer's focus in water. It has been the most common focus of essential healers of recorded history in Elaria. I theorize it is because the body is composed of so much of that element. Another example is a prophet who might have a focus in thought or communication, as prophecy is a mental ability.

"There are varying degrees of power among those able to manifest, just as the magai vary in their strength with magic. I believe there are two elves alive today who possess an essence powerful enough to manifest. In Annalla's case, it seems her essence is concentrated in the earth element with the manifest power to influence the growth of plant life. I am making an educated guess here. Only one with a concentration to manifest essence itself could see the connection and confirm my hypothesis."

"I know both Lord Jarin and Lady Morena. Morena is from the Palonian," Orion said. "Their unique abilities developed slowly over years. They were far from the destructive display we saw earlier, even when their powers first emerged. There are often irimoten with gifts, whose abilities developed in the same slow manner.

"Annalla appeared to be in pain. It was as though her own abilities overwhelmed her. What makes you call this an essential ability rather than untrained magical potential?"

"All magai know how to identify magical potential, but we cannot see essence. I found no magical potential in Annalla. As to the sudden and violent emergence of her power, all I can offer are theories. The first—and I believe best—theory is that whoever or whatever changed her form and now blocks her memory, also caused her manifest power to become...dormant.

"From the fragments she has of her transformation, it too was a violent process. I suppose that with her form returned to its natural state, her essence is beginning to reassert itself. And it is doing so at full strength. I believe it is not developing slowly because, as far as her essence is concerned, at her age, it should be fully developed."

"So, my own ability tried to kill me?" Annalla was not certain she wanted the ability if it was so dangerous.

"Essentially." Gregry chuckled at his own joke. Though she raised a chastising eyebrow, Annalla had to purse her lips against a smile.

He sobered again. "If you were a mage, death would not be a concern. The main difference between magic and essential powers is that essential powers are a part of the individual. It is only the ability to *utilize* magic in the world around us that is part of the mage. Magic itself exists independently from us.

"Using magic is like running. Those with greater strength can use magic quicker, longer, and on a greater scale, but if we exhaust our ability, it will not kill us. We can simply no longer run.

"The same is not true for those with manifest powers because a portion of essence must be connected to the other two parts of life for that life to continue. If someone were to put the entirety of their essence into one action, the action might be accomplished if they are powerful enough, but they would die in the process. Committing the whole of your essence is a desperate, final gamble."

"Theoretically," the irimote woman said. "Right? I've never heard of it happening."

"I am afraid not, Matriarch Patrice," Rolandor said with a shake of his head. "We have in our records two such instances of elven essentials dying upon a sudden and significantly stronger outpouring of their power than they had previously demonstrated. In those instances, we were not able to determine if their manifestation, or the effort itself, killed them, but it was not the enemy they faced."

"Irimoten have more essentials than the elves. If we have never seen this, is it likely a matter of strength? The elven essentials are fewer, but far stronger," Patrice asked and looked around, but most of the elves were shrugging with expressions, saying it sounded plausible enough.

Annalla saw Gregy shaking his head in a negating gesture. "There have been magai scholars in the past who researched essence," he said. "Many are interested in how magic and essence might intersect or interact.

"That is a separate topic." He waved off questions before they could start. "But the research has shown how essence in each race presents in fundamentally different ways. The differences are primarily within how integrated essence is to maintain the physical form. Irimoten are more integrated to the physical than elves, which means it is highly unlikely an irimote could sunder 'essence' from 'body.'

"It is theorized by these scholars that elves are *less* connected to their physical form. The connection to their Woodlands, and life around them in general, helps to anchor and sustain them. A more tentative connection means the sundering is still challenging, but very much possible." Gregry turned to look at Annalla. "I believe now that you are *aware* you are a manifest essence, you can avoid this risk."

And yet, he did not look relieved. "But…?" she asked.

He sighed. "There is another difference between magic

and essence. Magai tell magic what to do and direct the flow of power. A person with manifest powers is the conduit through which the element passes and changes. Again, the fact that all three parts of life depend on each other is critical.

"As the essence is taxed to greater extents, the body compensates by giving its own strength, which is why you were physically weakened, as well as losing control of your ability. All three parts work together to compensate when there is a need. If a manifest essential is injured, their power will be limited to some extent until the person recovers."

"Gregry, why does this matter? Why does it raise concerns?" Larron asked, narrowing in on the fact he had not yet stated the specific risks.

"The first threat I described is only dangerous to the individual when that person has control of their essence. It would need to be willfully and intentionally released from the physical connection to put forth their entire power into one massive act. Only the soul can drive such a sundering. The second threat might not be a threat at all. It depends on if the extent of Annalla's power has been released or not." He sighed again and rubbed at his temple.

"Let us say holding...this," he pointed to the ceramic water basin on the table by her bed, "is a task you wish to accomplish. It is a task you could easily perform thousands, millions, of times throughout the course of your life. If, however, we were to ask you to lift all of them at once and dropped them on you? The result would be your crushing death beneath the weight. For Annalla, making a seed sprout is like lifting the basin. Having her power return all at once is that mass of basins crashing down."

"Keeping with your imagery, it would seem she was able to gain control of the fall of basins before it was too late?" Larron's statement was said as a question.

Patrice pointed at Gregry with a quick finger jab gesture. "Two! She is half elf, and elves usually have either more than one ability or a two-pronged ability."

Gregry tipped his head in agreement. "Just so. I believe

Lady Morena has two, and Lord Jarin has two aspects of the earth element."

"If this was the strength of her full essence, then she has the ability to control it, even if another power or aspect does emerge."

Gregry looked thoughtfully at Marto, considering his statement, but Annalla answered before the magai could spring back into theory.

"No. It would be a valid point, but your analogy was a little off, Gregry. It neglects to consider the different aspects of each element. While magic might all be the same, such is not true for the elements as you described them." Her objection combined the knowledge and theories he had shared with her single experience. Even with those limitations, Annalla felt confident.

"Earth is fixed, stable, solid. Very rarely would we consider the earth violent. The growth of plant life is not something we think of as the earth *becoming* violent.

"I was not dealing with my full essence all at once. It came as a rushing flow, but I did not need to fight for control immediately. It was more like picking my way up an unstable slope. I slid back a step for every two forward, but I had time to make progress. Another element might not be so friendly."

She paused and looked for some optimism. "But Patrice said elves were the ones most often with multiple elements, and I'm only half-elf."

Gregry nodded. "Yes, I have met more irimoten essentials. While more frequent, they are less powerful on average and usually concentrated within one element. The few elven essentials are immensely powerful and there is often leakage if they are not careful. They have been known to start compensating for or using their abilities before they consciously know they have them."

Oromaer chuckled and commented, "Morena's family always had the most refreshingly cool house in the summers."

Gregry grinned but continued with his thought, "I cannot say where the fairy would fall on this spectrum."

"Do you have control of this one, at least?" Oromaer held

her eyes.

Annalla still felt lost and on unstable footing. Unlike her weapons, that was not something she felt trained to handle. She remembered climbing against the growing tide of her power, sliding back with every step she gained.

In the end, she *had* gained control, stopping the growth and stabilizing it so rescuers could reach her. It was probably safe enough, but she wanted a test. They likely *needed* a demonstration along with assurances.

At a gentle extension of her fingers, the plant by the window slowly flowered into full spring bloom. "I do," came her answer.

"Very well. We will leave you to rest. The winter hall will be set up by mid-day tomorrow. Our council will resume after the meal. Until then, relax, and everyone else can think further on Marto's proposal."

Annalla gave her friends an encouraging smile as they grabbed the extra chairs and left.

"You are not going to rest, are you?" Gregry asked when they were alone once more.

"I know I need it, and I will…later. I feel more restless than relaxed right now and lying about is not going to help the feeling go away." She paused. "How did you know I changed form?"

"You mean from a human form?"

She gave an answering nod.

"When I healed you the first time, I could find the recently healed injuries as well. Ears, eyes, wings. Each suffered from some sort of manipulation I could not explain with a wound."

"But this is what I'm supposed to be?"

The old mage reached over and took her hand in his own dry and wrinkled one. He gently squeezed. "Even essential powers leave traces in the body. There is nothing unnatural about you now. Extraordinary, yes, but nothing unnatural."

It helped to hear out loud more than she thought it would. Knowing it brought an embarrassed smile to her face. She gave his hand a squeeze in return, in thanks.

"I think I am going to go for a flight. I need to feel the air around me, clear my head."

"Not too long, young one. You did almost die today." Then, shaking his head, he too left.

Annalla slipped from her window and up into the sky. Flying took as little effort as walking. If the wind was right, it took less. The act was made easier by the fact that when her wings were spread for flight, she became lighter. Her weight lifted from her, and the effect translated, to a limited degree, to anything she carried. She knew this fact and could feel the truth of it more with every flight.

So many truths, and nothing to support them. What if everything she believed came from some show or other fiction? She was proceeding as though what she believed was fact, but there was no guarantee of the accuracy and certainly no guarantee it was complete.

Annalla might think things she carried became lighter, but what if there was some function of lift increased upon takeoff making it seem so? What if at some elevation the effect wore off and she either let go or plummeted to the ground with her load?

With the dance, she at least had the option of comparing her knowledge with Geelomin's to validate her understanding before trying something dangerous. Without the second opinion, she would have been putting herself and Larron at great risk.

Thanon had asked to fly with her. If she was wrong, she risked the life of her close friend. There were no fairy around to stop her from making a mistake or catch him if they fell. The implications of that last dream-memory were disconcerting. It meant unless she could recall from where her conviction originated, she needed to weigh the risks more heavily in case she was wrong.

CHAPTER TEN

Larron sat with Oromaer, Arbellie, and Orion in the king's home. It was nothing like outsiders expected. Of all the races he visited, the royalty and leaders of the elves lived in the humblest of manors relative to their people. The king resided in a five-room building just off one wing of the palace complex. It held two bedrooms, a kitchen doubling as a dining room, a water closet, and the parlor they sat in that night. There were no distinguishing characteristics outside or within the structure to identify it as belonging to royalty, which is exactly what the elves loved about their homes. They were homes rather than frames for status.

Larron, too, felt at home there with those people. They had spent many evenings together like that, relaxing near the small fire in conversation during his fostering years. That conversation, however, was more serious than any in the past.

"I will go as the representative of the elves. My orders from my own acting king were to seek aid. If two of the elven kings agree on a representative, the third follows. It is the agreement set forth by the three kings long ago in anticipation of situations such as this." Larron looked pointedly at King Oromaer as he spoke.

"You are also a prince and commander of your people. It would be optimistic to call this a shot in the dark. Why would we risk one of our greatest leaders?"

He shook his head and laughed at Oromaer's heavy-handed flattery. "Thank you, but I think we are past the point a 'great leader' is going to make the difference in this conflict."

"Maybe we are simply not at that point yet." He spoke the words, but Larron wondered if he was trying to convince himself.

"If we ever hope to get there, we cannot continue as we have thus far and hope for better results."

"Larron is right, Father. We both know it every time we look at the map. An entire battalion, or half of Kahnlair's magai, could turn in our favor and it would make no difference. It feels like every battle we win is one he allows us, raising our hopes before destroying them again."

"You think allowing Larron to go on this mission of hopes, dreams, and *bedtime stories* will bring us victory?"

"I think a shot in the dark is fast becoming our only *hope* of victory. We do nothing, and we lose. If they find the fairy, we might have a chance."

Larron pressed further with Orion's support. "There is only one person here with the potential to be able to represent all three Woodlands. We may need our full bargaining power if we do find them."

"A valid point," Lady Arbellie's soft voice called the attention of all three men, "but that is not the reason you want to go."

"A life bond is not a geas or some other magical compulsion. It places a marker in one path and limits access to others, but you know as well as any it does not control us." Larron would not deny the bond, but it was not the driving reason behind his push to be named their representative. "Our personal situation might be the reason I *want* to go on this mission, but there are many reasons I *should* be sent on this mission. I am a prince and commander of my people. I know my duty and would not forsake it."

"You are bonded?" Orion asked, his eyes turning gleeful as they had when he was younger and finding trouble. "To Annalla?"

"I am."

His eyes narrowed. "She does not know."

"We do not know if the bond will happen for her, being only half elf."

"I heard she was not pleased you withheld your status as a prince of the Derou." Orion gave him a look, clearly indicating his actions were a mistake. "Do you believe keeping *this* from her as well is the best approach?"

There was no good answer. If she asked, he would not lie. The timing was the greatest complication. They never seemed to have any time alone since entering the Heartwood.

"Her understanding of life mates for elves is limited to the few mentions of them as we journeyed. It might be different if she recalled the relationship between her parents, but those memories have not returned. I fear she would see it as an expectation or an inescapable trap. We know what this means for me, but not for her. I need time to explain in a way to avoid placing any additional burden upon her."

"I should have known when she was injured today." He grinned. Having conveyed his warning, Orion settled in to have fun at the expense of his honorary cousin. "You never behave as out of control as you were after her power emerged. At the training ground, with anyone else, you would have been treating them before Mage Gregry was even close."

"Thank you for the sympathy," Larron responded dryly.

"Ha!" He laughed, and his parents chuckled while enjoying the show. "It seems like she will travel with you, which was always the greatest hurdle for your relationships. I must warn her of your bad habits though, so she is not taken in by you saving her."

"I do not believe that will be necessary, and there are no bad habits of which to speak," Larron said, holding back a smirk as Oromaer scoffed at his proclamation.

Orion continued as though Larron had not spoken, "She probably already knows how bossy you are, and how you tend to keep secrets."

"We were on a mission," he responded in exasperation. "I had orders."

"But does she know of your love for odd-smelling cheeses and propensity to exaggerate your own prowess?"

"Orion..." He was not sure there was an appropriate response to the increasingly absurd accusations.

"Oh! And about how you become weepy when you drink more than a sip or two of wine?"

"You are simply making things up," he said dismissively while mentally assuring himself that he never gave Zeris that much trouble. "Arbellie, I would appreciate it if you could control your offspring."

Larron looked over at the woman struggling not to laugh as her son continued listing more outrageous personal failings, of which Larron was the apparent owner.

She forced a straight face, and he knew he would be receiving no help from this quarter. "I do not know, Larron. My son paints a devastating image of you. These are things a woman should know before entering a relationship. Perhaps Orion could help you explain the situation to Annalla and offer her some of your finer points. To aid you, of course."

The royal family burst into laughter, and Larron could not help joining. He had no doubt Orion would attempt to put stories in her ear if given an opportunity. She would probably see through it...he hoped. The conversation would more likely result in *her* telling some outrageous story about *him* to Orion, who would then spread it among the elves. He would have to make sure they were given *no* opportunity to talk. His reputation would not survive otherwise.

"Your concern for my bonded and our relationship is touching. I assure you, we are perfectly well without the need for aid or interference."

"Hmm," came the non-committal response when Orion regained control of his laughter, still grinning as though he found the situation hilarious. "With her skills and power, you have certainly met your match."

Larron smiled to himself and stared into the fire. "I have."

Orion gagged and Arbellie put a hand to her chest. Larron realized how sappy he had sounded and could only shrug.

"You are a brilliant leader, my friend, and it was my hope to call upon you here when we break our own siege," Oromaer finally broke the silence. "However, you are needed elsewhere for all the reasons you and my son have stated. You already have the voice of the Derou king. Now, I give you voice for the Palonian in this matter, and with it goes that of the Auradia. So long as you work toward the mutual good of all the Woodlands, you represent us all. Go with hope, Prince Larron."

"Live with grace, King Oromaer." The brief formality was all the ceremony needed, belying the import of what Oromaer had done.

With the authority of all three Woodlands, Larron could bargain away the sovereignty of elves if he thought it necessary. They would hold to it. To be a mere representative or ambassador was to be a messenger. He had the voice of kings, which meant he bore all the power and authority they possessed in any negotiations.

No other race knew of that long-standing agreement. Until that moment, it had never been enacted. They stared at each other for a moment until he nodded acceptance of the immense responsibility to all of their people.

CHAPTER ELEVEN

"I will be coming with you." Tyrus joined Annalla at the table she previously had to herself.

She had slept well and left her bed early to break her fast. His face told her his night had been filled with more thinking than sleeping. A day and a half had passed since her accident. The first afternoon of meetings produced two additional volunteers for her pending journey with Marto. Despite the lack of experience, the young mage remained relaxed as the discussion progressed the day before. Annalla simply tried to ignore the tentative glances cast in her direction the entire time.

"The human kingdom will be represented, then?"

"It will."

"Yet it took some convincing to allow you to go at all," she guessed with an amused twist to her mouth.

His tired, youthful face crinkled with a grin hidden beneath a growing beard. He could not be much older than she thought herself, and it was times such as those that the serious leader became a charming and handsome young man. She enjoyed their flirting. It felt like an easy escape for them both, like her joking with Thanon.

"I'm a prince. People do not *allow* me, they *obey* me," he said without conviction.

"Naturally. Especially when your decisions involve

traipsing off into the dangerous unknown without most of your guards."

"I suspect without any guards, actually. We will already be at six, including you, if each race sends a representative."

"You think twelve would be too many?"

He nodded. "With that many, you start needing to bring a supply cart, which is more complicated in winter this far north. We lost most of our people on the journey here in the first attack against our wagon. You could have some races only send one and others two, but that can send the wrong message, or at least an unbalanced image, in negotiations."

"So, you talked them into letting you go alone?"

Tyrus smirked at her with an air of smugness. "I talked them into my going with as many guards as the other ambassadors take and no more. Harndorn believes they would never send their leaders without guards."

"You believe otherwise? Larron came from Derou with a group of five."

"I believe the council will come to the same conclusion I have today. Stealth is going to be a critical asset, which means a smaller party, which means one for each race," he held up a finger for emphasis. "Marto, you, and I are already in. If the local magai council approved the mission, they clearly already agree with me. Otherwise, it would have been two magai proposing the expedition."

"Any guesses for the rest?"

He seemed to be familiar with the people represented in the council. If Tyrus did not know all of them personally, he was aware of the nuances differentiating the groups. Annalla would be surprised if he did not have direct experience working with the various peoples of the realm in his homeland.

"The dwarves will send their second if they send anyone. The first is stationed here for his assigned duration and would not abandon the posting. Irimoten are traditionally in smaller, more independent and disparate tribes. They would have to elect someone from among their leaders." He paused to take a bite, looking up in thought as he ate.

"It might end up being Patrice—the one on the council—or one of her advisors," he continued. "Both the irimoten and dwarves will be limited in their negotiating power. They would only represent the tribes and clans from this area. If the fairy are in this direction, it might be good enough, and the others are likely to pitch in later."

"What about the elves?" she asked, wondering if she might have a friend in the group.

"Elves tend to treat royalty like ambassadors rather than figureheads, so I suspect Larron, Oromaer, or Orion. If they send Orion, then Oromaer and Arbellie would become restricted to the Heartwood. They never risk the entire royal line. It is also more likely for them to risk the current king rather than the heir, but with Orion not yet bonded, the matter becomes less certain. I would wager my coin on Larron's selection."

"And, of course," he became exaggeratedly puffed up, "I'm the only human here who can speak for my father, so it has to be me to have weight. My father and brothers would hold to any agreement I might sign and push the council to follow through. I have told my guards a fourth son is good for nothing if not ambassadorial work."

Tyrus sobered. "While I am a younger son, my king gave me an order to seek aid in the north *beyond* the supply situation, if possible. There is none to be found for us here, in the Palonian, so I must seek elsewhere. I will not risk the lives of my men. If they stopped to think about it, they would agree that a few more people would add to the danger, not decrease it."

"It is sad and telling of the times when fourth-in-line for the throne is no longer so distant. They may be right to treat you with as much concern as they would the heir to the throne."

"We all face risks," Tyrus said with a grim shrug. "This is a task I must undertake to accomplish my mission."

"That is true enough," Annalla agreed. "What tasks have your brothers been set to?"

"Valdas, the second eldest, is safest from Kahnlair. I worry more about some greedy council member sending an assassin after him than anything else. He stayed behind to serve as regent of Ceru while the rest of us left with the army. Fortunately, Valdas is exceptionally good at reading and managing people to his needs.

"Humans in Ceru, and especially those on the council, hate the war and how much it is costing them. They are shortsighted, but it is not overly surprising when the fighting is so far from the safety of their homes."

Annalla agreed with that assessment and would likely have said something more biting about such individuals. Instead, she kept her silence and let him continue.

"My father, and Valdas as his representative, are not popular among our people within the city. It is why he set Valdas upon the throne as regent rather than Albertas, who is his heir."

"He is setting up your eldest brother as the bringer of peace," she said, seeing the wisdom in the approach. As long as Albertas survived, it might work.

Tyrus nodded. "Exactly. Valdas would much rather work from the shadows. He will be more than happy to relinquish his role as soon as we can manage it. Lukas' job—my third brother—is to ensure Albertas survives the war. They can't stay safely on the sidelines or the soldiers would never follow him if my father is killed. Lukas trained most of his life with some of our best royal guards. He would die for Albertas. We all hope that is never necessary, especially Albertas. I don't know if he could ever forgive himself if Lukas died because of his actions."

Annalla gave him a moment of silence, thinking about the danger each of his brothers faced. "And you are the messenger rather than another guard?"

"I studied other cultures in the realm to become an ambassador before the war began. Representing my father as a messenger is an extension of my training. I face less direct risk, but there are so many more unknowns."

Annalla nodded. "Like bandits on a river thought to be ally-controlled."

Tyrus tipped his cup in her direction with a groaning sigh.

She tilted her head in curiosity. "And you do not want to go home?"

"Willing or not," he said, "the way home is closed to me unless I want to go back with the provisions next year. I would not choose to remain here, hoping I might someday return home. King Oromaer would allow me to stay, likely even increase the number under my command. That was not my assignment. Call it what you will, my decision stands."

"I call it a very restrained and political response." Any lingering reservations about him melted away at his words. "If you have fighting skills to match, our situation will be even more improved. Though if not, I might be able to hold your hand through the frightening parts."

He gave his eyebrows an exaggerated wiggle. "I can't say I would be opposed, but I'm afraid we'll both be preoccupied if there are any *frightening* parts."

"I…" She felt herself blushing for no reason. It deepened with a surge of guilt—*though why I would feel guilty, I have no idea*—when she recognized familiar footsteps. "Larron, would you care to join us?"

"You are both awake rather early." He emerged through the open doorway to the smaller room in which they ate.

"You are not exactly waking to the mid-day sun," she replied. "It looks like Tyrus will be coming with Marto and me."

"Not unexpected." He addressed Tyrus, "You are the most logical choice if the humans decided to send representation. I am pleased to hear you will be joining us."

"Kahnlair may be a slow and festering disease upon the realm, but this disease is killing us. We need to try something different." He paused. "Us? You are coming for the elves, then?"

Larron collected a plate of his own and took a seat on the bench beside her. "I am. I convinced the king last evening."

Annalla was not sure whether it comforted or worried her. Like Tyrus, he was the logical choice. He would have the blessing of two elven kings to trade for aid on their behalf. If Larron came though, he would not be tucked away in the safest of the

Woodlands away from the dangers everyone who came with her would face. Would it hurt less if he died there unbeknownst to her, or at her side?

How about not dying at all? the small, optimistic voice in her head asked.

"Will the other Derou be with us as well?" she asked, again uncertain which answer she would prefer to that question as well.

Larron shook his head. "No. They will join the Palonian forces until it is safe to return to the Derou. Geelomin will remain as our representative on the council."

"Do *they* know this?" Tyrus asked him in a voice both sympathetic and amused.

With a wry smile, Larron replied, "Geelomin does. He will help me stop any objections. Though, he was—admittedly— initially vocal with his own displeasure." He gave a short laugh. "How desperate are we that ambassadors are dispatched to seek out a child's bedtime story?"

"Very," Tyrus said with a grave nod. "Very desperate, but not yet hopeless."

"Even Marto said he never would have gotten approval for the journey without some evidence the fairy *did* still exist somewhere." Annalla gestured at herself. "So, it's not entirely based on a story anymore."

Tyrus shook his head at her optimism. "Are you able to spar with me this morning? You did agree to give me a lesson."

"I'm busy today. How about tomorrow morning?"

"I'll mark the date… And eat a light breakfast."

She chuckled at his tone. "Don't worry, I won't go too hard on you."

"What plans do you have for today? If you do not mind my asking," Larron inquired.

"I had Thanon ask if I could visit the boy injured in our fight. Oh!" she exclaimed, having a sudden brilliant idea, and grabbed his forearm, knocking food back to his plate from his fork in her enthusiasm. "You should come with me. They said, 'anytime before noon.' Apparently, he thinks we are 'so amazing.' It would be a treat for us both to show up."

Larron's smile was small, but she could read so much meaning in the expression. He was pleasantly surprised at the invitation, amused by her behavior, happy, and beneath it all faintly relieved and a little boastful. Larron had always been easy to read, but she thought she might be seeing too much that time.

"Very well." He inclined his head.

"Really? You're not too busy?" She was a little worried she was asking him to skip something important.

"I will tell the Commander I am unavailable today. It is nothing to worry over pulling me away from," he assured her. "I appreciate the invitation."

It was like he read her concern straight from her head. Something was going on with him, but she would not push with Tyrus sitting across from them, watching the exchange with a smirk on his face.

"Okay, then. You can help me find where they are staying."

"Where are your usual guides this morning?" Tyrus asked.

"Doing elf things. I told them I would be fine on my own."

"*Elf things?*"

Annalla smiled at Larron's dramatically offended tone while he blinked at her. "They have been spending too much time worrying about me. They need to spend time away from me and each other, to do their own activities and relax. Which, for Geelomin and you, might just mean more work, but Thanon and Bealaras need free time."

"Geelomin will likely teach today. He loves children."

"You're joking. Geelomin?" Annalla thought about the taciturn elf and could not reconcile the image of him with little kids.

Larron nodded. "He possesses a calm demeanor that serves him well with the more volatile emotions of youth…and fairy."

She wrinkled her nose at him, but otherwise ignored the final comment. "Huh. Well, I guess he should enjoy all the refugee children starting their training here."

Tyrus finished his meal and bid them farewell as they continued talking.

"He will, yes." Larron paused. "Thank you for thinking of them."

Annalla shrugged. "Of course. They're my friends. Now, you should hurry up and finish eating so we're not late."

CHAPTER TWELVE

Annalla turned in her seat, sitting in a way allowing her to face him fully. She had felt bad for the boy getting injured during their dance. With combat being one of her best skills, her performance with Larron presented a rare opportunity to use those skills for something other than harm. He had been so eager to watch them he ended up climbing into a dangerous position to watch. She suspected her interest in that visit to be primarily vanity, but it would be more interesting with Larron along to help her with small talk.

"You asked me mere minutes ago," Larron said in response to her enthusiasm, "and said we had until noon to arrive."

"Yes, but we also need to find a practice weapon for him. I'm thinking a knife is best. I've been told it is an appropriate gift for an irimote child."

"It is. Though you will be expected to give him his first lesson with the weapon as well. Gifts among the irimoten are meant to include a transfer of knowledge between giver and receiver with the passing of possessions. An heirloom usually has a family story shared, craft gifts might be accompanied by a lesson in the associated textiles, and weapons require a lesson in use."

"For safety as well as tradition, I imagine," she said. "And *we* will be expected to give the lesson. This will be from both of us."

Larron chuckled and shook his head as he polished off the last of his meal and indicated they could clean up and go. It was easy enough to pick out a practice knife. Larron knew exactly where the armory was.

The two of them narrowed in on the same one immediately upon looking around, making Annalla laugh. It was blunted, like all the practice knives, with a smooth edge. The blade was only as long as the handle of the short hunting knife and curved like an orange wedge. It was too small to be a battle knife as the boy grew, but it was perfect to hide away upon one's person in case of emergencies.

"The two sections allocated to the irimoten refugees are on the other side of the Heartwood," he pointed as they exited.

They had plenty of time and settled into a leisurely pace. Alone, with no pressing business, it represented a perfect opportunity to dig into his growing oddities.

"Larron, can you read people's minds?" Annalla asked into the companionable silence. She was determined to get to the bottom of whatever was going on.

"I am skilled at reading people from different cultures because of my travels. Is that what you mean?"

"At breakfast, it was like you knew I was worried about taking you away from something important with my invitation today. There have been other times too. Maybe I'm reading too much into your responses. Were you just reading my expression?"

"Ah."

She was about to take the explanation at face value. It was plausible to expect his experience interacting with different people over centuries of travel could result in higher skills in interpreting varied expressions, body language and verbal cues. Annalla knew he was not lying to her about it, but the abbreviated sound of understanding meant something more.

"Aaaah?" She dragged out the sound. "So you *were* reading my mind?"

He pursed his lips and his brow furrowed in thought as she saw him carefully considering what to say, or rather, how to say it.

It hit her, as they kept walking in silence, that *she* was not experienced at reading expressions, so why did she think she could read his?

"Can I read your mind?" she blurted out and continued rambling. "I feel like I know you are trying to figure out how to say what you are going to tell me without upsetting me. Which is a bit unsettling at the moment. Am I getting another essential ability?"

"No." His voice was firm. "This is limited to the two of us, and there is nothing over which to be upset. We will work out how to approach the situation, and it requires no immediate decisions."

Annalla stopped him with a hand on his arm and met his eyes. "Larron, what's going on? What 'situation' do we need to deal with?"

Larron let out a breath and ran his free hand through his hair in a rare display of agitation, messing up his neat, if overly decorative, braids. "I have no idea how to have this conversation, but I want you to know there are no requirements or demands because of this."

Nothing about his statement was comforting or clarifying. "Okay. What is *this*?"

"You are my life mate," he spoke quickly and flinched back as though she might lash out at him.

The words did not make sense. His words were riddles. "What?"

"You are my life mate. We are bonded."

She felt the blood leave her head as comprehension set in. Her heart stopped.

I'm the only way he can have children. What if I'm not immortal and die before I'm okay with that? Annalla felt a responsibility for which she was not ready settling, weighing down upon her. *I like Larron and asked Thanon about him, but he is a prince, and I don't know if we will become more. Do we even have a choice now?* Her head spiraled with questions. *Is anything I feel for him real? What if I don't feel a bond too? Will he resent me? What if...*

"Annalla, breathe," Larron interrupted her rapid-fire thoughts, both hands holding her arms and giving a gentle shake. "No requirements, no demands, no expectations. Look at me."

She had not realized her head drooped to stare wide-eyed at the ground. Larron half held her up with his grip.

At his words, she heaved in a stuttering breath and peered at him again, her vision remaining tunneled.

"Come over here. You should sit down."

He led her to a little grassy area with some fall wildflowers still blooming. Annalla sat down in the grass, not caring if her rear became immediately soaked from the damp ground. She was quiet for a while, playing with one of the flower stems while her thoughts continued churning. Larron sat next to her, waiting patiently.

"Larron, this is…"

"Big? Frightening?"

She nodded and swallowed. "Are you…"

Larron had plucked one of the flowers and twisted it in his fingers. He stared at it rather than at her as he responded.

"Sure? Yes. I do not know how to describe it, but there is a hum or buzz? A knowing. A tug…something. It has been…not growing exactly, but…solidifying since we met. That you asked if you could read my mind means you feel the bond on some level as well."

"What is it doing?" How much was it manipulating them?

"It is not forcing a relationship. If you were murdering babies, the bond could not force me to love you." He glanced at her. "It does, if we choose a relationship, make communication easier. We understand intent, so there is less chance of misunderstanding. There remains the very likely chance we will disagree and fight, but it will happen knowing full well what the other meant to say."

Annalla gave a breathy, slightly hysterical chuckle. "I'm not sure if that is a good thing or a bad thing."

"Neither am I." Larron glanced at her once more before refocusing on the little white flower. "I will admit—however much

I regret you are in this position—I am glad to know you feel the bond in some way. That I am not alone in this experience. It is selfish of me, but I have been feeling some trepidation at the concept of being bonded. And some fear that it would be one-directional."

That, more than anything else could have, eased some of her tension. He was not jumping into some fantasy relationship where they were magically perfect. He was not demanding children from her.

"I don't—" She breathed out through her nose in frustration and tried again, "I don't know what to say."

"You do not need to say anything."

Annalla nodded in acknowledgment. "I'm going to need time to think. This… This is a lot to think about."

"Take however long you need."

"No demands, no expectations," she repeated his earlier promise to her, forcing herself to unwind a little.

His smile changed to something heated as he reached over to touch her cheek and met her eyes. "Hopes, dreams. As with anything new. But I will not even try to stop your flirting with the human prince. Who is nowhere near your match in anything, I might add, with absolutely no ulterior motive."

Her stomach dipped. "While I admire your restraint, I can't say I will be so forgiving."

There was something more between them. They stared at each other, and she knew they could jump in and find their way. She also knew that was not who either of them was, nor was it what was best in that moment.

"I need to know more about who I am and about my people. You need to find help for yours here and in your home Woodland. There is a war going on. Some might say that is a perfect reason to not hesitate, but…"

"Neither of us is one of those people." He smiled and leaned forward on one arm to press his lips to her forehead, still cradling her cheek.

Larron pushed to his feet, dusted off his hands and

backside, and held out a hand to help her up. "Let us find this boy and present him with his gift."

She fell a little more. The bond might help him understand her words and intent, but that demonstrated an understanding and acceptance of her as a person. Annalla would take time to further contemplate his revelation later. For the moment, she set it aside, trying to pretend the entire situation did not continue to poke at the back of her mind.

"Absolutely." She rose and started walking again, Larron at her side. "You can be the opponent as I show him how to attack someone larger."

***

That went better than I feared, Larron thought to himself as they made their way into the irimoten section of the Heartwood. He had been terrified of an extreme reaction in either direction. Running away would have been the worst response, but he probably could not have handled an expectation for them to immediately become a family unit.

There was so much going on. A relationship deserved attention and effort. Even a bond could not compensate for divided loyalties.

Larron should have known she felt the same, but few elves would be as reticent toward entering into something longer term as he. His desire to travel often placed relationships second in his priorities. Partners who understood the draw he felt were few. Those who might travel with him were, thus far, non-existent.

Annalla understood his need to travel. She made no demands of him.

"Excuse me," Annalla called to a passing irimote female, and when she turned, Larron recognized her as Patrice from the council. "We're looking for Sherdan and his mother. Would you know where we could find them?"

Irimoten grew to only about four to five feet in height. Unlike their balance, the canine windani who ran on two or four legs, irimoten walked primarily upright and were as graceful and agile as any cat. Their other feline attributes included retractable claws on thicker fingers and feline facial features, with tufted ears slightly higher on their heads than humans and elves.

It was not a cat's head on a person's body. The features were an elegant blending of the two. An irimote's pupils were vertical slits, like the gilar's. Both races possessed superior night vision. Irimoten also had the connected nose and mouth muzzle, but it was elongated and thinned from that of wild cats, and less pronounced on the facial profile. Their ears were also more human than feline, though higher on the head with soft points and fur.

Some humans saw them as a grotesque aberration. Larron had seen some of the more ignorant humans treat them as little more than animals, and he would not be surprised if most of those humans fought for Kahnlair in the war. How they justified supporting the gilar, vampires and windani escaped all logic. To Larron, the irimoten were a beautiful combination of forms.

Patrice's head perked up and her smile flashed a fang. "The dancers come to visit? It is good to see you remain well, Annalla. Always a pleasure, Prince Larron."

Annalla and he inclined their heads at the greetings, and Patrice continued, "I'm not sure Sherdan deserves such a treat after he was specifically told not to climb that tree. Any of the three of you could have been seriously injured."

"Isn't it said, 'fortune favors the bold?'"

"And kills the stupid," Patrice finished, making Annalla laugh with her. "Let's hope he learns something from this experience."

"And you would not have climbed that tree as a child. I am certain," Larron said, tongue-in-cheek.

"Hmm," Patrice grunted and looked at him side-eyed.

Annalla laughed again while Patrice shook her head. Larron grinned.

"I believe we can help with the lesson," he offered.

"Perhaps you should. Khalie, Sherdan's mother, happens to be the matriarch of one of our holdings. It should not be difficult to find them." She introduced herself to Annalla, since they had not formally met, as she indicated the direction they should walk.

"Thank you for helping. Sorry about all the destruction lately."

Patrice chuffed. "Every day is an adventure with you in the council. Stuffy elves always want to wait, wait, wait. No offense."

She spared Larron an unconcerned glance and carried on. "The Palonian is the supply base. While that makes it safer, it is also all about supplies all the time. I swear, every council meeting is about what crops are coming in, what crops are shipping, and what crops have shipped. The siege came in, and they took one look at it before deciding it was not worth the effort of eliminating. I told them my people could take out the patrols as quietly as any elf scout."

"Better than," Larron interjected.

Elves might be great at camouflage, but irimoten were the stealthy assassins. If you knew what to watch for, you could pick up signs of elven scouts. An irimote had her claws at your throat before you knew they were there. Training and fast reflexes were the only things that might, perhaps, save you from one set on killing you.

Patrice flashed her fangs again. "Thank you for saying so. We are grateful to the elves for their hospitality. There are nearly as many refugees here as there are elves at this point, but this is not our home, not our land. We live in houses belonging to others and conform to the rules of this land in which we live, but these are not our homes and not our ways. My people chafe at so much...structure."

"And it is too crowded for your comfort here."

Irimoten lived in close-knit groups, but they were smaller communities and semi-nomadic.

"So much so," she vehemently agreed with him.

"If we are the land, you are the creatures living in it. I will share, should it be any consolation to you, that this is too crowded for the elves as well."

"Ha! We have whole families packed into where one or

two elves might have lived, so I can well imagine." Patrice shook her head and sighed. "Much is being lost, but we are gaining an understanding of each other I hope will carry into the future."

"The elves will remember, and your heirlooms will carry the stories," Larron said in a traditional irimoten promise of remembrance.

"Of new friends and those lost." Patrice picked up the ceremony his words began. "I witnessed the murders of my father and husband since the war's beginning. Now it is my son fighting. Derek, Stathan, Nedral. Should Nedral not return, my heirlooms will go to another matriarch. We will end this war, and those lost will be remembered. Who do you remember?"

"I will remember Derek, Stathan, Nedral," Larron offered. "My brother, Zeris, was captured this spring. We do not know if he yet lives."

"I will remember Zeris." She turned to Annalla, who had followed the conversation but looked pale, as though seeing the ghosts of her forgotten past. He could intercede on her behalf. There was a polite way to cut out participants in a remembrance, but he knew she was not there yet.

"I will remember Derek, Stathan, Nedral," Annalla finally breathed out. "My parents were killed by gilar. I do not know their names."

"I will remember the parents of Annalla, and they shall be Named."

It was an honor he would explain to her another time if she wanted or needed it. To be Named by the irimoten meant to be given a title in your stories passed down. Klarhie Seer was so Named in their stories for the visions she had, saving an entire tribe's village. Until Patrice knew more of Annalla herself, they would remain *to be Named* in her stories, but the stories would begin then, and be passed on quickly. Sherdan and Khalie would be the first to take up the naming, and the little practice knife they carried for him would become an heirloom with a story attached.

"Here we are." Patrice turned to knock on a thin door. "Khalie, you and Sherdan have visitors."

"I'll answer it!" The cry came at the same time pounding feet could be heard tearing through the house in their direction. Someone ran full speed. Larron guessed it was the boy, despite Gregry telling him to take care for a while. The door flung open.

"Mom! They both came!" Sheridan yelled over his shoulder. "That fight was so amazing! You were both so fast, like *phew, shing, fwap!*"

The sounds were accompanied by exuberant, if not entirely accurate, demonstrations of fighting forms, nearly banging into the walls of the enclosed entry.

Patrice laughed at their faces. Larron was sure his eyes were as wide as Annalla's. "Good luck!"

Khalie came out of a backroom as Patrice left them with a wave, still laughing to herself.

"Sherdan, I will not have you breaking things in this house. You can break more limbs outside after we entertain our guests."

"Yes, Mother," he said and ran back to her side, grinning enormously as she greeted them.

Larron could tell he exerted an enormous amount of will to remain relatively still. His wiggling shoulders betrayed his only moderate success.

"Please, be welcome in this house."

Larron shared a look with Annalla as they thanked her and entered. That look made him supremely confident they were aligned on one thing. Neither of them was ready to consider children anytime soon.

CHAPTER THIRTEEN

The four travelers met daily, preparing for their journey in a room quickly filling with maps, scrolls, ledgers, and books. They studied the information available on known enemy disposition and rumored sightings to the east of the Palonian. Annalla specifically reviewed maps of the area to gain an idea of what the landmarks might look like from above. Larron had previously traveled the area, but she was considering requesting one of the dwarves walk her through their recollection as well.

A week had passed since the announcement of the addition of Tyrus and Larron to their mission, but neither the dwarves nor the irimoten had yet decided to send someone. On the day she and Larron visited the ball of energy known as Sherdan, the council discussed the merits and requirements of the journey. They decided the search party would meet daily, but with the overarching approach to the siege and river roughly scheduled out, the council would return to meeting only every three days to work out those details. Most of the documents in the room came in over the last few days, so they were rehashing the route yet again with the new materials.

"Let us go through the landmarks again," Larron said to groans from Annalla and Tyrus. Marto's enthusiasm had not abated, but the two of them were close to banging their heads on a table.

Larron became the leader of their small team when Tyrus suggested having one person in charge. The human even suggested Larron, as he was the most experienced traveler and familiar enough with the area to the northeast of the Palonian.

"Somewhere along the northern portion of the Nierda River here," Marto recited, pointing to a curve of the river on the map spread before them. "There is a bend in the river with a large rock outcropping sheltering a small, calmer pool of water. From that point, we head due north toward the Trazine Range, continuing in a straight line into the forested hills. If we have maintained the correct course, we will find the right gorge winding the rest of the way through the forest. From where the gorge exits the hills, we again head straight to the north, this time into the mountain range. There should be a pass or trail leading up, but that is where the story stops being fact and starts being just a story again."

Annalla stifled a laugh as Tyrus mimicked Marto. At that point, any of them could repeat the story verbatim. She flung a pencil at him to make him stop, and she swore Larron's eye twitched at their antics as he leaned over the map with Marto.

"The hills ha' many g'rges. Ya canna' know which be right," Sub-Controller Nurtik spoke from the doorway, surprising most of them.

"No, and we can't know where in the range to look, either. We have to start with the river." She switched to Dwarren, "How are you, Nurtik?"

"As well as can be expected, Annalla, thank you. As Controller Karntag was sent here to aid the Palonian, it has been decided I shall represent my clan in this expedition. The Controller wished me to make it clear I am not a representative of dwarves, but of the Trazine Range Clan only."

Annalla translated for the rest of the group, and they welcomed him to join them, settling into the discussion once more. Maybe they could uncover something new with a fresh perspective involved.

"We know we can't go straight to the hills," Marto said,

"so the river is our only possible starting point. We are going to have to follow my story through each step."

"Will the point on the river be recognizable after so long?"

Annalla spun around, dagger in hand, at the unexpected voice behind her. Patrice had crept in without a sound. Her sudden movement probably startled everyone in the room more than Patrice's arrival.

"By all the gods, Patrice! You are stealthy."

Patrice laughed as Annalla sheathed the knife and reclaimed her seat. "Thank you. It's a skill I learned on hunts."

"I hear *everything*. Water flowing miles away," Annalla emphasized, caught up in her wonder. "And with you, nothing. You're even wearing boots!"

"Fairy possess very sensitive hearing," Larron tried to explain in face of their confused amusement.

Tyrus snapped his fingers. "Vampires... I should be making these correlations faster by now. Welcome, Patrice. Are you to join our merry band as well today?"

"I am. The matriarchs voted to replace me on the council so they could send me on this mission instead."

"It is good you will be joining us," Larron said and postured in a way to bring everyone back to the table. "We were going over our route with the maps specific to the areas on which we will be focused. To answer your question, we have no way to be certain it will be recognizable or not."

Marto shrugged. "There is a limited amount of river in this stretch for us to search. I believe I will be able to recognize it with basic weathering of the features. If the river has shifted away from the prior path, then I probably will not."

"The historical maps I reviewed and compared did not show a significant deviation, so we hope for basic weathering," Annalla told them. "What's the plan if nothing we find along this stretch is similar enough?"

Her preference would be to press on, taking a guess and heading north anyway. Marto was correct that it was not a wide stretch of river they were looking at inspecting.

"We either turn back or guess," Larron summarized with a shrug.

"Which stretch of river is it?" Patrice kneeled on a chair and leaned over the map as Marto pointed it out. "And you head north from that point?"

Marto nodded. "Due north."

"The way it curves means there is not a great distance between the furthest east and west points," Tyrus said. "Guessing might get us close enough for Annalla to find them by flying around. The path through the hills winds and stretches in all directions, though, so there is no guarantee."

"That is the direction in which I would lean for the decision," Larron agreed, "but I want everyone to have the same understanding before we leave and ensure any orders from your people will not conflict with mine in the field."

He looked around, and everyone nodded except Nurtik, who would need to confirm with Karntag.

"For today, we proceed under the assumption we will head north, either from the specified location or the mid-point, if no better option is presented," Larron said. "Ideal conditions, re-mounts... It is a trip of at least three weeks. We will have neither of those, so we should adjust the estimate to a couple of months, minimum. We cannot carry enough supplies with us for the entire journey."

"I will be scouting ahead, flying most of the time, so we can pack extra on Moonshine, but it would still not be enough. Not by a long shot."

"We can't rely on the villages either. Karntag reported the gilar forces in the east moving north, so they might be in a position to limit that source of re-supply," Marto reminded them with a nod to Nurtik.

"Hunting and gathering could add another month or more. We will be on the waning side of winter when we enter the mountains, maybe early spring."

"But, Larron, we can't know if the timing will matter until we know what terrain we would be facing in the mountain path, right?" she asked.

"True. Winter would firm up a slushy slope, while spring would clear up a rockier path. In general, of course. And the northern mountains are never entirely safe to travel outside of the dwarven passes further east. Waiting a few months would make the journey safer against the weather."

"An' less safer 'gainst the 'creasing gilar threat."

"Agreed, especially with the bandits holding the river to the south. Which is why we are leaving in two weeks instead of two or three months."

"At least we are carrying less since I will be growing food for the animals," Annalla offered. "Are there any local edible wild plants I could grow, too?"

"Nothing that will not stand out in winter, but there are some options we could utilize without disrupting the ecosystem. I will speak with Oromaer about having one of the local farmers meet with you."

"Nurtik and I will need ponies. Will that add to the time estimate by slowing us? I can ride double on a horse, but it is not comfortable for long trips."

He shook his head at Patrice's concern. "Ponies will keep up. We will be breaking through snow often enough, anyway. The horses will need shorter and slower durations."

Larron handed out assignments for the next few days and dismissed them. Annalla could tell he was as excited with their new teammates as she. With a full party, they would head out early if all the provisions and packing could be completed to his satisfaction ahead of schedule.

***

"Why did we push to leave early?" Annalla asked no one in particular as she yawned again. "We're certainly forgetting something, and we have done zero scouting of the enemies around us."

As the days passed by, she had gone from feeling they

were wasting time, to feeling there was not enough of it. They stood with the horses and ponies they would be riding in the cold bite of the early morning air. The sky might be lightening, but the sun was still far from rising.

Patrice grinned at her and chuffed as she mounted her pony. "We are barely two days ahead of schedule. That is not exactly 'rushing things.' Besides, the elves and irimoten scouted for us and found an easy path out of the incompetent siege line."

She frowned and mumbled, "Last time I passed the line, I nearly died...and was shot in the leg."

"The order in which you say that makes me wonder which you thought worse." Larron stopped by her side and smirked down at her.

"The arrow," Annalla assured him. "The arrow hurt worse."

"The scouting was thorough." Larron's shoulder bumped hers and he lowered his voice. "You have been anxious to leave. Why the hesitation?"

She leaned into him, tilting her head against his shoulder. "I'm not just tagging along this time. Marto and I are critical to the success of this mission."

"It helps to separate *you*, the mission asset, from *you*, the person in your mind. You have no difficulty protecting someone else's life. What else?"

He was doing the not-mind-reading thing again. "Remember when I told you why I was afraid to enter the Palonian?" A nod. "If we find the fairy, I won't have you and the rest of the Derou to speak on my behalf this time. I must speak for all of you. They might not be so welcoming to a half-fairy, and we know I'm not as good as you at being diplomatic."

Larron's arm came around her shoulders. "I will be there to support you, no matter what comes. Many also find your direct speech refreshing."

"As far as support goes, maybe wait until after you negotiate their aid to help end the war before rescuing me when I'm arrested. I can handle prison that long."

"I am certain you could, but I believe you would more likely contrive your own escape long before my aid became necessary."

Annalla laughed and grinned up at him. The absurdity of their conversation removed some weight. "Okay, I'm ready now. We can go."

Geelomin, Bealaras, and Thanon had said their farewells the night before to both Larron and Annalla. They wanted to continue with them. No one was pleased to be splitting up, but their orders were to join the ranks of the Palonian elves and fight for Oromaer. If there was ever a campaign to free the Derou, they would join without hesitation.

No one said *if*, but the word hung between them like an unwanted guest. They were at war, and it was likely the last time the five of them would be together. She would miss her friends for that new journey, but Tyrus was correct about adding too many people to the group. None of them liked it. Agreeing with their reasoning did not mean they accepted it easily.

"A group of strangers will not work as well together," Bealaras argued.

Larron tilted his head in patient agreement. "I am familiar with the martial skills of the other races. I also interviewed each of our party members to discuss their capabilities. Annalla assisted with Nurtik's interview, as she is fluent in Dwarren."

Annalla shifted over to where Thanon leaned against the window.

"Hey," she said, leaning against the wall next to him without looking at him.

There was a smile in his voice when he responded. "Hey."

"Do you remember the conversation we had in the marsh about relationships and worrying about one person becoming bonded?"

"The one where I told you not to worry about bonds? That we do not enter relationships as placeholders, taking up our time while waiting for our life mates? Yes. I remember the conversation." Thanon shifted so he could look at her. He wore a cheeky grin when she dared a glance. "Are the two of you finally going to stop dancing around each other? Is there a whirlwind romance in the making?"

She rolled her eyes at him. "No. There is not. We both acknowledge higher priorities right now, and we are still learning about each other. I do need some related advice, though."

"You know you can ask me anything."

Annalla took a deep breath. "If Larron and I are bonded—"

"I knew it!" Thanon exclaimed, and all conversation in the room stopped.

She saw resigned amusement in Larron's eyes as Thanon waved the other three back to their own conversations. Geelomin and Bealaras sent confused looks in their direction as they took up their argument again, and Annalla fought against an irrational blush.

"Are you able to contain yourself now?" she asked through clenched teeth.

"Perfectly," he said, unable to clear the exuberant grin from his face. "You were trying to speak hypothetically about your bonding. Please, continue."

Annalla shook her head as she started over. "If we are bonded and one of us is seriously injured or killed, what does that mean for the other person, either now or as the bond grows?"

"Nothing. From an immediate perspective, there is no impact on the other party. You will not be distracted in a fight or feel overwhelmed in any way beyond what you would feel at losing any other companion or friend. If you are separated, you would not know their fate better than anyone else. There is no tactical weakness due to your bond."

"From the innate understanding it conveys in our communication, there may actually be a tactical benefit," she noted.

"Yes. It will likely reduce the possibility of misunderstanding orders given."

"What about longer term?"

"Emotionally, it is a relationship." He shrugged. "The two of you are responsible for putting in the effort to make it work or not. Physically, if you both sense the bond, the only restriction it imposes is fertility. Neither of you will likely have children with any other person. You are young enough that the bond will take years or even decades to shift your biology enough to produce children. There is no reason to rush."

Thanon's face was serious as he looked from her to Larron and back. He pulled her into a hug and spoke quietly, "Is Larron pressuring you? As your best friend, I will speak to him about such behavior."

Annalla laughed against his chest and hugged him back. "No. We're good. I just wanted to know how selfish I was being by accepting his patience."

"Travelers are the least likely among us to bond and have children. Larron is less than a millennium old. I can assure you that the probability of him, at this moment in his life, wanting to settle down and begin a family is remote to nonexistent. You would also know if he was attempting to lie to you."

"That is fair." She squeezed him again. "I'm going to miss you."

"I will miss you as well. I wish we could go instead. You need people you can trust watching your back."

She laughed and pushed him back. "Are you saying we can't trust the other races, Thanon?"

"Yes," the response came from three voices at once.

Her louder voice on the last question invited the others into their conversation. Larron looked like he had already had that conversation with Geelomin and Bealaras and lost.

"It is not *trust*, specifically," Geelomin clarified and shrugged.

Annalla smiled at him. "But they have not worked with us before."

Again, three voices responded to her in unison, "Exactly!"

"We will adapt," she assured them. "I had not worked with any of you either a few months ago. I'm more worried about leaving you three here to wreak havoc on the discipline of the Palonian's guards."

Four pairs of eyes turned on Thanon.

"Why are you all looking at me?" That set them off laughing.

Throughout the rest of the night, they enjoyed each other's company. Annalla promised to sit for a portrait with Bealaras when they were back in the Derou. She asked Geelomin who would rescue her the next time she ran off on her own. Thanon asked her to promise to name her first child after him. She promised to think about it. Eventually, the three of them pushed Larron and her off to their rooms to sleep for their early morning departure.

After a night's rest, they were departing before the sun cleared the horizon. The enemy encampments on the east side of the Woodland were neither set up—nor observant enough—for discovering and stopping small groups from coming and going.

An elven and irimoten guide remained with them for the day it took to leave the Woodland. They waved farewell and melted back into the forest once they reached the border. From Moonshine's back, Annalla looked ahead at her new traveling companions. She did not know them. If she was honest with herself, even Larron remained mostly a mystery to her.

Mage Marto was in the lead with his sandy head held high and his young, sturdy frame held erect in the saddle. He was a powerful, if inexperienced, combat mage forced to grow up fast. Marto's greatest weakness was his lack of confidence. He was thrust into a position of power soon after receiving full mage status. The death of the only other combat mage in the Palonian due to old age put Marto on the northern council. The one thing his confidence did not waiver on was his memory of the story's details. He would hear no argument about how young he had been or how long ago he last viewed it. He *knew* the landmarks in that tale and would recognize them.

Following Marto in line came Patrice. Over the last week and a half, Annalla discovered that most people guessed her age on the young side. It could be difficult to tell the age of an irimote because they did not turn gray and their fur hid signs of aging, like wrinkles and discoloration. Patrice was middle-aged for an irimote, about 70, and still toned enough to wrestle with the tribe's children. Her fur was a soft, downy white. She had bright yellow eyes that shone at night and faded in the light. Patrice had brought a cloak with a veil to cover her face at night if they needed to avoid being seen. She would blend in perfectly without it once it began to snow.

The much easier to read, Sub-Controller Nurtik was next in line, armed and armored. His eyes matched his dark brown hair and beard, and with all the metal encasing him, he was nearly as broad as he was tall. Dwarves tended to speak their minds without care of the consequences, as he had demonstrated when the two of them first met. Their emotions were quick to change, and you often saw them go from jovial to angry at a word. Given that volatile nature, some found it surprising they were often loyal to a fault. Nurtik's first loyalty was to his clan, but barring any betrayal on their part, he would do whatever they needed or asked because the very act of volunteering garnered his loyalty.

Tyrus, once more clad in his own armor, came next. His thick, dark hair and his steely eyes set into a masculine face would have been the envy of the king's court in happier times. Although she guessed his age in the late twenties, his personality ran through a wide range of maturity levels. There were times he acted younger than Marto when he joked around with his men, sometimes stooping to the bawdier stuff of a young man. At the other extreme, she caught glimpses of a soul exhausted beyond his years. His people and his family were on the front lines. He needed their mission to succeed as much as any of them.

Marto may have grown up during the war, but Tyrus had been near the age between man and boy when the war began. The age when responsibility battled with childhood in earnest and you were torn between striving to be older and clinging to a carefree life. The war left him little choice other than to grow up, but it likely made him cling to youth harder.

Finally, just before her, was Larron, who would also

sacrifice a great deal for aid. His own people were besieged and dwindling. The Auradia were in a similar state to Tyrus' people. The Palonian had sent so much aid south that they would be a tempting target for any significant forces moving north. It was not simply a few immortal lives cut short, but an entire immortal race dying out. He would utilize all his years of experience and training in any negotiations.

Annalla would help all of them with whatever support and leverage she could offer. She smiled at their backs as she pulled her feet up to crouch upon Moonshine's back. Her line was tied to Dusk's saddle. With a push off, Annalla rose into the air and flew ahead.

They would all be riding except Annalla. Three on horse, and the smaller two on ponies. Her wings could take her further and faster, so she would be doing most of the scouting. Moonshine was laden with additional supplies, and they brought four pack mules along. It would become more difficult to find food as the season progressed, and their water would be in the form of snow.

They hoped to be able to carry more with them on the mules and not have to hunt and gather as often. Between the provisions they brought and the food growing, she diligently practiced over the last week after speaking with some elven agricultural experts. They should do well enough.

She took one last look back at her companions below and thrust forward. It rained moderately. With her speed through the air, the wind and water pounded her face and body. Wearing her cloak would only make flying more difficult as it flapped around, so she left it behind with Moonshine.

Annalla was grateful her elven blood made her less affected by the cold. It was uncomfortable, but she did not lose feeling and was unlikely to take ill from exposure based on her time sitting in the rain in the Claws.

It was her fairy blood, however, allowing her to see despite the wind and rain lashing her face. She felt it the moment a thick, transparent film spread across her eyes like a second eyelid. Though thick enough to protect her eyes, it was clear enough to see through. Her elven sight became slightly limited with the membrane, but she could scan the path a fair distance ahead for signs of trouble.

Unfortunately, her hearing was greatly hindered unless she hovered. She suspected it diminished to around the same level the other races possessed due to the wind and rain obscuring other noises. Still, the reduction had been expected based on their time in the Claws.

The eastern side of the Woodland bordered a patchy forested area. As she could not see through the branches from above, Annalla needed to fly below the canopy. Raptor wings might be better for speed and strength, but butterfly wings could outdo them in agility any day. It was another fact she seemed to simply know.

Her path beneath the trees took her in a tight zigzag pattern, scouting ahead and to the sides. It was lonely work, but she did not allow her mind to wander from her task. Mid-day came and went, with a break for a bit of bread and fruit before returning to the sky.

The only signs of recent activity appeared to be the result of natural fauna in the region. Rather than returning directly to the campsite, Annalla headed back down their trail a short distance to coax a tiny bit of growth. The broken twigs and crushed moss or grass left by the passage of her riding companions could not be mended, but she covered it enough to be dismissed as old or the work of animals.

"You are late," were the first words said to her when she arrived at the seemingly abandoned campsite.

Annalla winced. She might have been offended by the sharp tone if she had not spent three months traveling with Larron previously. That was his Commander's voice, and the sharpness concealed concern and relief. It would probably have worried her more if he reacted pleasantly to her delay.

"It's good to see you too, Larron. I trust your trip was pleasant." She gave the all-clear, so everyone emerged from where they hid and put away weapons. She watched for Larron to come into view. "Sorry for the delay. I was taking care of something before joining you."

Tyrus' head shot up and his body tensed with a hand over the hilt of his sword. "Something or some *thing*?"

"A task, not an enemy. I saw nothing to indicate anyone in our path. Let me change and I'll explain." Shivering, she walked to Moonshine and dug around in her pack. Finding what she sought, she stepped behind her horse and stripped off her sodden clothing.

She wanted to be dry. The cold seeped into her more as the day wore on with the wind of her flight driving temperatures lower. With her cloak wrapped around her, she hung the wet clothing on nearby branches. All the moisture in the air meant they were unlikely to dry overnight, but better they hang there than soak everything else in her pack.

Turning around, she surveyed the place she picked out for their camp earlier in the day. It was a more densely canopied area, with enough space free of brush for them to gather. The surrounding brush was thick enough that it would hide them if she had missed some sign of an enemy. She also thickened the canopy further in that spot to help keep the rain off.

"Comfortable?" Larron asked, humor in his voice, handing her a portion of the food being passed around, and she noticed Tyrus and Marto blushing. Tyrus probably rarely traveled rough with women like that, and Marto was so young.

"Much better, thank you. I suppose you are wondering what task made me late?" A nod. "I was covering your tracks."

Three voices responded at the same time as she took a bite before continuing.

"Clever."

"How?"

"New growth will stand out in late fall."

"I doubled back a distance and used my ability to grow the foliage over them," she responded to them all, "covering tracks and broken branches left behind. You don't have to worry about the growth looking out of place. Plants do some growing all year, and I kept it minimal. Taking the time to do it carefully and make sure it blended took longer than I anticipated. It was easy enough, just slow work, so I will start sooner tomorrow."

"You said there was nothing to note ahead of us?" Larron asked for confirmation.

"No sign anyone has traveled through here for some time. I went as far ahead as you will likely travel tomorrow. Not even the forest changes much ahead of us."

Tyrus smiled at her as he polished off his meal. "You better not be late tomorrow. Larron made us wait for you to eat. I don't know if I can go so long without food on a regular basis."

"It will do you some good." She grinned. "All the food in the Woodland was starting to ruin your fine muscular physique."

"A fair point. Out here in the rugged terrain, we can lean down and bulk up. Isn't that right, Patrice?"

Her yellow eyes rolled. "I'm not sure that is how it works."

"I might bulk up," Marto said. "I forgot riding a horse all day was so much work. I already ache all over."

He gave a tentative smile as they laughed with him and Larron went to get something from his pack. Likely it would be something to help the young mage heal enough for another long ride in the morning.

They were still hesitant with their conversations, but she felt the group easing into companionship as they threw gentle comments around, feeling out sensitivities and personalities. They might not be her group of Derou, but they had the potential to become friends.

CHAPTER FOURTEEN

"Something has changed," Kahnlair said to Tiria when he returned to his own body.

The two of them sat alone in an elegantly furnished room, softly lit by flickering candles along the walls. There was no window. No one except Tiria would ever see him work that spell, and he permitted her attendance only in case his own body began to fail and he needed a sacrifice.

He erected shields no one could penetrate, but it would not do for him to have even the slightest appearance of weakness. When Kahnlair took over the body of the dying, he left only a sliver of himself behind, and he knew how he looked at those times. Tiria possessed little magic of her own, but she was a powerful conduit. Her body provided more of an amplification for his own magic than any other mage in his army.

Tiria craved, feared, and admired his power, which she was incapable of possessing alone. She stretched seductively on the couch across from him, her dark hair cascading over her shoulder to drape teasingly into the low neck of her thin robe. Her hunger for pain and destruction kept her loyal to him; one desire only he could fulfill.

You wallow here, the voice in his head scolded.

That day, he had joined his army on the battlefield, once again choosing an elf as his vessel. The first time he tortured an elf, the subject believed itself too pure for him to use. The conviction, the belief in elven purity, kept the elf strong longer than Kahnlair believed possible.

He fed the hope eagerly and without hesitation. Torturing the elf, then backing off as though conflicted. Kahnlair allowed hope to mingle with the pain; blend with it until the two were one. Even then, thinking back on the moment the first elf broke for him was arousing. Elves became his favorites. Their strength, their purity, and their self-destructive naivety made it so much more fulfilling when they shattered at his hands and gave him more power to collect for his purpose.

That time, he sent word for the strongest elf in the southern work camp to be moved to the front line. In front of the elven and human forces, one of his men stabbed the elf through the heart from behind. The life faded before their eyes as Kahnlair took possession.

To see and feel his power emanating from the image of purity never failed to gain a reaction from the opposing forces. That enemy wore their clothes, wore their face, but cut through them with more ferocity than any others set against them. Kahnlair used the elf's dead body as his own, drawing weapons and cleaving into the human front line.

Their hesitation to strike at the animated corpse of their dead ally cost them more lives, and he reveled in their blood until they gained desperation enough to hack a former friend's body to pieces. Only then would Kahnlair leave the fight and return to where he remained safely concealed.

Crush them. End them.

Humans first, he thought to the voice. The humans not under his thumb needed to be eliminated first. It was his whole purpose, and the voice knew he would not deviate.

Toying with them is not bringing power.

The voice was wrong. Hope and destruction brought as much power as ever. It only felt like not enough. His power in the world lingered upon a plateau. He could push for more, but over predation hurt the predators as much as the prey. Waiting was boring, but he possessed enough patience to ignore the voice.

"What is it, Lord?" Tiria asked when he did not immediately clarify his initial statement.

"I do not know, but something within our enemy has changed. They destroyed my body too quickly. They were more focused and careful about the outcome of this battle."

"We have seen the enemy accept that they must kill their friends before this."

"They fought and drew us on as they have before, but their purpose was different. I believe they may have gotten it into their heads again that they can win this war." The idea brought a smile to his lips. "It would seem the little deception I sent over is working. I grew tired of their hopelessness. The captives brought to me are near useless."

"I take it we will make another push before the next winter. Regain the territory they claimed this spring?" Her words were filled with eager anticipation.

"Yes, just enough for their will to grow. For now, we wait." The last order came out a growl, and Tiria shied back.

It was not her at whom he snarled. The voice chafed at waiting. It pushed him to conquer and expand, to claim more territory and search for weapons to secure his victory. What the voice constantly failed to recall is that he needed no further weapons. Kahnlair was the force driving the war. He was the greatest weapon, crushing all who stood before him in his power. That would end when he chose, and he enjoyed the games they played.

CHAPTER FIFTEEN

The weather had taken another strange turn the night before. The temperature dropped to the point it fell as neither snow nor rain, but a freezing rain latching onto anything it could and solidifying it in place. As usual in the morning, Annalla donned some of her chilled, still-damp clothing and took to the sky after a cold meal. The wet clung to everything, and she felt the thin sheet of ice coating her outer clothing crackle with every movement.

Previous exposure had not prepared her for such an extreme. Her teeth chattered against each other and every muscle shook. She flew with her hands tucked beneath her arms. Even with the precaution, they ached to the bone with cold when she stopped mid-day and curled up against a tree to get out of the drizzle. The wind told her little about when the arctic air would let up.

"I should head back now," Annalla told herself through gritted teeth.

Her jaw ached from clenching it against the shaking as she nodded in agreement with herself. She knew she should eat, but the cold meal in her pack sounded entirely unappetizing. Water was out of the question. It was another dumb decision, but she could not force herself to stomach something cold. Her shivering eased, and she felt like she could sleep.

Alarm shot through her at the thought of drifting off alone

in the cold. "No," she breathed out. "Sleeping would mean death."

Leaning against the tree would provide some shelter, but it should not feel comfortable still wearing the wet and icy clothing exposed to the freezing temperatures. Annalla pushed herself to her feet. She needed to reach the camp. Even if they were not there yet, they would find her and help if she fell asleep.

Exhaustion from the constant, debilitating cold meant it took longer than it should to get her bearings and take off in the right direction. Annalla kept moving, pushing toward camp. She slowed her speed to ease the wind chilling her, and because she was not certain of her control. An injury in her current condition would likely see her freeze to death, so she sacrificed the speed.

In ideal conditions, it would take her just over an hour to make a beeline for the camp flying high over the trees. She stopped twice to exercise her extremities and warm her face. Each time taking care to remain standing and moving. Looking around on the third stop showed she had overshot the clearing selected for that night's camp.

"I have one more flight in me," she whispered. "One more."

The shivering was minimal then. Most of her exposed skin felt numb instead of achy and burning. It became more difficult to concentrate and keep her eyes open with each moment, each breath fogging out into the air.

She needed to raise her temperature sooner rather than later. Annalla knew she could meet the others sooner if she followed the trail. She had placed the markers and knew the path they would take.

Annalla blinked.

When her eyes opened, her body toppled forward, barely closing her eyes before her face slapped the sleet covered ground. There was a dull knock against her cheek, but no pain. Annalla fumbled with a great deal less than her usual coordination.

Eventually, she pushed herself back to her feet and off the ground to move again. She stretched her eyes wide, straining against tears to give exaggerated focus to the landscape and repeating over and over in her head what she was looking for.

"Horses," she breathed out. She heard horses nearby and landed in her best estimate of their path. Her vision narrowed to the rhythmic splat of rain and bounce of sleet against the dirt and leaves.

"You are early," a concerned voice said as she neared the small clearing.

"Annalla?"

She looked up, swaying where she stood. They were off to her left. Part of her brain congratulated her for getting close enough to their path. The rest of her mind remained in a fog.

"Hmm...s'cold," she slurred.

Larron started issuing commands before she finished responding and flung his cloak around her. Annalla leaned into his warmth as he guided her toward the horses. With stiff fingers, she struggled with the ties on her clothing, frozen together into clumps of ice-covered string.

Patrice and Larron allowed her no more than a moment before their own hands were there to help. Without a thought for it, she allowed them to help her undress, and Patrice dried her off as Larron tossed the sodden clothing out of the way. Both worked efficiently, bending her chilled joints into dry clothes someone found in her pack. It was not until they tied them closed that she spoke again.

"I c'n do't myself," Annalla said with little conviction. Exhaustion had long past replaced the shiver in her voice.

A painfully tingling hand reached up. Larron lightly slapped it down, and Patrice snorted as she jerked on the lacing for the pants. Annalla offered no more resistance.

"You should have come back sooner if this is the state in which you return to us," he said quietly, and she was surprised at the anger in his voice.

"It's not that bad."

That was a lie. It was bad. The moment she stopped shivering, she knew it was bad.

"When you submit to having others do for you what you

could do on your own at only a cuff on the wrist, it is bad enough to say you should have returned sooner. I thought you were more practical than this, Annalla. It will not aid our cause for any of us to fall ill."

That was unfair. Anger brought some energy back to her, but not enough to do more than shake her head for the moment.

Larron sighed and looked again at his hands, settling her heavy cloak around her shoulders.

Patrice finished tying the trousers and peered up at Larron. "We need to get her in front of a fire," she said to him. "She will ride with you."

They allowed her the dignity of mounting, or at least the appearance thereof. Tyrus stood on the opposite side, waiting for her to fall forward, while Larron hovered behind, ready to assist. The cloak helped warm her some. The dry clothing helped more, so Annalla flexed her fingers, gritted her teeth, and heaved her creaky body up. Larron followed, and the rest remounted to hurry toward the selected campsite.

"The wind is deceptive," Annalla said quietly to Larron minutes later as she regained her wits. "It freezes so quickly you don't notice the cold. I didn't notice its effects until I stopped at mid-day. When I turned to come back, my pace was slowed, and I touched down frequently to work limbs other than my wings to keep the blood flowing to them. I've marked the signs now and will not make the same mistake again. I would not willingly risk our task in such a reckless way."

He froze, listening to her whispered retort. "I am sorry," he sighed. "You scared me. I have never known you to accept help so easily while still conscious."

"Call it practicality. It would have taken me twice as long to get out of that ice armor on my own." She smiled tentatively, hoping they were okay again.

"How are you feeling now? Any numbness in fingers or toes?" he asked, warming her hands with one of his own.

Annalla shook her head. "No. They hurt, but that is the feeling coming back. It is probably a good thing. Right?"

"Likely, but I want to look at your feet when you sit down by the fire tonight," Larron tilted his head to examine her face, staring at her cheek. "How did this happen?"

"How did what happen?"

Fingers gently brushed against her skin and there was muted pain from a scrape or bruise.

"Oh. That. I think I fell."

Larron pulled her back with an arm across her chest and gently kissed her hair as he breathed out yet another resigned sigh. He said nothing further.

The ride was nice. She turned her cloak around so she was blanketed with hers in the front and he and his cloak at her back.

As Annalla sat staring into the flames an hour later, she continued to work her stiff fingers and toes. Larron took care of her discarded things after declaring her fingers and toes safe from frostbite. Patrice seconded the declaration after her own examination.

Annalla hated the feeling of vulnerability the cold left her with. It would have taken her much more than twice as long to change without help. If there had been a need to defend herself on the way back, she would have failed.

"Annalla, dear," Patrice broke into her thoughts. "I am hoping I can have you for a fitting tonight, so I will be able to have modifications done in time for your departure tomorrow."

"I would be happy to help," she responded, a little sleepy, "but what are you talking about?"

Patrice flashed a fang with another smile. "I have something for you. Well, the irimoten refugees do. It seems I am already a day late in completing it, but there is no helping that now."

"I'm still confused."

Her only response was a smile and flick of her head to indicate Annalla should join her as she rose and went to her pony. Annalla followed, reluctantly walking away from the flames, and watched Patrice remove a bundle of skins from her pack. Without a word, the irimote began thrusting pieces up into her arms until she took out her needlework supplies.

"Okay, we will go back to the fire, so I have some light to work with."

"And so I can stay warm?"

That earned her a smile and a wink. "Cream for the cat."

Patrice took back the pieces one by one and set them aside until only one remained in her hands. This she told Annalla to put on over her clothing. It was a shirt...of sorts. Other articles of clothing followed until she was wrapped in the hide of an unfamiliar animal from head to ankle. As Patrice bustled around her, noting and pinning adjustments, Annalla was stunned into a grateful silence.

Balanced on her pony as only an irimote could, day after day as they rode, that was what Patrice had huddled over. The slightly oily feel of the bristly fur hinted that it would not collect water. Patrice made her a cloak she could wear while flying. All she could manage was a whispered thank you.

"Don't mention it at all. You may joke with us about the weather we are having, but you come in soaked and freezing every evening. When I told the other irimoten of our plans, they were concerned about you not wearing winter gear while flying, despite what elves say about their natural resistance. A collection was made to put together this gift. I'm a fair hand with a needle, so they agreed I could finish it along the way.

"This fur," Patrice continued, shifting her voice into that of a storyteller, "is that of a large beaver species found in the waterways of our lands. It is territorial. If they grow too prolific, they can denude an area and force other local wildlife away from a water source, so we watch their population closely. Hunting them is dangerous. They attack like alligators and pull interlopers into the water to drown. This is one of the hunts we use to teach stealth.

"As we have not been home in many years, the pelts provided for this gift were collected from all families living in the Palonian. Everyone with an unmade pelt provided it to the matriarchs, and we selected the pieces best suited for this purpose. Even before I was selected, they wanted to thank you for taking our message to your people. This gift is our opportunity."

"This, my friend, is more than I hoped. I will wear the gift of the irimoten with honor."

Patrice shook her head and continued with her work, but there was a look of satisfaction on her face.

"I know I'm from the south, but this feels like worse weather than usual," Tyrus commented from the opposite side of the campfire.

Marto shrugged. "Maybe slightly worse if the sleet lingers, but it's not outside a normal range. We might even be fortunate to have not yet had a multi-day storm."

"Not abnormal," Larron agreed. "But the sleet and freezing temperatures overnight mean we are going to see our progress slow more quickly than I would like. The snow will hide patches of ice that could injure the animals if we are not careful."

"A' leas' the land is fla' 'ere," Nurtik said.

"Yes, we still need to watch our footing, but the risk in such weather is much worse in the hills and mountains."

"I already need to cut my scouting back, even without the temperature issue. The weather limits the advantages of both my hearing and eyesight. I need to go slower, or I risk missing something," Annalla offered with a grimace.

"It should shift completely to snow soon. Will that help by showing tracks better?"

She gave Marto's words some thought. "Maybe. I think if it is actively snowing, the sound will be muffled, but I'm not sure how snow on the ground will affect noise."

"Snow will also cover older tracks quickly, and your new growth will stand out more until it, too, is covered," Tyrus pointed out.

"Good point. Is it worth continuing to cover our back trail if it starts snowing more, Larron?"

"Not if it is actively falling. That will cover our trail well enough, and anything you added would stand out more. If it is not snowing, use your best judgment."

"Head back if a storm comes in. There is no sense

traveling, or flying, in a whiteout," Nurtik warned her in his language, and Larron agreed when she conveyed the message.

"Or even if your sense of the air tells you a storm is coming. We do not have the ability to mount a search mission for you in a blizzard. Another hundred feet in either direction and we may have passed by you without noticing today."

"I will keep watch. If I get stuck, I will hunker down in my own shelter rather than stumble around to find you. Do not worry about me, especially now that I have a way to stay warm and dry out there."

In the end, despite all her fussing, the alterations Patrice ended up making were few and minor, and the outerwear sat ready in the morning. As Annalla took off into the sky, the sleet still poured down outside their sheltered area. Drafts and trickles of rain or melting snow still found their way under her clothing at the openings for her head and wings, but it worked magnificently.

Her rest breaks throughout the day continued to be more frequent to warm her face and ears. She needed them unobstructed to scout with, but she no longer risked death, and the storms held off. To the amusement of the men, the first night back with her new attire, Annalla grabbed Patrice up in a hug and spun her around before talking the entire evening about how well it functioned. A chorus of, "We know," preceded multiple people volunteering to take the first shift at watch that night.

CHAPTER SIXTEEN

Thankfully, the storms to which Marto alluded to held off. However, the sun took the place of the cold to give Annalla trouble over the next week. Sleet turned to gentle snow and covered the ground. As the clouds moved past, they left the sun shining down on the blanket of white.

From her vantage, she became snow blind almost instantly. Hidden sun breaks caught her unprepared frequently and left her stumbling blindly forward. The shine glared off the ground, off the layer on the tree branches, and from the tops of the bushes. Whenever it became unbearable, she squinted through the piercing light, seeking the ground. Even with her eyes closed, the painful brightness shone through. Enduring the glare for any significant amount of time drove painful spikes into her head.

During one of those breaks, Annalla glimpsed their first goal on her descent: the Nierda River. The Nierda River was large, cutting a path from the northern mountains before running on a winding course to the southeast until it reached Lake Nierda. Only three, much smaller, rivers lead out from Lake Nierda. The common opinion held that most of the water escaped through an underground river yet to be discovered. Even in the summer, the lake was too deep to explore the entire lake bed.

Along its winding way, the Nierda met with four tributaries. One joined with it further north, and the other three merged downstream. Marto stood confident that they needed to be on the north-eastern side of the river to continue toward their destination, so they intended to seek the ford closest to the Palonian Woodland to cross.

Annalla would have just enough time that day to make it to the river and scout the area. She shielded her eyes against the sun and strained her hearing to avoid being taken unaware, flying just above the ground on a serpentine path. The flight progressed slowly, and her movements were repetitive.

For the most part, her vision remained focused on where her shadow fell across the ground to avoid looking into the reflected sunlight as much as possible. She would scan to the sides and glance ahead periodically to avoid flying into one of the increasingly scattered trees.

Finally, the sound of running water drew closer, and Annalla flew out into the clearing along the banks to land. It looked to be running a little high, but still manageable. A cursory inspection of the ford indicated no one had attempted the crossing recently. A detailed search would need to wait until the next day.

We have made good time thus far, she thought to herself as she flew back to meet the group.

Taking less than two weeks to reach that point despite the questionable footing in the sleet and snow meant they were on or ahead of schedule. Other than the early turn in the weather, and her brush with hypothermia, it had been an uneventful two weeks. No enemies, no injuries; she would call the trip leisurely, were it not for the underlying tension and urgency.

"Stand."

"Hello, Marto."

"Annalla. Any trouble?"

"None, and you will reach the river soon."

He nodded and waved her through with a noncommittal grunt. Marto was as pleased with their progress as any, but his nerves grew with each passing day. As soon as they made it to the other side of the river, his decisions became critical. Tyrus had made it his personal mission to make the young mage laugh at least once every evening. As he often involved Larron in his antics, she and Patrice had a running wager on whether the human would survive the winter or if Larron would run out of patience.

"You have news for us?"

She had just walked into the camp clearing. "Larron, how could you have possibly known that?"

"Your face shouts it as clearly as if you had spoken aloud."

"It does not. I'm an enigma to all. Impossible to read."

"Perhaps. Let me see if I can read more… It is good news you bring us. Our journey approaches a critical juncture. The Nierda is near?"

Annalla heard Patrice snicker next to Tyrus and Nurtik and wondered if there was another bet on whether Larron would survive a winter with *her*. She mock-scowled and gave an exaggerated sigh.

"Taking my fun away to show off how well you know the area? Yes, you should reach it around midday tomorrow if you are not delayed."

"Good, we are making better time than I hoped. I know I do not need to ask, but you plan to fully scout the area?"

"Yes, that's my primary agenda for the day. I will not travel as far and plan to return to help you cross." She moved to trade her outerwear for her cloak. "Any difficulties today?"

"It was a close thing with one of the pack mules," Tyrus answered. "Lost its footing and went down on a patch of ice. We were lucky it did not result in anything serious, or we would have had to put it down. Snow is one thing, but preceded by the rain and freezing temperatures…" He shook his head. "How does the ford look? Frozen over yet?"

"No, it's as we expected it would be, too swift to freeze over much. If it ran shallow, I would say it might have had a chance to do so at the banks. Blessing or curse, the river is running high and only a little slick at the edges."

"We did not choose to cross it at the ideal time of year," Nurtik spoke to her alone, "but it is a rare occurrence when this ford is not passable, high or not. Though, it will not be a pleasant crossing or one without peril."

"We will be taking precautions. I am ferrying the supplies over to lessen the drag on the animals, and a shelter will be close by to care for them as soon as possible. A safety line will also be set. I see nothing more to be done."

"Agreed, and we will all see for ourselves tomorrow the conditions we face."

"Isn't it odd we haven't seen signs of other people in the area?" Patrice asked. "We know there are farms around, but even the few travelers' way stations are long abandoned."

"No struggle, no 'struction either."

Tyrus nodded. "And the reports I read through showed this area delivered the harvest tithe for the war this season, so there are still people living in the area."

"It is unusual," Larron confirmed. "Even during the winter months, there is often movement between villages and towns, hunting parties ranging further out, travelers choosing to defy the seasons. I hope the lack of destruction means the local people have sought each other out to form larger settlements. They will be better able to defend themselves should small groups of gilar push north."

"Farmers, 'erders, 'gainst gilar?" Nurtik raised a bushy, cynical eyebrow, showing exactly how much faith he put in their ability to defend themselves against well-armed gilar.

"Didn't the elves record something about local consolidation in the farming reports at the end of the harvest, Nurtik?" Marto asked his fellow council member.

The dwarf closed his eyes in thought. "After tha harves', somethin' 'bout concern on tha same repor's we hearin' in tha clan."

"That's right, and some of the families delivering the harvest this year remained in the Woodland. They volunteered to bring it because they didn't want to stay out there this winter."

"I read those later season reports," Larron said. "There was no evidence of gilar activity, but many in the area are frightened."

"The bandits were on the Yaziren, not the Nierda," Tyrus argued.

"Bu' tha gilar keep is east 'a Lake Nierda."

"How close is that to Ceru?" Annalla asked.

"It's not," Tyrus answered. "The Carsanje Wetland is between the lake and Ceru."

"Then how did the gilar get over there?"

Patrice shook her head. "They didn't come from the desert. All the races have held their areas pretty much forever. Kahnlair brought the evil ones together and is holding them under his authority somehow, but the gilar always held the eastern half of the Carsanje and the eastern and southern shores of Lake Nierda."

"It was a smaller contingent," Larron added. "Kahnlair did not spend any power bringing the eastern gilar slaughters under his command until recent years."

"Similar to the windani pack between my clan and the mage capital." The others nodded when Annalla translated for Nurtik.

"That's the pack we talked about in our planning sessions," she noted.

"Correct," confirmed Larron. "We are hopefully too far west for either to present a threat to our mission, but his additional attention on this side of the elven lands is concerning."

"At least the dwarves hold the attention of the Vampires in the mountains." Tyrus tipped his head at Nurtik, who probably grinned, but you could not tell for the beard.

Annalla rubbed her aching eyes as her head throbbed again when she glanced at the fire. "Alright friends, the sun glare was killing my eyes today, so I'm going to go close them for a while and turn in early."

Larron touched her arm to stop her before she walked away. "Please inform me if it becomes worse and you would like something for the headache. We can also look at creating some eye coverings you can wear most of the time and remove to scan the landscape periodically."

She nodded. "Based on this last week, that is going to be

necessary sooner than later."

"I will work on it with Patrice. We will see what we can come up with for you."

"Thanks." She smiled at him and waved to the others. "Goodnight, everyone. Wake me for my watch."

CHAPTER SEVENTEEN

They rose again before the sun. Judging by the rays thrusting up over the horizon, it threatened to be a blindingly clear day. Annalla imagined she could feel her eyes already cringing at the mere thought. She grabbed a cold meal of cheese, jerky, and fresh crabapples, grew something for the animals, changed, and went through her morning routine with her eyes mostly closed, trying to think as little as possible. She chose a stretching routine rather than one for combat training to try to loosen the stiffness that had settled in her joints overnight.

The fact the headache from the day before lingered that morning concerned her. She hoped Larron and Patrice would work out a solution for the sun issue that would not hinder her sight excessively. Tyrus left before the packing was complete to begin his terrain scouting for hidden, icy dangers, and Annalla departed not far behind him. She said her farewells before taking off for her own scouting.

True to its threat, the sun rose spectacularly to spread its light across the blanketed earth below. Shielding her eyes from the shine reflecting up at her, she scanned the horizon around camp before seeking the thinning tree cover below. Sweeping back and forth across their intended path, she began her inspection of the ground and surroundings. Annalla peered up and around periodically, careful to avoid looking to where the sun had yet to emerge over the horizon.

"Tyrus," she called ahead to avoid startling him as she approached his position. Even so, his hand moved toward his sword at her first sound. "Does the way present much trouble today?"

She slowed to hover at his side while he continued forward.

"The brush is thicker around here, as well as some of the thicker tree cover returning. We will make good time if the weather holds and the plants do not thin much. It could be taken as a good omen for our crossing today."

"Let's hope so. Be safe. I will see you at the Nierda," Annalla smiled and waved as she spun in the air.

A thrust of her wings and she sped off, leaving him to watch the ground they would travel. She wove between the trees, covering the same area she'd gone over the day before and looking again for signs of passage by any other than winter wildlife. Compared to the first forest she fell into, that one burst with life. As far as she could tell, none of that life was people.

With surprising speed, she arrived at the riverbank. The smell of water in the air was refreshing. Annalla moved to the edge of the river, closed her eyes, took a deep breath of the moist breeze, and listened to the movement around her.

There were rapids in the distance, but at hand was the soft gurgling of gently flowing water. It was a soothing sound. With only one tributary yet adding to it, the Nierda remained relatively manageable. The ford they would use was referred to as the Northern Crossing. Not very original—like most of the elven land names she found—but it was the northernmost crossing used by most merchants traveling along it. The name stuck.

At that location, the river widened out, and the bottom consisted mostly of sand, gravel and smaller rocks covering a firm base into which you would not sink or become mired. The absence of large boulders meant there were no close rapids, and the width prevented the current from becoming overwhelming.

Only in the spring, when the ice and snow collected in the

north began to melt, did it become too much. It would rise higher on the banks and move too fast for stable footing. Even with the near torrential rains dominating late fall, the ponies and mules should be able to make it across as long as they were unburdened.

The ponies would likely have to swim. That day it would be Annalla's turn as pack beast. She would fly the supplies over the river as the others lead the animals through the icy water.

There was still a significant time before mid-day. She intended to spend the remainder of the morning scouting around the ford in all directions. Annalla checked along the riverbanks first, but the shimmering water quickly fell behind as she headed beyond the far bank. There were fewer trees on that side, with longer stretches of open ground reaching out beyond even her elven sight.

Striving to squint past the mirrored sunlight, she swept back and forth on a path heading north. The story on that side of the river came up the same as they had seen since leaving the Palonian: there was nothing to tell. It was sad what had once been a well-traveled ford was nothing more than another abandoned stretch of river. As far as she flew, north, south, and east, she found no signs that anyone other than her and her companions had even considered passing that way.

The sun neared its zenith. She stopped her diligent, but tedious, scouting. Dropping to the ground, Annalla leaned against a lone tree, reveling in the shade provided. Without the sun on her, she could feel the cold more, but the glare gave her a headache growing more intense the longer she tried to peer through it.

Bracing herself with one hand on the trunk of the tree, she folded her other arm over her eyes, burying her face in the crease of her elbow. The pounding in her head beat in rhythm with her heart. She tried to ease it by concentrating on the life before her. Through the hand braced against the trunk, she felt the slow and steady existence connecting with the earth in her essence. Every time, it became easier and more natural. She understood more of her growing capabilities. For a time, any pains were forgotten, and she filled with a soothing calm.

It failed to work that time. The ebb and flow of the tree joined the beat of her heart. Annalla released the connection but remained positioned with her eyes shielded. Gradually, she removed her arm and readjusted to the daylight. The ache remained, but it did not worsen as she took to the sky and returned to the river.

***

"It's about time you all showed up!" Annalla called over with a smile as they emerged into the open.

Larron detected something wrong in her voice, despite the warm greeting. No one else seemed to notice anything, as they returned her welcome and dismounted.

"I take it all is well on the eastern bank?" he asked.

"Still nothing. I'm not sure I like how quiet it's been for us so far. Grateful, yes, but I would have thought covering a major crossing of the Nierda River a logical step for Kahnlair's forces."

Tyrus nodded, but shrugged in acceptance. "Perhaps our luck will hold as we head further away from their base. Or the reports of gilar heading north are exaggerated."

"Luck and I have not always seen eye to eye," she said as she moved to help unload the animals.

"What is causing your distress?" Larron asked her quietly, half expecting a denial, as they set supplies down to the side.

Annalla grimaced and put a hand to her forehead. "The sun glare off the snow is killing me. The headache is growing worse."

"How is your vision?"

"Still fine, I think."

He ran her through some limited tests and could not disagree. "How far were you able to scout this morning?"

"Far enough. I was going to ask to ride for the afternoon after we are across. I hope giving my eyes a break for the rest of the day will help."

"Done. You will also take something for the headache before we begin crossing. Give me a moment."

The smirk she gave him was halfhearted. "Yes, sir."

Larron opened the medical supplies from his gear and handed her something to dull the pain.

"This will make you a little drowsy," he told her, "but the activity involved in the crossing should keep you alert enough for what needs doing today.

Annalla chuckled. "Yes. My assignment does not require extreme focus."

He handed her a sufficient dose before joining the others in unpacking the animals. They stacked everything in small, neat piles Annalla could quickly grab to ferry across to a staging area on the other side. Once everything was removed and piled, they sat down for a quick meal before tackling the river, while the animals grazed.

"Everything okay?" Patrice asked, seeing Annalla chewing on the herbs he had given her.

"The sun is still giving me a headache," she answered with a shrug.

Patrice raised a questioning eyebrow at him.

"Annalla will be riding with us for the afternoon rather than scouting," he assured her.

She also possessed basic medical training. Her nod in response to his words told him she agreed with their solution.

"I know you probably scouted well ahead, but I will try to range further out after we cross. If you agree." Tyrus said the first to Annalla and directed the latter at Larron, who gave a slight nod of agreement.

They each gave Annalla a pat on the shoulder or word in sympathy as they crossed back over to the supplies. Everyone except her would be getting wet, so they changed into lighter clothing to keep their winter gear dry.

It had been decided the night before that Larron would be the first to test the crossing. He possessed the best combination of familiarity and skill with his horse and resistance to the colder temperatures. If there were complications, he was most likely to survive in the best condition. Both Larron and Tyrus would be making three trips, Marto two, to be able to lead all the pack and smaller animals across. Nurtik and Patrice would double with Larron and Tyrus on one of their crossings rather than burdening the ponies.

Once they were ready, Annalla grabbed the longest rope and tied one end off to a tree she grew at the bank, then flew the other end to the opposite bank for the same treatment. If, at any point, Dusk could not handle the current and lost his feet, Larron could cling to the rope until Annalla came in from above to snatch him out of the river. They would have to hope Dusk and any trailing animal could gain the bank on their own.

They cleared an area away from the riverbank of snow where Annalla created more small trees to tie off the animals and sweet grass for them to eat. The plants sprouted up with years' worth of growth at a flick of her wrist. Even there, when the growing served specific purposes like rope supports and horse tie-offs, it looked natural. Larron marveled again at her power.

He only felt less guilty about collecting Dusk for their impending icy bath for the fact Dusk and his fellows feasted on grass throughout their journey, while most of his rations were staler every day. Larron quickly removed all but his last thin layer of clothing and bundled the rest up tightly, handing them to Annalla. His cloak would be among the first supplies taken across so he could warm up in his cloak before making the trip back to lead the next pony or mule.

"The rope is secure, so use it for support if you need to," she said to him as she took the bundle from his hands. "I'll keep an eye on you, but don't hesitate to call out for help if you think you need it. Be careful, Larron."

"You as well."

She looked tired. Maybe it was his imagination, but it seemed even her wings drooped under some heavy weight.

"We'll finish this quickly. Oh!" She perked up with amusement. "Patrice agreed to allow me to fly her across. I think the sight of all this water got to the feline in her. Nurtik will have none of it though, so he is for the horses. The water will be over his head, and he will sink with all the metal he is still wearing, yet even that doesn't change his mind."

"To be expected. He will simply walk along the bottom and find his way out if that happens." He winked as she laughed. "I will see you on the other side."

It was brief, but before she turned away, her free hand touched his arm and slid down to give his hand a gentle squeeze as she gifted him one of her rare smiles that touched her eyes. Then she was gone, calling to Patrice. Larron gathered Dusk's reins in his hands, approached the water's edge, mounted, and urged Dusk into motion.

His horse's steps were reluctant, but Dusk obeyed and started into the river. The water reached Larron's feet, and it was like stepping into ice and became colder from there. With every pace forward, the water crept higher on Dusk's flank and his own legs. When it reached his groin, he could not quite hold back a hiss of shock.

Still, he pushed on. His breathing became more difficult in the icy water as the level crept up to finally reach its peak low on his stomach. They were lucky the current was easier there. Dusk had some difficulty gaining traction on the riverbed. They made it through though, and shortly after peaking, the bed rose again, and the water lowered. Emerging from it on the other side was not much better than being in the water. The chill air froze his wet clothing to his body.

"I would say we need to get you out of those clothes, but that will have to wait since you are making the trip again." She wiggled her eyebrows at him, startling a chuckle from him between shivers.

Her words brought some warmth back to him as he fought against a blush—*centuries of experience, and I am blushing?!* —as she walked over and helped him down, cloak in hand.

"Chest high on Dusk," she noted. "Is there any trouble I should tell Tyrus about before he starts across?"

He swallowed thickly before answering through slightly chattering teeth. "Easy enough to proceed. The current is steady, but not enough to push our horses off if we take it slow. The cold is the most shocking, and the water level is my greatest concern. Our smaller animals will end up swimming, but I think the horses will hold them on course as they push through. It is also best if we ride. Even Dusk started losing his footing a bit, and I think our weight will help keep them on the ground."

"I will let them know."

Along with his cloak, she and Patrice brought over some cloth to rub down the animals. While he gave her his report, the two of them had been taking care of Dusk. He and Patrice shifted over to work within another patch of freshly grown grass as Annalla took off to relay his words and bring another load of supplies. From the look of things around him, she already made a couple of trips in the time it took him to cross once.

"Go. I will help with the animals when Tyrus makes it across."

He smiled. Patrice knew he had not yet made his way back to the river in case they wanted help with the incoming animals, so he nodded his thanks. Larron set aside the cloth and mounted Dusk again to start his return journey.

Heading in on the opposite side of the rope spanning the river, Larron could see Tyrus already cutting through the water. He had Nurtik on his roan mare, and one of the mules tied behind. As they crossed paths near the middle, Tyrus gave him a look with wide eyes, clenched jaw, and shivering frame as loud as any verbal exclamation. Dusk shook his head, probably wondering why Larron laughed so hard.

With four pack mules, two ponies, and Moonshine to lead across, it would take seven crossings to get all the animals over to the other side. Marto was already entering with his gelding and one of the ponies in tow as Larron emerged on the original bank. Without pause, Larron tied off another mule and returned to the river, keeping himself and Dusk moving nearly the entire time to avoid either of them cramping up from the cold.

He looked up at Annalla. She carried light loads in case she needed to drop them, which was smart. It would take longer, but she was already nearly halfway done with the supplies. At that rate, she would finish her runs before them.

Marto approached the other bank on his first crossing, which was his sign for Larron to begin his third. He coaxed Dusk back into the frigid water, trailing one of the mules. While still unpleasant, he found exiting the icy water as disagreeable as wading through it thanks to the wind.

He was pleasantly surprised, upon reaching the far side once more, to find Marto erected some sort of shield around the animals' grassy area holding their own heat within. Patrice and Nurtik, saw to the trailing animals as they were dropped off, while he, Tyrus, and Marto quickly continued with their colder task.

They continued back and forth, above and below, and his last crossing was with Moonshine in tow. Tyrus would make the final crossing of all with the second pony as soon as Larron was nearly out on the far side. The other three tended to the animals, including Marto's horse, to get them dry and warm quickly. They also began loading up the supplies once more. As much as the area appeared abandoned, Larron wanted to be well away from the ford before nightfall. Annalla was nearly finished ferrying supplies over, so they would make quick work of it and be on their way once everyone dried off and dressed.

Larron stood in the warm zone, taking out his own dry clothing, when he heard a splash from the river. He spun around to look. Tyrus was still mounted and his horse still on her feet. The trailing pony continued pushing through the current behind them, catching up and even starting to pass Tyrus because he had stopped and gazed up.

Larron followed his line of sight to Annalla. Her arms stood empty of whatever she had been carrying, hands squeezed against her temples. She scanned the bank. A look of mixed fear, pain, and concentration consumed her face when she met his eyes. He recognized this look; it was the same one she gave him before turning the council room into a forest. She yelled out at the same moment he heard a distant rumble growing louder.

"Run!" was her cry an instant before she fell, fainting with a splash into the river.

Burying any emotion, he grabbed Moonshine's reins at his side and pulled her toward the river, leaving Dusk to catch his breath.

"Mount up! Get to higher ground now!" he yelled the order behind him without waiting to see if they obeyed. His attention focused on Tyrus. The man appeared about to dive after Annalla, where she could be seen floating downstream. He would never make it to her.

"Tyrus, no! We will lose you both in the rush!" Larron called out as he removed the rope from the tree and tied it to Moonshine. "Cut the rope behind you and wrap it about yourself quickly. Hold on as tight as you can!"

He hesitated only a moment before doing as ordered. Tyrus was still tying the rope as a wall of white-capped water rushed around the bend upriver. Larron mounted and looked back. The moment Tyrus grasped the rope, he kicked Moonshine into motion. She took off straight away from the river's edge, pulling Tyrus off his horse and through the water until he was practically skimming along.

Tyrus had cut the pony free and awkwardly slapped his mare into motion, but the onslaught of water overtook them before he or the animals came near the shoreline. The rope jerked against Moonshine's pull, but she fought it at Larron's urging, and little by little they won out over the high and raging river. After what seemed an eternity, Tyrus' head broke the surface. He coughed and gasped for breath as he tried to drag himself onto land.

Larron untied the rope, leaving Tyrus sputtering at the water's edge, and pointed Moonshine downriver. He frantically scanned the slowly settling water for any sign of Annalla, but there was nothing. Only after he was well beyond the ford did the river regain some semblance of its appropriate depth and ferocity, and he fought down his growing frustration and desperation. He passed the body of the horse, dead from what looked like a broken neck. The pony survived. Larron saw it running away from the opposite bank, back toward the Palonian. It might make it back to the

Woodland alone.

Finally, a flash of green and gray against the blue and brown of the churned-up water. Keeping his eyes on the floating form, he pushed ahead before turning Moonshine into the water. When the water reached her chest, he dove from her back and stroked into the river.

Larron lost sight of Annalla almost immediately and had to hope his estimates were accurate. He scanned the water briefly, fighting against the current and praying she had not already swept past him. Something floated ahead, coming down to his right. Digging in, Larron stretched as it passed.

His grasp found purchase in hair and he mercilessly grabbed a chunk in hand and pulled. Tucking an arm around her, he struggled to move them both through the icy water with his fading strength. The current continued pushing them downstream.

Larron could no longer imagine what waited for them ahead, his mind growing fuzzy. Still, he fought for the shore against the water sucking them down. Every muscle screamed. His lungs were on fire. He did not register when his frozen feet touched the bottom, only realizing he could walk when his knees scraped against stone.

He dragged her up, mostly out of the water, but that was as far as his exhausted body would take them. Shallow breaths condensed in the cold air, so he knew she lived and breathed. Of all mercies, she still breathed, though he did not know how much longer she would survive. The chill leached them both of strength, and he felt himself drifting off. Larron knew he had to keep moving or he would die, but his muscles remained shaky, limp, and ignored his commands. In his mind, he reached for her, but his hand barely twitched as he faded.

Those are hooves, he thought, floating in a warmer fog where the cold melted away. *She is still with us.*

"Help me take off her clothes."

That is a good idea, Patrice. That is necessary. Wet clothing will kill her. I will help you again. Larron was not sure if he spoke, there was too much fog.

"She is too heavy for me alone. Stop blushing and do as I say."

I am too old to blush. Mostly, Larron thought, defensive at her harsh tone.

"Alright, that's enough. Give me your cloak and take off your robes."

"What?"

"Take them off and make a little pile of cloth with them to sit on over here. Hurry up, boy."

Boy? I know what to do, Patrice.

"What now?"

"Help me carry her over."

Help? I can carry her well enough.

"Sit on your robes. Wrap yourself around her as best you can and rub her arms and legs. We need to get the circulation back and warm her up."

"She is like ice."

"Keep your shield up, and let's hope you can get her temperature out of the 'ice' range."

Fabric shuffled. Grunts and mumbles followed. Larron held her in his arms as instructed, but he was so cold. He knew he would do her no good. Someone jerked on his shirt, and he heard fabric tear as more horses arrived, and he still floated.

"Nurtik, see if you can't get a fire going over there. We are going to need it. Tyrus, can you carry Larron up next to Marto?"

His arm was grabbed, and the world spun.

"Sit behind him and wrap around, rubbing his arms and legs."

Hands manipulated his body and cradled him from behind. Someone started briskly rubbing, and he felt cloth wrap around his front and someone rubbing his head to dry his hair. His braid would look as disheveled as Annalla's after such treatment. Larron wobbled bonelessly in their hold, at the mercy of their movements. His arms and legs started to burn, then his hands and feet, then fingers and toes. He blinked his eyes to bring the fire into focus.

"Are you waking up?"

Larron lifted his head and peered over his shoulder. His tongue felt thick, so he swallowed a couple of times before trying to respond. "Tyrus?"

The man was wrapped around him. Larron leaned back against his chest, and he had his crossed legs covering Larron's toes and gently rubbed Larron's hands between his own.

"Yep. How are you feeling?"

He tested his fingers in Tyrus's grip. "Tired."

He turned his head slowly and let out a sigh of relief to see Annalla's hair poking out of a mound of blankets and cloaks with Marto behind her.

"Yeah, she's alive. I'm wrapped up with you, and the kid gets to hold Annalla in his arms. The only reason I am putting up with this injustice is because you saved my life back there."

Larron let out a breathy laugh, as he knew was the intent of the comment. "What happened?"

"Patrice grabbed Marto and rode off with him after you, telling me to dry off and follow with Nurtik and more supplies. Especially the bedrolls and flint. She took charge and got you both out of your wet clothes and nestled in with us to warm up."

"I...heard her?" The words came out as a question, as he was uncertain if the memories were real or imagined.

Tyrus resumed rubbing Larron's hands gently. "Sleep, Larron. Patrice and Nurtik are taking care of things. We have both of you safe and alive. We'll deal with the rest later."

Larron rested back again, his head falling against a blanketed shoulder as he drifted once more.

CHAPTER EIGHTEEN

Larron woke to the darkness of night still sharing a makeshift bed with Tyrus. The two of them were curled up on their sides together. He looked around, and his movement immediately woke the battle-hardened man.

"What?" Tyrus tensed and whispered before he recognized Larron beside him. "Oh, right. Is it a safe guess neither of us is going to freeze to death now, and we can cease our cuddling?"

"That would be most agreeable."

"Stay in the blankets. I am actually wearing something under here, so I will grab you some dry clothing."

He put on what Tyrus brought as quickly as possible, and the two of them joined Nurtik and Patrice beside the fire they kept going.

"Hungry?" Patrice asked them.

Larron stopped short at her question and was surprised to find his stomach growling in response on its own. He nodded and accepted what she offered before sitting.

"How is she?"

"I'm not sure. Her temperature is back up, and we can probably thank her elven blood she hasn't become ill and fevered. Once she warmed up enough to stop shivering, her breathing deepened and steadied. I have no basis to know how she will recover from the emergence of a new ability." Patrice paused, asking him, "I'm assuming that is what caused the flood?"

Larron nodded. "It is my assumption as well."

"Well," she continued, "she told us last time she was tired, but she did not lose consciousness during her struggle to control it as far as we know, only afterward from the effort."

"She also warned us the earth was likely a more gradual element to emerge. I believe it would be safe to assume this one is concentrated in water." Concerned eyes peered to where Annalla and Marto lay. "Thank you both for setting camp and keeping watch."

"We's not the ones as had ta travel 'cross the ice water 'gain an' 'gain. An' neither o'us got drenched under either." Nurtik shrugged.

"My mare and the pony did not make it out. What else did we lose?" Tyrus asked.

"The pony survived," Larron offered, but shook his head to indicate they would not be finding it. "I saw it on the other side of the river at some point, but it was running away."

"Along wi' yur horse, Tyrus, an' Patrice's pony, two o' the pack mules was caught in the flood 'cause they did'n run wi' us."

"We also lost the supplies we put back on those mules, the load Annalla dropped, what was left on the other side, and the supplies we had not yet repacked," Patrice concluded as Nurtik nodded with each addition.

"In total, our loss comes to the smaller tent, one of the medicine kits, most of our spare blankets and some of our spare clothing, the cooking gear, and about half of the remaining rations. The food worries me the most. Until Annalla revives, we need to ration carefully. Even then, it is a good idea to seek a village to provide supplies."

"I fear finding a village will be easier than convincing them to part with supplies. We will speak to Marto in the morning and see if he can make any direction for us from where we are now." Larron rubbed his eyes. "How late is it, by the way?"

"Past midnight."

"That is rest enough for me. I will take this watch while

you all sleep." He continued before anyone could protest, "Tyrus will be next and he can wake Marto for the last watch of the night, just make sure you have warm clothing in hand for him when you do."

This changes things, Larron thought as he settled into his watch.

With two of the mules gone, it was almost fortunate they lost half their supplies. The remaining two would not be overburdened that way. Moonshine would go to Tyrus. Patrice was small enough to ride with him and the mare would hardly notice, even if Patrice would be less comfortable. Annalla and the food were his biggest concerns, and the two issues were significantly linked.

Rationed, their current supplies could last a fortnight, but the horses would be without food in two days at most. Annalla's first ability enabled them to significantly limit the fodder they carried. With their portable harvest unavailable, they would need to begin the search for someone with whom to trade and hope they could offer enough to receive fodder in exchange. Their own food supplies could be supplemented by some hunting like the Derou did on their journey to the Palonian. It was primarily a time constraint.

The winter was not harsh yet, and they possessed skill enough to live off the land. Larron's greatest concern, and the one they could do little about, was Annalla's health. Of the entire group, she and Marto were the two they could not afford to lose. Marto had the closest thing to experience to guide them, but it would be Annalla's task to get them in whenever and wherever they arrived at the end of Marto's story.

No one knew how the fairy remained hidden. Maybe she needed to carry them over obstacles. Perhaps it was some barrier through which only she could pass. At the least, she might gain them an audience with the leaders of the fairy by speaking on their behalf. Regardless of the reason, the fairy lands were elusive. She was key.

He rubbed his eyes and sighed. As Tyrus mentioned the

day before, they were all safe and alive. He needed to remember the fact. There was little else to do until they made some decisions in the morning together, and worrying over them that night would accomplish nothing.

Larron's ordeal caught up to him sooner than expected and forced him to wake Tyrus early for his watch. The man waved off his apologies and shooed him toward the tent. His bedroll welcomed him, and he dropped quickly into unconsciousness again.

Morning dawned, and with it came the clouds and light snow absent from recent days. Marto made the rounds to rouse everyone for a small meal and decision time. The meal felt relaxed, and they took their time with tasks that morning. Most remained worn from the previous day's events, so their rest was well earned.

"Marto, have you had a chance to examine the area to see if anything looks familiar?

The young mage shook his head in response. "I looked around, but the river in the areas we passed is not what we are looking for. We still need to search for our first marker. I hope yesterday's flood didn't pull any of the features out of place."

"We will work under the assumption it did not," Larron said. "There is no use dwelling on the alternative, and we already addressed the possibility when we considered a shift in the river over the years.

"We have two choices before us. I do not have to tell you that with Annalla not yet recovered, our supply loss is temporarily compounded. One option is to make restoring our supplies a priority and focus our search on acquiring additional food for the animals. There were a few larger communities in the area the last time I was here, both to the east and north. If this course is our decision, I would suggest we make for one of those and hope people, or at least supplies, remain.

"A second option is to focus our search on the river for the first direction mark until Marto finds it. With this option, we may chance upon a village and be able to re-supply anyway, but it would be best to assume we would provide food for ourselves and the animals from what we find and hunt. Thoughts?"

Tyrus spoke first, "My choice would be to search for the villages and re-supply first. We otherwise leave too much to chance and taking the time now could save more time in the longer term."

"I 'gree wi' Tyrus. The risk o' a much grea'er delay is too much when we ha' the option of seekin' a place we ha' known t' be there 'fore."

"Do not forget, though," Patrice remained solemn as she spoke, "the villages could have been abandoned and looted based on the lack of people we have encountered. The gilar and Kahnlair's other forces in the east have been pushing into the area. We do not know if they have reached this far. If they have, then it is likely there will be little to find in most towns and villages."

"Valid point. That would cause delays, and if we failed to find any remaining, we would be forced to gather our own supplies anyway." Tyrus paused in thought. "I would still choose to seek a village, though with caution. The lesser reliance on chance and fortune remains with that option."

"Marto?"

"You stated there were humans to the north as well. After the river, north is the direction in which our journey lies. That is the direction in which I would direct our search for the beginning of the story. If there is a village or town along the river or within a reasonable distance upstream, we could follow the river to that point, divert to re-supply, then return to the river and continue. Should it happen the village we head for is empty of everything, we continue supplying ourselves and keep searching."

Larron nodded with the others. It was a sound plan and kept them moving forward.

"Any objections to following Marto's suggestion?" Larron asked. "There is a larger town upriver and north. The population was great enough that I believe it would be less likely to have been abandoned. At the pace we have been making, I estimate it is a week's ride along the river."

"Som'un els'll ha' t' scout if she's t' not fly today."

"I'll go with Moonshine," Tyrus offered. "Patrice can ride with Marto, and Dusk can carry both Larron and Annalla. You still have your pony, and with half our supplies gone, the mules will keep up."

He nodded approval, and Tyrus took off, quickly packing and leaving to put distance between them while the rest of them cleared the campsite. With each bag, he made note of what they had lost. Larron sighed as he settled into the saddle behind Annalla to ride. They were all still alive, that was what mattered.

CHAPTER NINETEEN

Annalla's head bobbed gently to the sway of a horse's gait. She was tucked in front of Larron.

It had to be him, she thought as her senses kicked back in.

Along with feeling warm, the pounding in her head was gone, and she wanted to keep it that way. Her legs were strapped to the saddle in case he needed to fight and allow her to sag forward, but he currently held her upright, leaning her back against him for support with one arm while the other controlled the reins.

She remembered everything to the point when she lost consciousness. The headache took on a different feel as she ferried supplies back and forth. When her essence had been concentrated in earth, the energy was steady and solid. The sheer volume of it became overwhelming, but its pace was not pushed and hurried, it simply existed.

Pain came from control, or rather the lack of it and the desperate grasping for it. The control she should have learned over time was ripped from her. A will to control it burned into her mind and through the essential channels in her body. When it stopped, when her control clamped down on the elemental influence to the earth around her, calm replaced the pain, along with peace, and fatigue.

Water had been the same, yet completely different. The struggle for control raged just as painful, more so even, and new essential channels burned within her mind. Rather than stable and steady energy, water ebbed and flowed, with a force leaving her mentally staggering. She reached out for those fleeting, calmer waters within her as a means of gaining a foothold for control. With every step gained in those moments, the pain at the next surge of power increased. It must have taken only seconds, but time slowed in her perspective.

That was the point at which she lost consciousness, the point when she left all but a tentative connection with her body and dove within another piece of herself to steady and firm up the control being established. The point she dropped the supplies was the moment she recognized the element gathering within her essence. At that moment, the ferocity of her headache became recognizable as a symptom of her emerging power.

Tyrus had still been crossing the river when it happened. She sat with her eyes closed, afraid to open them and not see him with the group. There was nothing more she could have done than yell out a warning, as the uncontrolled influence of her power had already found a manifestation. Her last physical sensation was a sense of falling—the river. Though her eyes never saw the wall of water, she knew it came. She should have died, drowned, within that lethal manifestation of her power.

"Are you feeling better?" Larron asked softly, his mouth at her ear. Annalla sat up slowly, breaking most of the contact between them.

"How did you know I was awake?"

"You always tense when you wake; instantly alert and prepared for an attack. It is as though your body falls back on training while your mind takes in the situation before it relaxes again."

"Always?"

"So far as I have observed, it was far easier to discern this time. The subtle tightening of muscles, the barely perceptible catch in your breathing. You have a talent for appearing more helpless than you are. I suspect you woke the same way when we first met, I simply did not notice it then. It would not be so easy to mislead me now." His voice took on a playful tone.

"You make it sound like I attack you all the time."

"Often enough, especially when tied to a horse."

She laughed. "That is untrue. It was one time."

"I had to take away your weapons in case you attacked. I am taking my life in my hands here."

Annalla turned her head to where she could see him in her peripheral vision and smirked. "Don't lie. You enjoy carrying me like this."

He closed his arms and pulled her against him in a hug. "I would enjoy it more were it not always preceded by some injury to your person."

As his arms wrapped around her, she could only offer comforting pats in return, but she felt them both relax at the contact. "How long was I out this time?"

"The river crossing took place two days past. We will be making our mid-day stop soon."

Her stomach rumbled. "Good. I'm hungry."

"As are the horses," he said in a dry tone.

"Did we lose the reserve supplies?"

Larron filled her in on their situation. "So far, Marto has not recognized the location, and there has been no sign of enemies reported. We are making for the nearest large settlement I can recall in the area as he continues to scan the river."

"Close to half our animals." She grimaced. "That's going to make planning our supplies trickier."

"Less so with you returned to us. You never did answer me. How are you feeling?"

"A lot better, just like last time."

"It is likely the headaches are an early warning, then."

Annalla bobbed her head. "Yes, but I think only the really bad one at the end. It was more likely the glare before, as we originally suspected. That morning it grew and grew as the day went on."

"We watch for sudden and growing headaches, then."

She twisted to look at him, holding up a finger at a time

for emphasis. "First, you think this is going to happen again? Second, what do you think we can do about it if it does? And third, you think I would survive another?"

"I believe you are very powerful, and I cannot say for certain your abilities will stop at two. That alone warrants watching for signs. If we ensure you are in a safe location as the headache mounts, it gives you a higher likelihood of survival."

"And you as well. To make sure all of you are out of harm's way." Annalla held her awkward position, staring him in the eye until he let out a deep sigh.

"I cannot help you control this. If you tell me to run, we will run." He paused. "As I have twice now, I will note, without question."

"That is fair. You've trusted me and saved lives both times in doing so. Thank you."

It made her think again of the life bond between them. There could not really be any secrets, so it was easy to trust when you read through lies. But would that be considered trust?

Annalla thought there was a distinction missing from a basic application of truth and lie. Trust was not about believing someone was being honest. It was also about understanding one's capabilities and knowledge and trusting they were not only honest, but right. It meant not needing to verify everything yourself when someone told you what needed to happen and acting on the word of another.

"So," Annalla broke the companionable silence, "what can you tell me about this town we are heading toward?"

"It was a small, but growing, village some decades ago when I was last in the area. I suspect it has become a reasonably sized town. The reports from the area I read in our preparations seemed to support the assumption. Though it is not set on the river, it is near enough to do business on it and centered among the farms and homesteads to easily act as a gathering and trading center for the locals.

"All the residents around here were human at the time. Good, hard-working people, with a few strong leaders. That could have all changed with recent generations, but I believe we will find someone residing there.

"The town itself did not sit in the most defensible position," he continued. "It was meant to be a welcoming place for trade and talk, not a fortified store of wealth. There was no wall, but the leaders pushed for one to protect against more dangerous animals.

"Even with a guarding wall, you would not want to be trapped there. An attack could come from any direction. The only positive defensive aspect of the location is that you can see a fair distance in all directions across the fields. You might have enough warning to make the river and escape if an attack came in force."

"A few might, but not an entire town," Annalla commented.

"Just so. Situated between the elves and dwarves, away from some of the rowdier human settlements to the south, this area should be safe."

"Nothing is ever as safe as you believe it to be. I hope they got the wall up and thought of more than just animals in its construction."

"As do I. Based on reports over recent years, the Palonian would have helped with construction supplies if asked."

"Larron," Patrice said as she and Marto dropped back to pace beside them, "and welcome back, Annalla. There is an easy ledge down to the river ahead. We were going to stop there and water the animals."

"Lead on," he acknowledged.

The ledge was only large enough for one horse at a time, so they had to lead them each down for their drink and back up when finished. In that area, the river was a good eight to twenty-foot drop from the bank as far as they could see on both sides. The fall-out from Annalla's flash flood was visible on the opposite bank, where a tree, with roots attached, had been thrown halfway between the drop and tree line. There was no evidence it came from anywhere nearby.

"The trees must have been closer to the bank further

upstream?" Marto's voice rose at the end, and she knew he tried to be sensitive about it and simply ended up awkward.

"Or we will see more destruction the further up we go. I do appreciate the positive thinking, Marto. I just hope no one was caught in it."

"I doubt it," the mage replied. "There is no one around *to* be caught in it. The village is probably as deserted as the land we pass through."

"Don' be so ser'ous, young mage. No need ta' borrow tr'ble from t'm'rra.'

Nurtik's words sent her spiraling into a sudden memory.

He was an odd dwarf. One of the rare few in history to sunder ties to any clan. Master Rokin, so he was known to her, worked as a smith much of the time to trade for the extravagances he could not hunt for or grow himself at his isolated cabin in the hills. He was a large, sturdy dwarf, graying before his time. At only two hundred, he would still be considered in his prime.

Master Rokin taught Annalla to wield an axe, or—to be more accurate—to use many different types and sizes of axes. Rokin was her first teacher other than her parents, and his style differed greatly from her father's approach.

She stuck to the lessons and drills with the same diligence she always gave to such studies. At times, it seemed to confuse and amuse Rokin in equal measure. He did not think of them as lessons or drills at all. To him, they were fun.

"Why'r you so serious all the time, Annalla?" he asked her in his own language one night as they cared for the weapons used earlier in the day.

"I must not die. To avoid such, I must learn all I can, as fast as I can, and as well as I can, Master." It was a child's voice answering him, but the words were those of someone far older.

"An' who'd wish you to die, little one? We're not at war."

"I am what I am. Perhaps war is upon us, we simply do not yet realize it has begun."

Rokin looked sad for a moment, but he let those ominous words pass by and started in on another story about his exploits with his favorite weapon. The axe was a serious toy to him. He thoroughly enjoyed playing with it, and he was brilliant. In his hands, the cumbersome weapon became a beautiful and fluid death, and he taught her all the finer points and personalities of each individual axe.

She would never reach his skill with that weapon. It was unlikely she would gain or maintain the strength necessary to work with the heavier versions in any serious capacity. Despite those shortcomings, she knew she could rival many who might claim mastery of such a weapon, even after her limited training. Annalla was a natural with a blade. Any blade.

She liked Master Rokin. His stories made her laugh and took her mind off the seriousness of the world for a time. How her father convinced him to teach her, she never discovered. Rokin enjoyed his solitude. Only one of the local farmer's daughters had permission to enter his land to do a bit of trading. The young woman would walk up the thin trail, leading the pony and cart that would take his smithy work back down the hill.

Annalla hid in the barn with the little donkey that helped stoke the furnace. No one was to know she guested there. He didn't even increase the amount of food he bought from the girl while she lived with him, in case it led to questions. She was fairy. Special. Secret. And she had a job to do.

"What are you thinking about?" Larron's voice broke into her thoughts.

"Huh?"

"You sighed and were not here with us for a moment."

"I remembered something. A dwarf named Rokin taught me to wield an axe. We hid out at his little cabin in the woods and he told funny stories."

"Rokin?" Nurtik asked at hearing the name. "He was one of the youngest master smiths in history. I was young when he left. His love died in a rockslide, and he could not remain with the clan. We thought he died when he never arrived at our kin in the south."

"He became a hermit instead. I remember wondering how my father convinced him to teach me, but I can't remember finding out."

"A fine teacher. It explains your skill with my weapon and with our language."

Annalla laughed with Nurtik at the memory of their first meeting. "He taught me well and kept my secret. And he gave a child laughter. I am even more grateful for that now I know his history. I hope I was able to offer him some comfort as well."

"It is good to hear he lived, and still might today."

"I hope he does. Finally, a face I might recognize!"

Nurtik laughed again and slapped Annalla on the back with enough force to send her staggering had she not braced for it. Larron and the rest looked at them in confusion. She smiled over at him. She would explain later.

CHAPTER TWENTY

Larron worried Annalla had overestimated her recovery, but after resting the remainder of the day, she was back to scouting the next. Two more days passed without incident. They settled back into the old rhythm as though nothing had changed. He checked in every day, but it looked like the headaches were minimal. The clouds may have returned, but he and Patrice had produced an eye cover for her during the time she slept after the river incident.

"Anything?" came the usual inquiry from Tyrus.

"Yes," she said with a huge smile and began to hurry through her usual routine upon arriving at camp. Even her words were rushed. "I think I found it."

"Found what?"

"Our actual starting point!" she exclaimed. "I use a zigzag scouting pattern rather than going directly on the path you will take. The river came into view on a return sweep, and I thought it resembled Marto's description, so I risked more height for a better overview. The bend in the river, the rocky outcropping on the southern bank, the pooled area sheltered by that outcropping. There was nothing extraordinary about any of the characteristics. We've seen others just like them spread along the Nierda, but *together*? In just that way?"

"How long until we get there?" Marto wrung his hands and looked at her with eyes wide with excitement. "Maybe you should take me with you tomorrow."

"I would estimate late afternoon tomorrow," she replied. "If it were out of the way, I would fly you there, but this is right on the river we are traveling."

"If we hurry some, we might make it there by mid-day," Tyrus offered as consolation to the young mage.

"Give me some credit for my foresight, Tyrus." She looked mischievously at him. "I knew you would speed up a bit and included that in my estimate."

His poor attempt to glare at her had them all bursting into relieved laughter. Everyone grinned then, slapping shoulders and ruffling Marto's hair. Finding that place represented another piece validating the mission. More than a pair of wings and a spot along a river would be needed to *prove* anything, but they approached a significant milestone.

"Any sign of other visitors to the area?" Larron asked, joining them after finishing with the horses to allow them time to celebrate.

She shook her head. "It would appear no one else thought the place significant. I only found tracks of animals coming to the river to drink."

Larron watched her purse her lips. "But?" he asked, gesturing for her to continue with whatever she was holding back.

"There is something else," she said in a heavy tone.

Everyone sobered.

"Trouble?" Tyrus asked.

"I can't be certain yet. Another half-day's ride along the river, a road strikes north from the bank. There is an old dock that may have been used to moor shallow river craft. Most of the damage from the flood I caused happened around the sharp bend in the river. At this place, it looks like the silt had previously built up. I think my flood cleared it out again. It is difficult to tell for sure if it was still in use or not as a result."

Larron nodded. "That sounds like the road to the village to which we are heading."

"The road itself is overgrown with grass, brush, and

bushes beneath the snow, indicating it is relatively unused in recent years. There are, however, signs of recent travel on the road."

"The harvest this year?" Tyrus asked.

Annalla shook her head. "Within the last few days. New snow obscured the tracks, but there was at least one wagon with many people."

"If you had to guess at their number and direction?"

"More than thirty, less than fifty, but I'm not trained for such tracking. More than a handful of people and I feel like I'm making up the numbers. They set up a clear perimeter but milled about. I would guess they were armed in defensive positions, but few, if any, are trained soldiers. The latter is based on how they remained clustered, while we would send lookouts. A trip to and from the river. Dual wagon tracks tying to two passes of the road, but I have no guess as to their reason for such a trip."

"And you found no other sign of passage between here and the road?"

"None. I will investigate further up the road tomorrow."

"Do so, but stay close to the ground and do not allow anyone to see you in the sky or even gain a glimpse of your wings," Larron ordered. "I would prefer our enemy to have no forewarning that the fairy may be joining our side. Also, return early to the spot you found on the river. If it is the right location, we will have another decision to make."

That night and into the next day, their excitement grew palpable. Though it was tempered with caution, the animals even picked up on their mood. The marker Annalla left for them was unnecessary. Larron could see exactly why she thought that to be the place from Marto's story. It sat just as he described, if a little weathered by time. They were lucky the river curved between there and where they crossed. He was not certain the rocks protecting the pool would have remained in place against the full torrent Annalla unleashed.

"This is it," Marto spoke reverently, whispering Larron's thoughts and running a hand gently over a boulder. So much awe over a stone. "There are some changes, but a great deal of time has passed since the story originated. The differences are nothing time can't account for. This is where we start."

"Good." The two of them turned north together. They would need to take sightlines regularly, but even such efforts might not be enough to maintain a true course with the open and empty plains around them.

"Annalla left a marker to indicate a possible camp location in that direction." Tyrus passed over the stone from where he stood at Larron's side, having made a sweep of the immediate area. "Is this the place?"

"It is, and yes, we are heading to the campsite and stopping early today. Leave a marker for Annalla in case she heads here first."

Those on the ground mounted again. It was not long before he saw Annalla skimming the ground, flying toward them. She gained on them with surprising speed.

He watched her, cutting through the air like an arrow in flight, with just as much compact strength and lethality. It was a vast improvement over when she was learning to fly. Larron recalled when she still dangled in the air and ran into a tree and laughed quietly to himself at the memories.

She caught up to them, circled once, and went ahead with no more than a wave. As the representative of the elves, what would he give to have an army of fairy on his side? He would negotiate, barter, bluff, but there was a more appropriate question. What would he not give for such an army? What line would he draw?

By the time they arrived, she cleared an area to pitch their one tent and grew their usual meals. The faces entering the camp around him beamed with their first significant success. It was a major step toward validating why they were out there. Annalla's expression, however, remained guarded. There was a smile, and words of congratulations were exchanged, but he knew she found something muting her own pleasure. She did not want to dampen the spirits of the others.

"What is it?" he asked her quietly, off to the side.

"They were attacked, Larron. Not recently or I would have spoken sooner, but there is clear evidence of gilar activity in the area."

"You do not believe there is an immediate threat?"

Annalla shook her head.

"Alright. You can make a full report to the group after camp is set. That way you do not need to repeat yourself too many times."

"I'm going to make another circuit around the immediate area before we pull our guard into the conversation. I just want to be sure," she told him when they were finishing the daily chores.

He held her eyes and saw only caution, not alarm. "Very well, bring him with you when you return."

"Hold on the fire," Larron said to Patrice as she stacked wood after Annalla left to scout.

She paused and turned to him, her head cocked to one side. "Oh?"

"Annalla is making another perimeter check," he explained. "I want to be more cautious with recent signs of others in the area."

"If she found anyone close today, she would have said something immediately to warn us," Tyrus pointed out. "Or did she tell you? I know we have been exuberant over finding the river mark."

"She would have told us if she saw any immediate threat. However, she saw something concerning. We will hear the details upon her return."

There were solemn nods all around as they resumed camp activities. They remained hopeful, but everyone shifted to high alert.

"First," Larron began after Annalla and Nurtik walked into the campsite and settled in to join the rest for their meal, "a sighting will need to be taken, some new landmark we will work toward. We did not remain there long, Marto, but did you see anything specific or know of something from the story we should make for?"

"No. We will need to sight on something stationary due north. Until we are within the forest, I do not know of another landmark other than direction. Everything else along the way was too...temporary."

"I saw nothing either. The land is too flat and the mountains too far away to provide adequate bearings." Heads turned to Annalla. "What about from the air?"

"I can see the forested hills and the mountains to the north, but the hills just look like a forest from above. I will fly back in the morning and find a couple of markers for us to use."

"Even if you need to align something closer with a mountain peak, we can always chain landmarks along the way." She nodded at the recommendation, and Larron moved on. "Please share what you saw today to worry you."

"Death," she said, sorrow coloring her voice. "So much death and destruction."

Everyone sat straighter and a few looked around.

"What do you mean?" Patrice asked.

"There was no immediate threat. They've been dead for weeks, possibly months," Annalla rubbed her hands down her face, regrouping mentally. "I went up the road today. Homes, farmhouses, fields...all destroyed. Most of the homes and outbuildings were reduced to scrap or rubble. There are signs of some burned to the ground, others were bashed in. No matter the method, nothing is left remotely resembling shelter. The animal remains I found were mutilated and half consumed. Blood stains the ground so thickly you can still distinguish it beneath the snow."

No one among them remained a stranger to death and destruction, but it never muted the impact of the next tragedy they encountered.

"Some of the homes burned down were occupied," she continued. "I found skeletons the fires did not consume among the charred remains and ashes. Anyone who came to bury them could not have reached them without endangering themselves because of instability or simply not seeing through the rubble. Graves were made for the ones they could reach. Gilar did this. They are this far north, perhaps further. I cannot tell how large their numbers are, only that they are great enough to obscure their tracks beyond count. But I have said before I am no tracker."

"You are certain it is gilar?" Larron asked her.

"The signs are clear enough," she said. "There were piled bodies further into the fields as we saw in the Claws. Whoever dug the graves I found near the houses did not find them. No wild animal did this."

Gilar were brutal, strong, dangerous, and by far the most cunningly cruel of the races following Kahnlair. Humans were their favorite source of food. That they were that far north in large numbers would make crossing the rolling farmlands ahead of them dangerous. Extending their time in the open with having to forage would only increase the risk. Everyone sat then. Their brief joy was replaced by serious consideration and not a little fear. Larron felt proud of them when he detected no panic.

"What else?" Larron spoke as the silence dragged on.

"I believe the town is held by humans still and safe enough for us, so long as they do not take us for gilar before we can be identified."

"With all the destruction you found upon the road, why do you think the town survived? The wagon tracks you found yesterday?" Tyrus's voice was quiet, hope and sorrow both evident. Humans who had left the kingdom proper were still his people.

"I believe the intent of the group recently passing on the roadway, at least in part, was to dig the graves and bury the victims they could find. Two sets of tracks for there and back also indicate they still occupy the town. You will see more tomorrow where the river meets the road."

"You did not see anyone in the town, though," Tyrus pressed.

"I did not. It still stood with evidence of previous attacks against it. It is not well fortified, but what can be done to shore up its defenses is in place, or possibly being repaired or replaced. Hastily erected walls span between buildings, and obstacles outside the town's perimeter have been set up. Despite that, it is still an open farming community.

"The gilar know tactics as much as we do, and the town is not a position I would choose to hold. It is weak and has no strategic impact. Were I in their position, I would destroy the town and those hiding in it and move on. I saw smoke from chimneys, so it is occupied. I want to run a higher sweep over it tomorrow. I think if I am high enough to avoid detection myself, I will not be able to see much, but gilar are distinctive."

"It sounds like you continue to favor resupplying at the town if possible?"

"In addition to supplies, current information is something we could find useful now we know the gilar are around."

"I have to agree," said Marto. "Information is a tempting incentive."

"After facing all of that," Patrice asked, "even if they could help us, do you think they will be willing to risk depleting their own store?"

Larron had the same concern whenever he thought of trying to trade for supplies. They had little to offer in exchange. A difficult winter would mean little to spare. Such shortages could make people aggressively defensive. The latter, however, was something he was not as concerned about in this situation.

"They might not have what we need, but I believe they will help us if they are able."

"What makes you say that, Tyrus?"

"They went back to bury their dead. They are holding their town. They are thinking with their hearts instead of their heads. I would simply suggest we keep in mind, constantly, what they have been through should they not be as trusting and congenial as we would like."

Patrice tipped her head, but her words were still of caution. "We will also be providing information to people about us if we go. As much information as we get from them, they might leak information about us."

"If gilar thin' ta question 'em at'll."

"We have a cover story for our journey." Larron shrugged. As long as Annalla is not seen for what she is, their cover would work well enough in that area. "Sending important information by both bird and messenger is not unheard of."

"So we go," Nurtik summed up the conversation. "We go, an' we get information an' supply."

"We go."

CHAPTER TWENTY-ONE

Their group reached the dock, heading there first, before traveling down the road to investigate the destruction. Both Larron and Tyrus possessed better training for tracking, so the two of them looked around the area while Patrice, Marto, and Nurtik held the animals away from the area.

"They were here for the boats," Tyrus said, pointing at the mess around the dock, "but the gilar had already burned them. You can see where one moored closer to the dock here and charred the wood."

The small burn appeared new enough to support his assessment. Larron said, "Annalla's flood washed this evidence down the river."

Tyrus nodded. "The people came hoping to find the boats still here. Maybe they planned to send some of the old or infirm from the village down the river."

"Agreed. They set up a perimeter and searched the immediate area. Deciding it was a lost cause, they turned around."

"At least we can tell Annalla *she* did not destroy their boats." Tyrus looked at him.

Larron appreciated the man's consideration. It would have hurt Annalla if she destroyed a means of escape for those people when she flooded the river. He looked back at the dock and then out over the road ahead.

"Shall we see what the road has to tell us?"

They started back toward the horses as Tyrus spoke, "I'm not looking forward to reading this story."

The road held as many horrors as Annalla claimed. Her descriptions the night before did nothing to blunt the impact of seeing the devastation.

Passing over the first rise in the land brought them to the site of the first home, a burned-out shell of what it had been. The roof was gone, sunk to the ground between the scattered remains of a charred and blackened frame. Within, Larron could make out bones buried among the ash; a hand emerged from the rubble, curling in on itself and blackened by the fire to claim its owner's life.

He doubted any of the others could distinguish the hand from the rest. The house sat back a fair distance, but the details were clear to his sight. That harsh image stood in stark contrast to the peace and beauty of the landscape. A soft light filtered through the clouds above, shining off the snow in a glow as scattered flakes floated gently down to join the blanket of white. The winter weather slowly claimed the gilar's destruction, as the blackened building became covered in white.

As they followed the road, the scenes became more heart-wrenching. More destroyed homes, some with corpses, others he could not distinguish anything. Larron knew by the size of the bones he identified that many of the trapped had been children.

It was a better fate to burn than being taken by the gilar, but not by much. Near the barns and stables, they found frozen carcasses of animals. Then came the sorrow of the scattered graves, and they paused for a moment in silence as tears were shed for the fallen. Larron would never be able to tell how many died based on the mounds of earth they passed. Most were large enough that he did not doubt they held more than one person.

He did not begrudge those people for not taking the time and care for individual, marked burials. The ground was frozen, turning an already emotionally difficult task into one of impossible labor as well. In his heart, he praised their valiant efforts to keep their dead from becoming forgotten carrion. Those people risked further attack, exhausted themselves digging so many graves, to honor the fallen in what way they could.

"This is why we left," Patrice said from her seat before Tyrus. "Many wanted to stay, protect our villages, but the matriarchs stood together and would not allow it. We are semi-nomadic. The villages were not who we are, only where we occasionally lived."

"Save people by sacrificing land. It spared your fighters to join the allied forces as well." Tyrus nodded in agreement. "My father has not been well-liked for telling people to leave their lands and consolidate. His conscriptions and orders would have been ignored were it not for martial law and the support of the military."

"It was the right decision for us," she said, "as it would have been for these people if they had known of the dangers, but I do understand that some cannot make that sacrifice."

"It is likely they were unaware of the threat," Larron offered, "and waiting for the harvest to come in. Their food is part of the supplies sent down the river to Ceru. They may have wanted to have as much of their own store as possible before begging asylum from a neighbor. If the gilar did not want to give warning of their coming, these people would have had none. Oromaer feared they grew complacent in the north, including the Palonian, but he had few options."

Patrice nodded. "Everything becomes clear in hindsight, but it hurts to see this."

No one had a response, and they rode the afternoon in silence. It was quiet as they camped well off the road. There was little comfort in the fact they had, just the day before, found the first step to lead them on. Most of them had seen such destruction before and witnessed it brought upon their own people. In recent weeks, their lives centered around their own survival and mission, but the *why* behind it shrank to a distant idea. It was especially true for Patrice, Marto, and Nurtik, who had lived in the Palonian for an extended time.

They were out there to stop that from happening, to find

help for people such as those, who suffered with no means of protecting themselves. It was a sobering day. Bedrolls were sought early, though he suspected they all found sleep elusive.

Morning dawned cold and cloudy and found the group still subdued but with a renewed sense of determination. They packed silently, and Annalla took off for a brief scouting trip around the town. She would be joining them before they came within human sight of the walls.

The scene around them shifted as they continued. The destruction remained, and the slaughter, but signs of armed defenders leading a retreat increased. Larron saw no fallen gilar upon the ground, but if Annalla was right about the town being held by the land's rightful inhabitants, then they succeeded where it mattered. They provided time.

Movement out of the corner of his eye made Larron tense, but he relaxed as quickly. The speck growing in the distance to the right of their party was Annalla skimming the ground at a speed no rider could match. He watched as she swung around behind them to come up in their trail and slow to match Dusk's speed as she reached him. He did not stop or slow, only moved forward and leaned down to pat Dusk to tell him something was coming. She stretched out her foot to stand lightly on his back, just behind Larron. In one fluid motion, her wings wrapped around her as she placed her hands on his shoulders and swung herself to sit behind him.

"I found nothing in the surrounding area beyond some smoke rising to the northeast, likely a smaller village or homestead. There is a guard posted at the town, but they are not soldiers."

"The first is good to hear. We will proceed with caution. When do you suspect we will be within hailing distance?"

"They will see us over the next rise. We should hear their challenge an hour or two after."

He nodded and waited for Dusk to climb the hill. At the top, he made out the battered town in the distance. Scorch marks showed attempts to burn the walls and the town down. The people there must have been prepared and found a way to counter the fire. It was difficult to judge from that distance, but it did not look like much of an effort had been made to take the town. The arrows speckling the walls were few and scattered, and the hasty barriers showed limited damage.

"You did not expect what you saw upon the road," Annalla said, breaking into his assessment.

"I am never prepared for it, despite the report you gave us and all I have seen." She left the silence alone and waited for him to continue. "This area is behind our lines, away from the enemy. It is supposed to be a pocket of land protected from war. The possibility always existed, and we spoke of it and planned for it. I do not think I believed it would come to this. You can never really prepare to see pointless slaughter."

"All war is pointless slaughter, but sometimes you have to fight more to end it."

He sighed but could not disagree.

Their mid-day rest was given up, ensuring they arrived with plenty of light remaining in the day. Larron could see the walls lined with men and more arriving. While there were not an insignificant number visible, he suspected the other walls were not currently guarded; they were all there.

Trained or not, they had the advantage of numbers, cover, and height. There was no warning shot to frighten them away, so at least they were not jumping at shadows. It was a tense progression as both sides waited for the other to strike, but neither did. Larron continued to the front of their group and stopped just outside the makeshift gate.

"Name yourselves, and your purpose here," a voice shouted to them from an unidentifiable source.

"We are travelers from the Palonian Woodland seeking rest, shelter, and trade, if you have it." They agreed Larron would speak, as there had been no sign of elves joining Kahnlair's cause.

"We have little enough for our own. Travelers with light bags, as I see yours to be, likely have little with which to trade."

"Perhaps, then, a trade less tangible. We need information

from these lands you might be able to provide. You, it would seem, could benefit from advice from a trained soldier on how to best defend this town from a larger force."

Silence was the only answer. Larron did not fill it and waited patiently for them to decide on a response. "Leave your weapons sheathed as they are, and you may enter. Move to draw them, and we will kill you without pause."

A gap opened in the barricade across the road. Larron nodded and Tyrus nudged Moonshine forward slowly. Emerging on the other side, he saw they were surrounded by guards with arrows trained on them. Their small group took care to give no hostile or sudden movements that might startle someone into firing upon them.

Dusk was the last to pass through the gap, and the barricade closed quickly behind. As soon as they stopped, an unarmed man emerged from the crowd. He was of late-middling years with the gray beginning to dominate the brown of his hair and beard. His figure was that of an active farmer used to working his land as long as the light touched it each day. In contrast to the farmer image, his eyes spoke of someone familiar with a soldier's training. Before the recent raids, he may have simply been one of the area's prominent farmers. He was obviously the one in charge. The defenders listened to him without question and followed his orders swiftly and efficiently.

He paused as he scanned the members of their party. "Why would you risk your women traveling in times such as these?"

He felt Annalla bristle, but she held her tongue this time. "All those with me are capable of defending themselves. Any information you can share with us would be helpful. We believed the gilar had not reached so far north."

"They have, and they will be back."

"Perhaps we could see to our animals and then continue this conversation?" Larron suggested.

He felt uncomfortable negotiating from an elevated position. It was not his intent to attempt intimidation, nor would such a tactic benefit him in this situation. At least, not yet.

"I must say I am not entirely comfortable with you walking armed in our town."

"Surrounded by such dangers, we would not feel comfortable leaving our weapons out of our presence, but we might compromise by setting them at the threshold."

It was not the greatest plan if he was trying to avoid intimidating them. He knew how many weapons they carried. Perhaps they would find it reassuring instead.

After a moment's thought, the man agreed. "The stables are this way."

He indicated to their right and waited for them to dismount before leading the way, the drawn arrows followed at their sides and behind them. As they were seeing to their animals in the stables, he saw the man speak to another, who then ran off on his assigned errand. His nerves made him wish for Annalla's hearing, but he relaxed at a nod from her. Nothing said was a threat to them.

They fed the animals from their stores and came together in a defensive pattern of their own, shielding each other's weaker sides, prepared to defend against a surprise attack. Their leader noticed, but did not stop it.

"Could you escape if we decided to attack?"

Larron had been wondering the same as they followed him back into the streets of the town, but it was Annalla who answered him.

"Not all of us," Annalla shrugged, "but more of your people would die. You crowd numbers in here against skill. Better coverage would be to place your archers along the path ahead and along escape routes, preferably at a higher level with an unobstructed view. That would place them in unknown locations and out of reach of blades."

"And you volunteer this information?"

"Part of the offer was advice on improving your defenses. You shared your belief the gilar will return, and I shared a piece of what we can offer."

Larron was again impressed by the man leading them. He

was obviously not accustomed to or pleased to be taking the advice of a woman. Rather than dismiss her words because she did not conform to his expectations, he gave her an assessing look. The people there might stand a chance if he could learn and apply their tactics.

No further questions were asked as they wound their way to the town's inn. It no longer served as a place for guests. Even the inn's stable housed former residents of the surrounding lands. They were led past and through the door to the common room, where he wasted no time indicating where they could leave their weapons.

Judging by the faces staring at them, it was an impressive sight to watch them disarm and see the growing pile of weaponry stacked—in an organized and easily accessible manner—against the wall. Each had a primary weapon. A few carried a bow and quiver of arrows. Then there were the smaller blades they continued to draw from hidden pockets and straps within their clothes.

Their leader recognized it in the way they moved and worked together, but the weapons told the rest of their audience they were dangerous people. Dangerous people who might be able to help. One by one, they indicated they had completely disarmed themselves. Even Larron was surprised to find Patrice the last to finish. Their little feline friend had small knives hidden everywhere and made a show of finding each one. It made him suspect at least one remained hidden on her person when they moved to a table in the corner.

"An elf, dwarf, and two young men traveling with two women, you say, from the Palonian Woodland. What in this world could be your reason for risking their safety by leaving that haven?"

"My name is Larron, this is Tyrus, Marto, Nurtik, Patrice, and Annalla. We are here specifically to re-supply as much as we can before continuing with our mission, which is one of information to the dwarven clan," he offered their cover story, which would not be untrue if they succeeded. "To say any more would not be wise. The fewer who know the details, the better it will be, and we are not at liberty to share the details of our message with anyone until we reach the clan."

"Convenient. I suppose, true or false, you would not tell me what brings you this way. I still don't see why it is necessary to bring women on any sort of mission."

"Sir, as I stated, every member of my party is fully capable of defending themselves. Gender is not an issue."

He eyed their weapons again, sighed, and shook his head. "No, I don't suppose it is. Call me Hamton. Please, what is it exactly you are hoping to find here?"

"As far as supplies are concerned, we need food for ourselves and our animals. As we are traveling to the north, anything you know of the surrounding area and further in that direction could also be helpful."

Hamton listened and smiled wryly at Larron's summary.

"Not much I see," was all he said as he waved a server over.

It was lean fare, bread, and mead, with a small portion of smoked meat and cheese. Despite the hints at limited provisions, a small meal was passed to all. Larron took that as another good sign. They were still inclined to be giving and hospitable. Everyone ate quietly, waiting for Hamton to respond more specifically to their request.

"You were right. The gilar were not known this far north until recently, perhaps a month back. Before that, the worst we had to deal with was the few windani to come down from the north range. There is no denying they are dangerous enough, but simple precautions were taken to protect the people and their land.

"We are at a loss to deal with what has happened. Out here, we are farmers. That is how we have tried to support our side in the war. Every harvest we kept only what was necessary. The rest was sent down the Nierda or to the Palonian. Now, the enemy comes upon us, and any who chose to fight left to the south years ago." Hamton sighed. "Though I am not sure it would have made a difference had they been here."

He looked toward the door of the inn, but Larron could tell his eyes were seeing the day of the gilar attack again. The anger and frustration at losing so many of their neighbors were plain to read on his face.

"They came from the south, as you would expect, and made their way up to the east of us. We have since heard rumors the main contingent that passed was headed to the dwarven clan. I could not give you an estimate of their number. Only a couple of survivors have passed through here with stories of gilar, and they were mostly hearsay. The telling expanded on and exaggerated out of fear and having a captive audience. It was said they are beyond count, the gilar between you and the clan. This warning did not come soon enough for our people.

"We sent word to the families on the neighboring farms that gilar had been sighted as soon as the news first came to us, but that group was not the only one traveling north. A smaller group broke off from the main force and followed the river as it wound around toward the west. They must have already been where the river meets the road when the messengers were dispatched.

"I was fortunate to still be here after delivering my portion of the harvest. My brother and his family were caught in their home." Hamton's jaw clenched, and he took a deep breath through his nose. "One of the messengers came speeding back to tell us. He is a smart lad and gave us good information. There were only about thirty gilar. Only thirty were able to do all that damage and kill so many."

"I am truly sorry for your loss," he offered, knowing it to be inadequate.

Hamton nodded and visibly brought himself back. "From what Kelly told us, our scattered farmers did not stand against them. They are stronger, brutal, and deadly accurate. Not until they neared the town proper were we able to mount any resistance.

"We organized as best we could. Set up lines to slow them down while those fleeing made it behind the barricades we put up. You saw them when you passed through. We manned the walls. They were smart enough to know they could not take the town as easily as they had the farms. I'm sorry if you were hoping for more details, but we don't travel far in our work, and that is all to come our way."

"What makes you believe the gilar will be returning?"

"They told us they would. We belong to them now, as our sheep belong to us, they said. When they return, they will take what they want, and if we try to run, they will track us down. Traveling in such a large group would make us slow and vulnerable, so we chose to stay and defend ourselves as long as we could."

"They must have a larger force circling down from the north to meet up with them and take care of any resistance left behind," Tyrus noted.

"What do you mean 'a larger force?'" Hamton asked, sounding resigned.

"I would estimate no more than two hundred in the second group. Larron?"

He nodded at Tyrus, agreeing with his assumptions. "Yes, this first was a hunting party, likely sent to track down anyone fleeing and pinpoint resistance. Two hundred trained gilar would assess the resistance and either end it or send scouts."

"We have been preparing carts and provisions to run with everyone in the town. Do we have enough time?"

"How soon could you depart?"

"A few days."

A few days. Then they would be traveling with the elderly, babies, provision carts, and about a thousand total people. It took their party a month to make the trip without such constraints. The gilar were already a month gone to report and return. He saw his thoughts echoed in the faces of his party as everyone did the math.

"That's what I thought," Hamton said. "We have too many to move with speed. The able-bodied remaining will leave none behind. It is why I have been trying to prepare the town defensively."

"For the time we are here," Larron leaned his head forward toward Hamton, "should it be accepted, we will do what we can to help you."

There was agreement around the table. They would need to leave those people and continue their mission, but they would leave them better prepared. Many of the townsfolk standing around listening to the conversation looked skeptical. They were not trained soldiers, and his party did not look like their expectations of soldiers. Even Tyrus was in lighter traveling armor rather than the heavier items standard for human infantry.

Hamton saw more than the rest. There, before him, was a small group, confident with their weapons and comfortable in a situation where they were unarmed and outnumbered. The people there trusted his judgment, and it would be his decision to trust them or not.

"I regret to say we have little to offer in the way of supplies. No one has dared hunt since the raid, and the meat we shared here was near the last of that supply. Grain is the only part of our harvest we have more than enough of because we had not sent the last shipment south when the attack came, but you cannot survive well on grain alone. I tell you this because we will accept any help you are willing to offer without the promise of much travel fare waiting in exchange."

"Two days." Larron sent a stern look at his companions, knowing they would want to linger longer because he wanted to as well. They would have enough of a delay having to hunt for themselves regularly. "We will stay and help with your defenses for two days, and whatever you can offer will be payment enough. Thoughts?" He looked around once more.

"The perimeter needs to be secured; the barricades will not hold against a larger force. The gate is a particularly weak point," Tyrus offered.

"Trainin'. Nu'in fancy, jus' 'fective fer farmers t' use."

"Organized support to free people for defensive roles. Ambush locations and traps within the town for any gilar that breach the walls," Patrice added her thoughts.

"See to it. Marto and I will sit with Hamton to review his resources and discuss possible tactics they could employ. Annalla, could you help with the training—archery and techniques for lighter and smaller combatants?"

"After midday tomorrow."

He tilted his head. "And in the morning?"

"I hunt."

Two words hiding so much meaning. A good hunt could help them and the people in that town. It might have the added benefit of giving them enough meat the town would provide them with another pack animal. Within those words, he also heard 'I scout.' She too believed the gilar would be back with numbers, and she believed it might be soon. Annalla was the only one who could cover sufficient ground to be successful at both tasks in half a day.

"Agreed. Hunt, then train."

"Alone?!" came Hamton's strangled protest. He had said they were afraid to send people out to hunt.

"Alone. The rest of us will start with you and your people at first light."

CHAPTER TWENTY-TWO

Larron managed to quell further questions about why Annalla would go alone, and Hampton had wisely taken that as an end to the conversation. A handful of men arrived at the stables as she exited the next morning before the sun rose, thinking to go with her. She told them to go train with the others and left without waiting. She covered more ground flying to hunt, and ended up bringing back a stag and a few hares around mid-day.

Her trainees were already waiting for her when she arrived, following a boy named Cory who led her to her students. The boys and young men assigned to her for the afternoon were smaller, and many began the session with an air of superiority to them. Annalla gained a measure of satisfaction knocking some of them on their butts. At least Cory seemed to like her and listen to what she taught them.

By the end of the day, she was exhausted from all the people and talking.

Annalla departed town to hunt once more before the sun rose the second morning, but that time she headed north after making a wide circuit around the town. North, she suspected, was the most likely direction from which the gilar would come. Some vague knowledge had been nagging at her since the first time they spoke with Hamton about the gilar. Annalla knew she had seen or heard some important but overlooked piece of information.

Unfortunately, she could not bring it to the front of her mind.

She hoped everyone was wrong about gilar to the north because it was the direction in which her group had to go. There was no cover for days on the ground crossing the open farmland. Should they need to hide, they would have to crouch behind the curve of a rolling hill and hope to be dismissed as bumps on the horizon.

There were no trees for miles, so she had to *create* a place to leave Moonshine. Leaving her horse with more grass, Annalla turned left and began her circle around the town. The west was clear. To the south, she only encountered an unfortunate hare straying into her path. The east proved just as calm. In every direction, the destruction left by the earlier gilar hunting or scouting party remained clear. It was also not recent.

On the way north, she swung out in a wider arc. Her heart and momentum stopped when she sped over another rise and saw what the early morning rays illuminated. A shiver ran down her spine.

Moving down from the northeast, like an elongated shadow, was an approaching mass of gilar. With nothing else in the area, their destination could not be mistaken. A quick count told her the estimate of two hundred had been high, but not by much, and there was absolutely no time for the townsfolk to flee without detection.

Annalla had seen them earlier. She knew she had. That was why she was so set on scouting while they were helping the town. When she had flown high above the town to check the inhabitants, there had been a village in the distance.

Not a village or homestead, she thought, realizing her mistake. At that elevation, she would have seen that group, but the distance and weather distorted them beyond recognition.

Before rushing back to Moonshine, she lingered a few moments longer to observe details. It did not take long to see they were far better trained, armed, and prepared than she dared to hope. Her horse was not pleased to be pulled away from her unfinished meal, but Moonshine did no more than snort her displeasure as Annalla turned her head for the town and set a hard pace. The sun had not fully broken free from the horizon when she arrived at the gate and requested entrance.

"Cory," she called, recognizing the boy, "see that Moonshine and this rabbit are taken care of. Do you know where any of my friends are?"

"Yes, ma'am, and someone was sent to fetch Mister Tyrus when they saw you returning quick."

He had no sooner said it and hurried off with rabbit in hand and horse in tow when Tyrus came around another corner, his face serious.

"How long?" was all he asked. Between her premature return and the look on her face, he correctly assumed what news she brought.

"We convene at mid-day, at the inn. I suggest you complete what you wanted to accomplish here today, a few hours after we meet would be ideal."

Annalla knew they had an audience and attempted to select words to avoid a panic. There would be rumors, but they were already supposed to leave that night if they held strictly to Larron's two-day timeframe.

"Understood. Nurtik is at the training ground, Patrice is at the inn and Larron and Marto are with Hamton in the northeast corner of town. I'll send runners to the other two about the meeting if you want to meet with Larron and Hamton?"

Annalla gave Tyrus a curt nod and left him shouting orders at the men standing around. She hurried between the buildings in the direction given and relied on her ears to pinpoint their location. There was activity around every corner, people working on the walls and running errands. The work was steady but relaxed.

A sense of urgency would spread with her news. Hopefully, it would not turn to panic. Acting and preparing would help, and the six of them remaining calm and confident would help further. Up ahead, Hamton's voice was the first she distinguished, but Larron's shortly followed. They discussed where and how many archers to position at the top of a wall she could not yet see.

Three more turns were between her and them, but she covered the distance quickly.

"Larron."

"You're back early today." Hamton offered her a small smile.

"How long?" Larron sighed but kept his expression neutral.

"Word is being spread to the others to meet at the inn at mid-day. Tyrus is accelerating his work on the front walls. One hundred seventy or eighty will be here before the sun sets. Well-armed, well provisioned, well trained."

Larron took a deep breath. He shifted a glance at Marto and looked around at the town, the people, the walls, and back to her. Letting out the breath, he said, "We will discuss your discovery with the others when we meet later." He shifted to make introductions. "Annalla, this is James, one of their best hunters. He has been designated captain of the archers, and we were going over their placement in the areas already reinforced. With the information you have brought us, we should accelerate our plans as well. I would like you to continue with James, so Hamton and I can finish the rest."

"Of course," she said with a nod.

"Marto, would you move on to setting up the special ammunition you want now rather than waiting for us?"

"On it." Marto nodded to the three of them before heading to his task.

Larron and Hamton soon did the same, and she was left with James and a couple of his archers. James was a lean man and looked like he was in late middle age, so around seventy. His sandy brown hair and beard were speckled with gray. His brown eyes looked sharp and scanned her from head to toe and back in a quick assessment. Whatever his impression of her was, he kept it to himself. The other two took their cue from him, so all three stared at her impassively.

Annalla thought back to the conversation she heard when following Larron's voice. "He was telling you to set up a crossfire situation with multiple archers there and there. Correct?"

"Yes, ma'am."

"And you already covered a few such positions today?"

"Yes, ma'am."

"Wonderful. I propose we proceed to the next and you describe how it would be arranged. I will comment when beneficial, but I suspect Larron already covered most of the standard points."

"Yes, ma'am." James held out his arm to indicate the direction they would take and started walking at her side.

The six of them could not be everywhere that night. Leaders among the townsfolk would need to be capable and confident, and their people would need to have confidence in them. James seemed to fit that need as he led her around and gained more confidence with every position they visited.

At the first few, he was hesitant, but thoughtful, as he tried to remember every detail about positioning and command. She waited for him to finish his own assessment, agreed with most of it, and adjusted one or two details if needed before he relayed the orders to his men. Quickly, her changes became fewer and less frequent. Soon enough, he gave his assessment directly to his men to be carried out immediately, only asking if she had anything to add at the conclusion.

"I think my grandson is a little taken with you," James broke the silence between one location and the next, catching her off guard.

"Uh..." Annalla stole a less than subtle glance at the other two men with them, wondering if he was talking about one of them.

One of them laughed and slapped James on the back. "Aww! Little Cory found his first love."

James grinned at her. "I am fairly certain I heard your entire lesson from yesterday recited word-for-word over dinner and into the evening."

"I heard you put Mevin Baker on the ground," another man crowed with delight.

"Someone needed to. The arrogant fool keeps talking about how his father should be in charge. At least Melgor has more sense than his son."

The three of them continued their conversation, including Annalla by their positioning around her rather than bumping her to the side. James turned to her again as they wound down, approaching the next position.

"You won't have any trouble with the archers tonight."

"I appreciate that." She glanced at the sky. "How many more positions are left?"

"Two more after this one."

"I need to head to the inn. You have this well in hand, I think. Are you okay finishing up?"

James nodded. "We'll manage."

"You know how to find us if you have any questions. Good luck tonight."

"To you as well."

Annalla waved and made her way between buildings to meet for the planning discussion.

"Annalla, how do our archer positions look?" Larron asked as she walked in. It looked like they were waiting on her and Nurtik to arrive, and the men gave them space for now.

"James is a good captain. They will be organized well enough. Though I must say, I do not like how open some of the positions are. He has some of his men nailing boards to the posts, but there is not much we can do. I would not say no to having a few straw men up there as decoys."

Patrice smiled and leaned forward slightly. "We have some people we could put to that task. I cannot guarantee many. Let me know where you think they would best serve."

"That would be great." She took the available seat next to Larron, and before they spoke again, the door opened to Nurtik. He took the last open seat at the small table with a meal already laid for them.

Once Nurtik settled, Larron lowered his voice and began, "So, do we leave now?"

The facial reactions conveyed everything from reluctance to derision, but Larron continued before anyone could reply, "Our small group could swing wide to the west and hug the river on its path north. Annalla has already taken landmarks and could lead us back on course for our objective."

Patrice sighed. "It would rely on the gilar not sending out large parties to sweep as far as the river, but the boats were destroyed on the first run. The land remains relatively flat, but we are a small, skilled group and could easily avoid detection or eliminate any scouts stumbling upon us. Leaving the town now is the smarter decision with a significantly higher chance of surviving to continue our mission," she admitted.

"I hate that you're not wrong," Tyrus said through clenched teeth, "but we have a responsibility to consider our mission as well."

"We do," Larron agreed. "What are the chances of survival if we stay?"

"Remaining here, the gilar will be significantly outnumbered," Tyrus said, "but those numbers have little to no combat training, and most of them are not in prime fighting condition. Do they have magai?" he asked Annalla.

She shook her head. "Not that I observed."

"Tha's good," Nurtik commented. "Magai wi' 'em woulda been zero chanc'a survivin'."

"'Not zero' chance of success is not good enough," Larron said dryly, "but having Marto with us raises the chances to about half, I think."

"A little more than half, if the rest of us are fighting with the town as well," Annalla said.

"So," Patrice broke in to summarize, "the chances of surviving if we stay are slim to reasonable."

They all looked around at each other, eyebrows raising, shoulders shrugging, all in a gesture conveying a sense of resigned determination. Finally, all eyes settled on Larron, who gave a half-smile.

"Reasonable is enough."

They let out a collective breath. Marto grinned and relaxed while Tyrus slapped Larron on the back and waved over the men hovering across the room. Nurtik's hands worked the grip of his axe, while he and Patrice shared a glance filled with fierce anticipation. Annalla smiled at Larron and nodded her agreement at his decision.

"Hamton told them to be sparing with what you brought yesterday, so there will be plenty to share."

Hamton approached with the rest, swallowing and bracing himself. No one harbored any illusions about what the group had been discussing.

"Are you leaving us now?" he asked, keeping his voice impressively calm, without a hint of the anger or fear he must have felt.

"We said we would stay for two days," Larron responded, "and so we shall. I hope it is not imposing too much on your hospitality if we extend our visit through the night?"

Hampton had to swallow again before he could speak through the tears of relief held back. "We are honored to have you."

"Introductions are in order," Larron began again as the men settled into seats at an adjoining table. "I do not believe everyone around the table has met. This is Trey…and Collin. They will be acting as Hamton's commanders. I believe the two of you know Nurtik from training yesterday. The rest here are Tyrus, Marto, Patrice and Annalla."

The two men he introduced inclined their heads but said nothing. Like all the people there, they were terrified but hardened into action. Both men were of middling years for a human, slightly younger than James. They looked used to laboring, and she trusted they had minds enough for what would be required if Larron approved of them.

Larron continued, "The attack you have been expecting will arrive this evening and likely commence when darkness falls.

Annalla saw them this morning, so I will let her give a full report."

She looked around the table briefly and focused on Hamton. "By my best-estimated count, there are around one hundred eighty gilar marching toward your town. These are trained soldiers, marching in line, and following commands. All of them are well armed, wearing as much armor as gilar ever do over their own scales.

"Two provision carts follow at the end of their line. I saw no humans among them, though I would venture to guess the carts are packed with people. They bring no siege engines with which to batter the walls, but I saw ladders and pots. About a third carried bows, and another twenty with crossbows, so we face a significant number with the ability to attack from range. All bear weapons for melee combat."

"Do you have any estimates on how they will attack?"

"Strike for the gate as a few small teams test the perimeter." Annalla shrugged. "The gate is the weakest point. We cannot concentrate our forces there without opening access points elsewhere. That allows them to remain grouped, limiting how spread-out and thinned their own forces become, while we are forced to do the opposite."

"I agree," said Tyrus. "They will strike at the gate and hound us elsewhere randomly, likely starting fires and using the ladders, to draw our attention away from the main force."

"Other possibilities?"

"Siege?" asked Trey.

"Possible, but unlikely. They did not bring enough provisions. I do not think this town is significant enough for them to set up a supply route," replied Marto.

"Coordinated multi-point attack," Patrice offered.

"It sacrifices their ability to overwhelm one point, like the gate. They would have more ground to cover from the lower position, and it would spread their ranged cover. The approach has merit if they use a strike and retreat method to get us starting at shadows and not knowing which attack is real," added Annalla.

"Burn us down," came Nurtik's blunt offer.

Collin was the first to respond to that, shaking his head. "The majority of the wood we use is treated against fire. It is a substance we traded for with the people from the Carsanje wetland because we build primarily with wood and did not want a fire to take the town. Unfortunately, we had little extra to treat the reinforcements of the last weeks."

"They might not know of it and could consider it an option. Do you think they have enough tar to attempt it, Annalla?"

"Not that I saw, but it's something to watch for based on the pots. The amount would not be enough to successfully burn the town if the treatment works as you say. Another possibility is that there are additional reinforcements on the way. This group might be to track the runners and keep us here until another larger force arrives. However, I believe it can be eliminated by the same reasoning as the siege. This town is not significant enough for so many resources."

Larron made a face. "They are unlikely to send two separate groups scouting. This is most likely the response to the exploratory group from before."

"How is it you saw them, with so much detail, that far away?" Hamton asked her.

"Elven sight."

"Hmm, I was not aware elves could see through hills."

Her smile was all teeth. "Only the females."

"They are coming." Larron cut off their verbal sparring. "That is what matters. I think we are agreed they will likely focus their attack at the gate and use smaller groups to keep our forces spread out to some extent. What are the resources we can bring to bear?"

"Two hundred sixty-nine men and boys from our town," Hamton offered, "and the six of you. We have swords enough for twenty. The rest will need to work with axes and hatchets, and even a few with scythes when we run out. There are enough bows for one hundred forty-six archers, of which about fifty have had no more training than you have been able to give them in the last day. We have to keep in mind which people have experience when we are doing placements."

"Our own fire jars are complete," Marto added. "It's nothing compared to what a chemist could accomplish, but it will burn until consumed completely upon whatever they break. Twelve were created in the time I had earlier. I hope to have twenty or more by the time they reach us. I would suggest they be used on the main force because they can hurt a larger number with one shot, especially if I supplement the damage."

Larron nodded to acknowledge the reports. "Hamton and I drilled some of his captains this morning on what to do in a variety of situations: if they make it into the city through the main gate, breach the walls, start fires, and other surprises they might try. I believe they are more confident now about making decisions in these situations, which will benefit us in damage control. We do not have the numbers to open the gates as a bottleneck and take the fight to them. Instead, we must rely on our archers until the gate is breached. Pikes have been set up in their most likely path."

"We place our men in a gauntlet around the pikes to contain the few making it through fifty-three of us, including the three of us and the four captains you spoke of. The rest are the youngest boys who will be stationed further back as a last resort. Where will you place yourselves?"

Larron started going around the table, "Nurtik will be stationed with the fighters around the pikes. He helped train many of them and will give them some measure of confidence. Marto can best direct and project the fire jars and utilize his own arsenal from atop the wall. He will also provide some protection to the archers, so he will remain with them for the duration. Tyrus and I will start with the archers at the gate. When it is breached, we will head down to join the melee fighting."

"And the ladies?"

"They will be everywhere else." Larron laughed, and their group shared a smile.

"Everywhere?"

"The rest of the walls where there will be only isolated archers to defend them. Annalla is faster than most, has better hearing and sight than anyone else here, and can drive off small groups on her own. Patrice is perfectly equipped to eliminate any threat that infiltrates the city in smaller numbers. We cannot spare a larger force. Hopefully, with Annalla and Patrice patrolling, it will not be necessary."

The men looked skeptical but said nothing.

Annalla's eyes met Larron's, and both knew there was another reason for sending her out on her own. Their mission could not risk them dying in exchange for secrecy. If she had to use her wings or an essential ability, she would not hesitate. The less chance there was of someone witnessing it meant there would be less chance of their enemies finding out.

Larron continued, "We need one of your captains to direct and defend the support from here. It is close enough to the gate, but still central to the rest of the positions. Runners will be available to carry messages and supplies for that person as they deem necessary.

"If it turns out they do not attack the gate with their main force but focus on smaller strikes around the perimeter, I suggest we redeploy half our archers to other positions and have a third of the fighters fall back to the inn. If they breach the walls, it is easier to deploy them from there."

"We will relay the contingency orders at the same time the primary orders are given, so there is no confusion should that event arise," Hamton assured him.

The remainder of the conversation passed with a few questions and exchanges. With the final dismissal, they paused for a moment to look around the table before leaving to complete what preparations they could in the time remaining. There were fires to prepare, people to arm and place, and arrows to fletch.

"Annalla." Larron's call stopped her. He continued when she joined him at the far side of the room with Marto. "If this battle reaches a point where our defeat is certain, the two of you are to leave."

"You want us to abandon you?" Marto asked, clearly confused.

Larron looked at her. "You will grab Marto from the wall, and the two of you will fly north. You will finish our mission."

"If defeat is certain, I will grab Marto and go," she agreed. Annalla was sure her definition of certain would not match his, but there was no point in arguing.

He narrowed his eyes at her, looking like he was preparing to argue.

Marto broke in before he could speak, "I do not like it, but if the two of you agree, then I will concede the point." He shook his head, turning to go. "I have fire pots to make."

Annalla made sure to leave the room with him. Everyone stayed busy to avoid thinking about what would come, or who would still be alive when morning came. It was one of the moments in life where time seemed to be moving at opposing speeds. It dragged on as they waited for the enemy to arrive, but it also sped by so there was not enough to do everything they needed and wanted.

The faces around Annalla were grim. Everything may have been happening well before it was expected, but there was no sense of the unreal among the people. That was as real as anything they'd ever faced, and they knew it might very well be the last thing they ever faced. Terror could have frozen them, but they used it to push them on, to get the last arrow made, the last brace against the wall, the last blade sharpened before their work was tested.

Annalla wanted to be more nervous, more afraid, but she felt herself settling into a calm state. She was afraid—a little fear was healthy, and she *could* die—but she had more options. If she wanted to, she could fly away from the battle. Somehow, the possibility of avoiding it made the battle seem less frightening.

Late in the afternoon, the first call sounded. The gilar had arrived. It was the signal to meet at the wall to survey what they would face. The falling sun hid behind thick clouds, cloaking those assembled below in a growing shadow.

When the news of their arrival spread, there was some level of panic, but the people placed in charge calmed those few and kept everyone on task. Not until the call indicating they were attacking would the final few leave off preparations for defensive positions. The gilar continued toward the city, stopping outside firing range and waiting. They spread out enough they appeared to fill the immediate area. A handful turned to one of the covered carts, and Larron looked toward the nearest captain.

"Turn your men around, Captain. They do not need to see this."

"Sir, we can handle…"

"Do it." He cut him off. "The only purpose watching serves is that of the gilar. Turn your men around."

He gave the order and turned back. "You will watch?"

"These are not our people, our friends dying. It is the gilar I watch."

"Well, I gain no insight by watching, so I will not," Patrice said before turning and sitting with her back to the outer wall.

The screaming started then. Gilar pulled three people from the cart. One tried to run while the other two begged for their lives, but the gilar cared not for pleading. The runner's legs were cut out from under him, and all three were slowly and brutally slaughtered. According to the reports shared with her, Kahnlair's forces discovered early on that doing so in front of an enemy had a devastating effect before the first arrow even flew. The people screamed as they lost limbs. They cried when they watched parts of themselves consumed even as they bled to death, staining the snow red.

Annalla glared at the gilar, fisting her hands at her sides against the urge to fly down and try to kill them all. It would be suicide. Even she was not that talented.

"You see them?" asked Larron, tipping his head.

"Thirty, dropping behind the hill. I will try to pick them up later… Or I could go hunting?" It would ease some of her violent desire to hunt them down.

"No, I want you both patrolling within the walls."

Night crept in, and visibility became more limited with every passing minute. Screams died down to whimpers as the gruesome display lost its spotlight. The gilar lit no fires, so to everyone other than Patrice, Larron, and Annalla, there was no more than a vague outline.

"You see them like the elves do, Lady Patrice?" Annalla heard one of the watchers ask.

"As I understand elven sight, their eyes make distant images appear closer. They see the gilar out there relatively as though they were standing up here with us. The eyes of irimoten use the light available more efficiently. I cannot see the details the elves can, but even to elves, the gilar are wrapped in shadows. For me, dusk is no different than day, and I imagine night is the same for me as dusk for you."

"But you all see them. Yes?"

"We do, but you also see them out there. The difference is only a matter of degree. You will see your targets well enough once they are in range." Patrice assured the man, patting him on the arm. "I should head down. They will come soon."

"If some of them have not already." There was a feral smile on Annalla's face as she turned with Patrice to leave the gate. "We might have some work to do."

"Be careful out there tonight, Annalla," she said when they reached the bottom of the wall. "I know all of us are worried about secrecy for our mission. It is an advantage we do not want to sacrifice, but do not forget you must remain alive for our plan to have the greatest chance of working. Do not take unnecessary risks."

They stopped at the entrance to the inn, and she gave Patrice a hug before they split up. "I fight to survive and to win. I appreciate your words of caution and offer my own. Stay alert, stay armed, and know your escape routes should they breach the town. It would be preferable for us all to be around to continue our mission. Stay safe."

Patrice shared her own feral smile, the fangs making hers more dramatic. "Always."

Annalla laughed as Patrice ran off, and she hurried toward the nearest wall, reaching it when the call that the attack had begun sounded. A roar of gilar and the twanging of bowstrings reached her ears, muffled by the distance and buildings between. Her ears remained open to everything, and she began the first of what could be many jogs along the town walls.

Little enough time passed before she heard the first cry from a direction other than the main battle and turned toward it.

CHAPTER TWENTY-THREE

Larron walked among the archers on his side of the gate, offering advice and encouragement when the second call sounded. He did not need it to tell him they were coming; he could see the charge from his vantage. Gilar swarmed forward, those with shields leading with their archers following only close enough for their fire to reach the top of the walls. By the time they were shooting up, Larron had hit three. He thought only one was a killing shot, but every injury counted.

When they halted their forward progress, he finally gave the order for those standing with him to open fire as well. They did not have the arrows to waste on shots they could not make, and stationary targets were easier to hit. One of the concepts he emphasized was for them to fire carefully, not quickly. He took a few moments between shots to look around and was pleased to see they followed his advice. Few found a mark often, but it was more frequent than he expected against shields and armor.

Two lines of gilar archers formed up to provide cover as the main force moved in. Men fell from the walls or cried out when struck, by arrow or bolt, to crumple where they stood. Larron hoped most could be treated and recover, but some were shot or fell in ways likely fatal.

Gilar charging forward hit the gate with the strength of their numbers, and those closest began hacking at the structure.

Others carried springy ladders and worked to raise them against the walls to either side. Half of the gilar at the wall held up shields to provide cover. It was enough to deflect most of their shots from those in key positions.

Without Marto, they would have presented zero threat at range. A combat mage, as Larron understood, worked with force and energy. Defensively, they could provide a dynamic wall more adaptive and versatile than any permanent construction. Offensively, their attacks often bore similarities to fire or lightning. Combat magai were each assigned to units, and they were all high-value targets for both sides. Often enough, whoever took out the other's mage first won the field. Their power on the battlefield made the loss of the southern academy as much of a strategic loss as it was emotionally devastating.

That night, Marto provided a generic shield above the edge of the wall that dropped when and where an archer reached through it to fire. Larron did not know exactly how, but through Marto's will and power, the wall became interactive. All their own archer's hits had to have been firing when it happened, when the wall before them dropped, so he could imagine many more would be down without the mage aiding them.

When the first ladder stood up against the wall, Marto demonstrated the first of his offensive capabilities. One of their fire jars, infused with his magic, was thrown perfectly to the base of the ladder where gilar converged. Before any could attempt to climb, the area burst into orange-yellow flames.

Nearby gilar became flailing torches in the dark night. Their pain-filled squealing growls pierced the pounding and chopping at the gate and the whistling of arrows through the air. It was some time before the patch of flames died down. Larron counted five gilar falling to the fire, and the ladder warped and cracked from the intense heat. Two more ladders went up in flames before the gilar abandoned the tactic in favor of closing ranks and protecting their flanks, but they also started fighting fire with fire.

While the gilar there might not have any magai with them, the same was not likely true of the main forces to the north. The first jar they flung over the wall broke barely ten feet to Larron's left, and about half the liquid fire came through the mage shield where one man was shooting. It covered him and the man next to him, and their tortured screams filled the air.

Larron moved the moment he saw the fire break through. A nocked arrow was still in his left hand as he drew his sword with the right and cut short their suffering. Silence followed, and shocked looks came from the men around him.

"Were I so far gone, I hope you could do the same for me. Keep shooting."

He retook his position and did exactly what he told them to do. There was hesitation, but the men around him overcame their shock and fear one-by-one to follow his lead. In the short amount of time that took, Marto must have thrown more fire jars into the mass of gilar close to the gate.

The shields deflected some of the fire, but there were more burned gilar bodies littering the ground. Despite the threat, more gilar quickly filled in the gaps to continue the assault on the gate. Marto would need to act to relieve the pressure soon.

The moment he released his next arrow, the dark split by a flash of light, and a group of about twenty gilar near the front flew back. Singed, injured, or dead, the blast from Marto sent their bodies soaring into the lines behind them. Larron quickly took advantage of their exposure as shields were dropped or flung to the side with the impact.

They had to choose how Marto would focus his power. In a drawn-out battle, he could not defend a large, spread-out group and attack continuously with his magic. If he tried, he would quickly lose consciousness like the architect magai back in the Palonian. That was one of the few blasts he could give them while maintaining the shielding. It was why they heavily relied on the fire jars he'd created earlier.

With the gate cleared for a moment, men below quickly brought in additional beams to shore up where it had weakened. The support would not last much longer, but they needed every moment it bought them.

More gilar fire hurled over the walls. Some of it broke harmlessly against the shield to rain down at the base of the wall, but Larron heard the screams every time one made it through. He pushed the implications away and continued firing on the enemy, lessening their numbers as much as he could, adjusting for the rougher arrows brought by runners when he ran low.

How long has it been? he wondered.

Larron needed to take a moment to see how they held across the line. There were not enough trained fighters to have him standing down to assess and give orders, but they could not afford him *not* giving orders either. Larron had to remind himself he was critical to the latter.

Shouldering his bow, he backed up and ran along the wall, assessing as he went. Calling over to Tyrus at the other side of the gate gave him a similar story. The gilar had discovered the weakness in Marto's shield and were waiting to concentrate fire on the men aiming and breaching the shield. They needed to adjust their tactics.

"Pair up!" he shouted over at Tyrus, bobbing his hands up and down opposite each other for emphasis. "Tell them to pair up."

He was grateful the human prince nodded, quickly catching on without him having to explain further. The less they told the gilar, the longer they would be effective. Trusting Tyrus to handle his side, Larron turned to explain things to each captain he passed. Pair up the archers, one to sight, one to shoot. It would not eliminate the risk, but it should decrease the amount of time each stood exposed.

Battle was always oddly quiet to him. Gilar growled. Men cried out when they were hit. Arrows hissed. Bowstrings hummed. Steel clanged against steel. There was even the hacking of axe on wood as they battered against the gate, but he always expected more volume. A louder crack below told him the gate was finally failing under the onslaught. More fire was thrown down, and more gilar died.

How many gilar have we eliminated? he wondered, thinking. *At least fifty.*

Even if they had greater numbers when the gilar broke through, the gilar were more skilled and better armed. He had hoped for more. They were losing too many because of how quickly the gilar adapted, and that placed Marto at risk. Larron would not fool himself into thinking they reduced the number enough to ensure victory, but it was better than it had been. It was as much as he could ask, and he would help hold the line.

The cracking and groaning grew louder and more frequent until even the walls shuddered with the pressure against the gate. There was a loud crash when the wood buckled inward. Larron put away his bow and turned from the wall to swing down and join the defenders below.

A number of bodies already littered the ground behind the gates; bowmen who had fallen backward when struck or charred corpses of victims of the fire thrown by the gilar. Larron took the briefest of moments to wonder at how little the wooden structures suffered from the fires. Whatever the substance they treated the buildings with performed beyond his expectations.

The moment ended, and his feet touched down amid the smoldering tar and broken arrow fragments. A few women and young boys scampered around, keeping the fires contained, but most defenders in the area held positions against the gilar surging forward through the gates.

Larron pushed toward the front in time to see the gilar leading the charge impaled on the braced spikes waiting for them, unable to stop and hold against the force of their fellows pressing in from behind. Spikes broke under the weight or became completely sheathed in bodies. There were not enough traps to hold back the full tide of attackers. The melee began.

There were two openings, one on either side of the defensive spikes, where gilar could pass through with relative ease. Both were small enough that they could—at least marginally—stem the flow of attackers entering the town. Nurtik covered the opening opposite Larron, and Tyrus would soon be dropping down for support.

That side was his, and he had to reach the gap before too

many men died and too many gilar made it through. Too late and he would be surrounded, and of little use in slowing their advance. There was limited enough time before the gilar identified the biggest threats and prioritized their elimination. He needed to keep his attackers in front of him as much as possible.

Larron pushed through the crowd with his sword in hand. He took the head of one gilar, pushing against two men barely holding their own. They were injured, but still alive and standing, so he continued without a second glance. Two more gilar were taken down on his way to the front line. After that, he lost count of those he faced.

His sword flew from one point to the next with an almost unnatural awareness. Sharp pain on his arm told him he let one under his guard, but the smaller injury had been necessary to avoid losing his head. He shook it off, shook blood out of his eyes, and dove into the next confrontation. The minor pain evaporated into the background as the fight continued, and he felt his muscles straining.

Have we been at this for more than an hour? The strain said as much, but fighting the gilar, with their greater strength, took more effort.

There was an ebb and flow to the battle. The gilar pushed forward, seeking weaknesses, then drew back to try another course when they failed to penetrate the line. Each time they withdrew, Larron tried to regain some of the ground they lost in the previous thrust.

Still, they were being overrun. Even though only a limited number could make it through at a time, three men fell for every gilar eliminated. That did not count the injuries and fatigue affecting the men in the town more quickly than the gilar. Too many were winning through. With every moment passing, they put Larron more on the defensive.

The next advance was well coordinated. The gilar managed to establish a firm line inside the gap beside the gates and used the protection it provided to build up forces behind the walls. A group thrust forward from behind, even as it looked to be another withdrawal by the gilar front line. Two were sacrificed to Larron's sword, but the men around him were cut down, and gilar surrounded him.

All his focus and effort were suddenly needed to simply stay alive. Whenever he managed to land a fatal strike, another gilar sprang forward to take its place. Step after step, he worked backward in a steady retreat to avoid becoming too separated from the rest of the men.

That surge broke their line. Gilar forces had a foothold and allowed the inexperienced farmers to bring the attack to them, killing them as they came. Larron did not have breath to spare to call for them to pull back and form up a new line. It was all he could do to keep from being sucked into the maw. There were others trapped beyond him with no path of escape for whom he could do nothing.

An unexpected call of retreat from further in town nearly made him lose concentration. Larron swore under his breath at whatever idiot was about to start a rout. A gilar on his left took advantage of the distraction and lunged for his side. He curled out of the way and used his attacker's momentum and weapon against it, pushing it across and impaling the gilar at his other side. A brief opening remained in their wake. Larron earned a cut along his ribs from the move, but took the escape.

If his forces did not hold the entrance, all would be lost. They would be hunted down within the confines of their streets and buildings. He was furious at the retreat order—they should be regrouping, not retreating—but he could not stand against the gilar alone. Too many on the lines wanted to retreat, but they did not have the training or discipline to do so in an orderly fashion. Half the men around him turned and ran, while the other half followed his example and slowly gave ground.

If they made the building line, and if some of those fleeing returned, he might be able to reform a coordinated defense once more.

CHAPTER TWENTY-FOUR

Annalla found the wall guards under attack in the northwest section of town. It was one of the locations she had passed earlier with James, near one of the closer 'rises' in the landscape which the gilar could use to move in further without detection, but not the closest location.

There were only two men at that post—probably why the gilar chose it as an initial attack point—and only one place from which to shoot along the straight edge of the wall. Gilar had already shot down one of the men; the arrow-pierced body dangled over the ground. His clothing had caught on one of the wall bracers halting his fall mid-way down. Blood dripped from his collar and down his cheek, sticking in his hair. The dead eyes stared at her, the only observer of her quick and silent approach.

Crude wooden steps were built against the interior side of the wall periodically. Originally for the night watch, they served as a means for the guards to reach their posts. None of the stairs were constructed with railings, leaving only a rope and hope to keep children from climbing and falling. Annalla made for the stairs.

A ladder knocked against the wall. Gilar climbed it to breach the city even as she started up the steps on this side. She reached the top as the second gilar topped the ladder. The lone archer cowered, backed into a corner, scrambling away from an attacker descending on him with arms raised, ready to strike.

Elven steel swept up, gutting the gilar before its strike could fall. Annalla swept around to take the head of the second as the first hit the ground. Its parts fell back over where the ladder stood. She heard the body collide with something on the way down and two larger thuds hit the ground shortly after.

"Try to take out their archer!" she yelled at her only backup and jumped over the side to slide down the ladder, her boots and gloved palms squeezing the outside of the posts to slow her descent.

There were only three gilar left, including both the archer and the one regaining his feet after falling next to the headless corpse. Annalla let go for a controlled fall in that direction for the last handful of feet. Her sword ran the rising gilar through, the downward momentum adding force to her stab. An arrow whisked by her as she kicked the body off her blade, the coarse feathers cutting a line in her cheek.

Her only option was to position herself with the remaining gilar between her and the archer. Had it been Larron or one of her other elven friends on the wall, Annalla would have ignored the archer and taken the last fighter down quickly. With an unknown human with potentially zero combat experience backing her, she had to use more caution.

The gilar tried to dance around, either to give its backup a clear shot or bring it within range for a strike. Annalla swayed with its movements and parried its blows until the man on the wall managed to land a shot on the other gilar. She heard the hit and the grunt of pain.

Hoping her opponent had not heard the same, she gave an opening, and the gilar obliged. Her wing shifted up to deflect the blow like a shield, and she ducked under its reach and arm spine, bringing her sword up and into its chest in the process. It snarled at her, making feeble attempts to bite her in retaliation as the last breath left its body.

A quick glance showed her the last gilar was still alive, and there was no longer a body between them. It had a crossbow, probably the only reason it missed her with the last shot. Such skill with that weapon was impressive enough to raise her level of concern. Annalla could not count on another miss.

She charged as the gilar pulled the human's arrow from its shoulder and reloaded, not at all slowed by the wound. The crossbow rose, and the gilar pulled the trigger. She brought her sword up, but the bolt punched her in the chest. It swerved to the side off of the armor of her wings. Without pausing, she reversed the movement of her blade to drive it back into the neck of the surprised gilar. Its gurgling ended, and she froze to look and listen for others in the area. From the wall, the man called to her, asking if she was hurt, but there were no other sounds or movements she could sense.

Annalla touched her chest where the bolt had struck directly over her heart and rotated her left arm. It hurt. It hurt to breathe, but the pain was nothing she could not manage. However, it would be best to avoid another hit to that spot if possible. She turned and headed back to the ladder, only to find the archer starting down.

Who does he think is going to stay on lookout? She shook her head.

"Go back up, stay on alert. There are more out there, just not around here right now." He glanced over his shoulder, nodded, and reversed direction. Annalla scrambled up after him, and he waited there to give her a hand over.

"That was amazing… Insane."

"Thank you for your assistance as well. Help me pull this ladder up." They strained against it, but it was too heavy for just the two of them to lift over the wall. There was no leverage at the angle they had to work with, and her chest protested the effort. Annalla caught the sound of one of the town's messengers making rounds and called out.

"Runner! I have a message for you. Runner!" she called out toward the dark streets.

The little girl—she was so young—stopped abruptly and perked her head up, listening for the origin of the summons. Annalla called out again.

She sprinted over. "Lady?"

"We cannot leave this ladder here. Tell your coordinator it would take the strength of five men to lift it, and that an archer is missing from this post."

"Yes, Lady," she said. And the little girl of no more than eight ran off as instructed.

Had she ever been that young? Annalla did not think so. She was born with a blade in her hand and lives on the line. That little girl was learning some of what that meant.

Annalla turned back to the archer. "I have to keep moving. Keep on watch for more gilar. If you see them before the others get here, push the ladder away from the wall. More people will be here soon, but they will not live long if any gilar make it up the wall before they arrive. Even before firing at them, get that ladder away from the wall. When others get here to help, do not help them; stay on watch and protect their backs."

"You're leaving?" The tremor in his voice was a result of fear.

"You're doing great. I might not have survived down there without your help. You already hit one, the next will be easier. Remember what we told you."

"You saved my life." His face begged her not to leave.

She hardened herself against it. "I did what was needed, and the same may be needed elsewhere. Do you have everything under control here?"

He shook, but did not look away. Tears threatened, but did not fall. He swallowed, nodded. "Yes, I know what to do."

"Good. James will be proud of you."

She left him, terrified and alone, but determined to do his job, and she continued around the perimeter. The sounds of pounding at the gate had started a while before, but it was eerily quiet elsewhere. There were people in watch posts she passed, but they looked out and did not see her below. A few more times, she had to go up the wall. She took out her bow twice and only used it once.

Most of the attacks she saw, either in progress or in the

aftermath, were hit and retreat strikes. No other ladders were brought since the first. They shot from different directions, taking out defenders along the way. From reports she received, only two gilar had been hit. A groin shot—torso shot where the aim was a little low—by one of the men finding a target, and a neck shot by her hand.

She had been aiming for the eyes, as their chests were all well protected, but it moved at the last moment. That one would probably die soon, but it was still on its feet when they disappeared over a rise. The other injured gilar was only in trouble if the arrow found a main artery. Otherwise, it would be back in the fight.

Where that fight might be, she did not know. Of the thirty she and Larron saw sneaking off from the main force, at least six, maybe seven, were dead or dying. The rest were like ghosts. One moment they would attack, and the next they were gone. There was no pattern to their strikes that she could see, but their objective had to be to eventually get into town to take the defenders from behind. There were other ladders out there, and she needed to find them.

A distant cracking and groaning told her the gate was failing. The gilar were taking their time. *They are probably surprised we have been able to eliminate as many as we have already.* Those were farmers who ran before a slaughter, not seasoned fighters. Still, they had not let their estimation of their opposition skew their planning. She kept running but could not mistake the sound of the gate failing and the clash of steel to follow. They were in, and more men were dying.

It was not long before she had her own problems to deal with as screams arose much closer to her than the gate. There was the second ladder she sought. The gilar were unmistakable silhouettes atop the wall with no men to be seen. She guessed the archers posted were dead, and it had been their screams she heard.

Her bow was in hand, so she had only to grab an arrow to be ready to fire. Two gilar descended the stairs into town. Annalla let her arrow fly, nocking, and firing a second in quick succession, thankful for her elven sight in the darkness. Their archer fell first from atop the wall, and she continued taking them out one by one. They had little time to react, and she was unlikely to miss at that distance. One managed to pick up a fallen bow and take cover on the wall.

The defenses put up to protect the town worked against her then, though they were less effective in that direction. The gilar was clearly an experienced archer. It released an arrow at her before she could take aim, and only her ducking behind a water barrel kept it from finding its mark. Annalla found herself pinned down in the middle of an open road, cursing her arrogance at thinking she could take them all before they recovered from the surprise.

A brief, patterned horn call went out from its position. It called to other gilar, letting them know a ladder was secure. More would come, archers among them. Annalla needed to make it to the wall before that happened. It would aim for her chest like the last one. That was the largest target, and it probably thought her a soft human.

I hope, she thought, also hoping Larron never found out she did what she was about to attempt.

Annalla puffed out her wing over her sides, putting space between it and her body to hopefully absorb some of the blow if she *was* hit again. The bulk would make her movement slightly awkward.

Taking a steadying breath, she dove to her left, rolling, and came up running toward an empty building. Even as she jumped for the open doorway, she felt a punch to her ribs. It was enough to knock her balance off and end the final jump in a sprawling tumble.

Nothing broken...probably.

She would have a second glorious bruise, but she was alive and hidden. Surprise was on her side again. The archer would be watching the approaches to the steps up the wall, but she would not be using the stairs. Rather than maneuvering to another building, she slipped out the back window and down a parallel road toward the wall.

Her wings got her to the top of the wall, and she crept silently along it. Annalla brought a hunting knife to her hand and snuck up, low to the ground, behind the gilar. She would rather have stuck with her sword instead of the knife, but she was afraid of leaving too much of a target for any potential archers on the ground.

The first stab into its neck was fatal, but it thrust back with the spike on its forearm in reaction. That blow would have taken her out had her wings not saved her life yet again, but the hit landed right on her new bruise from the arrow and knocked the wind out of her.

Ignoring the lack of breath, she grabbed the gilar tighter and yanked back, slicing into its spine. Blood sprayed, and the body dropped to the ground, taking her with it. Annalla wheezed for a moment, trying to stretch out and breathe deeply. Wincing, she rolled to a crouch and risked a quick look over the wall.

Their friends had arrived, and ten gilar approached quickly across the open ground. Annalla spotted the ones with bows, sighting on them first. They would reach the ladder before she could shoot them all, but maybe she could avoid being picked off from below while she fought on the wall above. Her ribs protested each draw of the bow, but she steadied her breathing and fired as quickly as she could manage.

Half went down, mostly injured rather than dead, before the first gilar made it up the ladder. She dropped her bow to bring her sword up in time to block a blow to her head. That part was made easier by the width of the ladder. It only allowed one gilar up at a time. As each emerged over the ladder, the one preceding it went down to her blade.

When the last fell, Annalla breathed a sigh of relief and flopped down for a moment against the wall. Some of the injured below slunk away into the night, but she hoped the injuries proved significant enough to keep them out of future engagements.

The enemy there had been taken care of, but no one was left on watch, and she could not remain. Already, she could hear another post under attack. Annalla looked up to her left at the top poles of the ladder still standing against the wall. It could not be left there undefended.

With another sigh, she stood up and looked it over, then looked around. She unfurled her wings, gripped the top of the ladder, and flew out away from the wall. Dropping it to the ground, Annalla quickly followed it down and pinned it there with vines and brush, called at a wave of her hand. It would serve well enough for a time.

She collected unbroken arrows as she checked on the gilar on the ground, finishing three that were still alive and in the area. Then she flew back up and collected arrows on the inside. Annalla lifted off again to rush toward the shouting, risking continued use of her wings in exchange for speed.

When she arrived, she found her rush unnecessary that time. Both archers still lived. Not only were they alive, but they had killed one of the gilar and were driving away the others. The two men worked well together, calling out shots and communicating tactics. They told all the archers to do exactly that, but those had two obviously practiced. Only a quick glance was spared by either to identify the person joining them before they were back at their task.

"Situation?" she asked them.

"Three are still alive," the elder of the two said, "but they are backing off and we can't identify clear targets anymore."

"Direction?"

"It looks like they are headed north, but we can't be certain," the second answered. He had the same dark brown hair and tanned skin as the first. Similar features between the two had her wondering if they were brothers.

Still within range, she noted the gilars' positions, but not within human sight in the darkness. Her bow was in hand as she stood tall and sighted north. The three gilar had stopped their evasive swerving when the two men stopped firing. Annalla released, and the one at the back fell as she sighted on the second. When she let fly again, a small voice started shouting up at her from the town below, but she ignored it for the moment longer it took to aim and fire.

"You need something?" she called down.

"You are needed!" came the excited response from another child runner. "Mister Gredall asked me to find you and tell you they are losing at the gate. Too many are making it through!"

"Understood. Let the coordinator know the post two positions west of north is unmanned, but the threat there has been taken care of temporarily." The little girl nodded and ran off again, and Annalla turned to the two archers. "Good work here. I need to head for the gate, so make sure to keep an eye on your backs as well in case they make it through another point."

"Yes, ma'am. Are the three that ran off dead?"

"Injured one. I think the second shot went wide." They nodded and resumed their positions.

As Annalla ran, she wondered if the rest of her small party knew about Larron's orders to her to grab Marto and leave. Her heart fell at the thought of leaving them there to die. She would do so if necessary. Larron was mistaken, however, if he thought she would just pick up and go without the situation being hopeless unless no other option remained according to her own assessment.

If they were at the point of calling her, it was best to get there fast and not worry about her wings being seen. Annalla flew through the streets and over buildings, heading straight for the gate. It was a mess, with men on the ground, dead or dying, amid a growing swarm of gilar. They got past too quickly for the line to hold, and no one formed a second after the first broke.

She could make out Marto on the wall and hear the grunting efforts of Nurtik somewhere among the fighting horde swelling the street. The only positive was the men still alive seemed to be falling back before the gilar instead of fleeing. It put them at the edge of the battlefield and kept it relatively contained so far. Unfortunately, her blade would not make enough of a difference. She shifted to take flight to grab Marto, but froze at an insane notion before her wings opened.

"RETREAT! To the buildings, retreat!" she yelled and ran forward with her sword in hand to help free some of the men enough to follow her command. Continuously she called for a retreat, and the call was quickly taken up by those around her and spread through the survivors.

When she thought enough time passed, when as many were clear as safely possible, she worked her way to the top of the street and climbed onto an overturned water barrel to see. There were still some townsmen trapped in the middle, but she could not help or wait until the gilar expanded too far into the spaces opening around them.

Jumping down to kneel on the ground, Annalla thrust out both fists, using the physical movement to mentally push at the earth around her. She kept it simple. Short, spiky trees erupted from the ground at an angle, mirroring the spikes set earlier in the day.

Through the elemental connection, she felt the impact when bodies were impaled, but she needed more. Annalla stretched her fingers, grasping forward. The motions followed images she formed in her head and the vines twisting and clinging to everything they touched. She clenched her fists and drew back her arms. The ivy tightened down at her command, strangling and pinning gilar where they stood trapped and cocooned.

Unlike the emergence, that time the massive use of power left her feeling light and heady. Annalla felt like she had been holding a heavy burden and finally released it. She became drunk on the relief, and her gaze drifted across the street as her awareness re-centered. A vague realization she had not gotten all the gilar in her attack floated just beneath the surface. The part of her mind remaining self-aware wrenched at the part drifting in essence, shouting about immediate threats.

Men ran down small groups or individual gilar, and still, the monsters fought and dealt death until their last breath. One broke free on an attack and ran toward her, already too close. It knew, or sensed, or maybe it just wanted an easy target. The blade was in motion before she initiated a futile attempt to dodge. Her reactions remained slower than usual. Her second mistake in as many hours would cost her life. She should not have lost herself in her power. It was not necessary, but she lacked experience on a larger scale.

An arrow erupted from its neck, spraying her face with blood. The strike was diverted, and the blade fell to her side, slicing her thigh on the way down. Around her, men rushed back into the fight to finish gilar running or struggling against the vines. The injured moaned in pain. People shouted cries of relief. Fires flickered here and there, but it was the beginning of the end.

CHAPTER TWENTY-FIVE

The fighting ended. Moans of pain echoed in the night, but the ground settled and the clash of steel faded. Hours had passed, and torches burned against the dark of night.

"What were you thinking? You were nearly killed!" Larron's voice was not raised, but she could feel the fury, and the worry, as he strode to her side.

Larron's green eyes flashed with frustration and his posture radiated stress. Smooth tan skin pulled taut over cheekbones sharpened by gritting his teeth. The elegant side braids pulling back into one tight fighting braid at his back were only slightly disheveled, despite the right side being caked with blood.

Breathtaking, she thought as she watched him approach.

"You were told to take Marto and go," he continued his tirade, "not to expose your abilities and risk your life. Your life means too much." He paused. "Too much to the mission to risk in an attempt like this."

His pause, the momentary slip, brought her fully back to herself. While he was correct about her having made a mistake, it was not her decision to act. Annalla would not allow him to believe otherwise.

"If you think," she said calmly, "for one second, I would pass over an opportunity with a suitable chance of success to save what I can of this town in exchange for limiting the risk to my own life, then you are mistaken. Yes, if there had been nothing I could have done, I would have left with Marto as instructed. I saw an option we hadn't discussed, and I needed to act quickly."

"It was an option that left you completely unaware of your surroundings and vulnerable to an attack you would have otherwise avoided... Annalla, if I had not shot it..." his thought trailed off into silence.

"The mission would have been seriously harmed," she finished for him and pursed her lips.

Larron shook his head and looked disappointed in her like she was being intentionally obtuse. He was not wrong, but being valued by others remained relatively new to her and somewhat embarrassing.

She sighed and softened her defensive posture. "I have never consciously used my power on such a grand scale and was pulled further into the effects than I expected. It can be avoided in the future now that I know what happens when I expand my influence, and how far I can go. Thanks for saving my life, again."

He snorted a breath in a sound she would describe as a frustrated sigh. "Many were saved today. I would ask you to never do something like that again, but I know it would be a pointless request. I cannot deny I am grateful for your intervention."

"Annalla! Larron!" Tyrus called as he limped toward them, aided by Nurtik.

He had a large gash in his right leg and a variety of other cuts and bruises beneath a covering film of blood and dirt. Pain and exhaustion clouded his eyes, mirrored in the eyes of Nurtik and Larron both. She may have been running about town, but they had fought for their lives since the gate had been breached.

Nurtik looked just as battered as Tyrus. The worst of his injuries was where his chainmail had been bent and driven into his shoulder by what must have been a fierce strike. She also took the time to really look at Larron. He walked and moved without difficulty, but appeared to be stiffening with the adrenaline, anger, and fear leaving him.

Out of the three, Larron looked the least battered. In fact, his injuries could have come from nothing worse than a vigorous bout of sparring. With others, she might have thought they stayed out of the fighting, but Larron would have placed himself in the middle of it all.

"So much for secrecy," Tyrus commented. "That was impressive."

His words brought her attention to the humans circling them, having been diligently staying out of their argument, but likely listening to every word and watching Larron's concern and anger. She fought against an embarrassed blush and focused on the human prince.

"Yeah, it could have gone better. If I keep my head, none of them escape."

"Ya' loss control?" Nurtik asked.

"Not of my power, but I lost focus." She knew she could do more with her abilities, but she needed to stay locked more to her body rather than retreating—extending? —into the elements. "I should be able to remain aware of my surroundings, but I got lost in the essential connection. I need to practice manipulating the element rather than just letting it move through me."

"It will be kept as a last resort for now." Larron visually scanned her, his eyes snagging on the cut on her leg. "Annalla, how bad are your injuries?"

She poked around the leg wound and tested her movement, assessing the level of pain and restriction. "I should wrap it, but we can treat it later."

Larron nodded. "Very well. Help with the search for any remaining gilar within the walls. I will work with Hamton to start organizing the surviving men and then join you. Tyrus, Nurtik, I want the two of you to go to the healing area Patrice established earlier today. No arguments, we have a long way to travel and your injuries need tending."

They had saved what people they could, but still, they wanted to do more, even as injured and bleeding as they were. Only their training and mission allowed the two soldiers to follow Larron's orders and head for the inn, leaning into each other as they went.

"You should have Marto follow them," she told Larron as she watched them walk away. "He looked near ready to fall over when I caught a glimpse of him earlier and is probably running dry."

"What about the rest of your injuries?" he asked. "The ones you did not call attention to."

"Bruises, nothing broken that I can tell, and I had less fighting than any of you."

"More running," he countered

She shrugged, feeling every bruise as she did. "Eh. Some of it was flying."

Larron stepped closer and took her hand. He studied her face and spoke softly. "You will allow me to check your injuries later?"

Annalla wanted to reach up, touch his face, slide her arm around his neck and bring him in for a hug, but her face burned, knowing they had an audience. She swallowed and tried for a cheeky smile. "As if you would allow otherwise."

"Go on then," he said, shaking his head and breaking eye contact.

She shivered at the loss, but settled for squeezing his hand, and turned to march deeper into town.

***

The full length of the battle took no more than three hours from the first the gilar approach, attacking the gates until Annalla ended it and the gilar outside the walls fled. Larron found Marto looking as exhausted as Annalla said and sent him directly to find a bed. He and Hamton then saw to the coordination of the clean-up.

Instead of helping clear the town after, he went to where the wounded were being treated. Patrice came in sometime later, presumably after she cleared her section of town.

He and Patrice labored there through the night, and he suspected Annalla took over with Hamton, as he saw neither again.

When the sun emerged the following morning, it found them still working to pick up the pieces left behind. They continued treating the wounded, despite their exhausted state, until a townswoman ushered the two of them into the inn.

"Have you two slept at all since the fighting?" Marto asked. His tone said he was already fully aware of the answer as Larron blearily blinked his eyes to see Marto, Nurtik, and Tyrus sitting at a table with simple food laid out.

"We were not seriously injured nor as drained as the rest of you." His tone belied the words.

It was a long night, and his clothing remained covered in blood. He absently thought about needing to clean and dry that set of gear before they left the town. His hands and hair... Everything felt grimy despite having quickly washed up before being pushed out the door of the medic room.

"I suggest we move on from here tomorrow morning rather than today," Patrice said. "All of us need time, and a day of inactivity would help the injured recover more quickly." She did not try to hide her exhaustion as she plopped down on a seat and started picking at food.

Larron held himself to more restrained movement as he sat beside her. "How serious are your injuries?"

"My leg will not keep me from riding, though in a fight it could be a hindrance."

"If we need ta' fight, my injury'll not bother me," Nurtik boasted, straightening in his seat.

"Then we will pack today and leave at first light. I will speak with Hamton to see what he can offer to add to our supplies."

"Hmm." Tyrus gave him a look akin to the one he saw often on Annalla's face. "I think Nurtik and I will talk to Hamton while you rest."

The dwarf nodded his support of the plan, and Larron was not going to argue. "Deal."

Behind him, the door opened again. Annalla walked in, pulled forward by a boy gripping one of her hands in both of his above his head as though pulling on the lead of a stubborn horse. Larron smiled at the sight and laughed silently, too exhausted to make much sound. His own exhaustion must have been catching up with him, as the image struck him as much more amusing than it should. He could not stop the huffing laughter, struggling to catch his breath.

"Here you are, ma'am. A meal and rest, as Hamton ordered. I'll see you later!"

She looked around at them, they looked at each other and back to her. "So...that was Cory."

That set all five of them off, and there were tears in Larron's eyes when he tried to get control. Tyrus met his eyes, also struggling for breath. His nostrils flared and lips pursed against a smile, and it set them rolling again. They were alive. They were safe, and people like Cory lived because of them.

Annalla cleared her throat. "Cory was one of my students. Hamton sent him to fetch me, thinking I might be less likely to argue with a child."

"Looks like he was right." Tyrus bumped her shoulder, his smile lingering.

"Eh, I was hungry."

"Riiight," Patrice murmured to another light round of chuckling.

"Are we still leaving today? I can't say I'm up for much scouting. My burning eyes tell me I need sleep, or they might not see any dangers."

Larron shook his head. "Tomorrow morning. These three are going to arrange things while you, Patrice, and I rest."

Annalla nodded and yawned. "Good. Hamton wants to talk to us later about fleeing to the Palonian. Most of their stores were kept safe, so they want to clear the gates and leave, but there are still gilar out there and the bandits around the Woodland."

"Maybe he can dine with us tonight. There are considerations either way, but I do not think they can hold here any longer."

"We'll help where we can today," Marto promised.

Larron felt himself drifting. The rest of the meal and conversation became blurry. Somehow, he managed to fall down on a cot before plunging into sleep. He thought his friends did as well, but it was a distant thought.

Some daylight lingered when he returned to consciousness. He felt horrendously disgusting and knew he was about to shock and appall yet another human village, as he did frequently during his travels. Though, with the war holding him in the Derou, it had been decades since he last tested humans' prudish sensibilities. If they were on the river, he would have cleaned up there because there were no public bathing houses to be found. There, he would seek another alternative.

"Excuse me. Do you have a bathing or washtub you could spare?" he politely asked a passing woman.

"You wish us to draw you a bath, My Lord?"

While he might enjoy it more, heating enough water would take hours. "No, thank you. The tub will be sufficient."

She found a large wooden basin, and Larron dragged it out to the wash area near the well. The open space stood between two buildings, with thin rope strung between them just above his head. While a few articles of rougher cloth hung to dry, most of the laundry would be set to dry in front of fires indoors during that time of year.

He gathered a couple of spare buckets strewn about the area and started drawing water, filling those two and the draw bucket before stripping down to his underclothes to sputters and giggles from passing humans. Larron did not care. The leather items were set to the side for separate scrubbing, while his clothing went into the basin.

He grabbed the first bucket and stepped into the basin on top of his clothes before dumping the bucket of freezing-cold water over his head. Larron sucked in a breath from the chilling shock and felt his teeth start chattering. Without hesitating, he grabbed the next bucket and dumped that one over his head as well.

Larron grit his teeth against his continued shivering and

used a spare bit of cloth to scrub at his exposed skin and hair. He would remove most of the grime before getting out to fetch the third bucket at the well. Another two or three buckets would rinse him off well enough to feel somewhat normal.

"Want some help?"

He turned to see Annalla struggling not to laugh at his shivering and knew she had not yet realized other implications for her question. He did.

Larron raised an eyebrow and gave her a wicked grin. "You want to help me bathe?"

His meaning sank in with all the heated implications he could pack into one innocent question. Her smile dimmed as her blush grew. Larron watched as her breathing sped and she swallowed, sending darting glances around and stepping forward.

Her voice was rough and quiet, but her words were direct. "I meant my water ability. They know I have power, so I can use it, right?"

"There are reasons not to, but they are minor in comparison to knowing you are an essential at all. I struggle to find a compelling reason at the moment. This water is very cold."

Annalla laughed. "Spread your arms and legs a little, hold your breath, and close your eyes."

Larron did as ordered and felt water swirl around him, pulling his clothing and twisting it on him as it passed. It was still freezing, but after about thirty seconds the water splashed to his feet in the bucket.

"Can you pull the water out of the cloth, too?"

She gave him a playful grin. "I'd probably pull the pants with it."

It was Larron's turn to flick glances at their audience. "Hmm. Best to not then."

"Go get dry and change. I'll finish your clothes here and we can hang them by the fire."

He made his way inside to his room. The gasps and tittering giggles followed in his wake, and he heard Tyrus comment on elves having no sense of propriety to someone he passed along the way. None of it mattered once he changed. He was clean, dry, and warming by the moment. When Larron returned to the large fire with his wet undergarments in hand, Annalla entered, carrying two stacked baskets, likely with his other clothing items.

"Are all elves so...brazen?" Hamton asked with tentative humor as they hung his clothing before the fire. His attempt at a joke held the awkwardness of someone trying to make friends across very different cultural lines. He wanted to smile and laugh with a comrade in arms, but remained hesitant of offending one of the town's saviors.

"Only travelers have a need." Larron glanced at him, offering a small smile and a shrug. "I always say it would not be necessary if humans built proper bathing houses."

Hampton's shoulders eased at his lighthearted response, and he said, "I doubt the women would support bathing houses *now*."

Annalla snorted, but offered no comment.

Hamton sighed and shook his head, shifting topics. "We have decided to leave for the Palonian," he announced. "We plan to set out in three days. I am grateful you have agreed to speak to us tonight about your thoughts and advice for the journey. Lord Tyrus and I have also spoken today about your needs, and we are adding provisions to your supplies." He drew himself up proudly. "I wanted to ask what else you might have of us before you leave."

"Thank you for whatever provision you can offer. The only other request I have is that you ask your people to remain silent about what took place here except to King Oromaer of the Palonian. We have a task to accomplish, and the less known of us, the greater our chance of success. I know you cannot control everyone, and I have no power to stop stories from spreading, but I would be remiss in my duties if I did not ask you to try."

"I will ask for their silence and will work to enforce it as much as possible," he promised. "As to the supplies, they will be brought to you as you are packing today and tomorrow morning. What we can spare, we will offer. It is truly the least we can do."

Larron stood there for a moment, watching him walk away. The people there could not ask for better in their leader.

"One of the stable boys said he knows how to work with leather," Annalla broke into his musings. "He offered to clean our armor today while I was finishing up out there."

"That will help. I wanted to return to the injured today. I want to see if I can help more and—now I know they are leaving soon—prepare some of them for traveling injured."

"I'm helping them pack while I stow our gear as well. They are going to slaughter and prepare most of their remaining herds today, keeping only a core few to intermingle with new livestock later if possible, so they are giving us all the prepared meat."

"Smart. They will not want people going off alone seeking missing livestock."

"He knows," Annalla pointed her chin to where Hamton had left. "that they will likely be attacked on the road. Hopefully, they will be vigilant enough to fight them off without too many dying. Their trained archers are going to be the most important people in the group."

Larron nodded. The humans stood the best chance of surviving their exodus if they could injure or kill from range. "We will include that information when we speak to them tonight."

They hung the last of his clothes. Annalla stood on her toes, scanning the room on the other side of his laundry, making him nervous with her behavior. When she started biting her lip, he looked at her sideways and was close to asking what was wrong. Before he decided to speak, she walked determinedly over, wrapped her arms around his waist, laid her head on his shoulder, and took a deep breath as she hugged him.

"I'm glad you survived too," she said quietly, squeezed gently once, then stepped back and gave him a small smile. "I'll see you at dinner."

Larron held onto one of her hands and gave her a pointed look. He saw the confusion leave as understanding set in, and she rolled her eyes at him and reached for the bottom of her shirt.

Annalla's wings slid to the side as she lifted the shirt to show the wrapped bandage beneath. A bruise already colored her ribcage, peeking out over the top above her heart and coloring down the left side below. He could only imagine what it looked like dead-center.

"Patrice dealt with the cut on my leg and wrapped my ribs and shoulder earlier today. This is just a bruise as far as we can tell."

"As far as you can tell?"

Annalla shrugged. "There might be a cracked rib," she said. "Patrice said it can be difficult to tell, and there is nothing any of us can do if it is. It is wrapped up tight enough that you can wait to inspect it until I'm changing again."

He palpated around the injuries, asking for reactions, and felt satisfied with Patrice's diagnosis and treatments.

"How much will this impact your flying?"

Annalla grimaced. "It is not going to be fun, but I think as long as I keep the swelling down, it should not be a hindrance."

"Very well," he conceded. "I will see you at dinner."

With a lighter heart, Larron set about his tasks for the remainder of the day. He would help where he could, and in the morning, they would leave.

CHAPTER TWENTY-SIX

They were up and dressed to travel before the sun rose. When they reached the horses, it seemed even the animals were ready to get out and move again. They packed and saddled in silence, tying off their two remaining pack mules, and took the leading reins of their mounts. Outside the crowded stable, they mounted, with Patrice riding before Tyrus and Annalla once again behind Larron.

She could have flown, but not everyone had seen her wings, and they *might* keep their silence even among each other. It was unlikely, but she did not need to be flashier with that secret than she already had been. The empty streets were a stark contrast to how they entered the town. No guard. No escort. Not one person lingered along the way.

Winding between the buildings, they rode toward the broken gate at an easy pace, only to find a crowd waiting for them amid the lingering evidence of Annalla's power. The bodies were gone, and a path barely wide enough for one cart had been cleared. People lined their path or stood upon the defensive wall once more.

There were no cheers, no cries of joy. Many had died for others to survive. What greeted them instead was a group of people showing heartfelt gratitude. Men touched their chests and nodded, tears brimming unshed in their eyes. Whispered words of thanks reached their ears from all around as they passed among and through the men, women, and children who had come out to see them off.

Cory stood with James and a man and woman who were most likely his parents. The bandage on his arm from the day before remained in place. It covered a burn he took helping battle the fires at the gate started by the gilar attacks. She had seen the hurt in his eyes as he shrugged it off and helped with the work throughout the day. He saluted in the human way as they passed, with a hand held at an angle at the head, and both she and Tyrus returned the salute.

The night before, after supper, Annalla had given him strict orders to stay safe on their journey. *This better be his way of promising to obey those orders,* she thought to herself.

The experience left the group in thoughtful silence well after they passed beyond the walls, some wiping silent tears from their faces.

"They have good fighters still, and Marto protected most of the experienced bow hunters," Tyrus noted after a time.

"Hamton will keep them alert, and the children did well staying calm in the chaos to carry messages. They will help with keeping watch," added Patrice.

Marto laughed. "And unlike us, they are heading away from the gilar."

"Yes, if they do not linger here, there should be time enough for them to reach the sanctuary of the Woodland. The defeated gilar will need to report their failure before another warband is sent."

"That is my hint to get in the air." Annalla said as she unwrapped her wings. She felt lighter out there where she did not have to hide that part of herself. "I took a sighting from the first marker we found. Make for the tree line below that up-thrust of rock in the mountains behind. I will adjust our course each day if we stray. If I'm lucky enough to find anything resembling shelter, I will let you know, but I don't think it would be wise to create it out here."

"Stay safe," Larron said to her as she took off.

Annalla abandoned the zigzag pattern for that stretch of the trip, and instead remained either high up or low to the ground when she flew. High in the sky, she should look like nothing more than the spec of a soaring bird to someone below. She might not be able to see details, but movement and other specks against the white snow appeared clear enough to draw attention.

She circled, riding the drafts taking her north, attempting to look as much like a hunting raptor as possible. There was nothing but rolling farmland below her, abandoned, or destroyed in the wake of the gilar. Wisps of smoke could be seen rising lazily to the northeast. If the wind blew just so, the acrid stench of smoldering wood and flesh reached her nose. Weeks, or months if they were lucky, would pass before that small army was missed and a larger one sent. That did not mean smaller groups would not block their way, however.

Annalla dropped down slightly, noticing movement below, and started to track a group of people. Her best guess was a party fleeing the attack on the town to report to the main contingent that was, potentially, surrounding the dwarves. It was unlikely any humans in that direction would have survived the gilar march south. Any lower elevation to allow her to see more details would also be more likely to raise suspicion, so she wound back to her group to confer.

"Trouble?" Larron asked when she settled in behind him shortly after mid-day.

"A bit. There is a small band of what I suspect to be gilar heading northeast not too far from here. We might pass close enough that topping any of these hills would place us in their line of sight. I believe we can avoid them easily enough."

"Probably fleeing the battle."

"My guess as well. We are heading somewhat in the same direction, so I don't think we will be out of visual range anytime soon."

"You want to eliminate them." It was not a question.

The way he phrased it made her feel slightly guilty, like some part of her *good* nature was missing. It was the gilar they were talking about, not innocent bystanders. They were part of the group that butchered and ate people alive to frighten villagers they were going to attack and then eat them, too. Her group was not capable of taking prisoners. Leaving them alone and alive meant leaving them to become someone else's problem and, likely, someone else's death.

"They will rest during the day, so take Patrice with you and plan to attack them close to midday."

Annalla blinked in surprise. She leaned around and forward to peek at his face, holding his waist to keep her balance. "Seriously? I'm not horrible for wanting to eliminate them?"

"The ways of the gilar and the elves are diametrically opposed, Annalla. We might offer them a chance to return to their lands closer to the border in better times, but they have declared war on us and are actively invading our lands and raiding our allies. Their lives are forfeit."

Part of her still expected 'good' to be synonymous with 'pacifist,' but the elves surprised her every time with a willingness to fight and actively defend. It was as though she expected them to hold themselves up as too good to dirty their hands, but nothing about any of her friends demonstrated such thinking. Which meant it was probably her placing them on some level better than her own. Larron would probably berate her for *again* not thinking her heritage worthy if he could see her face at that moment.

"I'll take Patrice with me tomorrow then," she spoke to keep him from turning further.

"If you think their numbers are too great to risk with only the two of you, we can discuss other options. Only engage if you believe the risk to be minimal."

She smiled. "There are at least five of them. You think Patrice and I can take them on our own?"

Larron glanced back, and she felt him laugh. "Five? You or Patrice could eliminate them individually, but doing so might require some amount of surprise or luck."

"Is that why you had Patrice patrolling as well in the fight at the town?"

"She is best as a stealth hunter. If they entered the streets between buildings, she could take out more from there than on the front lines of an open battlefield."

Annalla thought back to when Patrice surprised her when she joined their planning meeting for their trip. She could easily imagine her walking up behind someone and taking them down without a sound. They would put it to the test the next day. Annalla smiled fiercely and took off to scout further as the day progressed. When there was nothing else of note, they spent the evening planning and discussing how the main party would remain below the rises in the land to stay low on the horizon.

After quickly scouting their position, Annalla picked up her partner for the mission and brought them close.

"Eight," Patrice noted late the next morning as she and Annalla lay in the snow on a hilltop.

"Stay or go?"

"Stay. In an ambush situation, we have the advantage."

Annalla grinned over at her. "I'm glad you said that. Now I can tell Larron it was your decision if he is mad at us later."

"Are you two still dancing around a romantic relationship?"

She could feel her face scrunch up. "We're not dancing."

Patrice gave her a very disbelieving head flop before continuing to watch the gilar on the next hill over.

"Apparently," said Annalla, "I'm his life mate. Which is supposed to be no pressure and does *not* mean the love of his life, but it complicates things. As does his position and my lack of memory."

"There are always complications in relationships." She shrugged. "Elves can live a long time, so taking things slowly is not a bad decision. As long as you don't expect me *not* to poke fun at you for being embarrassed about hugging him in public. I hope you are stealthier today than you were in the inn's common room." She gave her a toothy grin, and Annalla felt herself starting to blush.

"Oh, Larron, you're so handsome," Patrice continued in a whisper. "I love it when you walk around without your shirt on."

Annalla's face was on fire. "Okay, stop."

"I do not believe that was his response."

The two of them were reduced to silent giggles curled up in the snow and trying to keep one eye on the enemy camp. They wiped tears from their eyes as mid-day approached and worked through a quick and simple strategy.

Annalla dropped Patrice off behind the gilar, where she would come up the last rise and into their camp, then flew opposite and prepared to crest a hill, be seen, and act shocked and terrified so they would chase after her. They planned for her to act as the initial distraction, drawing their attention as Patrice came in close from the other side.

She set her sword down in an easily accessed spot so it would not be obvious in her silhouette and headed up the hill, affecting an exhausted stumble. No shout of alert came when they saw her, only a hiss to notify the group. The two on watch charged while the rest made ready.

The shock on Annalla's face was not entirely feigned as she watched Patrice eliminate two as they grabbed weapons to join the attack. Patrice sprang onto the first gilar's back and it crumpled to the ground. A second quickly followed.

Annalla could not see the exact motions, but from her positioning, it looked like she jabbed a blade into the back of their necks. One strike for a kill. Two were dead before Annalla even had a chance to fully react and turn to run from the gilar as the lure. As soon as she was far enough, she grabbed her sword, dropped to the ground, and crawled back to peer over the top to watch their approach.

A third died before she saw them again, with Patrice leaping onto the back of a fourth. When that one fell, Patrice changed. She put the knife in her mouth and dropped onto four feet, her hips and shoulders shifted until she was a sleek feline bolt flying over the ground.

There was no other word for it. Patrice *pounced* on the next unsuspecting gilar, and that one went down with a grunt that had one of the runners turning to call out to the rest even as she shifted back and jabbed her prey's neck, killing the fifth.

Annalla charged as they turned to face the new threat. She and Patrice quickly eliminated the last three pincered between them before they could coordinate a counterattack. It went better than Annalla could have hoped. A masterwork of ambush skill and tactics she felt privileged to witness.

"What was that?" Annalla jerked her chin at Patrice as she cleaned her blade with a spare cloth.

Patrice's smile was feral. "We are less powerful on average, but irimoten have more essentials than the elves do. About a third of us can shift our joints to run like that. It also helps with climbing and balance."

"A third of all irimoten?"

She shook her head. "A third of our essentials. Another third is telepathic, but usually only either sending or receiving and only with each other. The rest have a variety of other minor gifts."

The two of them went back to the gilar camp to rummage through their belongings for anything worth salvaging.

"Why is this not mentioned more if there are so many of you?"

"We're not strongly gifted." Patrice lifted a shoulder. "Our leadership makes use of our skills and lets the chain of command know, so it is not unknown, but it is more of an asset, like a skilled archer. Not one of us could churn up a river as you did or call a forest of trees out of nothing."

"You took out five gilar with a knife and ran them down like they were children taking a leisurely stroll."

"I didn't say it wasn't useful," she laughed. "We are ambush hunters and are wasted on the front lines. Most of my people fighting in the south are behind enemy lines, with telepathic partners on our side to report in."

Annalla winced in sympathy. "Do they return periodically, or is it not worth the risk of crossing the lines?"

"Most remain in position, but there is a system of secret safe locations set up to allow them to rest. They operate in cells in case anyone is captured."

She nodded. It would be riskier for the individuals, but safer for the broader organization as they attacked supply lines and harried small groups of enemies. It was likely a similar organization to the bandits along the river. After seeing Patrice in action, though, she knew the irimoten could do more with fewer people.

"I don't see anything of use for us here. You?"

Annalla agreed. "Nothing. I think we leave all this as it lies and fly back. Unless you want to scout with me the rest of the day."

She said the last with a grin. Every time she flew with Patrice, she ended up with claw marks on her back and arms. Patrice had zero interest in flying, and she suffered through it by holding on as tight as she could.

Patrice made a hacking sound. "No. Thank you. Heading back sounds like the best plan."

She laughed as she gathered Patrice up in a bear hug and took off. They both hissed as she rose and the claws came out once more.

CHAPTER TWENTY-SEVEN

She was young to be creeping silently over bare rock alone on a night without a moon. She felt her way in the darkness, cloaked in shades of gray from head to toe. The cold stone cut into her hands, but she forced herself to move slowly. It was the more difficult route, but she was less likely to be discovered.

That was not to say she was safe. At all times, she remained conscious of her breathing, keeping it slow and steady and avoiding the large puffs of exhalation that become visible in the cold air. It was unlikely she would be betrayed by such a small thing, but better not to take the chance.

Daylight was the bigger threat. Her clothing blended with night and shadow, but stood out more against the lighter, gray rocks. That was when she slept—or tried to. It was her first mission alone. She remained on edge; sleep was always long in coming and short in duration. For the three days and nights it took her to cross the open distance, it was all she could do each dawn to find a crevice to curl up in and hope she appeared as barely a shadow in the landscape to any watchers.

Finally, she reached her goal undetected a few hours after the sun set for her fourth night in enemy territory. It was a large stone castle, but its size was more width and depth than height. There was nothing ominous about the building itself, but a shiver went down her spine, seeing it close for the first time.

A scream came from within, and it took a moment before she felt sure it was real and not imagined. The young girl pushed through her unease and crept around the base of the castle wall, looking and listening for a safe spot to ascend. After the first loop around, she knew the gilar were well prepared against even the smallest incursion.

She spent hours watching and studying their patterns before finally finding a crack in their perimeter, a gap in their watch rotation. It would not have been enough to scale the wall, but it was just long enough to allow her to spread her wings and fly to the top. Something that took all her concentration, as she only recently began flying on her own.

She teetered on the edge of the battlement but pushed against opposite merlons to pull herself forward. A moment after she was hidden, the next patrol passed. She had to remain in a small, shadowed alcove for nearly an hour before the next gap allowed her to move and make her way inside.

The layout of the structure was completely unknown, and she found herself surprised at the amount of activity within, despite the hour. Those were not creatures whose days were determined by the rising and setting of the sun. Inside was a flurry of activity, and she scrambled for momentary blind spots whenever more gilar passed.

She found gutters, cracks in the walls, and barrels stuffed into corners. It took all her training to avoid being discovered. It was not so much the risk of being seen and killed that concerned her. She could probably kill the smaller patrols, but such action would put an end to her mission. Secrecy was critical, and she could not remain secret leaving a trail of bodies in her wake.

By the time she worked her way down to some musty and unused rooms, it had to be nearly mid-day. The dust on the ground grew thicker with every step down the last corridor, so she was certain they had not used that part of the castle in at least a year, probably more. Still in enemy territory, it was as secure a location as she could ask. Constant tension from the last day and a half helped her drift off to sleep quickly for the first time in days, and she was fortunate not to be discovered over the following hours of drifting slumber, dead to the world.

Days passed, and she explored and observed. The screams came regularly, though less frequently than she expected. It was not long before she discovered their stock of prisoners. From the cries for mercy and release, their screams of pain cut short. The scene before her was not as anticipated.

There were hundreds of them held in three separate groups in and around the building, but they were unharmed and well provided. A few irimoten were scattered among the people, but most were human. She had been told of the gilars' preferred food, but that was her first experience with a gilar herd.

Those were not people to them. They were not treated as slaves. They were livestock. You do not mistreat your food source. The gilar provided for them, fed them, treated their illnesses, and made sure they lived healthy and content enough to face the end intended for them.

It was confusing, to know what was to become of those people but not have a great deal of sympathy for their immediate situation. Cattle might not know what fate they faced, and might not be able to organize and use their numbers against their captors, but they were people, not animals.

She knew there were ways they could escape. It would mean taking risks, and not all would survive, but it was possible. A part of her knew they were afraid acting would speed their deaths. They spent their days enjoying what was given to them and always hoping it would be someone else taken.

Could she blame them for taking what comfort they could find and accepting their lot in life? Did they deserve that life, and its end, simply because they accepted it? Surely being born and raised to this life precluded any uprisings?

They were kept illiterate, given nothing with which to read or write, and the gilar watched for signs of dissent. She understood the explanations, the clever ways in which the gilar kept them down and dependent upon their captors, but their behavior made her angry. The docile acceptance sickened her to watch nearly as much as those who kept them prisoner. On her own, it was something she thought about often during her time in the gilar stronghold, feeling angry and guilty for feeling angry in turns.

Three months, that is how long she spent hiding and sneaking around the castle, a silent witness to all taking place within those walls. She watched and learned more than she ever wanted to about the gilar, but she stayed the entire time as instructed until her mission succeeded. Only at the end, before she left, did she go against those instructions. She snuck down to each group of people during one of the times they were loosely guarded.

"I can set you free. I could get you weapons to fight them with. They do not know I am here, so I could help you coordinate your attack with the other groups. No more of you need to grace their tables," she whispered to one she thought a leader, the one the gilar treated like an alpha stud, among them.

"Child, we do that, we all die. I have food and bed here."

"They will take you eventually."

"But not today." He smiled at her hungrily. "And maybe not ever. I am strong. I give them many children."

The response she received from him was echoed at each group. She opened the gates on the possibility they might change their minds, but left without waiting to see. Sorrow already settled into her heart at the exchanges.

It was fortunate she did not hesitate longer. A signal sounded from within as she jumped from the wall and into the sky on shaky wings. No one could have seen her and raised an alarm so quickly. Someone told the gilar of her presence, someone sacrificed a chance at escape and freedom for a chance to avoid being chosen. They would not find her, nor would they find evidence of her presence, and that person would die.

She thought them weak and hated them for giving her a reason to think of them that way. It made her angry, sad, and confused, but she had accomplished what she had been sent there to do. She understood them now, the gilar. Had she the ability to change her form, she could become one of them...and suddenly she was.

She looked down, and her hands were scaled and clawed, clutching a broadsword. The world moved in slow motion around her, and she watched the muscles in her arms ripple as she raised the sword, pulling back to strike. A grin stretched the leathery skin of her face, pulling her lips back over pointed fangs. The blade swept across her body. It sliced through skin, sinew, and bone, parting a head from its body. She watched her father's head tumble to the ground beside his body.

Annalla inhaled sharply and opened her eyes, but otherwise gave no indication she woke. Her heart pounded in her chest and her lingering bruises throbbed in time to the beat. She suspected Larron knew she continued having nightmares, but he made no mention of it, and she no longer woke up screaming.

The ones preceded by a new, returned memory always left her with a bit of a headache, like an echo of the headaches before her powers emerged. Tyrus and Nurtik would be on guard. She silently emerged from the tent and began dressing for flight.

"You're up early. Trouble sleeping?" Nurtik asked her in Dwarren.

"A bit. Patrice and I spoke yesterday about some of her people behind enemy lines and it brought forward a memory of the gilar herds."

"You mean the prisoner camps?" Tyrus asked.

She wiped sleep from her eyes. "No. The herds. The ones they keep in their lands. Prisoners are slaves and *then* food. Their herds are just food. I tried to free some of them once and they betrayed my presence. It made me so angry. They just accepted their fate in life of being eaten someday, along with their children. I spent so much time watching the gilar there that I missed the herd dynamics. When I tried to free them, I went and talked to the men I thought were in charge."

"They weren't in charge?"

"They were, but only because they were big and strong. I realize now I spoke to the pampered bullies of the herd. The people who took what they wanted and gained benefits from the suffering of others. I should have looked for the protectors among them."

"People who shielded the weak from the bullies and the gilar and cared for the children."

"Exactly. I would see it now, but children can become so narrowly focused they miss the bigger picture. I thought of those men like my father, but they were nothing like him."

"How old were you?" Tyrus asked incredulously.

"I could fly solo, so probably eight or nine. No younger than seven."

Nurtik's beard twitched. "What were you doing in a gilar stronghold at eight or nine?"

Annalla understood their feelings. Seeing the children, even older than she had been, running around the town during the battle fighting, or simply carrying messages, struck some protective instinct within her. She had buried it like everyone else and let them do their jobs, despite the risks.

"Learning to speak their language, of course," she said with feigned chipperness. Though, their responding sputters brought a smile to her lips.

"I'm going to head out early," she said, pulling on the last of her winter flying clothes, "use the time to settle my brain. Keep an eye on the weather. There are some tricky currents up north. They are headed east right now, but it doesn't feel firm."

"Yes, storms in my mountains is tricky, sudden, fierce." Annalla smiled as he continued. "I'd 'av words fer yer parents if they were 'ere, Annalla."

"I do not doubt that, Nurtik." She shook her head. "Some things are bigger and more important than one person, even if that person is your child."

Annalla pushed into the sky and away from further conversation, but she heard them wonder what might be so important. She had no answers yet, but pieces were coming back.

There was a nearly audible sigh of relief when they reached the comforting, concealing shelter of the tree line at the northern edge of the rolling farmland. A distance that would normally have taken a couple of days at an easy ride turned into six days of slogging through thick snow.

It became different under the trees. Deeper drifts collected in places, and nothing more than a dusting in others. While she could not cover their tracks in the snow, at least the tree cover would allow her to grow shelter for them from the cold without it appearing out of place.

"I see you found what I was able to grow now that there are trees again." Annalla grinned as she entered camp and started helping with the last of the chores. "How was your ride?"

"Slow work. A great deal of snow fell today, and what the branches cannot hold drops to become thick, wet mounds." Larron's tone was gruff, but she could tell he was happy to be better hidden again.

Tyrus grunted. "At least the trees should keep some of the wind off us. It was cutting right through my clothes out there in the open. I'm surprised I still have my nose."

"There was wind?" Marto asked, struggling to keep a straight face as the rest of the group paused to glare at him.

Annalla did not even attempt to restrain her laughter and cracked up at the sight of the young mage blushing at the attention and beaming at his own joke.

"Tell me again why you can't shield us all?" Tyrus shook his head.

Marto shrugged. "I'm not really shielding myself. It's a basic healer skill we all learn to maintain body temperature. The bigger shield I use around the camp requires more effort to maintain when moving. I'm not powerful enough to do so for extended periods without draining myself...and Larron told me not to."

The last was said tentatively, with a sly look over at their party leader. That was part of the real Marto. He was not just a stoic council member and representative of the magai, but also a young man with a sense of humor who wanted the friendship of those he respected.

"No. No pinning this on Larron." Tyrus pointed at him

exaggeratedly. "We all know I'm his favorite."

"Favorite fool, maybe," Patrice muttered to Nurtik's amusement.

Tyrus continued, "So he would never order something so detrimental to *me*. This is clearly retribution for some imagined slight we have made against you."

Marto laughed at him. "If that was the case, I would be *accidentally* dropping the shield at night, so don't tempt me."

Tyrus boomed out a laugh and slapped Marto on the back, leaving the mage staggering, but grinning. "You should come visit Ceru with me, Marto. We would have so much fun torturing my brothers!"

"That's because you stopped aging emotionally at twelve." Patrice gave the long-suffering look all parents seem to master.

Nurtik said something about challenging them to some sort of drinking game, and the four of them were quickly trading boasts as Annalla made her way over to Larron. He wore a contented smile on his face as he watched them.

"It is good to be in the cover of a forest again. I will no longer feel like a rabbit stretching up to peer around for predators."

Annalla leaned against him. "You'll still feel that way, you just won't see as far when you do it."

"Are you not supposed to comfort me? Ease my mind?"

"Hmm. I'm afraid I didn't hear about any such rule for a life bond." She felt, more than heard, him laugh. "You really should have done more checking and preparation before going and getting yourself bonded."

"You are right. I will do so next time."

"Next time?" She leaned her head back to look at him and found him smirking at her. Another verbal battle lost. She was simply not good at them. Rather than responding further, she made a face at him and leaned in again.

Larron chuffed and lightly kissed her temple. "How was the flight?"

"Back to winding. There is a game trail you will be able to follow tomorrow. That should ease the way a bit and help mask our trail. Such things could help mask the trail of others too, though. We were probably safer when you all had to play rabbit out there. I could see for days in every direction."

"Tyrus is correct. At least it will be warmer for us with the chill of the wind reduced."

"That's something. We can't all have my fancy coat and pants."

"Ha! No, but I will be forever grateful to her people for thinking of and making that gift to you."

"Annalla," Nurtik called, and they both looked back over at the group. "See ya' sign'a tha next marker?"

"No," she answered as she stood straight, "but we didn't really expect it this close. Marto, I know you said it was a small gulch within the forest. You wouldn't have happened to see it from above, would you?"

"Unfortunately, no, and this is the point I'm most concerned about us missing. Nurtik mentioned this forest has many of these small valleys scattered and crossing throughout. There is nothing I can recall from the story that might differentiate the one we are looking for from any other. If we are wrong, it could take us out at a completely inaccurate spot."

"We will stay on course as best we can and follow the marker as we see it. If we mark where we go down, it will be easier to backtrack if we find we are off course," Larron responded without concern.

"I'm also checking my reference points and marking a spot parallel to where we camp along that line. If we run into any dips, I will check it against that line to see if we missed something. I scout far enough to either side ahead of us. I am fairly certain we will not miss it."

CHAPTER TWENTY-EIGHT

Nearly a week into the forest, she had found no sign of any significant dip in the land, at least not in their path. Winter was thick around them. The snow frequently stalled their progress. Annalla flew ahead, winding through the close branches, but there was nothing for her to find through the new snowfall unless it was very recent.

She was at her midday rest when something changed in the air. A light wind had been flowing from the east, but an unstable system shifted and brought a harsh wind toward them from the north-northwest. It sent a chill down her spine, and Annalla lifted herself above the trees to gain a better feel for what the currents might tell her. Above the shelter of the branches, the wind gusted, and she saw dark clouds in the north speeding onward.

Still above the trees, she turned and rode the leading wind south, seeking her companions below. The stormfront had been close for days but hovered away from them with no sign of turning. She never expected it to change with such speed.

The clouds outpaced her, and with them came hard-thrown snow hitting the back of her head and building up in her hair. White whipped around her, cutting visibility to arm's length. The ferocity posed a new danger, forcing her to drop speed and make her way below the sheltering canopy. Even in that relative shelter, the wind drove new snow down and stirred up the drifts already on the ground. Nearly two hours passed before she found her friends pushing through the heavy snowfall.

"Stop! Larron, we need to find shelter!" Their hands stopped the automatic reach for weapons when they realized it was her.

"We have not passed any location that might serve as a shelter against this," he called to her over the wind as he pulled up Dusk beside her.

"And this is only a taste of what we will face."

"We will have to dig in," he said, resigned.

Marto came up beside them and shouted at Annalla as he pointed. "It looks like level ground over there. You and I might be able to set up something. Unless you saw another suitable place nearby?"

"Nothing. That might work, but we should do it quickly."

Even in the short time she was on the ground, the wind picked up, and visibility rapidly diminished. They pushed through the snow, bowing their heads against the wind, and made for what they hoped was level ground.

"Everyone stay where you are, and try to keep the animals calm!" Annalla shouted over the wind and creaking boughs. She could barely hear herself and hoped they could at least see her visual orders.

She looked inward, seeking her essence as she reached toward the ground. Her fingers curled, grasping, and as she raised hands and arms, the ground beneath them trembled. Trees and plants came at her call, erupting from the ground at a steady but controlled pace.

The roots grew deep as trunks and branches threaded together above, leaning on each other, and combining their strength against the wind. It was over in moments, and there was an immediate difference in the gusts swirling around them. As Annalla looked around at her work, the wind lessened further.

"I placed a heat shield within the circle of trees. With them doing most of the work, it should be easy to maintain for a while," Marto answered her question before she asked it.

"Wer't not fer the gilar, travlin' wi' the two o' you'd be no challenge 't all." Nurtik let out his bark of laughter, clapped his hands, rubbing them together and set to unpacking.

His joy was infectious. For the first time since leaving the Woodland, they would feel safe. Not even gilar would travel in such a storm. They would take their turns on watch as usual, but the weather provided the greatest protection they could have against attack. With that protection, they could also have a fire to warm themselves beside for the first night in far too many. Even the animals edged closer to the crackling glow.

"In the Claws, I saw you predict a storm's beginning or end days in advance, what was different this time?" There was no accusation in Larron's voice as he sat at her side.

"The winds were more constant then. This shift was sudden. Pressure hovered to the north, but it just held there until it suddenly felt like a dam broke and it rushed south."

"It sounds like you are saying the shift was unnatural. Do you suppose Kahnlair can tamper with the weather now?" Tyrus asked.

Annalla had no idea about that and held up her hands. "Can the magai?"

They looked to Marto, who scanned the faces around him before staring into the fire. His voice became low and intense as he spoke.

"There is a magai legend, brought over from our homeland. Once, five great magai, gifted with strength such as Mage Gregry possesses and each the master of a different magic concentration, joined together to halt the greatest storm to ever hit the largest city on the eastern shore, saving tens of thousands of lives."

Some of his mother's story-telling ability carried over to him, as his voice and cadence drew you in. Annalla wanted him to continue.

Marto smiled, relaxed, looked around again, and laughed. "I'm joking! Kahnlair is powerful, but Elaria is not a high-magic realm so far as the magai are concerned. An essential with the proper manifestation might be able to do what you imply, but magic is too diluted here for one of my people to influence on such a magnitude."

"Windani'd be more likely an' be'er ta send. Fer a small group like us."

Patrice nodded in agreement. "They are the best trackers and could run us down even if they are currently further away than the gilar."

"An' wi' us an' tha magai stayn' close ta home, tha huntin' packs bin rangin' further."

"Let's hope they don't have hunting parties this far west," Patrice added. "They only hunt in what they consider their territory, and we do not want to be considered 'in their territory.'"

"Why?" Annalla asked. "I thought gilar were the worst?"

"Gilar are smarter and more organized, which makes them a greater threat in a larger confrontation like war, but the windani are extremely territorial and are near-obsessive about it. We could take down a hunting party easily as long as they don't surprise us, but doing so would bring all the hunters in the pack down on us, as they would see it as encroaching."

"They are not dissimilar to the trakin," Larron added to give her a reference. "Windani are relentless, fast, and hunt in packs. When their territory is trespassed upon and one of them killed, they will swarm and hunt down those responsible to avoid the appearance of weakness."

Tyrus looked grim. "There was a village to the south setting up near a border with one of the windani packs near Ceru. They were warned not to trespass. A handful of poachers went in, killed a few, and brought back the pelts to trade. This is against our law, as they are a sentient race, but some people care nothing for the law.

"Two families escaped. One was with the old guard we stationed down there. Instead of trying to arrest anyone, he packed up and told everyone to leave. Only one other family listened. They were on the road and saw when the windani swarmed out and took over the town."

"And they were not chased?"

"If it happened today? They might have been, but the town was the prey, and the people leaving had not touched the pelts. In the past, if they killed those escaping, we would have retaliated. The windani had enough food and the people who trespassed and those sheltering them were dead, so further encroaching on the territory of Ceru in pursuit would not be worth it to them."

Patrice lifted a shoulder. "Windani and irimoten are much closer to the center of good and evil, as we see it, than gilar and elves. Don't expect to reason with them on a hunt, though."

They paused while the wind howled around them, considering the implications of heading toward windani territory.

"How long do you think this storm will last?" Larron finally asked Annalla into the stretching silence.

"Through tomorrow night, at least. It might not let up enough for us to travel again until midday following. We have a bit of a wait as far as I can tell."

So, they waited. Annalla kept the horses fed, and they were happier than ever to be out of the cold and have a ready supply of fresh grass. It proved a welcome break for them.

After finishing her midday ration, Annalla went over and gave Moonshine a second brushing. It had been a while since she was able to spend much time with the horse. They were always taken care of first, so the chores remaining when she came back from scouting led her elsewhere every night. Since Tyrus and Patrice lost their own mounts at the river, Moonshine had become theirs while she occasionally rode behind Larron, so she was not even hers to take care of anymore.

Despite their distance of late, the mare had not forgotten her friend. She leaned into the brush strokes and listened to Annalla's random words with a patience few people could match. It was relaxing. Everyone left her alone with her thoughts, and Annalla moved from one animal to another before sitting down among them with her back against a tree.

The rest of the afternoon, she sat and listened to the storm. Although the wind could not penetrate the trees and Marto's heat shield, she felt it swirling, the strength and intensity. The storm spread vast and furious, possessing a force to knock down ancient trees, bury structures in snowdrifts, or strip the snow cover completely.

Animals would have run back to their burrows when the wind shifted, but any people caught in it would die. She wondered how bad the storm was to the south and if Hamton and his people had enough supplies to take shelter against the elements. Were they beyond the river? Had they delayed their departure that long? They were beyond her aid now, but she hoped they were safe.

For the two nights of the storm, they continued to set up the tent. Marto could not maintain the shield as he slept, and the trees kept the worst of the wind out and the heat from the fire in. They would not be leaving for a few hours, so they packed up and waited within their warm pocket of air.

"Say, for a moment, we find the fairy. What do you suppose they will ask for as concessions to provide aid?" Marto asked no one in particular, just to fill the silence.

"We sh'd give nothin', they'r be'in' saved too."

"Are they, though?" Larron replied. "If they still live, they have hidden from the rest of the world for countless generations. It would seem our fate is little tied to theirs. In fact, I think if they do help us, they may be placing their people at greater risk by exposing these hidden strongholds."

"You think they will just say to forget the rest of the world and concern themselves only with their own welfare?" asked Tyrus.

"Based on observations so far, or rather a lack thereof, the fairy are likely isolationist. This history of the realm would suggest they are content to rely only upon themselves and leave the rest of the world to progress as it will, without their influence. Our benefit, or harm, may not be enough for them to deviate from a philosophy of non-interference. It could also be argued the rest of the world proved content to do nothing as they were pressed to near extinction, as we for so long believed to have happened."

"Annalla has proven willing enough to interfere and help out since joining us."

"Whoa! Don't hold me up as an example of the model fairy citizen. For all I know, my mother could have been exiled for fraternizing with another race. As far as this conversation goes, consider me an elf." She heard Larron fail to suppress a laugh, but spared him only a fake glare as the conversation continued.

"Let's move away from this particular argument about what they might ask," Patrice spoke calmly. "If we ignore Annalla as a possible example of fairy behavior, then we have no idea at all what they will be like and what their reaction will be to our news of the war. Instead, it might be more worthwhile to discuss again what we could offer, or what we have that might interest them. I had such conversations with the other matriarchs, as I'm certain you did with your own people."

The six of them sat there, dismissing one possibility after another in their minds, until Marto finally said what they had all been thinking: there was little, if anything, the allies could offer, already stretched as they were.

"The war has already taken anything we could offer. Even if we win, it will take years to recover enough for our own people to survive," Tyrus agreed with Marto's assessment.

"Any offer we make would need to be long term to carry weight," Larron offered. "Trade rights, price-fixing, harvest percentage guarantees. Each of our people has something different to offer, and there are ways of wording such agreements to be beneficial to them without our people suffering unduly."

"The question is how long term any such agreement will need to be for them to accept," Marto cautioned. "They come back to the world as our saviors, only to cause discord by limiting or delaying our recovery with harsh trade agreements. I know it would not begin in such a light, but there are people with short memories who, after a time, would put pressure on leadership to think of their people instead of a war that ended years before."

"Elves have long memories; we will keep our bargain."

"You also have prosperous Woodlands that have not been razed to the ground to make it difficult to keep those bargains, as some of us have experienced," Tyrus pointed out.

"My clan'd never ferget a promise."

"I do not think he meant the rest of us could or would not, simply that the elves would," Patrice offered.

"I can only speak for the people I represent," Larron agreed. "I meant no offense. The Derou will also struggle to recover from this war. My own Woodland is not what it once was."

"What if they ask for more?"

"What do you mean by 'more,' Annalla?" Tyrus asked her.

"You have all spoken a great deal about mutually beneficial trade agreements. That is fine as long as they lean enough toward their naturally good side as the opposing force to balance the vampires in Elaria. What if they don't? What if they have a different perception of what is bad or wrong when it comes to risking the lives of their people?

"A request for such trade agreements for an unspecified duration to be determined by them alone. They might ask for a place on your council, perhaps with guarantees on influence. There are many things they could ask for, to which you might have trouble agreeing. I am not asking for an answer, but you should consider how you will respond to such demands. How far are you willing to take your people down a path of fairy control to gain these reinforcements?"

Marto, especially, looked shaken, his inexperience making a rare appearance. "Do you really think they would ask for anything so outrageous?"

"I don't know," she shrugged, "but I have the benefit of ignoring such possibilities. I am not going to have to agree to any of them. When the fairy were apparently killed off by the vampires, there was no help. The world let them fall, and now the world comes asking for the lives of fairy to be spent in its defense. If you were them, what guarantees would you ask for and how much would you trust the word of those desperate enough to promise anything?"

Annalla paused to peek out between the trees while her companions thought over her words. "The storm has stopped. We should head out."

She packed the last of her things and finished putting on her outerwear before stepping out into a completely different scene. There had been a fair amount of snow on the ground before the storm, and the trees held piles of snow in their branches. All that snow was on the ground in odd patterns. Some of it packed hard against tree trunks or thick plant growth, piled high, or covering the ground in a shallow blanket of white. Many of the branches joined the snow on the ground in jagged, broken heaps. As she looked up, gray skies changed to blue before her eyes, the snowfall fading to nothing.

"You are not going to enjoy traveling today," she said when she stepped back to where the others gathered the horses and tied off pack animals. "Movement is going to be slow through the higher snowdrifts, so you will probably need to take turns with which horse is breaking the path for the rest."

"There will also be little chance of you finding evidence of anyone else out here," Larron cautioned. "If there was anything to find before, it is gone now. Be careful."

They would not be traveling long that day, or far with their slowed pace, but Annalla kept her same speed in the air. As Larron expected, the only tracks she found were those of animals emerging from hiding with the passing of the storm. Her main goal was searching for the mark in the landscape, letting them know they were closer to their destination. With another day of no results, she could not help but think that for a forest allegedly filled with such drops in the land, their path was curiously devoid of them. It became increasingly frustrating.

Every night when she rejoined the group, Annalla could tell they were experiencing a different frustration. They covered little ground each day, but the horses and people looked exhausted. Even the smaller animals tired from trailing through what was left in the horses' wake.

All of them were realistic enough during their planning to acknowledge the detrimental impact of traveling in the winter and into the north. Knowing that did not make it easier physically, but it did allow them to approach the situation with a more rational frame of mind. At least, that is what they kept reminding themselves.

Periodically, Annalla emerged above the treetops to scan for any obvious depressions in height differences, but nothing stood out. Snow built up again on the branches, and ice where snow melted by the sun froze again. Breaking branches and falling snow clumps frequently resulted from the accumulation. The sound could be natural, or it could be caused by someone brushing against a branch and knocking down the build-up. If the sounds were too far away, she listened for a while for anything indicating people. When it was closer, she went to look.

One of her investigations finally resulted in something of interest. Annalla flew through an unexplored area when the familiar cracking came, followed by a wet thump. Approaching quietly and cautiously, she heard no sounds of people and found no visual evidence.

What she did find was a change in the landscape. The fact she could not discern that from above boggled the mind. The ground before her dropped off in a steep slope. Annalla floated down to the base of the gorge to test the snowpack, not liking what she found and yet unable to stop smiling. It was deep and soft, and it would be nearly impossible to move through. She would double-check her bearings on her return journey, but Annalla felt certain that was on course.

The excitement at her announcement made for a restless night, but no one complained in the morning.

"We will definitely need to remain up here as long as we can. Have you seen if there are still ways down ahead of us?" Tyrus asked when the full party arrived at the gorge a few days later and they stood at the top, looking down.

"As far as I have flown there are, but this does not continue on a course directly north."

"It shouldn't," said Marto. "Distance is difficult to tell in the story, but if this is the second marker, it should wind through the forest, ultimately curving north and west."

"Can we folla' it from 'bove?"

"For much of it, yes. There are places where the walls are sheer, and the trees give way to jagged rocks. I will start scouting for alternatives for us to consider at those points."

"What does it look like when it comes out of the forest? Or does the gorge end before the forest does?" Larron asked Marto. Annalla had not had time enough to reach the other end. They were only about halfway through the hills at that point.

"It takes us through to the other side of this small range of foothills above the plains to the north. That's why it's so important to find the correct gorge here. From where it exits, we head due north again, and somewhere in the mountain range is what we seek."

"If it comes to it, we will need to leave the horses behind," Larron said. "Shoes can be made for us to walk over the loose snow, but not for them. I hope that it does not become necessary, but if there is no other choice, we will do what we must."

"I will let you know as much as I can about the landscape ahead. If there is a place where that might be necessary, I will tell you. I would prefer we stay out of there as long as possible, but my concern is less for leaving the animals and more because that is a prime place to stage an ambush. A small number of people could overtake us down there."

"Have you seen signs of anyone ahead?"

"No, but that does not mean there is no threat."

"You are scouting days in advance of us and we set our guards at night. If there is a successful ambush against us, they will have earned it," scoffed Tyrus.

"As long as I can lead us back to this same gorge, we also have the option of going a longer way around obstacles, since I can keep us on course without delays."

"At least the snow will be starting to ease off and melt by the time we hit the open land again," the human sighed. "Maybe the wind won't be as bad on that side of the forest."

The exaggeratedly comforting pat Larron gave the human's shoulder had the rest of them laughing, even knowing they would be facing the same chilling wind themselves.

CHAPTER TWENTY-NINE

After twelve days—they were probably only about four or five days of 'good weather'—of unobstructed travel along the gorge, they followed based on how quickly Annalla said she returned each day. They made two detours to take safer paths through the forest rather than descending into the thick snow and ice at the base of the slope. Tyrus' comments about probably seeing the first of the spring flowers peeking through when they reached the other side became more likely with every passing day.

It would be faster crossing if they could cut straight through. Being forced to follow that one specific mar in the geography meant they needed to either continuously backtrack, or split up and send Annalla to scout a direct path alone before returning to guide them. Sending her further ahead might have been a viable option if she were not so critical to their mission later, but she was. It was all the reason needed to prevent anyone from suggesting such a course of action.

That day, they were back at the top of the gorge, and decided to continue their travel despite the moderate windstorm kicking up throughout the morning. The last few days of sun melted a good portion of the snow and ice from the branches, so the trees were less likely to break. Less likely, but not impossible. Marto had reacted fast enough to shield Nurtik from a tree crushing him and his pony. Since that jarring incident, they jumped and reacted to every creak and crack, even as the wind died down late in the afternoon.

"Did'ye hear tha'?" Nurtik whispered, just loud enough to be heard, and stopped walking.

Larron did, once they stopped pushing through the forward snow, and he called everyone to a stop on their way through the thick snow covering the ground. His heart stopped as his mind scrambled. What he heard should be impossible. Annalla scouted for days ahead of them, extending her range east and west in case someone might be on an intercepting course.

Despite all their caution and care, people approached, and from what Larron could tell, they came from nearly every direction and were not attempting stealth. There was no way they could outrun them in the thick snow cover. All of them knew it and drew their weapons to make a stand. The animals were left standing in the path they had broken, while his people scrambled as quietly as possible to a defensible position. They were backing themselves into a corner with only a small escape route, but they were likely outnumbered and soon to be surrounded.

"We do not know if they are friend or enemy," cautioned Patrice.

Everyone responded and spoke only with nods and hand signals as the people closed in on them. On his order, Patrice shifted. She used her white fur to blend in with the snow and her irimoten grace to slip up into the trees to where she might see them.

"You are surrounded. Lay down your weapons and step into the open with your horses. We might allow you to live if you do as you are told." The rough voice came from Larron's right. He did not answer. "You are severely outnumbered."

"There are at least fifty of them, possibly more. I cannot tell which side they support," Patrice whispered in his ear from above.

"We do not have a choice. There is no chance we can win against their numbers, surrounded as we are." Anger and frustration showed clear in their eyes, but he saw nods of agreement. Larron turned back to Patrice and ordered her to disappear again. With only one pony in their party, she would potentially escape their notice. Larron called out, "Stay your hand. We are putting our weapons away." One by one, they did so and stepped into the open, Larron leading.

"Take their weapons," the voice ordered, and men emerged from the surrounding woods to disarm them. Only after the men stepped back did their leader show himself. "I thought I recognized some elven beasts in this group, but what are you doing so far from home? Lost, little elf?" The mocking tone made it obvious they were not allies.

Their winter clothing appeared dirty, their hair unwashed and greasy. The leader wore a fur cap, but even the concealment could not hide his thinning blond hair. His sallow, sunken cheeks and eyes seemed more a product of bone structure than any lack of nutrition.

"We had word of gilar heading north and volunteered to take a warning to the dwarven clan," Larron answered without hesitation at the misdirection.

"Not that it matters," the man said, "but I'm afraid you would have been too late to accomplish anything there. I would take you to them to sell as additions to their herd, but I'm headed in another direction. Besides, you are lying, and finding out *why* might just be worth more to those interested in such things."

"I told you—"

"The cover story you devised," he interrupted. "It may have worked when you were further south, but you are past the point where your lie is believable, and your trail leads in the wrong direction. Bring them."

Trail, Larron realized. *They came from behind us.*

He breathed a sigh of relief at the knowledge because it meant Annalla had not been overcome while scouting. Memories of losing Palan in such a way were still too close.

He watched for a moment before being jerked around, his hands bound together and tied to one of their horses. Larron's companions were treated similarly, and once they were all bound and tethered, their leader ordered them to move out.

Larron plodded back through tracks left in the snow by their captors. He was not surprised at that point to find they led away from the gorge to the southwest. Annalla would have seen them and given warning if they arrived from the north. With the amount of ground she covered each day, even if someone overpowered her, it would have been days before they intercepted the rest of the party from that direction.

As they moved through the path, every few steps the ropes binding his arms jerked taut when his leading animal pulled too far ahead. They dug into his wrists, and he stumbled forward so there was some slack until he fell far enough behind for it to happen again. Larron knew Nurtik, with his shorter gait, suffered much worse in trying to keep up.

Marto had been intentionally handicapped by their captors. It seemed they knew how to prevent a mage from using his magic. His hands were in fists and wrapped tightly so he could not extend his fingers. His eyes were covered, and he was gagged.

A mage's magic might work through their mind alone, but they were taught to control its expression through the body: postures, expressions, words. Few, if any, could use their power without such things.

Even without being able to see, catch himself properly, or raise himself from the ground, they left Marto tied behind an animal to struggle in its wake, blind and impaired. Though he could not see them, Larron heard frequent falls behind him. He heard his friends dragged along the snowy ground as they struggled to rise even as their bindings pulled them down again face-first into the ground, accompanied by jeers and insults from the men.

Noise grew ahead of them, and it was not long before a camp came into view. They had circled back around south. It looked like the group had been shadowing them for some time. Remaining far enough away to not be noticed, tracking, flanking, and surrounding them without warning.

They were no mere bandits, but likely hired mercenaries.

They would be skilled and disciplined to some extent, which made the chances of escaping grow slimmer by the moment. Even if Annalla and Patrice remained free to come and look for them, they would be little help to the pair while unarmed and trussed up.

"Tie up the others and place a guard on them. Bring the elf with me," said the brigand captain.

The tent was tall enough to stand in, with a sleeping area curtained off, but everything in it was practical. They would be able to break down and pack the entire tent and its contents on short notice. He sat on a simple stool, and two men pushed Larron to his knees before him.

He removed his hat, tossing it on a thin, plank table, revealing a bald crown with the long, thinning hair dangling around his face on the sides. The man rubbed a hand over his pale skin and scratched his scruffy jaw.

"Now," he said, "why are you traveling north?"

"I have already answered that question, and my answer has not changed."

Something hard struck Larron in the lower back, making him fall forward in pain.

"Dran, that will not be necessary," said the leader calmly and without reproach. "Do not mistake the pretty visage of the elves as weakness. He will not tell us anything that way without more effort than I wish to spare. As I was saying," he continued, as Dran and the other man helped Larron back to his knees, "your lie is no longer believable. If you were heading for the dwarves, you would be further east of here, not continuing on a northerly course."

Larron groaned, giving his pain voice in an attempt to appear weak and cowed. "Only if you believe us stupid enough to follow the main roads, most likely to be patrolled by the gilar."

"I do not think you are stupid, and you would do well to recognize I am no idiot either," he scolded. "There have been strange reports in the area recently. Stories of an army of gilar defeated by a small group of farmers banding together. It was also told a few strangers helped lead them. That is the reason they survived. Stupid people would not have survived." He leaned forward. "I may not be bound to him as some, but I wonder how much Lord Kahnlair will pay me to get his hands on you."

Larron said nothing. Their balance of information was already tipped in favor of that man, and he could only worsen his position by speaking.

"We've been following you for some time now," he continued, undeterred by Larron's silence, "so I know you are more than mere messengers of something long anticipated. There are unusual aspects to the path you chose.

"It was not obvious when we began following you. Everything seemed normal, natural. We were more than a week on the trail before the *convenience* of it came to my attention. The snow covered most, but I have several talented trackers in my company." He leaned forward. "Every place you camped, the snow was dug out with evidence of some type of edible plant. Now, such things are not unheard of in our winters, but every time and always upon your path?"

His head tilted and the feral grin bared yellowed teeth. "Nothing to say?"

There was a smirk on his face as he sat back again. He waved one hand dismissively in Larron's direction.

"Keep your secrets, we know about your mage. You may have already guessed by our treatment of the young man. Less armor, few weapons. They always think they are better than us, but we know how to stop them.

"Lord Kahnlair will want him, and you—he is fond of elves—but the other two are expendable. Which do you think we should sacrifice for his Call tomorrow?" He smiled at Larron's glare. "The dwarf, I think. They are always the least important. Think on this tonight, elf. There are other ways to take a Call. Give me the truth. Give me the answers of value, and you could save his life."

He looked at the two men holding Larron down. "Put him with the others."

Larron entered a large, stripped-out tent with his two

guards. They guided him forward before shoving him down so they could tie him to one of the thick tent poles.

Based on the size, it was a tent he would consider standard issue for supplies or communal rooms. Larron would usually not expect to see such larger tents without supply wagons, but mercenary parties of that size rarely used wagons due to the lack of versatility. It was more likely they had few horses for riding, with most carrying supplies the men could not carry themselves. If the snow had not restricted Larron's party to a walking pace as they broke through the snow, that group would have never caught up to them.

The lack of movement stopped the ropes from biting deeper into his wrists. His companions were already each tied to a different post, and two guards remained, one inside the tent and the other at the entrance. He knew without even trying they would not be allowed to speak. Larron could finally see their faces though.

As expected, Marto looked the worst for their cold walk. The ropes left bloody cuts on his wrists, and his face and lower arms were bruised and scratched from where he had fallen and been dragged repeatedly. Nurtik was not much better.

None of the injuries appeared serious. He regretted their discomfort and pain, but their situation was the greater concern. Larron tried to show nothing from the encounter with their leader in case someone watched for such reactions. Without being able to warn Annalla or Patrice, they needed to act quickly, or one of them would die. The threat had been no lie or bluff.

***

Annalla frowned at the stone walls towering over the slope leading down to the bottom of the gorge they followed. That point reached the edge of her range for the day, meaning the others were days away from reaching it. That gave her time to look for alternatives. She would need to scout for a way around it the next day, though, because right then she felt tired, hungry, and had a headache coming on.

Maybe we can rig something up to pull the horses to the top, she thought, squinting up at the top of the wall.

Groaning, she rubbed her hands down her face before stretching her arms wide. For a moment, she considered asking for a day of riding the next day, but then she remembered how much work they put in every day pushing through the snow she simply flew over and dismissed the thought. They would all have earned their break at the end of that trip.

With a final stretch of her neck to relieve the pressure, Annalla turned to fly back, leaving the troublesome wall behind as she took more of a direct course toward the indicated campsite. She would finish her chores and turn in early. Maybe the next day she would skip her morning exercise in favor of sleeping in.

It was a great plan, and it fell apart well before she approached a silent camp. Through the course of her flight, Annalla felt progressively worse. By the time she arrived, she knew something was significantly wrong with her, but she set it aside in light of the new development.

While Annalla was slightly ahead of schedule, her estimate placed their expected arrival at least a half-hour before then. She could not even hear the animals, so she pulled up short of the small clearing, alighting upon a sturdy branch.

"Pssst," came a call from above her.

Annalla barely restrained herself from crying out and falling off her perch as she drew her weapon and spun around to face the sound.

"By all the—" She put her free hand to her breast. "Patrice, you scared me half to death! What are you doing up there?"

The irimote sat upon a higher branch, her fear of heights nowhere to be seen as she dangled high above the ground. When Patrice did not laugh at Annalla's surprise, she knew something bad happened.

"What is wrong?" Annalla asked.

"The others," she said, "they've been captured."

Sighing, she rubbed her eyes once more. "We should

probably go rescue them."

CHAPTER THIRTY

Hours passed and night fell. *Annalla will soon arrive at a campsite without a camp,* Larron told himself, *and Patrice is a fair tracker with an easy trail to follow.*

She would find the trail, they would follow it to the camp, and they would plan it out carefully and logically. If they could recover their horses, their group would escape over terrain through which they could move faster than the men on foot. It would mean backtracking later to recover their intended course, but they would live to do so.

Their guards grew relaxed, but they could afford to be with the prisoners' bindings tight and well tied. Larron worked at the ropes tying his hands together—and he thought the others did as well based on their shifting movements—but the moisture collected from the snow made them swell and tighten, leaving no space to work free.

The tent posts might prove to be a more promising means of escape. They were, by need, easier to pull out of the ground, but the tent was taut, and moving any post without arousing attention would be near to impossible. He hoped the noise outside meant the rest of their captors were as unconcerned about the prisoners as the two guards.

It was not an unreasonable hope, with the laughter and cheers coming from the direction of the largest fire and open area.

Someone provided entertainment and continued to do so well into the night. Based on the behavior, they did not suspect Larron's group was any larger than the four of them. The number of horses matched the number of riders. He never thought he would be grateful for their losses at the river crossing.

By the time the revelry died off, it was well into the night. The guard had already changed once. Their current interior guard sat on a stool just inside the entrance, facing out at the party he wished he could join long after the noise faded. He glanced back infrequently, seeing them dozing periodically in the awkward positions in which they were bound. The night wore on, and Larron's worry grew, but he could not manage enough of a grip on the post to free himself. With every moment, morning crept closer, and with it the death of a companion.

Movement in the corner of his eye caught his attention. A small section at the rear of the tent went slack, a tiny gap waving in the slight breeze. Someone changed the tie-downs at the two adjacent posts to keep the rest of the tent from showing the slack. At least three of them were awake, staring at the gap, sparing brief, nervous glances at the guard. Larron could not tell if Marto was awake with his eyes covered and his head dropped forward.

Fingers reached under the gap to grab the cloth and stretch it carefully away from the ground. Another hand and arm stretched through, followed by a head. He could not take his eyes off Patrice as she slid under the edge of the tent. Even with the slack, it was a tight fit for anyone other than a child, or someone the size of a child, but she did not rush things, stayed calm, and made it through without attracting notice.

She did not even look at them once she was free. Patrice moved slowly and purposefully, standing and padding toward the guard in silence. He stood no chance as she came up behind him, reached around with one hand to grab his face, and thrust a dagger into his neck with the other. Only after easing him to the ground did she look at the person closest to her. Tyrus beamed at her as she quickly cut the ropes binding him.

"How—" he started.

"Quiet, not all of them are asleep," she whispered before moving to the next.

"How did you get through to us so quickly?" Tyrus lowered his voice to ask just as softly. "These are not amateurs."

"They were overconfident and did not go through our things to see if they had our entire party. It also doesn't hurt that Annalla could fly us over the sentries." She used her dagger to slice open the back of their tent a couple of feet up. "This way is clear for a while longer. Follow me. Annalla is collecting our supplies and the animals."

She led them into the darkness, weaving between tents with sleeping men, stopping them and guiding them unseen through men still awake and patrolling the camp. It was not a direct route, but she managed to guide them out to the animals without detection, and Annalla stepped out of the shadows.

"They unloaded the animals but did not unpack our things," she said, "so it was easy to reload. I also stole back your weapons."

While Marto continued massaging his hands, the three of them quickly rearmed and took the reins of their animals as quietly as possible.

"Listen," Annalla took Larron's face in her hands, looking at him with remorse in her eyes, "I overheard them talking earlier, and there are windani to the north. This group is not allowed to travel much further in that direction because it has been claimed as windani hunting territory and only the gilar have free passage. You will need to be careful to avoid them, and do not linger in any one place. Go now and go quietly."

Larron narrowed his eyes at her. He knew what she meant. There was no way for him not to know with their bond, and he still wanted to deny it. "You mean *us*, right? *We* are going to go?"

"We cannot out-pace them, Larron," said Tyrus. "They will surely catch us again. With the windani in the area, we can't run and then return to find this path again later, not with any sort of safety."

He ignored Tyrus and watched Annalla massage her

temples, her eyes squeezed closed, before looking up again. She pressed her sword into his hands and swallowed. "Take my weapons with you."

Larron grabbed her hand and clenched his jaw, not knowing what to say. He shook his head in denial, refusing to agree. She was in pain, and he wanted to cry.

"I'm on the ground this time," she said, trying to assure them both, "with stable footing and no buildings around to collapse on me. I'm not giving up, but it's happening faster than before. These bandits will not survive, but you will not either if you do not run now. Larron...*run*, please."

He understood her meaning, and he suspected their friends began to as well, but he could not look away from her. There was pain; the headache was back, he knew. The one heralding another essential power emerging. There was desperation and fear for herself and for him and their friends. Regret. Determination. Too many emotions to convey.

"Annalla, we cannot leave you here." Patrice was the only one to question her aloud.

Larron took a deep breath to steady himself and gestured to the horses. There was nothing they could do to help her. Depending on the manifestation to emerge, they might all die if they remained there. She believed they would.

"Come on. We need to move quickly. There is not much time." He turned back to her. "What about the scouts?"

"I cleared a path while Patrice found where you were being held. You should be clear before the alarm is raised, and I will stall them as long as I can."

He nodded and pulled her tight against him. "We will come back for you," he whispered into her hair.

Her head shook slightly against his neck. "No. Larron, this is going to be bad. I can feel it surging. Unless you know for certain you will be safe, you continue north. Promise me."

He would try to do as she asked, but he could not force himself to say the words to make that promise. "Find us if you can...after."

Annalla hugged him back and nodded before they both reluctantly let go. She walked further into the camp, and he led the others out.

***

A weight settled on Annalla when Patrice told her of their companions' capture.

"How?" she asked. "I swear I have been scouting, covering the same ground over and over again. No one should have gotten past me, let alone a group large enough to threaten you all."

Patrice sighed and shook her head. "They were trailing us. They came from behind. We never considered... Since the snow began..." she trailed off.

Rubbing her aching temples, Annalla pursed her lips and pondered. She felt the power building within her; a lethal eruption would soon be inevitable. The best chance they stood would be if she could use the approaching destruction to eliminate the threat without killing her friends in the process.

"We will need to determine where and how they are being held," she finally said, "but I think our best option is to rescue them, get everyone clear, then I will use my essential power to prevent their captors from pursuing, killing them if I must."

There was no hesitation in Patrice's response. "If you think you are strong enough, that sounds like a plan to me. Come on," she jumped nimbly down from branch to branch until she reached the ground. "Their trail should not be difficult to follow; they were practically dragging Marto along." Her voice ended in a snarl as she recalled the treatment of their companions.

Annalla experienced the same anger as they followed the path, seeing where people had clearly fallen and been pulled along like dead weight. She had to fight against the emotion threatening to latch onto the fire building in her and pull the destructive force violently into the world. Her head pounded and her hands shook with the effort to keep herself contained. Essence became a caged animal within her, fighting for freedom with every beat of her heart.

Finally, she heard the sound of revelry ahead and held up a hand for Patrice to stop. They listened, then proceeded cautiously, listened again, and so on. Between the two of them, they had no difficulty avoiding sentries and approaching well within the camp's perimeter without detection.

"There are not many larger tents," Patrice said at a barely audible whisper, pointing. "I suspect our friends are held in one of those, while the horses are over there. If I go find and free them, can you take care of our escape?"

Annalla nodded and put her mouth to Patrice's ear. "Bring them to the horses. I will ensure a clear path."

She watched her melt into the night before making her way to the animals, finding them still burdened with supplies and unfed. While the fact they had not been taken care of irritated her, she felt grateful for not having to spend time and risk noise repacking them. A quick look around the area found their confiscated weapons haphazardly piled in the snow nearby.

As she went to pick up the first of them, a wave of power washed over her, dropping her to her knees. She became feverish, shaking, and sweating. Her body boiled hot and shivered with cold at the same time and she struggled for air. Annalla took a handful of dirty snow and rubbed it on her face in a vain attempt to cool herself down.

I cannot lose it yet, she ordered herself mentally. *They need time to get clear. Just hold on a while longer.*

Voices approached, discussing windani to the north and where they would head instead. Annalla rolled herself behind a pile of sacks, laying there listening as the two men passed by the horses. Her shaking subsided for the moment, and she heaved herself up to her knees, then to her feet. She needed to eliminate the sentries in the direction her companions would take and gather the final pieces of equipment for them.

Feeling temporarily steady, both tasks were accomplished quickly and silently, and she returned to the horses just before

Patrice led their group out of the shadows. Bruises and cuts marred their faces, hands, and arms. Marto stretched and massaged his fingers and hands as though they pained him, but he uttered no complaints.

Annalla released a held breath at seeing Larron alive, but her relief was cut short as another wave of power rose within, threatening once more to overwhelm her.

"Larron...*run*, please," she begged him to understand even as she desperately wanted him to stay and help her through it. They both knew he could not.

"I cleared a path while Patrice found where you were being held. You should be clear before the alarm is raised, and I will stall them as long as I can."

He nodded and pulled her tight against him and she clung to him. "We will come back for you," he whispered into her hair.

Annalla shook her head without letting go. "No. Larron, this is going to be bad. I can feel it surging. Unless you know for certain you will be safe, you continue north. Promise me."

As she leaned back, she saw in his eyes an inability to make the promise, but he would lead their group away as far and fast as possible. He would help her protect their friends. It would be enough.

She stole one final hug before releasing him and walking away, traveling far enough that they could not see her when she fell to her knees once more. Their departure fell to the distance as she fought against the power closing in around her, suffocating in its intensity. Her skin felt as though it cracked and broke under the pressure, but she endured, containing everything within. They were still too close. She needed to buy them an hour, more if possible. She toppled forward, her face planting in the snow. Annalla imagined it sizzling and steaming beneath her from the heat burning throughout her chest.

Time passed, and eventually, the wave of power did too. Annalla pushed herself up once more and sought out a hidden place to wait for the men to discover their captives missing. It bought her time and consumed the least amount of energy.

Annalla removed her outerwear, bundling the pelts up to use as a pillow instead. She no longer felt the cold. The snow at her back and the breeze upon her skin provided relief from the blaze churning within, kept just beneath the surface.

Her skin grew numb, and her head went from pounding to fuzzy. Annalla was aware of the pain. Her body hurt and ached all over, but she grew distant from it; her awareness floated beyond the physical out into the essential. The body represented a painful suit she wore, but she held onto the link with a tenuous, but stubborn grip.

Hold on, she repeated the mantra over and over in her mind. *Hold on.*

Shouts rang out across the camp, and she knew they had been discovered. A dead guard found. Missing prisoners discovered. Something gave them away.

She rose to her feet, fluid and graceful. The pain meant nothing anymore and proved no hindrance. Annalla walked silently up behind a man as he peered into the forest around them. In a smooth motion, she grabbed his sword arm, twisted her body, and broke his arm over her knee. He cried out in pain and surprise as she took his sword in one hand and the collar of his shirt in the other before striding toward the center of the camp.

Orders and shouting quieted as the men noticed her, pushing the whimpering man before her as he held his arm close to his chest.

"My companions are well beyond your reach by now," she said into the silence.

A sallow, balding man stepped forward with a condescending smile on his face. "My lady, we have you surrounded. Put down the sword, and I promise no harm will come to you."

Annalla was certain they had two very different definitions of 'harm' in that case, but it would be irrelevant soon enough. Another wave of power approached, and she barely had any connection left to her body with which to attempt to contain it.

She dropped the sword. "You should run," she told the

men. "I do not think you can get far enough now, but you are dead if you remain here."

They were not listening. Men surged forward, laughing, but stopped short as the wave crested over her. She did not know what they saw; her own vision went white, blank. Annalla's body dropped as her consciousness rose above it, connecting to the essential power gathered to her and igniting it into explosive force.

Running would not have saved them, she thought distantly as the world burned.

CHAPTER THIRTY-ONE

No alarm sounded. No one rose to threaten them as they returned to the path on which they arrived. It was well beyond the sight range of the camp when they allowed themselves to take the already broken path. It would allow them to make better time and hide their tracks.

Annalla would find other weapons to use, he had no doubt. She would hold them off as long as possible. Pursuit was not their greatest threat, which was why he pushed their group forward through the night-dark forest. Finally, hours later, they came again to the edge of the gorge.

"Which way do we go? Back down our own trail, or continue north?"

No one had time to respond to Marto's question. Even as he asked it, an explosion shook the world behind them, followed by the rapidly growing glow of an enormous and expanding fireball. The awesome sight would have frozen him in fear and wonder had he not expected something of that magnitude.

"Quickly!" he shouted. "Down into the gorge!"

Larron grabbed tighter to the reins in his hand and plunged over and down onto the steep slope. Dusk followed him, dragging the attached mule along. Larron did not stop to see if the others followed. He had to hope the urgency in his voice convinced them.

A few steps down, he sunk into the soft snow, falling

forward, and struggled for every additional foot deeper. He did not know how far they needed to be, but he did not want to risk coming up short.

The whooshing rumble grew louder, but it was no warning for the powerful force slamming into him. It felt like a gigantic wall of heat thrust forward, knocking him over, and smashing him deeper into the snow. He could not move. He couldn't breathe. The sound caught up a moment later, pounding his ears with a roar like some strangely intensified amalgamation of a raging river and windstorm. It lasted an eternity, and he fought panic at not being able to see, hear, or feel anything around him.

It stopped as suddenly as it came. A moment or two passed as he sat wide-eyed before regaining his bearings enough to stand and look around. What he found were his friends, struggling up from the melting snow, along with their dazed animals. Larron shook his head, trying to clear the buzzing in his ears, and scrambled up the slope, sliding back with every step forward.

Muffled shouts rang out behind him from his companions still lower on the slope, but he ignored them and continued climbing, slipping, and sliding on the slush. When he finally made it over the top, the change he saw rent upon the land was shocking.

Annalla turned a winter forest into the aftermath of a summer wildfire. All around him were charred husks of trees, most toppled away from the blast with a few still standing pillars of charcoal. In his life, he had seen many wildfires and what they left behind. The scene before him appeared unnatural. The fire had just…stopped, and it was as cold as if it had happened months before. Except for the center of the burned-out area. In total, the charred swath could not have been more than a handful of miles in any direction, but the center remained a wall of flames.

"Oh, my…" The whisper was so soft he could not identify from whom it came.

Larron was unsure how long they stood there, staring back at the pillars of fire before someone spoke again. "Why is it still burning?"

"There is still fuel for it to consume," Tyrus answered

Marto's question.

"There is still fuel around us too, but the fire went out here."

"She could not stop it," he heard himself say numbly. "Maybe she was reining it in, but it overcame her before she could put it all out."

Patrice fought back tears. "Mage Gregry said that would be lethal."

Part of him broke, trying to scream and rage and cry, but the mantle he trained to wear for centuries fitted in place. Larron took a deep, calming breath, buried the shattered pieces, and put need ahead of want.

She will find us if she is able, Larron promised himself. He had lost people before, and he would lose them again, but he trusted she would find them.

"That is going to burn for hours more, and we cannot guarantee it will not catch on the dried wood left in the rest of the burn zone. We need to secure the animals and supplies and continue along the top of the gorge."

"Larron, we—"

"We need to move," he cut Tyrus off before he could begin the thought, "or we may lose more than one today. Fire is too dangerous for us to attempt a search. She has recovered quickly before. She will catch up to us easily enough by flying if she survived. Let us bring up the horses."

He slipped back down the hill to lead Dusk out before anyone could respond. He could not handle platitudes or disagreements at that moment.

The fire did them a favor by clearing snow off the ground. There was no plowing a path, tiring the animals and slowing their progress. With the crevice curving northwest, their time in the open area extended and gave them a couple of hours of easy riding. New snow fell to dust the charred ground, transforming it to an ashen color, but they did not call a halt until they found where it looked like the snow was no longer only new-fallen flakes. Dismounting, the group waited as Tyrus walked forward to inspect the ground.

"Is she still alive?" Patrice asked quietly at his side as she placed a hand gently on his arm.

"I do not know, Patrice."

The forest continued burning behind them. Smoke curled into the air in thick black and gray clouds, blocking the skyline as the fire expanded toward them. The expansion progressed naturally then, so the snow-covered areas would probably be safe.

"She told me you were bonded."

He looked down at her and sighed, not wanting to talk about any of that. Larron held himself in a shell of a belief that she was even recovering. Talking only cracked the fragile shell.

"It does not work like that. I have no greater knowledge of her than anyone else."

"Oh." Patrice took a breath to continue, but stopped and frowned at him. Without saying more, she rubbed his arm and stepped away.

"We need to walk the horses through for a while," Tyrus said when he came back to them, avoiding meeting Larron's eyes as he spoke. They all avoided catching his eye. "It looks like this is the perimeter of where Annalla's...of where the fire reached. Unlike the snow further in, it didn't all evaporate. What melted has refrozen and formed a crust of ice."

Their concern irritated him. He knew it was unfair, but it kept scratching at the shell allowing him to move forward. At least some of them knew about the bond, and there were so many rumors about elven life bonds out in the world they were bound to make assumptions. Larron wanted to tell them to continue north without him and march back south. He wanted to ignore the fact Erro and Oromaer had given him complete discretion over the future of elven alliances. He wanted to erase the last two decades.

That last thought made him uneasy. It meant he would give up his bonded to undo all of this. To save them from the war, have his brother back, and see the Derou safe. Larron knew he did not love her yet. Even if he did, he was not certain he would not trade her life to save the rest.

I am an awful person, he thought to himself. It was not true. He knew it was not, but more loss, more pain, made it difficult to see beyond.

"Very well, please lead us through." His voice sounded flat.

The thin layer of ice thickened and remained solid beneath their weight. It felt like all the speed they made over the morning hours was lost by how slow they moved then. Each step was carefully placed, and they watched for areas that might be impossible for the horses.

Of the group, only Patrice and Larron avoided falling on the ice. The other three had to be well bruised from hitting the ground so many times, and Larron suspected Tyrus had reopened his injury. Fortunately for the animals, their four legs instead of two kept them slightly more stable and standing.

After a while of sliding along the ice buried beneath the new snow cover, they faced another new danger. The snow beneath the ice became deeper further away from the fire perimeter, and the crust of ice sat on top of older snow. The horses would break through as they stepped down, but a point came when the ice crust was nearly thick enough to hold the weight, increasing the danger dramatically. If it held them for a moment and then broke, they risked a broken leg from the drop to the ground. They also risked injury by pulling the leg back up. Done at the wrong angle, it could be cut, sprained, or broken depending on the force used and the edge on the ice.

Tyrus called another halt the first time the ice held Moonshine's step for a moment. For the remainder of the afternoon, one of them walked out in front, breaking the ice layer with an axe, staff, or the hatchet from their supplies, and another person behind cleared out chunks to the sides. Hours seemed to take days, and everyone was sweating and aching long before the sky darkened. It was tiring work, and they let out a sigh of relief when Nurtik called back from his position out front.

"We're through!"

It was a good thing they made it past when they did.

Clearing a campsite amid the ice shelf would have been horrendous. They pushed on a little longer in the waning light before stopping to make camp.

"We will see more ice as we proceed, though I doubt to the same extent," Larron noted.

"Why do you say that?" Marto asked.

"Spring is comin'," Nurtik answered. "Warm days wi' freezin' nights this far north. I 'spect more from here on."

"If we face too many more days like this one, we will need rest more than the horses." Patrice sighed as she flopped gracefully to the ground around the fire.

"This was an extreme version of what we might face, but it is something we must watch for." Larron tried to keep worry from growing too much in their minds, but he could not stop them from looking back south. The fire had expanded to linger in patches of the surrounding destruction, where the wood had dried but not been completely consumed. Flickers of light were visible through the trees, a painful reminder.

It should not have happened like that. Annalla was supposed to have been the one to reach the fairy, to find out about her family, about her life. The rest of them were holding her back since she could have been there already, flying directly instead of having to wait for them on the ground.

Guilt ate at him. He pushed it away. It was her decision to travel with them, but the thoughts returned. What if they had known something? What if they could have saved her from herself? It was not an easy night for any of them. Though he may have rested, Larron did not sleep.

The following day, they were back to the slow work breaking a path through chest-high snow in places. They spoke little and did their best to remain as quiet and inconspicuous as possible as they wedged through the snow single file. Patrice was light enough to walk on the snow without cumbersome snowshoes, so she ranged ahead, but still within visual or shouting range.

They had been spoiled with a scout who could fly so far ahead. The only attack that could have surprised them was the one that did, one from behind. Should Annalla return to them, they would not make the same mistake. *He* would not make the same mistake.

CHAPTER THIRTY-TWO

Zeris peeled bleeding hands off the handle of the pickaxe and deposited it into the barrel under the watchful eyes of the gilar guards. A whip-crack sounded behind him with a cry of pain, but he closed himself off to it as instructed and shuffled along in his chains. From what he could see of it, his already dark skin was as black as his hair and the dust lined his lungs more with every breath down in the mine.

He was tired and hungry. There were times on the field of battle he had ended feeling that weary and thin, but nothing that constant. Every night he cried, missing Tralie, Erro, and Larron. Every night he was grateful they were not with him there, wasting away in the mines until their turn for table or torture.

When Zeris arrived at the work camp, the elves there conveyed to him—with great emphasis and urgency—he could do nothing to lead them. Zeris, the elven king, needed to disappear into the middle of their ranks. It was an order from his people, and they would hear no objections. Zeris hated it. He hated that some of his people sacrificed themselves to keep the strongest among them secret and safe. It should be the other way around, but they gave no ground, and everyone united against him.

They knew the vampires watched them, listened to them, and they expected rebellion and plotting to escape. Their communication took forms the vampires could not eavesdrop upon, and through such means, his people told him their story.

The weak were killed and eaten, more useful to the gilar as food than in the mines or on the forge. The strong were made to watch as punishment for transgressions. Periodically, a leader was sent away. No one knew for certain, but they suspected those few were sent to Kahnlair directly. There were rumors of torture, but no one returned to confirm the suspicion.

After the first escape attempt, those too frightened to run had been tortured while the runners watched. Tortured until the people who instigated the escape either killed their companions or watched their continuous torture and suffering.

The order of things shifted in the camp then. Elves who were not leaders, who were not comfortable leading, took over. They argued that when the moment came, when the time for a real escape arrived, the strongest among them would be needed. They could not allow those warriors and strategists to risk themselves before then.

So, they took orders, but were the voices of the plotting. Or they spoke against such plots to make themselves appear weak. The fear was real, but they were anything but weak. The ones who spoke up did so knowing they would not run and would die horribly for their actions. Zeris hated it.

Their worth, their strength and cleverness, was so much greater than they gave themselves credit. Their resourcefulness, tenacity, and courage kept him from acting against their wishes. It was smart to fool the vampires and gilar, to make them believe they knew what plotting and planning went on while keeping them in the dark.

Kahnlair wanted the leaders among them for some nefarious purpose, and their plan kept him from achieving his desire. The approach was inspired. Were it a game, he would cheer the gambit, but those were people making sacrifices of their lives. Never should his people feel the need to die for him, and it pained him to bear witness to such times.

I will allow them their decision, he ordered himself.

Zeris would not insult their sacrifice and bravery by

undermining their efforts and sacrificing himself. There were times when death was the easier path, but not the path of valor.

"How many hammers have you managed to steal without them noticing, Lourantile?" Tremane whispered as they huddled around a fire pit the size of a torch with their bowls of slop.

"No more today. They watched too closely. We should leave that area alone for a few days."

Tremane shook his head. "That is okay, we can hold there for a while and focus on the picks. I think we are still a month or more away from having enough to make sure some of us escape."

"Quiet," Frendiran hissed. "You are going to get us all killed with your talk of escape. We need to stay as we are. If we do not rebel, they will find their food elsewhere."

Zeris ducked his head in feigned disappointment with the detractor speaking up. The entire conversation was a farce, orchestrated to be overheard and give them time before questions were asked. Frendiran had seen prior escape attempts and could be thought to have been cowed. He was also injured. A collapse in the mines broke his leg and it was set improperly. It naturally placed him in a weaker position. He could remain behind and either distract for an escape or be tortured to death as punishment to keep others alive. Frendiran thought himself already dead. If he could save another with his time remaining, he would take the chance.

"You. Elf," a voice called out across the yard.

It was an idiotic address, two-thirds of the men in the camp were elves since they made horrible breeding stock. Everyone in the area froze and looked at the gilar striding toward them without seeming to look at him. It was soon enough apparent he made for their little group. Tremane looked around and gave a gesture for them to remain calm, his eyes lingering on Zeris and a couple of others among them under the protection of anonymity offered by their act.

"You." The gilar stopped next to Tremane and grabbed his arm, jerking him forward. "Come with me."

Tremane grabbed the gilar's knife and stabbed it in the eye. He would have taken the sword, but the gilar had his hand on it threateningly. Gilar swarmed the field and vampires took to the sky, all yelling at the prisoners to drop to the ground.

It was not an escape attempt, so they did. Not because the gilar ordered it, but because that was the plan should Tremane be taken. That was why he was the leader of their open rebellion. That was why he spoke to the other leaders and coordinated the theft of weapons and other supplies. That was his sacrifice.

Zeris watched as Tremane held them off with his knife. They did not want to kill him, so he injured three more before they piled on him. Kahnlair did not want a dead or injured elf, he wanted one elf leader alive and well, so the gilar were relatively gentle as they tied him up and took him away.

Tremane knew what was coming. He would fight the entire way, killing as many along the route as he could, but also making sure he never had an opportunity to escape this fate. Tremane was a weaver. He liked beautiful patterns and colors. He was an artist. Before the war, he never held a weapon nor had any military training. Tremane was a good man sacrificing himself so those he left behind might have a better chance of surviving.

Zeris hated it, but he played his part and waited for his chance.

***

Close to two weeks had passed since their escape. If Annalla survived, she could have caught up to them by then. She *should* have caught up to them by then. Losing one of their number left them all shaken, and the mood remained subdued.

He knew the others would continue with the mission, and Larron would finish what Annalla started. Her secondary mission had become his. He would find out who she was and what happened to her and her family. It helped him deal with his own emotions to have a purpose that could help her. They needed to find the fairy because someone needed to find the answers, even if they refused to help in the war.

Unfortunately, they were not making great time through

the forest. There continued to be expansive heavy snowdrifts in their path, and moving through took time and energy. Already, they took two half days to rest the horses and attempt to hunt, with some success, before moving on again. Each evening they dug out snow anywhere there might be something for the horses to eat, trying to extend the limited fodder they carried.

If the gorge kept a straight path north from there, Larron estimated it would take them another six or seven days to cross out of the forested hills. Adding time for the twists and turns he anticipated meant at least another week on top of that estimate.

The weather had begun to turn, with signs of the coming spring more prevalent every day. In the north, the weather tended to be erratic at best as late winter transitioned to early spring. The last two days gave them a brief rain, some hail, and a minor blizzard the night before. It left the party traveling through soggy, heavy snow that morning.

Pushing through the puffy winter snowfall was one matter. It left them tired, but relatively clean and dry. Wading through proved altogether different. The heavier snow clung wet and dirty, and it left every article of clothing feeling the same. Temperatures were still below freezing most of the day. Along with weighing them down, when the wet penetrated to their skin, it provided a means for the cold to reach them even when bundled for winter temperatures.

They changed clothing at a break each midday and stopped well before the sun set. It allowed them time to dry off and start a fire to warm themselves by and hang wet clothes over. The heat given off was wonderful, and Larron settled in close to enjoy it, along with the rest, despite his greater tolerance for temperatures. Exhaustion from the day's efforts and cold sent him straight to sleep for the first time in days, but it did not last long.

It was not his turn at watch, nor was it time for a change in the watch, but instinct woke him at sounds outside their only tent. Larron held his breath and listened, as he suspected Tyrus, who *was* on watch, was doing the same. The horses were the source of the noise to wake Larron. Tyrus would be moving slowly and calmly toward them in an attempt to keep them calm.

That he did not speak told Larron they operated under the same assumption. Windani approached from upwind of the camp. Horses and mules reacted to their smell as they would to a pack of wolves. Even war-trained horses became uneasy at the scent of windani. Larron rose as silently as possible, waking everyone even as Tyrus entered to do the same. They gave the sign for windani and were acknowledged without words.

Windani were a wolf-like people slightly longer and much broader than the irimoten they balanced, which placed them at about the size of a small bear. Short fur covered their bodies, growing longer on their heads and backs, and they had short muzzles with sharp teeth, which were their weapon of choice. Their hands bore long, dexterous fingers, so they could use weapons in addition to their claws, but it was rare to see them carrying anything larger than a knife. The main reason for their limited use of weapons was that they were more comfortable walking on all four limbs due to a spine curved to support their higher center of gravity.

Patrice could achieve a similar form utilizing her manifest essence, but the windani were built to transition naturally. Their legs were proportioned more like wolves, and their shoulders curved forward at the edges. That positioned their arms more in front than to the sides while retaining a wide range of movement. Those two features gave them the speed and agility of a wolf with the strength and size of a bear.

No one spoke because, while their hearing was nothing compared to a vampire's, it was still better than most. They could only hope the noise the animals made would not be heard and continued to speak only through hand signals.

Patrice, circle around, stay downwind, try to get a count.
Acknowledged.
Marto, protect animals.
Acknowledged.
Tyrus, Nurtik, perimeter.
Acknowledged.

Acknowledged.

Me, up tree, vantage vision for bow. Go.

Scouting would not matter against several windani, but little could help them if it was a significant hunting group. Everyone went quickly about the assignments given, and Larron hefted himself into a sturdy tree upwind of their camp before peering into the darkness. They, fortunately, had let the fire go out hours before, or it would have stood as a beacon to their location. Everything remained silent in the night except the nervous shuffling of the animals, and they patiently waited.

Patrice's white fur blended so well with the snow that he barely made her out against it. She looked up at him. *Three, hunting us now. I circle, prevent escape? You draw here?*

He recognized the plan she proposed. Patrice had determined they were only scouts or distance hunters, and they were alone. They posed a danger to the group if left alive, and they could not be allowed to escape to tell of his group's presence directly. It would likely take longer for their absence to be noticed than it would for them to report a find, and they needed the extra time. Patrice wanted to wait behind them in case any made a run, while they lured the windani there to be killed.

Yes, circle around. He turned to catch the eye of Marto, who would pass along his orders. *Three windani, prepare to ambush. Marto, animals louder to draw, alert me when ready.*

Acknowledged. Larron saw him move to relay and waited for his return. It took only moments. *Ready here. You?*

Acknowledged. Go.

Marto did something near the animals, making them cry out briefly. When Larron saw the first windani slinking toward camp, the mules were just shy of bolting. He would need to wait until all three passed below to take them from behind as Marto, Tyrus, and Nurtik fought and defended from within. They approached cautiously and from separate angles. At some point on their way over, they split up to flank their prey.

He was finally able to make out their brown and gray fur against the snow, but the third remained well covered below the edge of the gorge to their right. Larron would not be able to target that one until it moved closer.

They crept forward, moving quietly, and heading toward the animals, who expressed their fear loudly as Marto fought to calm and control them. He expected Tyrus to be moving toward that side of camp, ready to help Marto where he played bait.

The forward movement of the windani stopped outside the perimeter as they readied themselves to strike. Those were not animals expecting only what they heard and saw in a campsite. There was little doubt at least one would head straight for the tent to take out any sentient threat. Nurtik would need to deal with that one. As soon as the horses began to panic, the windani would have sped up the attack to prevent those in the camp from waking and organizing.

Larron still could not take a sight on the third windani, and the first would not be in his view much longer, so he took aim at the second. The closest let out a low, throaty growl, and they sprang forward as a unit.

Even as they raced forward, Larron's arrow sunk into the heart of his target. Two windani made fluid and graceful entrances to continue their attack, while the last flopped to the ground awkwardly and did not rise again.

Larron heard Nurtik battling on the far side, but their tent blocked his view of the fight. He could see Marto shielding the animals while struggling to keep them calm and contained within the shield while avoiding being trampled. Both windani managed to get behind something and out of his line of sight, so Larron was forced to sight at the edges and wait for one to step out from cover.

The one attacking the animals darted back and forth, striking randomly, and trying to scare a horse loose or break the mage's concentration. It lunged forward in another attack as Larron heard a cry of pain and anger from Nurtik. The cry came closely followed by the whining growl of an injured windani, but the sounds were enough to send the two mules bolting back along the path broken earlier.

The shield dropped as Marto dodged thrashing hooves.

The windani ignored the escaping animals and lunged. Marto raised his hands in front of him, holding only the hunting knife Larron had given him back in the Palonian. The arrow was already drawn, and Larron released it as the attacker jumped. It sang through the air, passing a breath from Marto's ear, to sink into a gaping mouth, and the creature landed heavily against the young mage.

Tyrus came running from behind the tent, bloody sword in hand, as Larron quickly dropped to the ground. By the time he made it over to them, Tyrus already pushed at the body on top of Marto. Larron added his strength to the effort, and the carcass inched over. Patrice joined them, and Marto finally took a gasping breath as the dead windani rolled to the side.

"Lord, that smells like a bloody, wet dog. Where is Nurtik?" he managed, wheezing.

"I'm here. Mad thin' jus' got me injured shoulder and landed on my legs. Tyrus left me ta help out here."

"You are sure there were only three?" Tyrus asked Patrice.

"Only three. I checked for other tracks and found nothing to indicate more."

"Their behavior makes me think this was a ranged hunting party rather than advanced scouts." Larron added his earlier thoughts, with Patrice nodding in agreement. "We are fortunate in that. It will be some time before they are missed and another group is sent after them."

"We'll never outpace them in the snow. We need an early and warm spring," Patrice said as she frowned at the dark forest surrounding them.

If the windani pack was to the north, even an early spring would not help. Between the fire Annalla caused and encountering those hunters, they needed the pack to be far to the east and to not expect those pack members' return for many days yet. Perhaps two weeks to escape the hills, another three to six days across the fields, depending on their pace. They would need to find a place in the mountain's foothills to make a stand if they made it that far. Three weeks. There was zero chance they had that long.

"We will not be able to stay here the rest of the night. The horses will not settle down with these bodies so close. Tyrus, would you take Moonshine and see if you can track down the mules? The rest of us can pack up and push forward a few hours before stopping for a short rest in the morning."

"Sure, I'll catch up to you, follow your trail."

He and Patrice treated Marto's and Nurtik's injuries before they packed up and headed out into the night.

CHAPTER THIRTY-THREE

They walked until the sun returned to the sky and set up a hasty camp. Patrice took the first watch and was still there when Tyrus arrived.

"Only one?" she asked him quietly.

"Broken leg. It must've been moving too fast in that soft spot we passed yesterday."

She sighed. "One pack mule left... It's almost a good thing we are running so low on supplies. Get what rest you can. Larron wants to move again before mid-day."

Knowing there was nothing wrong, Larron drifted quickly back to sleep. He took the last watch before they set out again, letting Tyrus sleep through. It was not a relaxed afternoon after encountering the windani.

Unlike the gilar, who were—more so before the war—found as often individually as they were in groups, the windani were a race with a strong pack-hunting mentality. With so many to feed, the sources of food were quickly depleted close to where they lived. They sent out small, far-ranging hunting parties throughout their territory to bring back food. As soon as the pack realized that hunting party did not return, they would send out most of their forces to track and hunt down those responsible.

As Patrice said, they could not outrun windani in the snow. One on one, the other races they faced were more dangerous in armed combat, but their proficiency and ferocity as a group made the windani the greater threat to a small unit like theirs.

You might live through the initial encounter, but in many ways, that simply delayed your death. They had no way to counter a full-pack windani attack. One step at a time, they pushed the grave images from their minds, but the implications of the previous night's encounter could not be ignored. Larron allowed for an early stop in the evening. They were tired from the broken sleep, and the horses appeared in no better shape.

"We should give the horses a half day tomorrow. It was supposed to be today, but the timing became understandably delayed."

"Shouldn't we keep moving as fast as possible if the windani will be after us soon?" Patrice asked, trying to keep her voice from trembling.

Tyrus and Nurtik darted glances around as though the pack would swarm them at any moment. Fear was understandable and warranted, but they could not maintain that level.

"Our best hope is if the snow melts and the horses are able to run with us in the fields before the mountains," he said. "To do so, we need them healthy and rested. It is tempting to rush, but I believe it best if we continue as we have to this point. If the pack is close enough for the rest break to matter, then we have already lost. I will not choose to proceed under such an assumption. We act as though speed is important, but with a mind for speeding the entire journey, not only this part of it."

She sighed. "I understand, but I can't say that's comforting."

The horses may have been getting some rest in the morning, but the people were out early, using the time hunting and foraging to supplement their supplies. He and Tyrus headed into the forest, away from the gorge well before the sun rose. They remained alert for both game and signs of other windani in the area as they crept quietly over the snow, took up positions, and waited for winter animals to peek out of their dens and burrows.

When Larron arrived back at the camp, Tyrus already sat

there with a fire going and a skinny squirrel turning over it. He fared a little better, but the rabbit in his hands had more fat than meat on it.

"How are the rest of our supplies looking?" he asked.

"Low. Not much to forage right now, and this is all we caught." Tyrus shook his head. "It's a good thing we were rationing even before we lost Annalla."

"And that she had us take everything she grew each time," added Marto. They gradually began talking about her again recently. Larron ignored the pain and focused on his new mission during such times. Marto continued, "Maybe she knew it was going to happen again."

Patrice shook her head. "She would have made sure our packs were full, and we had plenty for the horses. It got worse the second time, so she would have known she might not be so lucky a third time."

"She believe it poss'ble tho.'"

"We both did," said Larron. "I guessed she was powerful, so we discussed how we might make it more likely for her to survive. The headache came on quicker this time, and we were not able to harvest anything, but we have been cautious and frugal. Which is why we have enough to reach the mountains if we are careful. Annalla gave us the chance to make it there, the least we can do is try to take it."

Larron did not think any of them expected to make it to and through the mountains, but giving up did nothing other than guarantee the worst outcome. No one had even stumbled across the fairy in the millennia since their disappearance, so the likelihood of finding them held to a depressingly low level. They had counted on a fairy guide making the difference.

It did not matter either way as far as decisions went. There was no help close enough to reach to even consider alternatives. They could head for the dwarven clan and hope they still had a large patrol out, which would require ignoring the fact they were likely besieged. They could turn and face an enemy they had no chance of defeating, one that was also probably in the direction of the dwarves. Or they could follow through with their mission and hope it to be more than a bedtime story.

There was only one option, so they continued, pushing as much as possible without reaching their breaking point too early.

"We have a problem," Patrice said a few days later.

She returned from scouting in time to help them set up the tent. Usually, she did not return until well after they were done with the camp, taking the extra time to go that little further bit ahead.

"Windani?"

"No, not yet. A couple of hours ahead, the way becomes difficult. Sheer walls, sudden drops. Nothing more than about twice your height, Larron, but there is no way the animals can make it across."

"Wha' 'bout goin' 'round like 'fore?" asked Nurtik.

"I followed the wall around today and was not able to reach the other side. At the speed you are making through the snow, it will be at least more than a day. We risk returning to the wrong gorge if we leave the edge here, and I can't verify the connection like Annalla."

Tyrus spoke next. "The gorge below is still blocked?"

"The snow is higher than out here, but nothing we can't push through, I think. The trouble is the snow hanging on the slopes and walls. One wrong clump melts off above, and we're buried with no one to dig us out."

Larron looked around. "We cannot leave the horses. They are our best asset against the windani in the open land between hill and mountains. It would mean losing weeks we do not have to save days." There were nods of agreement. "Taking the gorge means risking worse to save only days, but I do not see another choice."

"Not…necessarily…too big of a risk." Marto looked out into the dim twilight toward the gorge they followed.

"Marto?" Larron verbally prodded him.

He took a steadying breath, as though steeling himself

against an expected argument. "I can get us through the gorge safely for a while."

"I thought only architects could change the structure of the land, and only in groups for larger-scale changes." Larron was not disagreeing with him, but hoping for clarification.

"We all know a couple of basics from the different concentrations. I could use a bit of architect skill to strengthen the snow on the slopes, but I was thinking more of shielding us from any of the small avalanches Patrice was talking about."

"How would that work?" she asked.

"A few shield modifications we are taught for combat. I did something similar with the windani when they attacked because their attacks are different than weapon strikes. If you understand the basics of an application, you can alter them to suit your needs. The heat shield I use is an example I learned from my master. Not all combat magai learn it because it's something we are guided into rather than taught. I can make small changes to the reactive properties of the shielding—intensity, duration, extension—and we will not risk being buried."

His jaw was set, and a look of complete confidence was on the young mage's face as he stared into Larron's eyes. "We should expect a couple of days in the gorge. Are you able to maintain it that long?"

"There are ways. I will need to ride with someone else guiding the horse. It would not be necessary for a shorter duration, but for days without sleep, I need to meditate," he took a deep breath and let it out with one, decisive nod. "I can do this, Larron."

"Alright," Larron conceded. "We will head into it tomorrow, and you will not take a watch tonight. Patrice, you should stay with the group until we are out again."

Marto did not argue with the order, which earned him more of Larron's trust than pushing his limits ever could. He wanted to prove himself and stood confident in his abilities, but he would not place his pride above the safety of the group.

It was something the brash youth of better times might not have been able to do, but the current youth were all wise beyond their years. Marto was not a child still in training. He represented the magai in the council and on their mission, and he knew his craft better than anyone else present.

They rose early the next morning and set out as a group, coming to the place where Patrice said they should descend less than two hours later.

"The only other concern I have," Tyrus said as they looked down the slope, "is that we will present easy targets for anyone above or before us."

"I doubt we will see any ambush. With the windani ranging this far out, and the top impassable to all but those on foot, there is little chance of seeing an attack from humans. Even those mercenaries said they would not travel much further north on someone's orders or instructions."

"What about a windani ambush?" asked Marto.

It was Patrice who answered, "A windani revenge party does not set an ambush. They hunt you, then take you down like a pack of starving wolves on a rabbit. That is about all the threat we pose to them without better positioning."

A shiver went down their backs, but Larron did not let the silence reign long. "Let us proceed."

The work proved not much different at the bottom. They still had to break through thick snow, still had to watch for ice, and had to work with damp clothing as the day wore on. It was only when they looked up from the snow on the ground to the snowy walls surrounding them that they felt the weight of their claustrophobic position. Even with Marto's assurances, it felt unnerving, and Larron worried about the potential for an avalanche.

The first day passed relatively uneventfully and left them with a lighter heart. A fair distance remained, but each day brought them closer to the fields on the other side of the hills. The second day offered the true test of Marto's plan as he grew tired from a night without sleep. He served as their protection, going into a trance-like state as soon as he mounted up after the initial descent.

His eyes closed, and his muscles relaxed slightly, but he

remained seated on his horse without having to be tied. It looked like he slept sitting up, but Marto warned them not to try to *wake* him. He told them he would not be able to remain seated upright if he were falling asleep, and only then would they need to shake him alert.

Larron's feet started feeling the effects of the freezing inch of slush they trod through. Their boots were well made, which kept the water out, but immersion in ice water could only be endured for so long. It was probably only a bit of cold, muddy ground up above, but the gorge funneled the water to the bottom in one long, streaming puddle. They would need to massage their feet every night and take extra care with the horses.

All thoughts of feet and hooves left as a creaking from above turned into a *crack, thud,* and a groaning *creeeeek.* He looked up in time to see a large section of snow ahead and to the right break off the steep slope. As though in slow motion, it fell onto the next section, growing larger on the way down.

The crashing sound banged off the walls of the gorge and sent another section of snow above them on the left falling as well. Larron could not take his eyes from the awesome sight. Walls of snow rained down like an incongruously moving, frozen waterfall.

Speckles of snow hit his face, but nothing more as dark descended around them. His heart pounded in his ears, along with the neighs of fear from the animals, but Larron remained on his feet.

"Is everyone alright?" Larron received scattered affirmative responses, which was necessary because he could not see his own nose in the darkness. "Patrice, can you see anything?"

Her eyes made better use of light, so she might be able to distinguish something with only the pinprick at the end of the snow tunnel.

"Details are in shadow, but I can see enough to guide us on," she answered, anticipating his request.

"Good. We need to get out of here as soon as possible. Single file, find the animal in front of you, and Patrice will let us know if she needs us to stop or slow."

Larron had to close his eyes against the disorientation of walking blindly. Forward they marched through the day. The tunnel collapsed behind them as Marto let the shield fall away. He was not sure how long it took, but eventually, the darkness began to lift. When he opened his eyes, he could make out silhouettes of those in front of him.

When the group made camp at the top of the gorge that evening, having found it passable above once more, Larron's spirits lifted. Temperatures rose, and they made fair progress for a few days until Patrice returned early again one afternoon.

"We'll have to head down again soon," she said, grimacing.

"How far ahead?"

"Less than a mile. It curves around to the west sharply, and we need to drop back down about that point."

"Not today," Larron decided. "The slopes are more dangerous with the snow melting, and we will need Marto to shield us again. We take the remainder of the afternoon, rest the horses, and head down in the morning after a good night of sleep."

"You intend to hunt after we set camp?" Tyrus asked. "It would seem a waste of time at this hour, though snares might not be."

"Not making use of the time would be a waste," Larron pointed out. "If you can set traps, we can spare some time in the morning to check them."

"Catch anything?" Patrice asked when Larron walked back into camp later.

"Not a scrap," he replied. "We may have more luck with Tyrus' snares come morning. I am going to change."

She nodded and refocused her attention on their surroundings. Larron slipped quietly inside the tent, not wanting to wake Marto, and looked around for his pack. Nurtik had brought them all in earlier, tucking Larron's into a corner next to one with wrapped weapons strapped to it.

The sight made him stop, his hand rising to cover his mouth. Larron's heart sank into his stomach, and his throat closed, making it difficult to breathe. They could have discarded most of her belongings by that point. The weapons could prove useful, and he kept telling himself the clothing could become bandages at need, but there really was little they could do with most of it other than having the horses carry it around as a constant reminder.

Days had passed since Larron had that much of a reaction. Usually, it was a simple double-take, a brief constriction in his chest. That was the same as losing his brother almost a year before. Perhaps alive. Probably dead. Maybe he had still been figuring out if he was in love with her, but Larron had been falling quickly.

I set myself up for pain, he thought with a choked laugh, *falling for someone as prone to injury as she.*

"Is something wrong, Larron?"

He swallowed past the lump in his throat and ducked his head to wipe away an escaped tear with a quick swipe of his fingers. "I thought you were sleeping. I did not mean to wake you."

"No, not sleeping, just a mental exercise to ease the way for an extended working." Marto stood and walked over. Larron watched his eyes move to the corner and saw the sorrow and comprehension in them before they returned to meet his own. "Changing before bed?" was all he asked.

Larron cursed himself for having to fight against becoming choked up again. The young mage's intuition surprised and touched him. "I am, yes."

"Well, I'm heading to bed now to actually sleep, so I'll leave you alone. Goodnight, Larron." With a brief, comforting pat on the shoulder, he turned and went back to his bedroll.

"Goodnight, Marto."

Larron regained his composure by the time they headed out the next morning; no tears threatened or breakdowns pending. Annalla's things were once more safely packed along with his own on Dusk's back. Tyrus managed to snare a rabbit they dressed and packed with wet snow. They would cook it at the next opportunity they found to start a fire. The cold would keep it until then as long as they changed out the snow as it melted.

Once more, they headed down to the base of the gorge. With the higher temperatures, there were times they could ride for a time beside the stream forming at the bottom where they passed. It made the travel more comfortable, but the snow upon the walls grew heavy with water. Twice that day, Marto stopped large mounds from dropping on their heads, and Larron called a stop early at a place where the rock walls stood bare above them.

They roused Marto, having let him sleep well that night with the risks from above mitigated, and started out again early the following day. Marto went back into his trance, and they rode most of the time. The base of the gorge widened in places, and they stopped twice to allow the horses to eat and rest when they found—or thought they were likely to find—grass beneath the snow.

Most of the soggy snow must have fallen off the slopes over the last few days of sun and warming temperatures. It was mostly clear, and Marto only had to protect them in one spot better sheltered from the sun where the snow layer broke off and would have buried them. If they could find a way out to travel at the top again, the day would be almost perfect.

"Larron," Nurtik called from ahead, lifting a hand to the sky ahead of them.

Dear heavens! It was too much to ask? Larron cursed his previous optimistic thoughts, expecting the worst as he looked ahead to where the dwarf pointed.

The distant strip of sky peeking between the sides of the gorge above darkened to a deep gray, the clouds swirling in a wind yet to reach them. A warm spring might be hurrying toward them, but winter was not ready to relinquish its hold on the land.

The storm was not rushing directly at them with speed, as far as he could tell from their limited vantage. It might shift direction and avoid hitting them full-on, but they would be seeing foul weather before the end of the next day.

Tyrus whistled softly. "That does *not* look good. If that

thing hits us while we are still down here—"

"Then we push through it," Larron finished for him. "We cannot dig in and wait it out if it arrives before we find a path out. Marto would not be able to protect us, and we cannot afford the time with the windani threat looming. Maybe it will miss us, and we will only see a bit of light snow."

Patrice snorted. "Your optimism is commendable, Larron, but I think I'll hope to simply make it out of the gorge by the time it reaches us."

They watched the sliver of sky as they finished the day's travel, pushing on until it was dark enough to make setting camp difficult. The line of dark clouds crept onward. As night fell, they could only tell the difference between where stars could be seen and where they were lost to cover.

CHAPTER THIRTY-FOUR

"Wake up everyone. We need to go. Now." Patrice's voice was urgent, but not afraid in a way indicating an attack.

Asking why she woke them was not necessary, no one had been sleeping easy. Wind peppered the top and side of the tent with little frozen flakes and made the cloth flap and stretch. It whistled over the rocks around them and the trees far above creaked as they swayed, and branches brushed against each other.

"It's been getting stronger with each gust. I don't think we'll be able to pack the tent if we wait much longer."

"Then let us pack," Larron said. "Tyrus, I want Marto tied to his horse this time. I do not care if he believes he can remain in the saddle in his trance, not in this wind."

Tyrus nodded as each of them hastily rolled bedrolls and blankets. Another gust of wind pressed in on the treated cloth making up one side of the tent, shaking it all over. Wide eyes looked around, meeting before everyone quickened their efforts. Snow stung Larron's face when he emerged. Horses hung their heads against the onslaught, and he followed their example.

It took Nurtik standing and lying upon the tent to get it rolled up without flying away in the wind, but the two of them managed it while Tyrus manhandled Marto onto his horse and tied him to the saddle. Temperatures had dropped rapidly overnight, and patches of ice littered the ground.

Tyrus returned toward the horses with one of the last supply packs when his feet came out from beneath him. He went down hard on one side with the supplies flying out and up. Larron kept him down until he satisfied himself that nothing was broken. The young man rubbed his backside, grimacing, as Larron helped him to his feet once more. They were lucky Tyrus did not fall until after the mage was secure.

He glanced over at Larron. "No laughing."

"I am not." He was certain his mild amusement was not visible, but Tyrus only grunted in obvious disbelief.

Nurtik went down when they led the horses away from the water and icier areas, slipping and nearly being walked over by his pony as he struggled to roll out of the way in his heavy armor. The incident to finally break Larron's stoic expression, though, was when the wind knocked Patrice off Moonshine before Tyrus could mount behind her.

She shifted mid-air, still landing gracefully, and came up spitting and muttering about storms. Larron had to purse his lips and suck in his cheeks against the threatening smile. As though she could sense his mirth, Patrice's head turned his way with narrowed eyes before she told Tyrus to get up first and jumped up after him, her leap impressive in her shifted form.

Schooling his features, Larron shouted over the wind before they started out. "Patrice, if this does not let up after a few hours, we will need you to head up the side periodically."

She nodded. "To see if it is passable above. Yes, we need to get out of here."

The early start ended up rather fortunate, it made up for the fact their progress slowed to a crawl. No one could see beyond the next few steps. The walls funneled the wind, so it pushed them in random directions, forcing them to dismount, and making keeping their footing a serious effort. Cold bit every inch of exposed flesh and pushed through any tie or seam in their clothing.

There must have been snow still falling from the slopes. Maybe some of it had iced over, but Larron suspected the ice would only make whatever fell on them heavier. Marto's shield held. That was all Larron knew for certain because he could not see how much snow and ice the mage supported above them beyond the first layer.

He wondered if the wind made it worse. Did it increase the resistance required? Was the sleep two nights before enough to see him through? Larron was not even sure the shield was necessary, because they only needed it to save them from a slide large enough to bury them. He could be shielding them and draining his strength without need.

The sky lightened, and the wind began to die down as a ceiling of white could be made out above them, the shield building up a layer of snow through which he could make out the rising of the sun by glow alone. Larron waited what he thought to be a few hours, then a little longer—knowing a short time could feel much longer in such conditions—before he called to Patrice, shouting to be heard. Word passed up to her, and he saw a shadow head up on the right before she became swallowed in the white cloud.

No one stopped pushing forward to wait. If she found nothing, they could not afford to lose the time and momentum, and she could catch up over the snow. He wanted her to come back and point upward, but there had been no relief as far as he could see before settling in the night before, and he was not confident they would be freed so soon.

Patrice confirmed his doubts less than an hour later. She did not even try to make herself heard, just shook her head and passed him to resume her place in line. It was the same story every time he sent her up, and Larron could feel the sun descending, even if he could no longer see a sign of it through their snow canopy. Another few hours, and they would have to stop for another night if only to give the horses rest. He would send her up twice more before giving in and calling a halt to the day.

Marto held the strongest shield above them and slightly forward. Larron could tell he pulled in the range of the shield as the snow gathered above them and forward, but further ahead, there was no cover. It was different than the time he protected them from the avalanche, which likely meant he needed to adjust due to the additional strain the storm placed on him in other ways. There was no way to know if it meant he would or would not be able to spend another night protecting them.

The danger itself was less in the snow building up on top of the shield, and more related to the snow on the slopes above them. They had no way of knowing if an overloaded shelf of snowpack hovered precariously above from one moment to the next.

"Larron!" He turned to see Marto trying to get his attention and dropped back to the mage's side. It looked like that small physical effort drained him, and Larron had his answer. Marto leaned toward him. "Too much. Shield will go when I do."

Even as Marto finished saying it, Larron rushed forward, shouting a warning ahead. Nurtik looked back, received his warning, and passed it to Tyrus at the front. He hoped Patrice would not be taken by surprise and buried once the shield fell. They would not be able to dig her out if they did not know where she went.

The moment the shield fell, he knew. All the larger clumps and mounds it held off their path were released. It must have either been concave or the snow built up at the edges, as more snow fell to the sides and swept over them from opposite angles. Larron felt his feet go out beneath him as the snow hit harder from one side than the other. He toppled, losing Dusk's reins, and landing in the foot of freezing slush they walked through before the wave of snow buried him completely.

His mind went back to the icy river, but that time he could not move. There was no grasping Annalla or swimming toward shore, there was only snow and slush packed all around him. He had no idea which direction was up with the tumble. Larron tried to thrash, wrenching his limbs with all his strength.

Panic set in. He could not breathe. He could not think. Only snow existed. That is how they would all die, weakly thrashing about in a snowpack from which they could not escape. His foot jerked backward.

It moved! Larron thought as he fought more.

Pushing the opposite direction and wiggling the rest of his lower half, he inched backward out of the hole in which he was buried only a few feet deep. That was the amount of snow holding him down, and he knew a larger avalanche could have killed him under less than a foot. He wiped his face off with his hands and tried to shed the lingering panic along with the icy water.

The horses in front of and behind him were both standing, and he pushed himself up out of the freezing slush. Chill winds on his wet clothes made it feel like he was still sitting in the icy slush at his feet. A quick glance ahead told him the rest of the group made it through the deluge unscathed.

"Larron!" Someone called him for the second time in about ten minutes, and he turned. Patrice hurried toward him over the snow.

"I am glad you made it. The shield is down," he told her when she stood beside him, so he did not have to yell over the wind.

"I was above the shield and saw it fall. I have had to dig my way through up and down almost every time, but it dropped before I reached it."

"Marto is unconscious," Larron said. "He could not hold it any longer, so we will have to proceed without the shield."

Patrice shook her head. "We won't. We can head up here and look for a place to camp."

Larron sighed with relief and wiped away more water dripping from his hair down his face.

"Can you lead us out?"

She nodded.

"Tell the others," he ordered.

He was the only one to have fallen into the slush, so no one else shivered as badly. They went slowly, slipping and stumbling up the slope, struggling to reach the top through swirling snow and deepening dusk. He felt his clothing freezing against his skin, and his fingers and toes burned with cold.

When the ground finally leveled out, he turned his attention to looking around for some place to possibly break the wind enough to set camp. Tyrus found something first, and they followed him, quickly setting up the tent despite the driving winds. As soon as the tent was erected, Larron grabbed his pack and shouted over at Patrice.

"Take care of the horses. I have to change, fell in the water at the bottom when the shield fell."

Without a backward glance, he ducked into the tent and stripped off his clothing with as much speed as his freezing hands could manage. He was not surprised when Patrice followed him a few minutes later.

"The others are well enough to finish up with Marto and the animals. Sit down and give me your feet."

He didn't argue, sitting down with a blanket around his shoulders and started working feeling back into his fingers, even as she did the same with his toes. They sat like that for a while. Slowly, a tingling pain took the place of the numb chill, and he was grateful for every stab indicating he once more avoided frostbite.

"Okay, I am back enough to dress again. Thank you, Patrice."

"I would say you should have told us, but we could have done nothing before now anyway."

Larron pulled dry clothing out of his pack and pulled it all on. "You are sure the others are alright?"

"Yes, they are a little damp in places, but nothing compared to the soaking you had down there. They will bring Marto in with them. No one is going to stand watch tonight; we are all too tired, and falling asleep in that would be fatal."

The tent flaps opened before he could respond, and Tyrus backed in carrying Marto's top half, with Nurtik holding his legs. They set him down for Larron and Patrice and went back out for the remaining packs to be brought inside for the night.

"How are the horses doing?" he asked when the five of them huddled together.

Tyrus looked over at him. "Tired. Cold. We brushed them down, got them dry, and wrapped up as tight as we can without shelter. A good night's rest and they should be fine...unless this storm lasts days."

"Thank you for taking care of everything."

"We think ya close ta losin' fingers ta let us take car'a Dusk."

"Hush, Nurtik." Tyrus grinned at the dwarf and winked. "You don't want to ruin the perfect reputation of the elves with such rumors of gracelessness."

Larron scowled at them for having a laugh at his expense, but since he was fighting back a smile of his own, it was not convincing.

"No respect," Larron muttered, shaking his head.

"Oh, we're just happy to know the elves aren't actually perfect, Larron. Most of us smell like we haven't bathed properly in months,"

"Because we haven't," Patrice commented as Tyrus continued.

"And you walk around fresh as a spring rain shower. We slip and slide on the ice—"

"And in the wind," she added.

"—and you don't even wobble. It only took a small avalanche to knock you over and have you flailing about."

"You could have helped me."

"No. No," Tyrus said placatingly. "I would not want to have startled you and received one of your flying feet to the gut or this handsome visage."

Patrice only snorted as Tyrus gestured to his face.

Now Larron could not stop the smile. "If you are all done having fun at my expense, I am getting some sleep. It has been a long day, and *this* handsome and perfect visage needs rest."

Patrice rolled her eyes, shook her head, and curled up on her bedroll. "Not one of you is handsome," she muttered, receiving a chorus of exhausted laughter in response.

CHAPTER THIRTY-FIVE

Nothing attacked them in the night, so risking no guard as they slept paid off. The storm dissipated at some point, leaving an overcast but calm sky in the morning. Larron had slept deeply and felt better rested than he recalled in recent weeks. Patrice proved correct about their exhaustion, and they all seemed better for the rest.

"How are you feeling, Marto? You still look drained."

"I'll be back in a few days, maybe a week. We are usually ordered to bed rest for a day after reaching our limit. It will simply take me a little longer without being able to take things easy."

"Would you like to ride again?"

"I might need to later, but I would rather stretch my legs to start today."

He ended up remaining on his feet only a few hours before mounting. The storm made walking tricky, freezing the slush and adding to the snow cover so they were breaking a path once more.

It could have been worse, Larron knew. With the sun and warmer temperatures returning in the afternoon, the ice and snow began to melt. Each day following saw them moving a little faster, and their spirits lifted as those days passed without sign or hint of pursuit. No one deluded themselves into thinking they were safe, but every day they survived became a victory. After about four days, the land beneath them started to rise more sharply.

"We're almost out of the forest," Marto told them, staring at the slope, while they waited for the evening's rabbit to cook. Tyrus' snares had proved fruitful of late.

"Why do you say that?" asked Patrice.

"The hills. In the story, what I saw of this part of the gorge is pretty much straight through. They are taller at the north edge of the forest, right? So, we should be out of the hills soon."

"How long until we reach the mountains?" Patrice looked at Nurtik when she asked.

"Dunno, we stay'n main roads 'n not come out this way. Larron?"

"I have never been in this specific area, but from the maps and other points of reference, I estimate less than a week to cross the final hills and the land between, so long as the snow has sufficiently melted."

A week did not seem so insurmountable all of a sudden. About twice as long had passed since the attack. Soon enough, the snow would clear, and the land would open enough for them to ride constantly.

Meat was shared out, along with a bit of bread and cheese gone hard and stale. Only the freezing weather kept some things from becoming inedible. Despite the lean fare, there were smiles and conversation Larron noticed had been lacking lately. The fact they could practically see their goal made the burdens and difficulties along the way ease and have some meaning.

Larron smiled, watching for a while longer before reminding them they would not make it through that week if they did not get to bed. Calm settled over the skies, the group, and settled into him. He drifted off, finally feeling more like himself, even if it was a different self than the man who'd left the Derou, or even the Palonian.

When Nurtik woke him later, the calm and contented feelings withered. It was not time for his watch.

"What is wrong?" he asked, and others woke around him.

Nurtik nodded toward the tent opening. "Listen."

They followed him outside, watched him face south, and

copied his example.

No one spoke. They waited, watched, and listened for whatever brought him to wake them. Nothing happened, but that did not make them dismiss his concern. Larron was on the verge of asking him to describe the sound instead when he heard it echo through the forest.

His blood went cold. They froze in place. No one would ever mistake that howl for a wolf.

"Windani," Patrice whispered. "They've caught our scent."

"So it would seem," Larron replied.

"How far back do you think?" Tyrus asked.

"They would be at the edge of the gorge to follow our trail," he said. "That will make it more difficult to determine with the sounds echoing off the walls. Four...five days, I think. They know our race now, and how many, and will pick up their pace to try catch us. We will gain some distance on them over the plains tomorrow."

"Earlier, you said less than a week," Marto pointed out. "We can still make it."

No more storms, he thought. *We are lost if another storm delays us.*

Larron would not speak those concerns aloud. Instead, he said, "We will have to. Back to sleep. At least rest if you cannot sleep. We will need it in the days to come."

He did not bother worrying whether the others would take his advice. Experience taught him to take sleep where he could find it in battle. And that had become a battle. The opportunities to rest would become fewer over the coming days. Back in the tent, he lay down, emptied his mind, and drifted back to sleep until it was time for his watch. When his shift ended, he slept again in moments.

Their goal was in sight. The enemy no longer remained a vague idea and unknown factor. Larron shifted easily into the hardened soldier persona that had subsumed his existence for the last two decades. When morning came, Larron was not surprised to find he was the last one up. Elves were, after all, masters of patience when needed.

They would want to push, which could overtax the horses and triple his estimate. The slightest margin would mean life or death, and he would lead them with escape in mind.

They needed the windani to be five days behind, not four, so he had to operate on that assumption. Five would give them a chance. If he accelerated their pace, they could reach the foothills in seven days, and extend the time it took the windani to catch them as well. Trying to increase it more would lame or kill most, if not all, of their horses, and he refused to leave anyone behind for lack of mounts.

"I know why you are doing this, Larron," Patrice told him when he had his things packed. "I appreciate it, but it is going to become irritating very quickly."

"Then we should get moving." Larron smiled at her congenially, to which she huffed and shook her head in response.

They traveled through foot deep snow in most places, though the mountains to which they headed remained covered in white. Somewhere in those mountains lived those they sought. It was only a question of if they could make it there.

With the clearer ground, they picked up the pace and rode most of the day. They were over the hill near mid-afternoon, and Larron kept them moving until they reached the bottom, well into the evening hours.

"We need our visual references," he said to Marto in the early morning. "A point we are making for from here?"

"Straight north. We'll end up somewhere between those two peaks there," he pointed, "and there is a small pass we need to ascend. They are somewhere at the top."

There was a wide swath of mountains between those two points. With the curvature of the land, even Larron's eyes could not make out a marker lower in the foothills, so he settled for selecting two higher points in a line due north to make his reference for their bearing.

"We will run the pony," he said. "That will help us pace

the horses. We will lose it sooner, so you will ride with Marto when that happens, Nurtik. It should last through tomorrow. Let us hope the windani do not reach the plains by then."

It was a marathon race they were bound to lose eventually. The windani were capable of covering twice as much ground in a day as the horses, even more, differentiated over snow. Even though the group was limited to the slower pace of the pony, Larron still varied their speed to stretch the endurance of the horses.

As night approached, they took advantage of the open landscape, allowing the very last rays of the dying sun to reach them. By the time the group stopped, they were again performing camp chores by the afterglow and firelight alone. Extra attention was spared for the animals before turning in, and Larron sent them to sleep with the promise of another early start.

He kept his promise. They packed quickly and left the tent where it stood. It added unnecessary weight. As they packed, they sorted through the rest of their supplies for other items to leave behind, but there was little expendable with a mountain hike waiting at the end.

"What about this?" Patrice asked, and Larron jerked back seeing her holding Annalla's pack and weapons. He considered that before he gave the order, and it still gave him pause.

"Keep the weapons—we may need them—and one set of clothing. The cut she preferred and holes for her wings might be the only proof we have to convince the fairy of her existence and that she sought to help us find them. Leave the rest."

The wind picked up the next evening, blowing in from the northwest, and the mule and pony slowed dramatically. By the time they stopped for the night, all the animals were sweating and breathing heavily. The smallest of them would die if pushed much further. Rather than taking the time to move the supplies later, they sorted one more time and left all the fodder behind, counting on the field grass to see them through.

Mule and pony were sent running in another direction. They would likely be run down by the windani, but it might take a small number away from the immediate pursuit. Patrice continued to ride with Tyrus, and Nurtik rode with Marto, with the dwindling supplies behind Larron on Dusk. Even with the extra weight, the horses made better time than before, no longer running at the slower pace of the shorter animals.

It was still morning when they saw the windani crest and descend the hill. The wave of muscled fur flowing over the land as they moved proved an awesome and fear-inspiring sight.

"They did not think it necessary to send the full force of the pack after us," Larron observed calmly.

"What do you mean? There are hundreds of them!" Marto shouted over the hoofbeats, his voice rising a little hysterically.

"Their den would number thousands. This is most likely a token force of that which initially set out to see what kept the three we killed. Three hundred is a great number to us, but for a windani pack of significant size, this is only a large hunting party."

"They're still two an' a half days 'hind us. We migh' make the pass yet."

"We might," Larron said, even as his mind settled with the knowledge they would be at least a half-day from cover when they were run down.

It was difficult to keep from looking back every few seconds to see how much closer their pursuers had come. Larron imagined the others only saw a blurry mass, but he made out the details clearly enough.

Their tongues lolled and flopped lazily in their mouths as they loped gracefully over the flat land. Powerful muscles in their legs and arms rippled to the beat of their strides beneath fur brushed back with the wind of their movement. In their eyes were hunger, revenge, and sheer joy of the hunt. There was an undeniable beauty in their motion, something akin to the wolves they resembled, but those were people making a choice to follow Kahnlair. They were people who cared nothing for the sentience of their prey and took such behavior to another level of greed.

Hating the races born to evil was difficult for Larron. He could not hate someone for their nature. Instincts existed within everyone and everything, and they could be nearly impossible to overcome. He had seen a pack of wolves hunt before, and they looked not so different from the people racing after him and his friends.

Both needed to eat and feed their pack, both had food preferences, and both hunted with the tools nature gave them. Never would he say he did not fear them. Windani were ruthless hunters who enjoyed playing with their food before killing it, if given the opportunity. He would not hesitate to kill them, but hate was something he could not manage.

It kept coming back to nature. Nature was a balance of all things, including good and evil. The windani existed because the irimoten did, and the irimoten existed because of the windani. The destruction of one could very well mean the destruction of both. Each was meant to work against the other, directly and indirectly, and by doing so maintained the balance nature created.

Larron could not help but think Kahnlair believed something along the same lines, but he amplified the destructive nature of the evil races to an extreme. Rather than balance, his desire for power and control took his opponents to the brink of extinction.

"They're stopping." Tyrus' voice broke through his thoughts as evening fell.

Larron took a quick glance back and saw them settling down. "We keep moving until dark again."

They managed another few hours before the light grew too faint to continue. The horses were lathered when they stopped and needed to be walked before they were taken care of for the night.

All the food and water for the horses were gone, so they dug a trough to fill with melted snow. Larron did not expect any of them would survive to reach the mountains.

They would be pushing the horses at or near their full speed for a portion of the next day, and more the day after that. He did not want to lose them, but he had learned many times that, companion or not, his horses would die in their own time. Giving a final pat on Dusk's neck, he curled up next to the fire with the others.

"We need to go." It seemed only minutes since he'd fallen asleep when Patrice woke him.

"What has happened?" he asked, instantly awake as battle readiness settled.

Others shifted around as well. "The windani have been on the run for an hour now. I don't think we can remain here through the night."

"The horses are not rested enough," Larron sighed and rubbed his eyes. "We will run ahead of them for a time. We cannot ride in the dark, anyway. There is not enough moonlight by which to see our footing."

"We are leaving?" asked Tyrus through a yawn.

"The windani run toward us even now," he said, nodding. "Patrice has been watching them come for an hour."

"I'll start getting the horses ready." He rose with a groan.

Marto came up beside Larron. "If you let me know when the horses are ready to ride, I can provide some light."

"Another way in which you 'change the basics of a working?'" Larron asked him with a small grin.

"Yes. Do you think they will rest tomorrow?" He tipped his head to indicate their pursuers.

"I do, but it will not be for as long as we need." Larron thought he managed to keep hopelessness out of his voice.

They finished harnessing the horses and began running. Patrice and Nurtik took the lead to set the pace. Patrice's night vision could help them avoid places on the ground that would otherwise trip them in the dark.

It was a crawl compared to the speed the windani made behind them, but every step delayed the moment of attack. Hours passed in the darkness, and they were slowing their run before Larron called for them to ride. As they mounted, a burning glow grew ahead of them. A little ball of fire shone above the ground.

"I did not think magai could make air burn."

"We can't. I dug up some of the dead, frozen grass and am slowing the burn on it. It is not much light, but it might help."

"I will take point," Patrice told them from her place in front of Tyrus. "It is more than enough light for me to see by."

Through the early morning, they continued, taking another turn at running ahead of their mounts in the twilight hours before the sun rose. The image greeting them as sunlight illuminated the windani was not encouraging.

If the windani continued to gain at that pace, Larron could not see the faintest hope they would make it through the next day. His estimates had failed to account for the windani pushing forward with little to no rest. Even when they continued on during the three hours during the day the windani took to rest, they did not regain enough of their lead.

That night followed the same pattern as the last, with their pursuers stopping for only a few hours before starting once it was full dark. They did not stop riding until there was not enough light for the horses to travel by, and then they ran for another hour before stopping to rest.

Not even bothering to set camp, they saw to the horses, then curled up in a pile together to remain warm. That time, when Patrice saw the windani rise to run again, they did not wait an hour to move.

"We can vary their pace, but they are still carrying double. The horses will not last," Tyrus said to Larron as he tied off the harness.

"They will take us as far as they can, and then it is our turn to finish it."

They shared a resigned look, and Tyrus nodded. They did not waste their breath with more idle talk, so it remained silent except for the clop of hooves, Patrice's relayed warnings and the faint sound of hundreds of windani at their backs. Marto burned more grass when they rode before sunrise.

When morning finally came, they saw they could not spare the horses even to vary their pace. The final sprint was upon them.

Larron set the pace, keeping the horses at a steady gallop,

the fastest speed he thought they could maintain for the longest time. He tried to calculate the odds in his head, but the windani seemed tireless. If their group could maintain all day and the windani stopped for their mid-day break, they would reach the foothills first, around sunset.

Each time he looked back, the windani closed the gap a little more, but the mountains they headed toward did not seem to be getting any closer.

About an hour before mid-day, whatever luck remained to them turned. A horse's sudden scream behind made Larron look back and pull up Dusk to trot back. Marto's horse hit a hole in the ground beneath the snow. It was on the ground with protruding bone, declaring a broken leg. Both Marto and Nurtik went sprawling forward when it fell. Tyrus also stopped and turned Moonshine around to come back with him to where the three lay.

"Are either of you hurt?" Larron asked them.

"Scrapes, bruises, nothing broken I can tell."

"Same wi' me, horse 's done though."

"I'll take care of her," Tyrus said as he dismounted. "Move Dusk and Moonshine away a bit more."

They backed off, and Tyrus quickly ended her pain. Every second there doubled as valuable time they lost, allowing the windani to catch up that much sooner. If they remained where they were, they would be dead inside a half hour. Patrice, still on Moonshine, spoke his thoughts aloud.

"We're not going to make it."

"No," Larron said as he laced his fingers at the back of his neck. "Running full-out, the journey is seven…eight hours to the pass, no more than four until they catch us." The words were barely out of his mouth when something made the three on the ground stop their rush back to where he and Patrice sat upon the horses. They stopped and stared.

"Please tell me you did not discard all my spare clothing to save weight." The voice, full of sarcastic exasperation, had Larron's head whipping around so fast he thought he might have snapped something.

It would not have mattered. His heart already stopped; he could not breathe or think. Nothing existed except her. Annalla. She was nearly in the same shape he first found her all those months ago. Hungry, tired, and completely naked but for her wings. The only things missing were the injuries and a look of frightened confusion, but the hollow cheeks indicated malnutrition.

"Clothing? Please?" She wiggled her fingers. "It is not summer weather out here."

Larron shook his head, swallowed a few times, and took a deep breath, but when he opened his mouth to respond, he could only breathe out one word. "Annalla?"

"We don't have much left for you," Patrice saved him, kicking Moonshine closer to Dusk so she could rummage through the remaining packs. "Only a shirt and some trousers. No boots, but I know Larron is wearing two pairs of socks, so he can give one pair to you, and you can ride."

"My weapons?"

"Those we still have." Patrice handed over clothing and weapons, and Annalla dressed, ignoring the uncontrolled staring brought on by their shock at seeing her alive.

Larron finally found enough of his voice again to ask a question. "How? It has been weeks."

It would not have taken her weeks to fly to them. Along with the shock and joy came anger that she would leave them—him—waiting so long, thinking she had died.

Annalla stopped buckling the sword around her waist and looked up at him. He felt his heart skip again and tried not to start shaking, crying, or both.

"By the time I gained control, I did not have enough strength to dampen the fire completely. I pulled back what I could—hoping it would be enough to keep you safe—then used what power remained to keep the fire from consuming me. It was a long road back from there, which is better told later. I came as soon as I could, Larron." Her eyes asked him to understand. "You four need to keep riding. Leave Patrice here. I will pick her up on my way back and drop her off closer to the mountains."

She did not wait for them to respond, but shot into the sky again, heading for the oncoming windani. It was surreal… Impossible. He was relieved and giddy, angry and frustrated. There she was, back from the dead like nothing happened, giving out orders.

Larron wanted to shake her, demanding answers. He wanted to hug her and demand she run away and not risk dying *again* with the rest of them there. That would never be her…them. Something in him snapped back into place, and it felt like his mind could function at its normal speed once more.

"Nurtik with me. Marto, you are with Tyrus," he ordered, even as he removed his socks. "Patrice, give these to her when she picks you up. Come on, we need to ride."

He eased off on the horses a little and said nothing when every head turned to watch and see what she would do. Larron peered back with the rest as Annalla tore across the sky and plummeted toward the ground without slowing. She hit in front of the windani with a force, shaking the ground where Larron sat, causing a dirt cloud to rise through the thin snow cover. The damp earth settled quickly, revealing Annalla squatting in front of a wide row of spiky trees like the ones with which she previously impaled the gilar.

Windani plowed into the spikes, unable to halt their momentum. From his distant seat, he saw her rise, uninjured. Annalla stretched her arms wide, and the spikes burst into flames, killing any nearby windani not already dead. Even as he heard death howls, he saw others jump the barrier she created. Most did not make it, but two managed the hurdle and attacked. He could do nothing from that distance except watch as they sprang at her. It was movement born of training that became instinct saving her life. Her sword swept through the head of one and plunged into the throat of the other before they touched the ground.

Her fighting skills might indicate she was unharmed by the last few weeks, but her next movement dispelled the notion. Annalla reached to pull her sword from the second windani's throat and nearly fell over when it did not come easily.

After cleaning and sheathing her blade, Annalla took to the sky again and headed away from the fiery wall behind her. The wall of wood and fire was not extremely wide, but the windani would be more cautious, slowing them. Annalla brought them a miracle—two, with her return—buying them time.

CHAPTER THIRTY-SIX

Annalla took a deep breath and shook off the lingering pain and exhaustion before returning to pick up Patrice. She was rushing her recovery, but hearing the windani howl those few days before pushed her into her decision. A day later, she would have found nothing but bloody, trampled snow. That still might end up being all that would remain of them. She pulled the mask back over her emotions and physical strain before landing.

The irimote surprised her by drawing her into a tight hug and bursting into tears. "We thought—we had—lost you." She managed between sobs. "Thought—you—were dead."

She patted her awkwardly on the back while Patrice held on, but the tears lasted only a few minutes before she regained control.

"Are you okay?" Annalla asked her.

A wet laugh escaped as Patrice wiped her eyes. "I should be the one asking you that. Yes, I am better now. How are you? What happened?"

"Let us walk. I am still a little too tired to be carrying anyone," Annalla said while gesturing forward.

Annalla was more fatigued than she wanted to admit, but she had experienced worse many times in her life. She hoped, in an odd way, it would not be the last.

Patrice caught up to her quickly, and she waited until then

to respond. "I am still recovering, but I came as soon as I could. I heard the windani howls and was not certain I would reach you in time."

"That was rather impressive." Patrice nodded back south across the plain.

"Do not expect another such display anytime soon."

"I take it you have some sort of plan?"

Annalla nodded. "I will take you close to the pass and leave you to run the rest of the way while I return to pick up another. The horses will not last, so eventually, everyone will be running. If I take the smallest each time, I will have less distance to carry the heaviest among you.

"You, and whoever else arrives in the pass first, should look for a defensible position. The windani will not stop simply because we are no longer in the open, so we need someplace where we will not be facing the entire pack at once."

"You cannot carry us all," Patrice said and peered over at her with a skeptical look. "You will never last that long. I may not be able to read you the way Larron can, but even *I* can see *that*."

"I will." She shrugged. "I have to."

Patrice grunted but made no further argument. "Leave me further back. I will shift and run. I'm as fast as most horses in my hunting form."

Annalla nodded again, and the two of them walked in silence for a time. She could almost hear the questions fighting to be the first off Patrice's tongue. There would be questions no matter what, but Annalla was not going to invite them, not when she still struggled with everything herself.

"What happened? It wouldn't have taken you weeks to fly here."

She thought in silence before answering. "The way you die—if your essence overwhelms you—is not directly through the manifestation's effects. It happens in one of two ways. You either consciously separate your essence from your body, allowing the entirety of your essential energy to fuel the manifestation, or you cannot control your essence, draining your body of what keeps it alive.

"I came near to experiencing the latter. Body and soul, diminishing to maintain an uncontrolled force struggling to break free. It did not leave me very well off and took a long time for me to have the strength to even stand. I am not certain how many days passed."

Annalla sighed and shook her head. She changed the subject rather than explain further. "Ready to fly?"

Patrice knew what she was doing, changing the subject, and narrowed her eyes. The shift had not even been in the vicinity of subtle, and she hoped her wish to move on would be accepted.

"Not my favorite way to travel," Patrice finally responded. "I prefer my feet firmly on the ground, but if you are ready, so am I."

"On my back this time. You are small enough to fit between my wings."

She kneeled down so Patrice could wrap her arms around her neck, and as she rose to her feet, Annalla held Patrice's legs to keep her from slipping as she took off. The arms around her neck tightened at their rapid ascent, but Patrice managed to refrain from clawing her that time.

Only once Annalla leveled off did she loosen the stranglehold on her neck as she was fully supported by Annalla's body below her. They flew in silence, the air rushing past, and Patrice's face buried against Annalla's back, making conversation impossible. It gave Annalla time to think, to remember the things she had not shared.

Pain.

It was too limited a word for what she felt as the flames licked at her body, seeking a way to consume it along with the surrounding forest. Every bone felt broken, every joint ached, and every muscle burned. Her entire body became agony, and that was only half the torture. Along with draining her physically, her essence strained against the connection her soul fought to maintain.

The result went far beyond her initial amnesia. She not

only lost her memory but the ability to think. All desires and basic instincts were gone. Life, death, fear, longing—they meant nothing to her. Her entire existence became the repeated mantra to keep the flames away without the ability to know why it was important.

Eventually, the flames around her died. That one, driving purpose was lost, and it stopped pushing for a continued manifest effort. She lost consciousness.

Things were not improved upon waking. There remained a constant ache everywhere, and movement of any kind shot bolts of pain through every muscle. Even breathing hurt.

She tried to stop breathing but found it happened involuntarily. Annalla later wondered how long she lay unconscious, but such considerations were irrelevant at the moment of waking. Hunger and thirst ate at her, but she was ignorant of how to alleviate them.

Little wisps of lingering smoke drifted over her, and she watched them without purpose. If any animals dared to enter the charred area to attack her, she would have felt every moment, but done nothing except watch with mild curiosity. She lost consciousness again.

Slowly, it came back. Instinct first, which was why she had not starved or died of dehydration. Though, her initial methods were nothing close to civilized. Annalla was lucky that her training and memory settled back into place by the time the last winter storm hit, or she would have died of exposure within minutes.

Her mind recovered much more quickly than her body and essence. She knew how to use her powers long before it was wise to do so, but sometimes she had to risk the use or starve. When she finally remembered her companions, she was far away, and walking or flying for any extended duration proved impossible.

The damage had been so great that it was still difficult. She could spend almost an hour in the air with Patrice before she needed a break and headed for the ground. The landing also made the irimote cling tighter to Annalla's neck. They angled with their heads toward the ground, and Patrice was not completely confident she would be caught if she slipped off, despite assurances that

Annalla would not let her fall.

"Can you not fly closer to the ground, Annalla?" Patrice asked as soon as she gained her feet.

"Not with the situation we are in, I am afraid. The higher air is easier for me to fly through. Down here, the ground itself seems to pull at me. I cannot spare the energy, so I cannot spare you the height."

She sighed heavily. "It did not hurt to ask. Are we walking again?"

Annalla smiled at her and started toward the mountains. They walked for a while and took off again for what she thought would be their last flight before they parted ways. She estimated it would be under three hours from the time she left with Patrice to when she made it back to the rest of the group. Her intervention would delay the windani maybe an hour. She did her best to estimate how far Patrice could run before the windani reached her and landed again.

"Will you be able to make it from here?" she asked.

Patrice nodded. "Be safe and get back quickly."

"I will bring you a running partner as soon as I'm able, but they will start out ahead of you when I drop them off."

Patrice shifted and began loping off as Annalla flew back the way she had come. It was amazing how much lighter she felt and how much faster she could travel without carrying another person. As quickly as possible, she sped through the air to reach the rest of her companions.

They were further than she expected when she caught sight of them, but Dusk and Moonshine were showing the strain. The two horses would not last much longer, and the thought of losing her friend and first mount had her swallowing past a lump in her throat.

Instead of making them stop, Annalla curved around, slowed, and flew beside them.

"Patrice?" Larron asked.

"Safe. I am grabbing another."

He nodded, and Annalla shifted to gliding beside Tyrus

and Marto. "Marto, I am going to pull you from Moonshine, so I need you to hold out your arms for me."

"Nurtik is lighter than I am. He should be next."

"Only by a small amount, but he wears armor and carries a heavy weapon, you do not. You are next."

"Alright." He nodded.

As she peeled off to approach from behind, he stretched out his arms. Annalla wrapped her arms around his chest and pulled him up and back, gaining a small shout of surprise as he flew from the horse's back.

"My lord! I thought I was going to fall," he exclaimed as she set them both down.

"I would not let that happen."

"I just wasn't expecting it. What do we do now?"

"You are bigger than Patrice, so I need you to do more work than her. You would be in the way of my wings, riding on my back."

"Oookaaay," he said slowly and nervously.

"Arms around my neck and wrap your legs around mine. You need to hold on tight, crossing your arms and ankles behind me."

He hesitated.

"Come on," she gave her head an impatient twitch.

He took a deep breath, as though bracing himself for something horrible, and did as he was told. Annalla grabbed his thighs to hold him steady.

"Larron will not be happy about this."

Annalla laughed, the act feeling new again for having been so long. "Nonsense. He told me directly I could flirt with whoever I wanted."

Marto's eyes grew big, and he squawked as she took off.

***

Annalla came back another hour later and took Nurtik from Dusk's back the same way she had Marto. She must have been pushing herself as hard as he pushed the horses. It concerned him greatly because the horses would not last much longer. She might not either if he believed what his instincts told him.

Moonshine, and then Dusk, both benefited from the lightening of their burdens, but Annalla's load grew each time. Larron suspected her plan the moment she left with Patrice, and his suspicion was the reason he risked pushing their speed after Marto left.

Timing would be critical. If they remained at the easier pace, they would be caught before she had a chance to come back for them all. If he pushed too much, the horses would give out before they were far enough to give her that time.

From where they rode, it looked like they *finally* neared the mountains when Dusk suddenly faltered beneath him. He was already sweat-soaked and taking heaving breaths. Then he shuddered and started to collapse.

Larron tucked up and rolled away to avoid being pinned beneath him as Dusk crashed to the ground. The wet snow cushioned his fall, and he heard Tyrus rein in and turn back. He jumped up and hurried over to Dusk's side to find his horse struggling to breathe. His friend would not be getting up again.

They had been through so much together in such a short time. Dusk gave Larron everything he had without protest—horses were fully capable of arguing—and he seemed to know what was at stake. His strength was gone. He had nothing left to give. Larron closed his eyes on the tears, finding it difficult to let go.

"Larron, leg up."

He stroked Dusk's neck gently one last time before ending his pain, speaking an elven death prayer for his lost friend.

"Coming," he said hoarsely as he stood.

Tyrus gave him a hand to pull him up on Moonshine. Larron would ride behind for as long as she could carry them.

That did not turn out to be long. She was used to heavier loads than his stallion, but the higher speeds hurt her. Her fall had them both rolling to safety, trying to avoid hitting each other as they did.

Moonshine was not his horse, but she had been Annalla's for a time, so he offered the same comfort and prayer for her, and cried for Annalla's loss.

"You should go with her next, Larron. We both know I'm the heavier of the two of us."

Larron gave him a wry smile. "We each run at the fastest speed we can maintain, and she takes the one furthest behind."

The look on Tyrus' face told him he knew an elf could usually outpace a human, but he also could not argue with the logic. "Makes sense."

It was not a race, and they both set the fastest pace they could sustain for hours if needed. Larron soon pulled ahead of Tyrus, his feet barely touching the ground. They ran for about fifteen minutes before he saw Annalla flying back toward them. He did not need to tell her their plan. She went straight past him, and when she passed overhead again, it was with Tyrus clinging to her.

Annalla would either return to him in time, or she would not. He did not risk tripping by looking over his shoulder constantly to see how close death was. Not until he could hear them at his back would he check to see how long he had until making a stand became necessary. The ground fell away beneath him, step by step, as he ran for his life toward the relative safety of the pass.

His eyes could make out three people running together and reaching the base of the mountain range. He saw as Annalla set Tyrus down with them just before they disappeared behind a rise in the land. He tried to avoid watching her to see how far away safety was, but that proved even more difficult than keeping himself from looking back.

The windani gained on him much more quickly without a horse, and it felt like no time had passed before he heard pounding feet, growling breath, and snapping jaws closing. A glance back confirmed his suspicions. He had mere minutes before he would need to turn and face them or risk being brought down like mindless prey.

Larron kept his breath even, his stride steadily increasing, and forced himself not to panic. Faster and faster, he pushed himself to stretch out how long he had, but they came on harder with him so close. The fastest few pulled ahead of the main force. There was no more time. Larron drew his sword as he skidded to a stop and turned in time to counter the first body crashing into him.

He slipped from beneath it as his blade opened the windani's gut and spun, decapitating a second attacking from his left. The leaders reached him in ones and twos, so for a while, he held his own and suffered only minor injuries fending off attack after attack.

There was a small break between the last of the individuals and the mass of windani. Larron backed up and moved behind the dead to give him a tiny barrier. He stood there, positioned to strike, as an overwhelming force closed upon him.

"Not this time!" The snarled cry came from behind, from a source he had momentarily forgotten, losing hope of help arriving in time.

Annalla swept past him and a small arc of flame burst to life between them and their attackers, but died as quickly as it flared up. The windani recovered from the moment of shock to renew their charge forward. She gave up on attacking and sprang back to fly toward him, the windani at her heels.

Larron was unsure of exactly what to do, and they would not have a second opportunity. He sheathed his sword and held out his arms as he had seen the others do when pulled from the horses as he watched her fast approach. She slammed into him with a force, knocking the breath from him and wrapped her arms around his back under his arms as she lifted them into the air.

"Hold on to me!" she gritted out into his ear, and he could feel her hold slipping. Without thinking, Larron wrapped himself around her to try and ease the burden on her arms.

"Better?"

"I thought I was too late." Her voice sounded shaky.

He eased his hold enough to look at her, their faces almost touching. "What did you mean when you said 'not this time?'"

"Please..." she took a shuddering breath, "not now,

Larron."

He suspected he already knew the answer. Larron brought her close again, giving her what comfort he could, turning his clinging hold into a hug. She did not protest, and they flew like that for some time.

"Moonshine... Did you?" she asked.

"I treated her end with the same respect I showed Dusk. She was your horse, whether you rode her recently or not."

"Thank you."

When he felt them dropping down to land, he looked over his shoulder and found they were not descending to join their friends. Hovering a couple of feet above the ground, she turned them into an upright position, and he loosened the hold of his legs to reach them toward the ground. She set him down carefully, but it must have cost the last of her strength because she collapsed next to him when she landed.

"It looks like it is my turn to carry you."

She tried to push him away and stand. "I can walk."

"Perhaps," he said, "but we will need you to stand when it comes time to fight. Rest for now."

"You know I hate being carried."

"Not as much as you hate being tied to a horse."

She laughed, as he intended, but sorrow lingered. The loss of her horse on top of the threat to him—likely reminding her of her father's murder—opened old wounds.

Larron picked her up, and in moments he carried a sleeping figure in his arms. She would not have taken them beyond where their friends were, so he headed up. Some of the footing was loose, but he did not need to use his hands to keep his balance and managed to let her sleep the entire time. He would have liked to have spoken with her, asked her how she survived, what she had been doing, and how she managed to reach them when still clearly weakened, but it was not the time for such a conversation. Simply being able to hold her eased a weight in his chest.

"Is she alright?" Patrice cried out when they came into view, and the worried outburst had Annalla reaching for the weapon trapped between them at her hip. Having witnessed her reaction to being woken suddenly, he did not hesitate to drop her and back up quickly as she rolled away, ready to attack or defend.

"She is fine, simply tired," he said, and Annalla relaxed.

"Have you found a suitable place, or do we need to continue hiking?" Annalla asked, fully awake once more.

"This is it," Tyrus answered. "High, flat walls from which they cannot reach us above, and a bottleneck entrance to this wider space giving us room to fight. It's as good as we hoped to find as far as defensible positions go."

"I'll keep watch," Annalla replied and took off to perch on one of the cliffs high above them, leaving no opening for questions.

Larron gave a small shake of his head before settling down with the rest of them to get what sleep he could. They'd had so little recently.

There will be time for answers later, he promised himself.

CHAPTER THIRTY-SEVEN

The area selected for their last stand boasted high walls surrounding a relatively flat and open area of bare rock. To the south, the walls narrowed into the opening through which the windani would approach, the path leading out of the mountains to the plains. The northern edge of the area squared off some, with a thin pathway leading to the north from the northeast corner.

As far as tenable locations went, they could not have asked for better. There would be room for them to move while the attacking windani would be restricted in how quickly they could press numbers forward. The escape path north was similarly restricted in size, favoring individuals over a mob. Their greatest weakness would be how quickly the windani could emerge and overwhelm them.

They were able to sleep for more than an hour, which made the lead Annalla gained them that much more impressive, having had to make the trip back and forth five times. Larron wished she would have taken the time to sleep as well. The fact she had not been able to fly them all the way to the others, and that she put up such a token protest when he carried her, told him she was worse off than she appeared. A part of him knew there was something weighing on her mind to keep her awake.

Annalla came back down to them. "Ten, fifteen minutes before they arrive. It looks like we caught a bit of luck. Some of them must have decided we are not worth the effort because there are only about a hundred thirty or forty following up the pass."

"Fighting against that number is lucky?" Marto asked, exasperated.

"Fewer to kill now than there were before." She shrugged. "I think that is as much luck as we could expect right now."

"Archers will work first." Larron addressed what they needed to do to survive. "We might be able to plug the entryway, and Nurtik can take care of the first few who make it past our arrows. Marto, how are you feeling?"

A look of guilt came across his face. "Good, but I'm not fully recovered."

"Do you think you could loosen those rocks on the cliff face after they begin their attack?" Larron pointed to a spot high on the rock wall back down the pass.

"If they are already loose, it should not take too much. Are you thinking to crush some of the windani below with them?"

"If you are able. It could give them pause before coming at us, and their hesitation gives us an edge."

"I'll do what I can."

They're here and listening now. Annalla motioned after gaining their attention.

Acknowledged, came five simultaneous replies, and they got into position. Three archers stood ready to fire.

The windani quieted down to stalk forward. For such a large group, they made little sound, with only an occasional loose rock scraping the ground, telling of their approach. To not waste their limited supply, he, Tyrus, and Annalla would take it in turn to release arrows at the windani coming through. Any not fatally wounded would be handled by Nurtik and Patrice.

Seconds ticked away. Their nerves were on end. Still, they waited.

With a sudden burst of movement, windani shot cleanly and rapidly through the gap in pairs. Each pair moved right on the heels of those before, making it difficult to keep up with the stream pouring in. Larron let fly his arrows, his fingers humming with every shot. At that range, there was little chance he would miss. Arrow after arrow found its mark, eliminating one enemy only for another two to take its place.

Before him, Nurtik stood like a rock in the middle of a raging river, slicing through necks and limbs with every swing of his axe. Patrice whirled around him, leaping, and striking endlessly with her daggers flashing. They took them down and built up the pile of bodies.

Marto stood behind the archers, remaining as protected as he could be under the circumstances. As the numbers crowding around them began to grow, a loud crack pierced the evening. A bolt of magic shot at the cliff face like lightning from the sky. Stones shattered under the assault, but the mass of them did not move.

Time passed, the number slipping past their attacks increased, and their responses slowed, hindered further by lingering exhaustion. Marto paused to gather more power and shot again. With the second blast, rocks broke loose to tumble down the cliff face. As they fell from sight, sounds of pain and death followed, and the stream of attackers eased. It offered breathing room, but not enough to allow them a break in the fighting.

Fifteen minutes? A half-hour? It was difficult to tell exactly, but eventually, their supply of arrows was expended.

They shifted to a formation more suited to melee combat. Blades sliced through windani flesh and crushed bone. Mage fire roared into the gap as often as Marto could manage, to burn and frighten. Each time, the duration and ferocity of his attacks lessened.

Larron became lost in the motions, his thoughts not extending beyond his blade and the victims within its reach. He trusted those he was with to take care of their own and concentrated his efforts on those within range striking at him.

Plunge it in. Withdraw. Take the one on the left, sweeping strike. Slide around as it falls. Do not forget the one circling behind you. Patrice just killed him. Two attacking, tuck and roll, rise, two heads in one. Duck back, you need more space.

So it went as he faced them again and again, losing track of his efforts and the passage of time. At some point, Larron saw Annalla take over for Marto to attack with fire, driving them back. Instead of a wall, she became a figure of flame with the blaze covering her body.

Seeing the image of a person ablaze startled him for a moment, wondering if someone caught one of Marto's attacks. There were, however, no cries of pain or distress.

Annalla danced on, a flickering beacon in the deepening darkness. She drove into the windani, setting fire to any she touched with the flames coating her and her blade. Some windani fled from her, many attempted to avoid her by turning wide, moving along the walls to attack others. She shifted to the front of their force, slowing the flood and disrupting their coordination. Smoldering corpses littered the ground around her.

Larron did not watch her for long, he could not spare the attention, but the blaze continued to burn, and every windani coming after them hesitated a fraction more than before. She provided light by which to see as the sun set and night fell, and still, they battled for their lives.

Tyrus and Nurtik fought back-to-back, their space closing in more with every attacker piling into the fray. Another mage blast sent several windani flying, not to rise again. The precise placement of the strike gave the two fighters room to breathe, but even as the windani hit the ground, Larron heard Patrice call out. "Marto's down! That was all he could give us."

Without his power helping to stem the flow of attackers, they would be pressed harder. It might not be much longer before they lost others. The light dimmed. Annalla was fading, but the windani were also fewer. Larron quickly injured two and jumped clear to look around and survey their situation.

Blood soaked everything and everyone. It was impossible to tell who might be injured. Marto lay on the ground, his leg torn open where a windani grabbed him to carry him off. Tyrus, still battling, stood over the young mage while Patrice darted in behind those attacking Nurtik.

Larron leaped back in to kill one of the injured even as he saw windani retreating down the trail. As many fled as were killed, and he found himself free again. Annalla fell to her knees to his right, her sword loose in her limp hand before it clattered to the stone.

A windani stalked forward, and Larron reacted. He ran forward to tackle the creature. One of Patrice's daggers thudded into its eye even as Larron's body slammed forward and knocked it off course.

Scrambling to his knees, he touched her shoulder. "Annalla? Are you injured? It is over, Annalla. The windani have all been killed or fled."

"Over," she breathed out in a sigh of relief and collapsed forward.

***

"Marto's down!" Annalla heard Patrice call out. "That was all he could give us."

He must have exhausted himself because she thought Patrice would have said it differently if he was injured. Annalla was close to exhaustion herself, but she took it one movement at a time and forced the weariness down. The short nap she had while Larron carried her up the trail had not been enough. She should have slept longer.

The weakness of her body made it difficult to maintain the smallest manifestation. In regular circumstances, keeping flames that close to her body would have presented a negligible effort, but at that moment, it was all she could manage.

The terrain there would not allow her to use any other element. There were rocks all around, but throwing the little ones would require concentration she could not spare, and the bigger boulders went deep. Nothing bigger than a shrub would grow for her. Water was also in short supply in the immediate area, as snow was not under her control.

Fire remained her best option, and it hurt their group then

more than ever if she could not maintain it. Windani had better night vision than Patrice, so if they lost the glow, she would hand the windani another advantage.

They were so close. She kept telling herself they could not lose, not with their goal in sight. With each kill, Annalla repeated *one more to go* over and over in her head. The smell of burning fur and flesh surrounded her, and she continued driving through them with blade and blaze. Gradually, she felt the fire dim and slow, no longer able to hold off the fatigue.

With each thrust of her sword, she accounted for slower movement and less force. She took more care with how much space she maintained for herself to maneuver because her reaction time lengthened. Annalla drove her sword deep into the heart of another windani. As it went to the ground, she fell to her knees on the blood-soaked rock, pulled down even as her blade slid free.

An eager growl rose to her right, but she struggled to open her eyes.

The others could still make it. I am not the last to fall. Our mission might succeed if they can win through. No, you know that is not true, she argued with herself. *They are outsiders and will never reach the sanctuary. I should have gone ahead alone. The fairy will not know until it is too late. I have failed everyone.*

"I'm sorry," she whispered to no one, her lips barely moving.

The creature padded closer and closer. Its steps were moist on the ground. Inside, she screamed at herself to rise, fight, move, do something to see her through that moment to the next, but she already pushed far beyond that point. Guilt and anger, and a little fear, clawed at her to no avail. Something touched her shoulder.

"Annalla? Are you injured?" It was Larron's hand, Larron's voice speaking. He kneeled beside her. "It is over, Annalla. The windani have all been killed or fled."

"Over," she said through a sigh of relief and collapsed, falling forward into him.

CHAPTER THIRTY-EIGHT

Horns sounded all around them. From the hilltop where her mother pulled up their horse, they could see gilar closing in, surrounding them. Her father's sacrifice bought them time, but it would not buy them freedom. There would be no escape unless she flew, leaving her mother behind.

They dismounted, and her mother grabbed her shoulders, shaking her gently. "Annalla!"

Tearing her tear-filled eyes away from where her father's body lay, she met blue eyes filled with sorrow. Both her parents were blue-eyed, but her mother's light brown hair came through in the darker streaks of Annalla's own. Mother had a curvy figure. Her fair skin clearly showed the scar on her cheek; a reminder of the accident in her youth that took her mother and her flight.

"Annalla," she said again, more gently that time. "You must take the oath. Do you understand?"

"Yes, Mother."

"You must believe it," she said. "It must become everything you are."

Annalla took her mother's face in her small hands, the hands of a child, and spoke the words to bind her fate. "Sanctuaries. Family. Friends. I swear to the order with everything I am."

Her life had never been her own. The oath was a mere formality. Destiny held her in its grasp, pressing the weight of an entire race of people upon her small shoulders. Annalla held her head high. That responsibility was why she trained, why she worked daily to become lethal.

Her mother swallowed thickly. "You are our Protector now," she said, bowing her head for a moment. "I am going to try something. It should see you safely away from here, but if it does not, you are to fly as fast and far as you can. Do you understand me, Annalla?"

"Yes, Mother," she replied, crying again. "I will not fail you."

"Take my hands," she said, reaching out.

Gripping her mother's fingers, Annalla watched her mother close her eyes. She spared a glance for the gilar approaching, judging how long she could wait before she had to fly away.

A glow began, rising from her mother's body. The light was not visual. It was not seen with her eyes but felt or known by something within her. It was pure power, and it emerged and rose. Streams of power gathered above them, forming tendrils from the orb to her body. When the final tendril broke free, her mother fell over to the ground.

Annalla watched her breathe. Once...twice...three times. Each breath came slower and slower, but after the third, she could watch no longer.

The orb of power enveloped her, and Annalla screamed in pain. Agony lanced through her as her body changed. Her wings shrunk and disappeared, and her head pounded. The power flared, and her vision went white. Then she was 'Annalla' no longer.

It was dark when Annalla woke the same night, or the next. She could not tell and brushed away the memory. Dreams taught her nothing new. The fog in her mind lifted with the last emergence, bringing back to her everything she had been and experienced.

No fire burned that night, and only the breathing of sleeping people could be heard nearby. Annalla remained tired, but the drive to stay awake the last few days had not faded. With her mind back in control, she needed information before she could rest more. She rose and looked around, finding everyone except Larron asleep around her.

"I expected you to sleep longer." Larron's voice came from the top of a jumble of rocks where he stood as a lookout. "It has only been a few hours."

She flew up to him and saw the normally composed elf still wearing bloody clothes and sporting bloodshot eyes.

"I cannot right now," was her answer as she sat beside him and looked out into the darkness. "What happened?"

They sat together in silence for a while.

When he finally answered, his voice was flat, dull. "Marto had fallen unconscious from his efforts, but you were alert for that. Hours of finely controlled magic use are difficult for magai, I have been told. He did well.

"I knew you were struggling when the light began to fade. You would never have reduced our vision unless you had no choice. There was nothing we could do to help either of you. The fight had gone on for more than an hour, and I knew the end of them had to be near unless they gained reinforcements."

Annalla placed a comforting hand on his arm.

"We were fighting the last of them," he continued. "Patrice noticed you on your knees and a windani closing in. She took it out with one of her knives, but before that, before the end, one tried to drag Marto away." Larron closed his eyes, and her hand moved to his back.

"Nurtik took its head, but not before it took a large chunk of flesh from Marto's leg. We dealt with the rest of them, and I grabbed the kit and tried to help him. There was too much blood, so much blood." Larron's words came quickly. "I pinched off the main flow, but he already lost so much and there was so much damage. He is so young, and still, he saved us countless times and weakened himself to do so. I could not do enough, Annalla. Marto is going to die for this stupid wild-goose chase."

"How long does he have?"

"I do not know. I have done all I can for his injuries, but

he lost too much blood, and I do not have the resources to repair the damage."

Annalla hesitated, and Larron's muscles stiffened beneath her hand. "It is not a stupid, wild-goose chase."

Neither was it as simple as asking for aid, however. She knew so much then, and the fairy were so close, but none of it could help them.

He turned a glare on her. "You know where they are? You could not ask the fairy to come to our aid?"

"I know, yes." She removed her hand. "It is more complicated than simply helping my friends, Larron. They cannot yet leave their sanctuaries. There is a process, but it will take time, and you all would have been dead by the time I returned."

Larron rubbed a hand down his face, letting out a heavy breath. "The fairy are really up there?"

"So I have been told." she looked into his green eyes, the color visible even in the darkness. "I remember everything now, but I have never been inside a Sanctuary. I know their approximate locations but have never seen my people. My last fifteen years were spent alone in Aryanna, and in the first nine, the only people I came to know were my parents and a few trainers. I have never met a fairy other than her."

"Do you think the fairy will help us? Help Marto?"

"They do not have healers like Mage Gregry, but they will host you if we arrive together. Whether you ever leave again, I cannot say."

"Another chance we already agreed to take," he said. "We should wake the others and go. Marto's only chance is if we can find better treatment than I can provide.

They woke their friends one by one. The rocks meant she could not grow anything for them, so they had to go without food. Larron explained to all that they still needed time to recover, but there might be help for Marto if they moved then.

It was not surprising that everyone was anxious to continue. The injuries they had sustained would take more than a day to heal, and Annalla had never fully recovered from her last manifestations. She still felt drained and could not conjure much of an essential manifestation. There was nothing for them there. Rest would not sustain them.

Tyrus received a deep gash on his arm where a windani's claws had dug into him. Nurtik was missing an ear, had two broken ribs, and broke his arm in three places. The bones broke under the pressure of two windani slamming him into the rock at the front of the battlefield. Patrice had the worst of it beyond Marto. A windani took a fair bite out of her leg as well. While Annalla had not seen the injury, Larron said it was unlikely the fur would grow back in that spot.

Despite her protests, Patrice was carried by Tyrus for much of their ensuing hike. With his arm injury, she had to cling to his neck as she sat on his good arm. Larron carried Marto, while Annalla helped Nurtik in the places where his broken ribs did not allow him the necessary mobility.

Unbeknownst to the others, Annalla had four manifest powers. Her air elemental manifestation would still be emerging at her age, so the force of it returning to her proved relatively limited. She thought of it as a baby power and suspected it would not reach maturity for six months to a year. Fortunately, she would ease into that one naturally.

If she had not exhausted herself at a time when she still needed time to recover physically, she could lift them all up the mountain on her own. As it was, she had to settle for stabilizing those being carried and taking some of their weight.

"How is it we are supposed to just walk up this path to find the fairy when no one has been able to find them before? Do they kill intruders?" Patrice asked when they stopped at a place where they finally found ground soft enough for Annalla to grow food.

It was a good question, especially considering the pass they walked had been relatively easy up to that point.

"Their policy for intruders will depend upon the will of the king, but it is mostly irrelevant." Annalla shrugged. "The Fairy Sanctuaries are imbued with a power akin to, but different in application from, that which lives within the elven Woodlands.

Unless led by a fairy willingly, outsiders are unable to gain entrance."

"Our Woodlands have the ability to defend us to a point, but what you are describing goes beyond that," Larron said.

"Not really. The Woodlands are far more active. The earth will literally move to protect you within their bounds, while the Sanctuaries have a barrier that cannot be penetrated."

"How is that possible?" asked Tyrus.

That was not a topic into which she wanted to delve. Sharing such information with outsiders could place the Sanctuaries at risk, and it was not the time to extract the oath of silence necessary for them to hear that truth.

"Sacrifices and promises made long ago," she said and looked around at each of them. "That is all I can say for now. I am sure they have historians who can do the story better justice than I."

So, they continued on. Even as spring rose from the south, they climbed to colder heights with every step. They were fortunate to have traveled through winter because it meant they already wore winter garments when forced to leave their belongings behind.

Unfortunately, they had limited equipment to deal with the conditions they faced. Over the first few days, their clothing soaked quickly as they walked through slushy snow dampened by the light rain often falling. Annalla started a fire during each break and each night to dry and warm them.

She spent most of her time hovering over the ground, since Larron's socks were no protection. The slush gained an icy crust as they went higher. At first, only a thin layer to step through in the mornings, but there came a time between the slush and the snow until they arrived at a wall of ice. After some argument, they allowed her to fly them to a flat area higher up the path.

Every aspect of the pass started to slow their progress, but nowhere did it seem impossible to continue. With each step, each day, Annalla became more worried about what they would face. What would she need to lead them through?

Annalla had never been so close to one of the Sanctuaries. Outsiders could not enter, which led her to believe there was some land feature a fairy had to help them cross in addition to the mystical barrier.

Otherwise, why would there be no stories about explorers running into an invisible wall? she wondered.

Her main concern was her lack of knowledge, putting her companions in danger. A fairy had to willingly lead others within, but to be willing, did they need to know what it was they were leading them through? Of everything she had been taught, the rules of her own land were where her knowledge proved the most lacking.

"Wait." Annalla stopped them late in their eighth day of climbing and listened back down the path.

"What is it?" asked Nurtik.

"We are being followed."

"Windani?" asked Tyrus.

"Yes, they are trying to gain the ice wall. Keep going. I will fly back and take care of them if it looks like they will make it over."

"By yourself, Annalla?" Patrice sounded worried.

"Larron and I are the only ones uninjured. One of us needs to lead, looking for sound footing, and Larron cannot fly quickly there and back. There are no more than ten, and they walk on ice right now."

"None of us could take on ten alone."

"None of us have the advantages she can claim either," Larron spoke on her behalf, then turned to her. "You are well enough for this?"

"I am."

"We have a couple more hours of light, so you will likely find us still walking upon your return."

Marto had gained a fever two days before, and Larron grew more concerned every time he inspected the injured leg. It appeared everyone else was healing well enough, but the mage did not have the strength to fight off infection. Annalla knew Larron tried to hide his concern, and she was likely the only one to see through it.

Annalla sped back down to try to reach the windani before they summited the wall and still clawed at the ice. She circled around, approaching the location from the top of a nearby cliff, and held up to watch their progress. Even as she landed, the ice bearing a climbing windani cracked and broke off, falling to the ground below and taking the creature with it on the way down.

The windani landed awkwardly, with a thump and a crack, and it let out a yelp and whine of pain. Annalla suspected a broken leg. No one helped the injured windani as they looked from the wall to their companion. Another made a run and leaped at the wall, reaching high and digging in with its claws, only for the ice to crack and break again. That one pushed to spring away from the wall and landed by rolling along the ground.

It appeared the ice would not hold them. Two of their number apparently thought the same as they broke off to head back down the trail. Another three followed a short time later.

Annalla considered killing them, but there were already many windani to see her who had already fled the initial battle. The pack had already lost enough people to hesitate to engage in battle for a time. Killing them would gain little and cost more of her slowly recovering energy. Choosing mercy, Annalla left the enemy alone.

Returning to her friends further up the path was a more leisurely journey. The wind fought against her, but she did not push herself for speed. They were not walking quickly through the thigh-deep snow, so she did not expect them to gain a great deal of ground beyond where she'd left them earlier.

When she passed a short way beyond that point, however, she began to worry. Fog or low clouds descended to where they walked and grew thick enough to conceal the ground at any significant distance. Annalla dropped into it and slowed to follow their trail in the snow. In and out of the surrounding rocks, she weaved along the path of least resistance Larron found for them. Finally, it started to clear and she rose higher, trying to spot them from above.

Through the clouds, white snow gave way to a dark rift in the landscape, directly in their intended path. Packed ice and snow clung to the edges of the chasm, obscuring where the stable rock ended and the drop began. Annalla quickly scanned the visible area and saw no one walking below. The thought immediately crossed her mind that they'd walked right off the edge with the fog obstructing their vision.

Even if the first had fallen, the others would not have followed mindlessly, she assured herself. *If I can see it from here, it is unlikely they would miss the contrast when closer and moving slower. Maybe there was a snow bridge covering the gap, but it broke under their weight as they crossed it?*

The bleak thought undid all the comfort from her previous self-assurances. She did not want to find broken bodies at the bottom and hesitated a moment before flying forward again. As she did so, shadowy figures bobbed into sight from behind a high snowdrift on the near side of the chasm, and Annalla breathed a sigh of relief. That place made her jumpier than the possibility of becoming windani food.

She would be able to see them over the gap and further on their way. With the limited light left, they should be able to find a place across to camp for the night and resume in the morning. No one noticed Annalla as she drew closer, but she gradually made out more of their familiar features through the thinning fog and dropped down when she was close enough to call out.

They were walking, it seemed, right to the edge to wait for her…but they kept walking well beyond what might be considered safe, and they were not slowing. Annalla could not believe what she witnessed and barely recovered in time to call out and shoot herself forward and down through the air.

"Stooooop!"

They froze and turned to look, but Larron already stepped too far. He walked in the lead still and planted his forward foot to turn. It was open air, with nothing for him to plant on. In slow motion, she watched the surprise come to his face as his body fell sideways into the chasm. His arms threw Marto back before whirling around to claw at the air.

She heard the others call out his name and reach forward to try to catch him, even though he was well beyond their reach. Patrice grimaced as she leaped forward and snagged Marto's collar before sliding until Tyrus gained a hold on her.

"Don't move!" Annalla yelled at them as she sped past and into the breach after Larron's falling form. People usually fell the same way when they were not prepared for it. Their arms and legs moved, trying to gain purchase on the ground that had abandoned them, and Larron proved no different. He could see then what he fell toward. Whatever had been at work keeping them from seeing the danger was no longer an issue.

Annalla folded her wings flat against her back and pointed her head straight down, pulling on his clothing with her power like the wind. Larron turned to look down and did not know she closed behind him. His speed picked up the longer he fell, despite her efforts, and it felt as though she gained on him far too slowly. She did not want to see how close they were to the bottom. If he hit, she was likely to crash into it as well.

Closer and closer she drew, until she could finally reach out to him. Annalla wrapped her arms around his waist, making sure she had a firm hold before snapping her wings wide. Larron turned his head to see what grabbed at him, but when her wings opened, everything pulled toward the ground violently and away from her.

Her arms and wings felt like they were being pulled from her body as he doubled over against her grip. At the same time, she struggled to stall their descent and grip the air with her wings. Slowly, slowly, she gained control and they began moving up instead of down. Larron coughed to catch his breath, and the movement pulled again at her sore arms. Her hold started to slip.

"Larron…" she hissed in pain. "Larron, I need you to turn around and hold on. There is nowhere to set down here, and I can't hold you." He coughed and gasped. "Larron!" Panic entered her voice as he slipped further.

He could not yet speak, but managed to nod and reached an arm back as far as he could. It was all she could do to maintain her tentative hold as he hooked his arm around her neck and grabbed a handful of clothing.

"Let go...I can hold on now."

Hesitantly, she released her grip and let him fall, but he caught himself and reached his other arm up to hold on as she flew them back to the top. Annalla started to topple again halfway up with all of the weight at her head, but Larron swung his legs up to wrap around hers, and she turned slowly upright as though standing in the air, rising straight up.

"Stand on my feet. It will be easier on us both." She steadied him as he did as told. "Are you alright?"

"Bruised around the middle, I suspect, but nothing to complain about in exchange for not plummeting to my death. Where did this come from?"

"You really did not see it?" She set them down at the far side of the chasm.

"I would have sworn to you it was not there before falling into it. I would have sworn I was falling to my death before you caught me. Once again, I owe you my life."

"If I had returned quicker, you would not have fallen at all." She breathed out a sigh of relief. "I will bring the others across before it gets too dark. Do not move anywhere."

"That will not be a problem," he assured her.

Annalla left him a safe distance from the edge and flew out over it again to their companions on the other side. They had done exactly as she yelled and not moved other than to draw in Marto's body. They must wonder if every step risked some danger only she could see. Annalla flew to the safe side and called them toward her.

"Can you still not see it?" she asked, gesturing behind them.

"See what?" asked Patrice.

"The enormous hole in the ground Larron nearly died in!"

"What hole? It looked to us as though you were both

swallowed by the ground until you emerged ahead of us," Tyrus explained as Nurtik tugged on his sleeve.

"Tyrus, tha' hole," he said.

"Oh, my lord... We could have all been killed." He breathed as he saw what the rest stared at, mouths agape.

"Mus' not be able t' see unless ya tell us 'bout it." Nurtik shrugged off the oddity. "How'd it go with the windani?"

"They will not be a problem for us, and I am fine. Any who later make it up the wall will be as blind to the chasm as you were, and I will not save them from the bottom." She looked over to where Larron waited. "I will carry you over one at a time."

On both sides, Annalla identified a safe area to walk in so they would not need to worry about further unseen dangers while she was away. There were no further incidents, but when they started walking again, she took the lead. She watched for anything dangerous and warned them in case they could not see it, but the path was relatively easy. She would almost say 'well maintained.'

"I do not see any better place to make camp for the night ahead of us. This will have to do," she said as she stopped in front of a short and slanting rock face.

They would be hard-pressed to find a place to rest for some distance when they continued in the morning because they were coming to the jagged and steep part of the mountainside. Annalla was about to start their fire when she heard something almost familiar on the wind. It was the soft flutter of a wing and the cooing of a bird so faint it was nearly inaudible, even to her ears.

Annalla froze, then motioned for the others to remain still and silent...no weapons. The cooing was repeated by another in response, and she offered the hoot of a snow owl—as well as she could—as her own response. She knew they were there.

Four figures emerged from the snowy landscape above as quickly and quietly as wraiths in the night to surround the party. Her friends heeded her warning, remaining still and unarmed, against all their instincts and training. Annalla did not know what would have happened if they presented themselves as a threat to either her or the other fairy.

The four winged shadows hovered above the ground, brandishing their own weapons at the intruders. All were raptor fairies, which meant their wings were feathered and jointed as a bird's. She had been told raptors were placed on patrol most often in higher altitudes. Their wings and coloring were often better suited to the snowy landscape.

"Why do you bring outsiders within the bounds of this sanctuary?"

He spoke Satarine, the language of the Sanctuaries. She knew it well, as it was one of the few pieces of fairy culture her mother could share. The fairy speaking to her stepped forward enough to be visible to them all and addressed his words to her.

"These people request an audience with the king." Annalla moved forward, standing before her friends and gesturing back toward them.

A second fairy stepped forward and gave her a look of disdain. "You have no authority to make such a request when you have violated our laws and helped these outsiders into our lands. And you should know to bow to the prince when you are introduced to his presence."

"Prince? How fortunate," she said as she looked through him toward his leader, feeling the start of a grin. *Mother said they emphasized martial service for all in authority. Perhaps this will simplify matters.*

"You will bow to show your respect, or you will face the consequences dictated by our laws. It is already enough you have risked exposure so close to the borders."

Her smile faded, and she drew herself up tall.

CHAPTER THIRTY-NINE

The five of them stood frozen in place as four fairy came into view. Their features remained hazy in the darkness, but Larron could see them well enough, and he suspected Patrice could as well. Three were male, and the fourth was female, but all appeared to be a member of some sort of fairy border patrol in the way they were similarly armed and clothed.

They blended wonderfully with the snow and rocks covered in white and gray furs. Their wings were better at blending there than Annalla's, enormous like an eagle's, with feathers of colors varying from white to mottled gray, to a light brown. Even after so many months of traveling with Annalla, those people felt completely foreign to him. She only represented the fairy as much as she did the elves, too unique to be held to either description.

One of the fairy stepped forward and spoke to Annalla in a language unknown to Larron. He rose to the same height as Annalla, but their coloring was completely opposite. Where her hair flowed a dark blond halfway down her back and her eyes blue, the fairy speaking had short dark hair, dark eyes, and skin a deep tan nearly matching Larron's own. His bearing told Larron he was a leader, not only of that group, but likely more broadly among his people.

This man knew the mantle of power, he thought. *Perhaps a military leader? It is not unknown for Geelomin, or even Erro or myself to join patrols often enough.*

His suspicion was confirmed when a second man approached Annalla quickly and threateningly. Larron wanted to move to her defense against whatever accusations were spat in her face, but it would not help and probably get him killed. Those were her people. He was only a possible guest or prisoner. They watched the foreign exchange, oblivious to the words being spoken until she switched to market speech.

"I bow…to no fairy," she said to the male in her face and looked around him at their leader as she continued, holding her head high. "My authority here is not granted by the king, but is my own. I am Annalla, daughter of Lana and Anor, last in the line of the Enchantress Fairies and Protector of the Sanctuaries. These people will share my customary audience with the king." The words were undeniably a title, but Larron did not know what weight or significance it carried.

As she spoke, she changed her stance into what must be a formal greeting. Her right foot was placed flat behind her left, and her right arm brought up to where her hand lightly rested over her shoulder with one finger angled toward the sky and the others feathered down. Their leader reflected her posture, and they bowed their heads to each other, but the other three made a full bow toward Annalla. Whatever position she claimed, he found, was equal, in some respect, to royalty.

"Protector Lucil was the last to enter the sanctuaries many decades ago, and Lana, her daughter." The leader's market came across surprisingly clear, despite a strong accent. "Without returning, how is it she has a daughter of her own, and why are you, Protector, so young?"

"Valid questions, Prince, but the answers are best given to the king."

The man's eyes flicked to their group, and Larron heard him sigh out through his nose. "The outsiders complicate the matter of your return."

He sounded put upon by the 'complication,' and Larron could sympathize with him.

"They are in the sanctuary with my blessing, they need nothing further. Though, on my word, I tell you they pose no threat to your people."

He nodded his head to the side to show a desire to speak to her in private, and the other three resumed their guard of the outsiders. Larron watched as they spoke quietly to each other for some time. The fairy prince eventually broke off and spoke to one of his men.

"Gweth, take the injured young mage to the hospital."

One of the men saluted and approached Larron with determination masking uncertainty. At a slight nod from Annalla, Larron passed Marto into the arms of the fairy and watched as they left into the sky after some words from the prince.

No one spoke in their larger group. The fairy around them were too suspicious of the outsiders and amazed by Annalla. Larron and his friends were just as awed by the fairy. They had been 'extinct' for so long, but there, five stood casually around them, guarding them. Larron felt himself gawking, but was comfortable with it. He let himself take them in until brought back to the situation by Annalla walking in his direction. Their prince called his patrol over even as she approached.

"Annalla," Patrice said excitedly, throwing her arms around Annalla's waist, "those are fairy! We made it, we're here."

There were tears in her eyes, and Nurtik sank down to the snow as he stared open-mouthed at the clustered fairy. Larron did not blame them. His own knees felt weak as he wrapped his mind around what it meant to be standing there. Annalla put an arm around Patrice's back and smiled at her words.

"We are," she said. "The four of us will bear you to the fairy domestic quarter…if that is still your wish. There you will be given shelter, food, and a chance to wash. Marto is being taken to their medics. I authorized them to do whatever is needed to save his life."

Larron nodded and grimaced. "They will need to take his leg. The flesh is already dying. He also needs nutrients, not having eaten in days."

"Prince Darrin passed along what I could share of his condition. I do not know the capabilities of their healers, but they will do what they can for him."

"Are you royalty?" Tyrus asked.

Annalla smiled and gave a small laugh. "No. I am not royalty. It is a complicated relationship, but I have a position equal to—but absolutely nothing like—royalty. My title here is Protector. You will have your audience with the king if you come. Will you accept their hospitality?"

Larron watched the faces around him light up at her words, and Patrice turned Annalla's comforting arm into a full hug as she started laughing. Her expression of joy spread to the rest, and they must have made a strange spectacle to the fairy, laughing and trading hugs and handshakes.

If Larron were honest with himself, he never thought that day would come when they set out from the Palonian. He expected they would fail and die, the war would continue, and their people would face death or slavery. If he was honest, part of him would rather die on a fruitless errand than watch everything he cared about destroyed. Something had changed since that time. He found hope again and could believe another future was possible.

He looked around, receiving nods in response to his unspoken question. "Our mission lies not behind us, but within this Sanctuary of yours," he told her. "We accept."

The fairy had their weapons put away as they walked over to join the larger group. Not all of them looked pleased, but they would follow orders.

"We will fly from here to reach the homes tonight," the man spoke to them for the first time. "Protector Annalla has told me you have all been carried before, though not all of you prefer our method of travel. I regret any discomfort, but there will be warm food and shelter provided for you at the end of this flight, so I hope you will excuse the journey."

"We have faced worse on our journey here and thank you for your hospitality, Highness."

Five of them, and five fairy, including Annalla. Each was

taken up into the air at the same time, and they soared quickly through the gathering darkness further into the mountains. Larron felt the cool air brushing against his face and smiled into the wind.

EPILOGUE

"Where is the alpha?" Kahnlair always felt off when he spoke through one of the other Elarian races, and using the body of a windani was no exception. They usually kept one of their human prey around at the times scheduled for his contact with them. It kept them from needing to use one of their own.

He would not forgive a missed contact and had demonstrated his displeasure at having to force contact in the past. Stretching his soul across the lands to reach and take control of a sacrifice was no small task, even for him. Though, putting the responsibility of meeting with him onto a common dog would not be well received either.

"I am Alpha," the windani replied with pride, in its own gruff, limited language.

"You are not even a primary here, and I will not remain patient with further delay."

"Primary are all dead. I am Alpha, and I kept the ordered meeting time."

Only a revenge party brought all the primary into a single confrontation. That was exactly something he was about to instruct the alpha to watch for and report back to him. A change was taking place within the ranks of his enemy, and he had yet to determine the source. Their tactics took the approach of an organized group concerned about the outcome of the war rather than the individual battles being fought—as he tried to keep them.

Even though he had not intercepted any messages that must be winging between them, they were coming together in a concerted effort against him. The only explanation he could think of was they discovered something they thought would cause a shift in the odds against them. He had been carefully keeping them at a level where they would retain hope of survival, but little belief they could actually win, while he eliminated the human center of power.

For the windani to have lost all their primary would mean whatever they discovered and faced in battle was easily overlooked in its significance. They were not the clever soldiers of the gilar, but even a hunt for revenge was called off if the group they sought appeared too large or too well-armed. It was a great satisfaction to know that, on his orders, they would set aside their instinct and throw away their pointless lives.

"Did they come from the dwarven clan?" His gilar in the east had been sent to besiege the clan, but it did not mean all remained trapped.

"Perhaps, we found their tracks coming from the south, but they could have traveled first west, then north, but only one was a dwarf. We should have destroyed them and feasted on what little flesh they could provide us tonight."

"How many were in this party?"

"Five." There was hatred and anger in the growled answer, but Kahnlair was well acquainted with the look the other emotion left on this creature's face, the emotion he tried to hide. Every victim he took to supplement his power feared him, and fear clouded that new alpha's sight even then, but it was not Kahnlair he feared.

"Tell me how a group of five decimated your hunters. Start at the beginning," he ordered.

"A hunting party failed to return, so we descended upon their territory as we have always done, and we found them dead. There was enough scent lingering to determine their number. It was such a small group the alpha dismissed half the hunters, though none of the primary would go.

Days we spent on their trail, for it seemed they had much time to place distance between themselves and the place of the killings. Finally, we saw five running across the plains toward the mountains, but the then-alpha pushed us on, and we knew they would never outrun us.

"The first night we continued running after dark. They heard us and started moving again as well, but it was how we discovered this that was most unusual. Far ahead of us, on the plains, a fire rose above the ground and guided their shadowy figures through the night. Our advantage was taken from us by mage trickery.

"We did not give up, but became more determined to run down those who would laugh at our efforts with their limited magic. If they had more than three magai among them, they would have faced us, so we knew they could not stand. Their animals were the first to fall under the strain of trying to match the stamina of the windani, so we thought we had them in our grasp.

"That was when the strange female vampire flew in over them and brought a wall of fire, pain, and death between us and our prey. We lost many upon that wall and heard the female slay those jumping it to attack her. We were delayed in our pursuit, and some even trailed behind to flee from her power.

"When we regained our ground on them, it was a shock to find there were only two left for us we could see. *Surely*, we thought, *they are riding two or three to a horse.* It was not so. One of the horses fell, and we saw only one person fly from its back, and when the last fell, there were only two running from us at their pitiful pace.

"That was when the sixth, the vampire, returned and plucked one from the ground to fly it off to the mountains before coming back for the last. We raced her to the final runner and would have had them both except for her power. She dove in front of the elf and more fire erupted from the ground, and when we could see ahead again, she had him in her arms and flying toward the mountains as well.

"More trailed behind to flee with the second demonstration, but the then-alpha told us the second blast of fire was much less than the first and she was weakening. Most took heart from his words and continued the chase, and we rushed up the mountain pass in pursuit of our prey. *Even with a defensible position,* we thought, surely, *they cannot defeat so many.*

"Their mage rained deadly rocks upon us, their blades killed us in numbers as we rushed in to face them, and the vampire burned and fought as though she were a flame brought to life. Those of us alive here are the ones who chose to retreat at the end, when it was clear only one had been taken down. I brought order, I sent a small group to track them silently for information. I am Alpha now."

"And has that group brought you information on these enemies?"

The anger and fear were still there. "Nothing, I fear they are also dead."

"What did she look like, this female vampire with power?"

"I was further back, which is why I yet live, but saw less from there. She has wings like the lighter color vampire wings, but looks human or elvish." He spat the names of those last two races. "I know no further details of her."

"Watch the pass, and make sure someone survives to report to me should they leave this place."

"But we…" Kahnlair gave him a look that returned his fear to its proper source, even through the eyes of another. "We will do as you say."

He left the new alpha and returned to his own body alone in his chamber. The greater distance and maintaining a connection to a race so different from his own forced him to cut the interrogation shorter than he would have preferred. It would have drained his power too far, but he gained enough information in the short time. The report would have been disregarded completely, and the new alpha killed for lying if it did not raise a memory of a similar report from years before.

The report came from the gilar, who were not prone to

exaggeration, so he had not dismissed it out of hand. Unfortunately, they were also not the greatest at providing detail beyond the disposition of forces. All the odd report said was they had chased down a family, but when they reached the woman and her child, all they found was one dead body, that she had a colorful wing—which they confirmed were part of her when they ripped it off—and that the child was nowhere to be found.

That they mentioned a child at all meant one had to have been there at some point, but because that was a singular incident against a male elf and his mate, it was not well recorded, and only that much because of the unusual circumstances.

That meant there was another woman with wings helping his enemies. It raised the question of whether that woman's child had finally been found. Her presence could be the source of the change he felt. Her power could be what called to him of late.

Perhaps she was a power strong enough and naïve enough to allow him to consume it and make it his own. He needed to change his orders quickly. She was to be taken, if possible, not killed like his orders for the irimoten. He needed her alive and fighting. Kahnlair would break her himself.

***

Zeris huddled with those also assigned to that sleeping spot, shivering against the cold of the night. Kalambaras lay at the center of their pile. Three days before, he'd developed a cough, growing weaker and slower with every rising of the sun. He was not the first to take ill that winter, and he may not be the last.

In the craggy land at the edge of the Kalachi desert, winter temperatures often dropped below freezing at night, and the gilar cared nothing about making the elves' accommodations hospitable. Larron had traveled that land before. He brought back stories of the stunning beauty of the sunsets across the open land and the tenacious life finding ways to thrive against hostile conditions. Zeris could not appreciate the beauty through all of the death and despair.

When the first signs of sickness appeared, his fellow captives guided him on how to help them: keep them warm at night, work in a rotation to cover for their reduced workload, and portion part of his rations to give them more. If fortune smiled on them, the sick recovered quickly. Five had not been so fortunate that season. They fought with their meager remaining strength as the gilar dragged them away, not to be seen again. Baerjormond, a seasoned warrior, killed three with one of their own weapons before they eliminated him. The gilar roared and cheered as they hacked at Baerjormond's body, thinking that a great victory while Zeris and the rest of the elves watched.

When their rage cooled, silence descended. Zeris felt his lips peel back over his teeth in a fierce approximation of a grin as the attacking gilar glanced around nervously. It was no smile of joy, but a representation of repressed rage, and he wondered if the gilar saw death in his eyes as they backed away. One elf, weak from illness and malnutrition, killed three well-fed and armed gilar.

Captive or not, they mattered. Every life there mattered.

Rolling over, Zeris tried to unobtrusively stretch his back, scraping his arm along the ground. Hissing at a sharp scratch, he placed a hand on the rocky dirt to lean over for a closer look, and the first real smile since his capture broke out over his face. With a watery grin, he peered down at the little sprout, holding his hand out to it.

A sweet beet, he thought with wonder. *Spring is almost here.*

THANK YOU!

Thank you for searching for the fairy sanctuaries with Annalla and Larron! I hope you are enjoying the series so far and are excited to explore the fairy people and their home.

What are the fairy people like?

Will they help the people of Elaria against Khanlair?

How will Annalla's returned memories impact her relationship with Larron?

Book 3, *Hidden Promise*, is scheduled to release June 2023.

Preorder the ebook now!

Great reviews are critical for indie authors such as me. If you enjoy the book, please leave a rating or review, and recommend it to your friends! I appreciate all your support. To keep up with all my new releases or learn more about Elaria and the other realms, please check out my website. You can sign up for my quarterly newsletter, find bonus material, or follow my blog at:

www.tiffanyshearn.com

ACKNOWLEDGEMENTS

This one feels different, and a big part of that is all the people who have invested time and effort into making the series a success thus far and continue to do so. I cannot describe how much your support means to me. As always, any and all errors are mine alone.

To Samantha Millan, I'm sorry an earlier version of this book was a little traumatic, but thank you for pushing through. I hope the final version was easier. Guy Parisi, you continue to rip into the early drafts to help make me a better writer and storyteller. I know it feels like work, and I appreciate every minute of it. Éva Rona, your enthusiasm for the story and desire for more description help me bring my world to life.

Jonathan Lebel, thank you for creating another beautiful work of art for my cover. Maxine Meyer, I appreciate all your quick and responsive editing work and continue to enjoy working with you.

To my beta readers, who helped me trim this one down a little in the end where it stuck a bit, thank you for your time and feedback Ellen Zuckerman, Divya Ramji, and Beba Andric thank you for reading through the final draft, providing excellent reader feedback, and enjoying my work.

This would not happen without all of you. Thank you!

ABOUT THE AUTHOR

Tiffany Shearn is a writer and author of the *Hidden Series of Elaria*, her first book *Hidden Memory* released in December of 2021 to great reviews. While working by day in business finance, Tiffany has spent more than two decades bringing her fantasy realm and characters to life. She is already working on *Hidden Promise*, the next series installment, to continue their story.

Tiffany is a lifelong reader with a passion for the fantasy genre. She began writing in college when the stories in her head were vivid enough to distract her from lectures, and now has two published works with more on the way. Tiffany lives just south of Seattle, Washington with her husband, Big Cat, and Little Cat. (www.tiffanyshearn.com)

Made in the USA
Middletown, DE
11 July 2022

68954480R00231